WHEN CROCS FLY

WHEN CROCS FLY

Stephan T. Pastis

Andrews McMeel Publishing®

a division of Andrews McMeel Universal

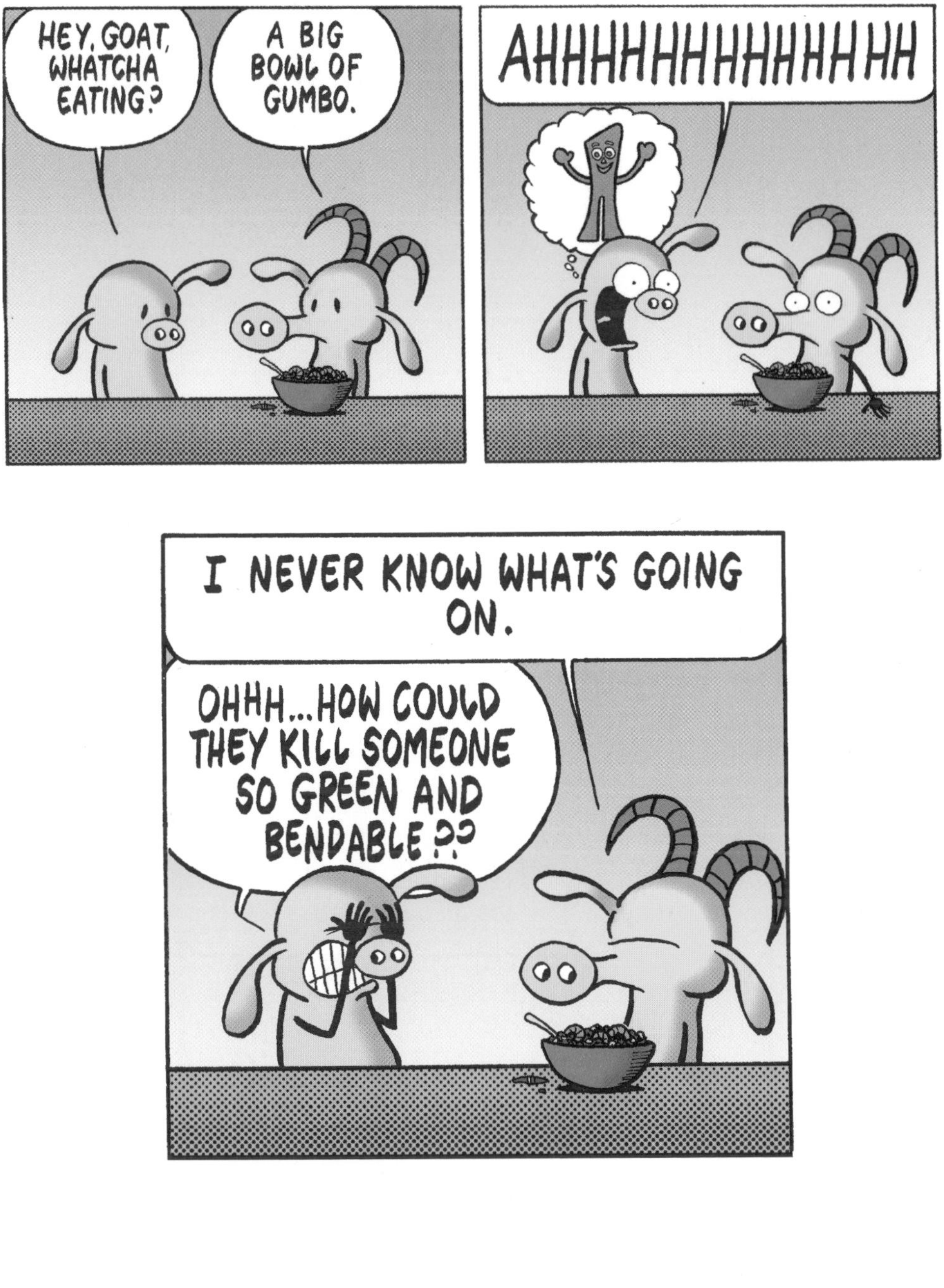
HEY, GOAT, WHATCHA EATING?
A BIG BOWL OF GUMBO.
AHHHHHHHHHHHHHH
I NEVER KNOW WHAT'S GOING ON.
OHHH...HOW COULD THEY KILL SOMEONE SO GREEN AND BENDABLE??

Zeeba neighba...Come heres.
WHAT DO YOU WANT?
Time geev up. Crocs find you mail slot.

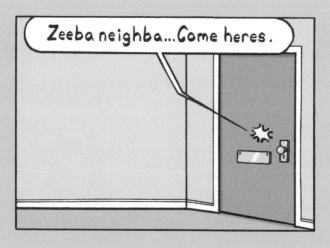

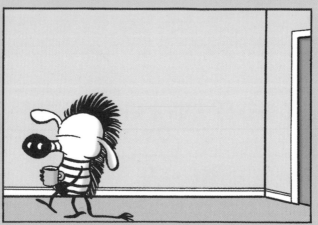

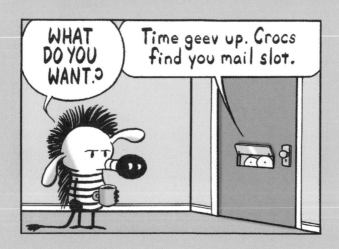

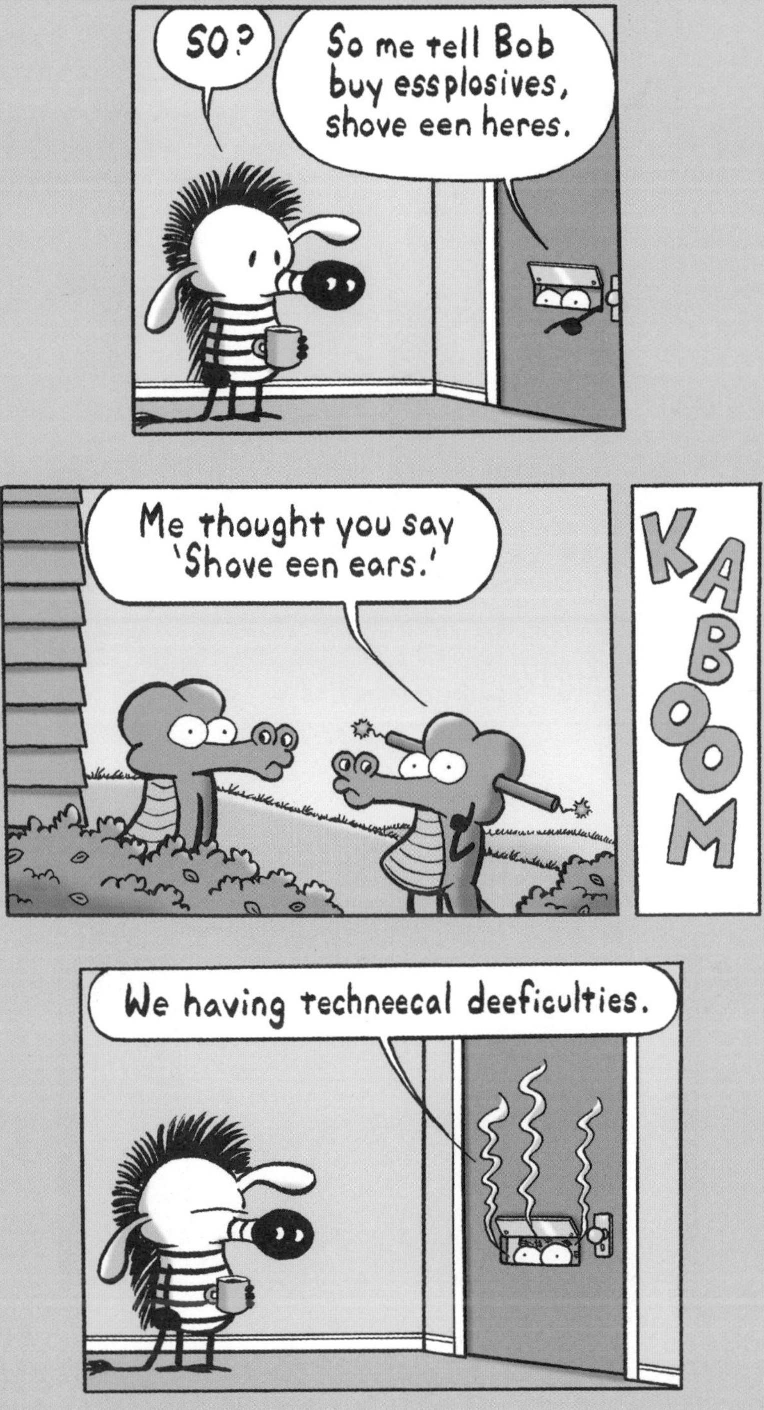
SO?
So me tell Bob buy essplosives, shove een heres.
Me thought you say 'Shove een ears.'
KABOOM
We having techneecal deeficulties.

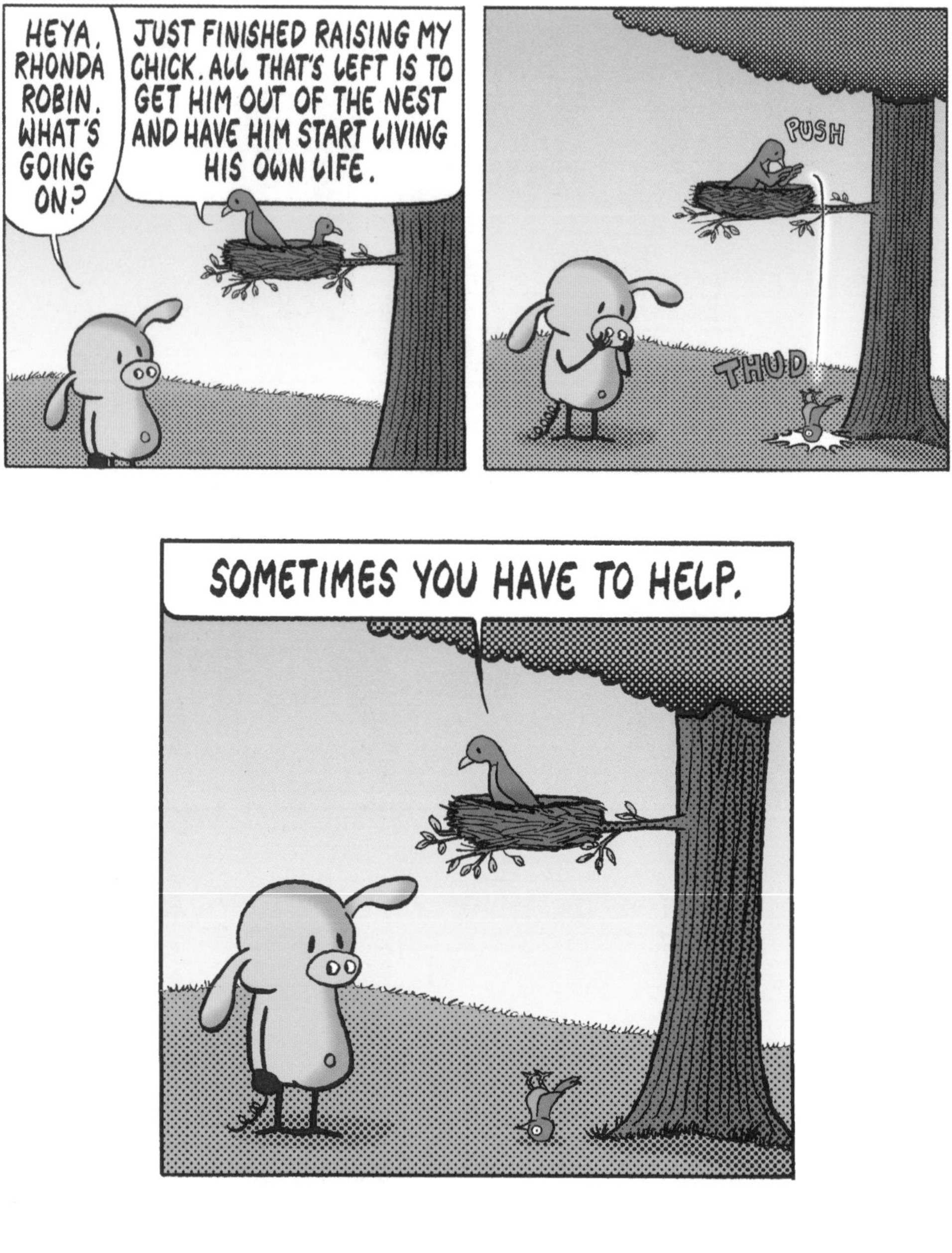
HEYA, RHONDA ROBIN. WHAT'S GOING ON?
JUST FINISHED RAISING MY CHICK. ALL THAT'S LEFT IS TO GET HIM OUT OF THE NEST AND HAVE HIM START LIVING HIS OWN LIFE.
PUSH
THUD
SOMETIMES YOU HAVE TO HELP.

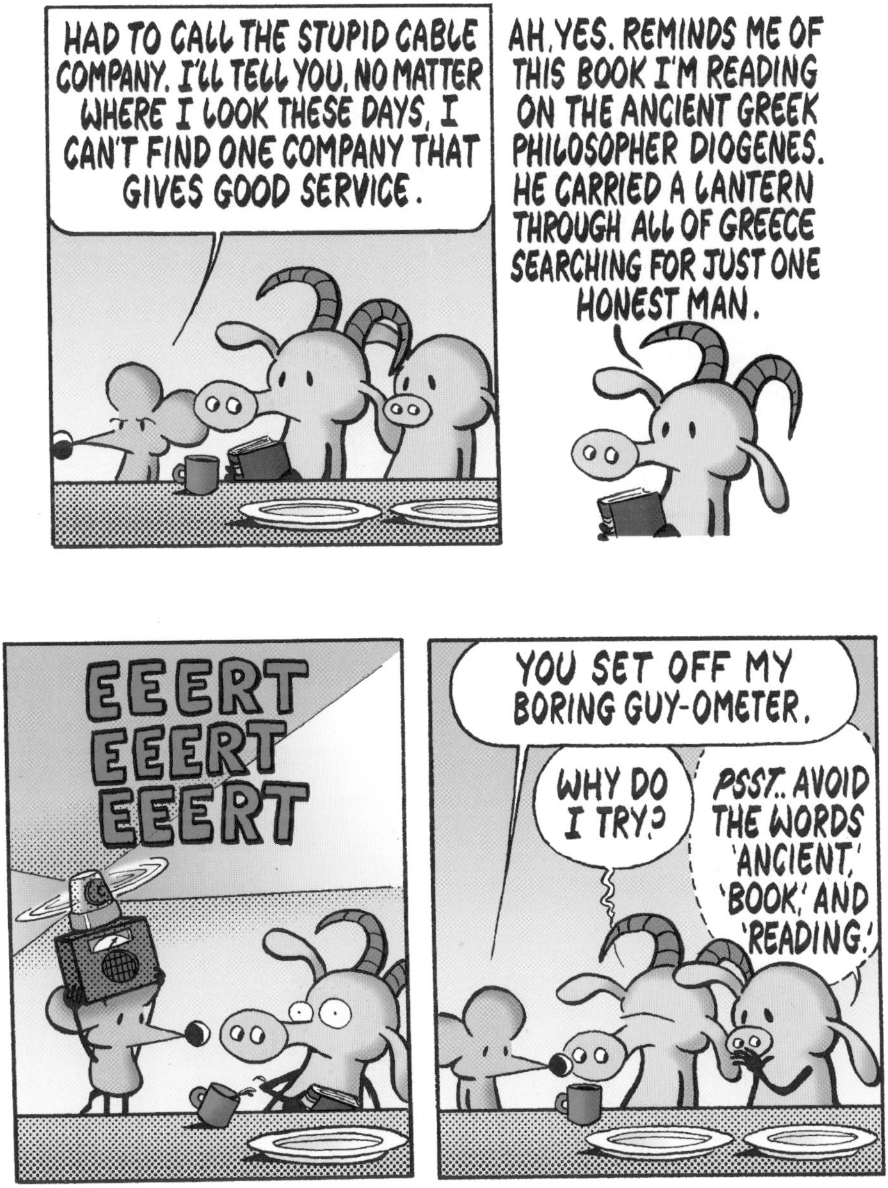
HAD TO CALL THE STUPID CABLE COMPANY. I'LL TELL YOU, NO MATTER WHERE I LOOK THESE DAYS, I CAN'T FIND ONE COMPANY THAT GIVES GOOD SERVICE.
AH, YES. REMINDS ME OF THIS BOOK I'M READING ON THE ANCIENT GREEK PHILOSOPHER DIOGENES. HE CARRIED A LANTERN THROUGH ALL OF GREECE SEARCHING FOR JUST ONE HONEST MAN.
EEERT EEERT EEERT
YOU SET OFF MY BORING GUY-OMETER.
WHY DO I TRY?
PSST.. AVOID THE WORDS 'ANCIENT,' 'BOOK,' AND 'READING.'

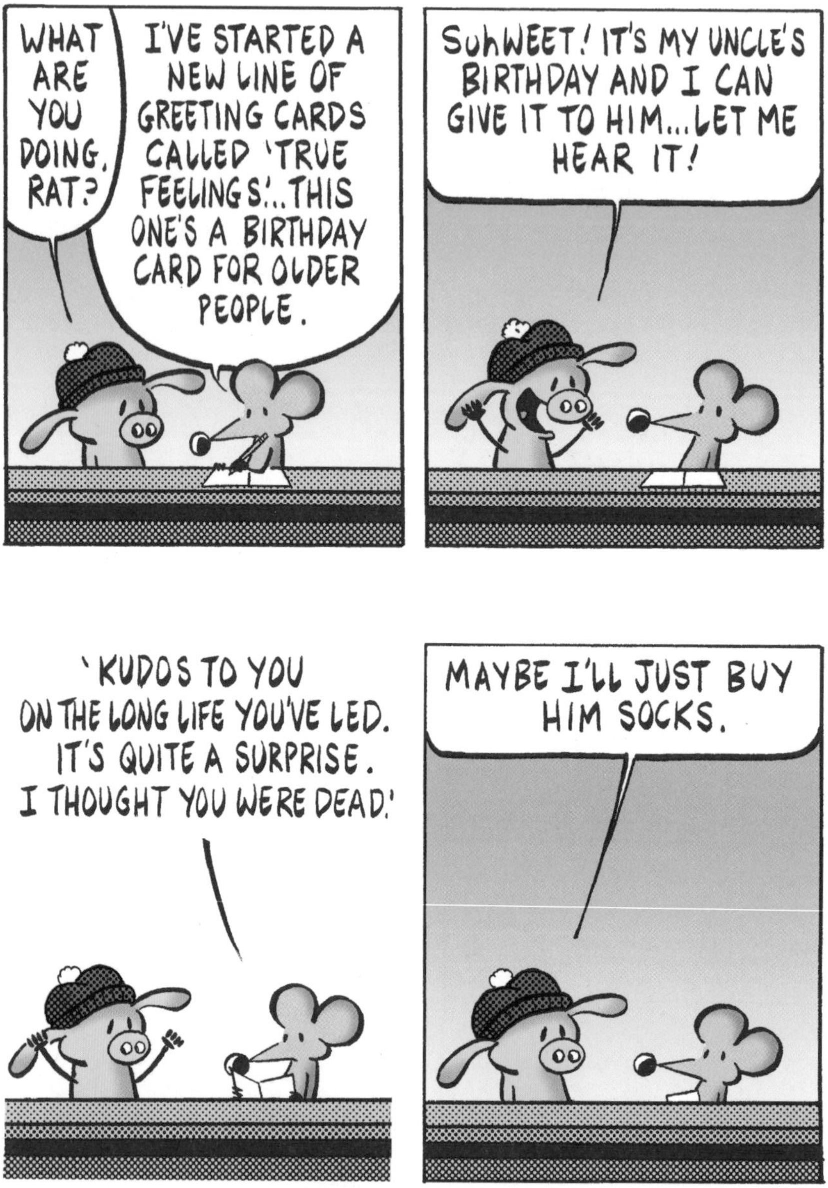
WHAT ARE YOU DOING, RAT?
I'VE STARTED A NEW LINE OF GREETING CARDS CALLED 'TRUE FEELINGS.'...THIS ONE'S A BIRTHDAY CARD FOR OLDER PEOPLE.
SUHWEET! IT'S MY UNCLE'S BIRTHDAY AND I CAN GIVE IT TO HIM...LET ME HEAR IT!
'KUDOS TO YOU ON THE LONG LIFE YOU'VE LED. IT'S QUITE A SURPRISE. I THOUGHT YOU WERE DEAD.'
MAYBE I'LL JUST BUY HIM SOCKS.

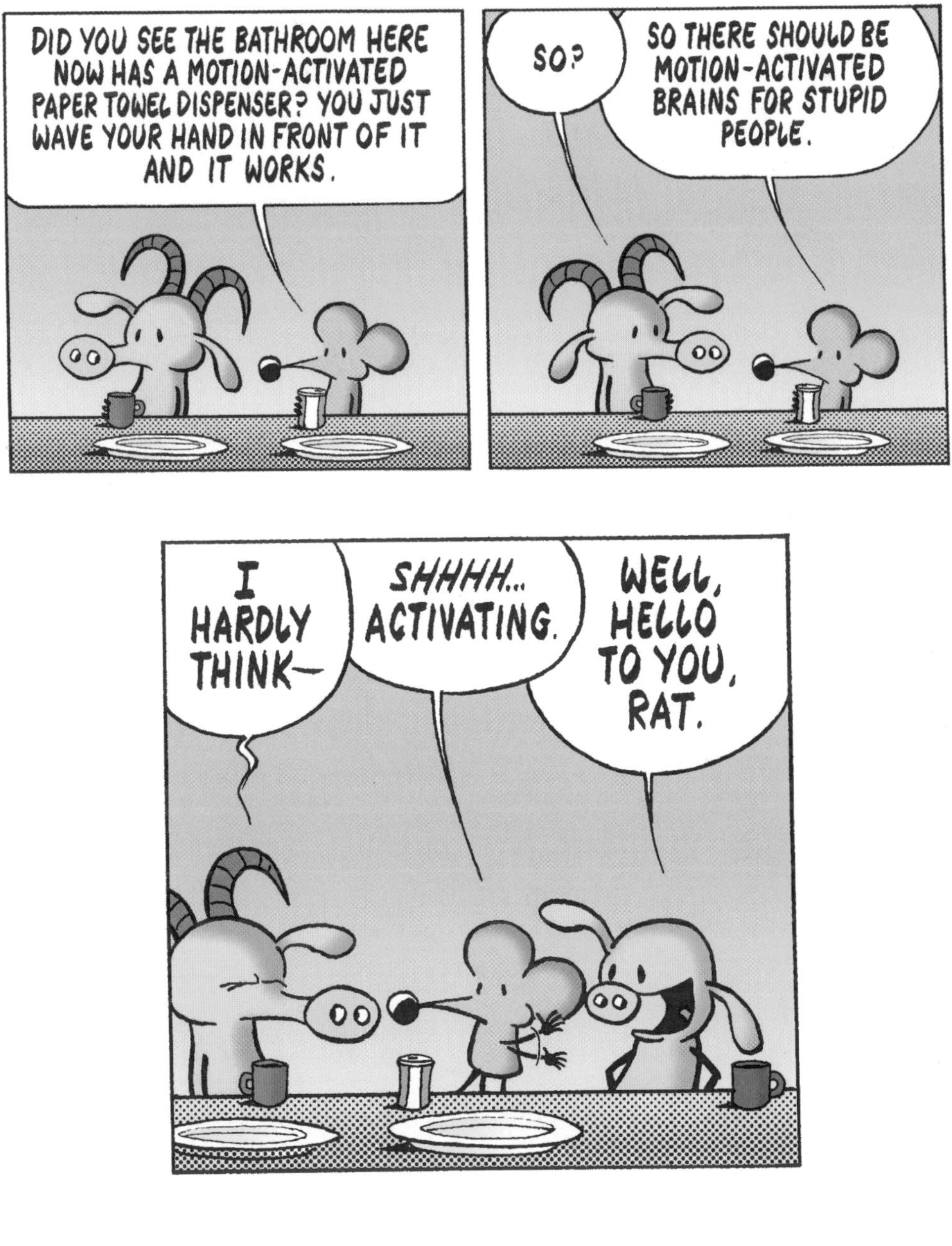
DID YOU SEE THE BATHROOM HERE NOW HAS A MOTION-ACTIVATED PAPER TOWEL DISPENSER? YOU JUST WAVE YOUR HAND IN FRONT OF IT AND IT WORKS.
SO?
SO THERE SHOULD BE MOTION-ACTIVATED BRAINS FOR STUPID PEOPLE.
I HARDLY THINK—
SHHHH... ACTIVATING.
WELL, HELLO TO YOU, RAT.

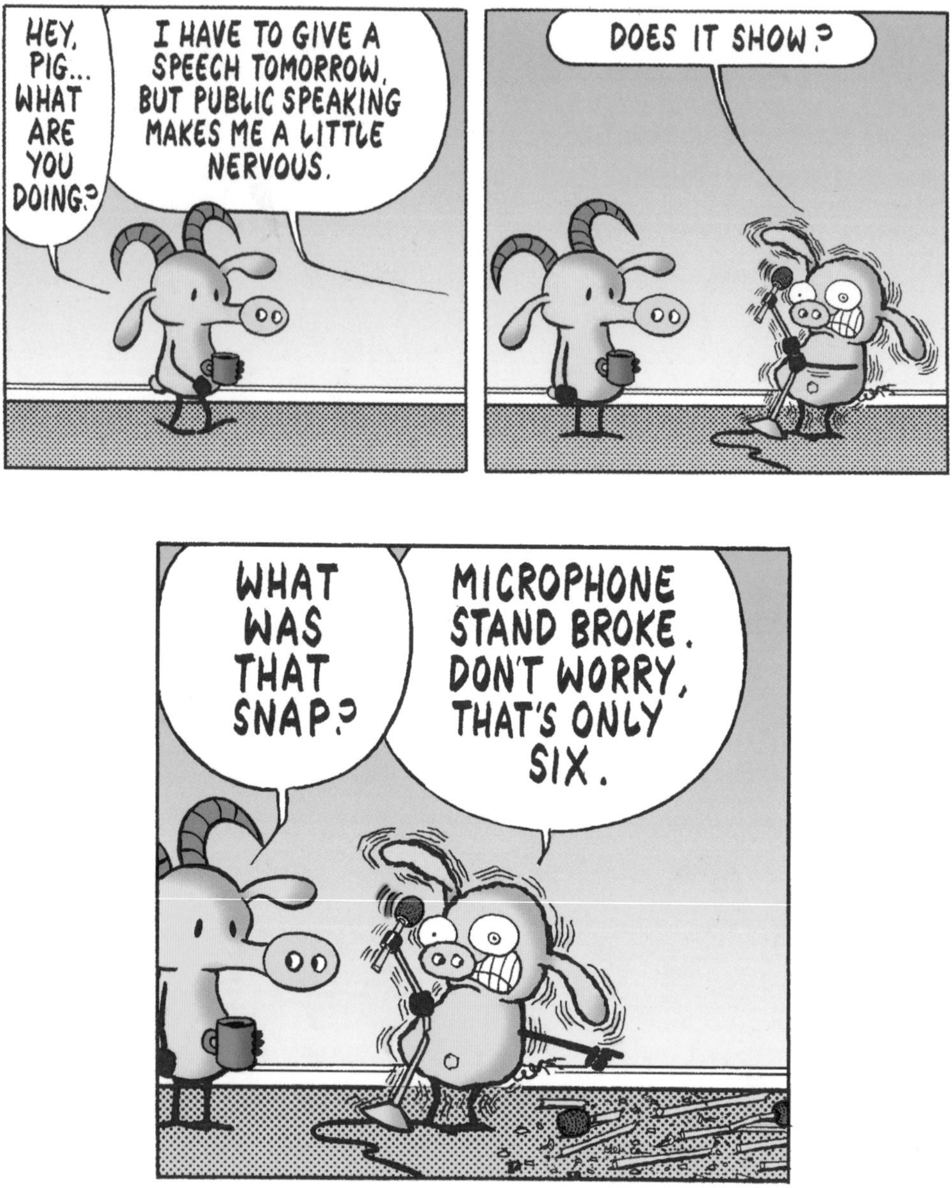
HEY, PIG... WHAT ARE YOU DOING?
I HAVE TO GIVE A SPEECH TOMORROW, BUT PUBLIC SPEAKING MAKES ME A LITTLE NERVOUS.
DOES IT SHOW?
WHAT WAS THAT SNAP?
MICROPHONE STAND BROKE. DON'T WORRY, THAT'S ONLY SIX.

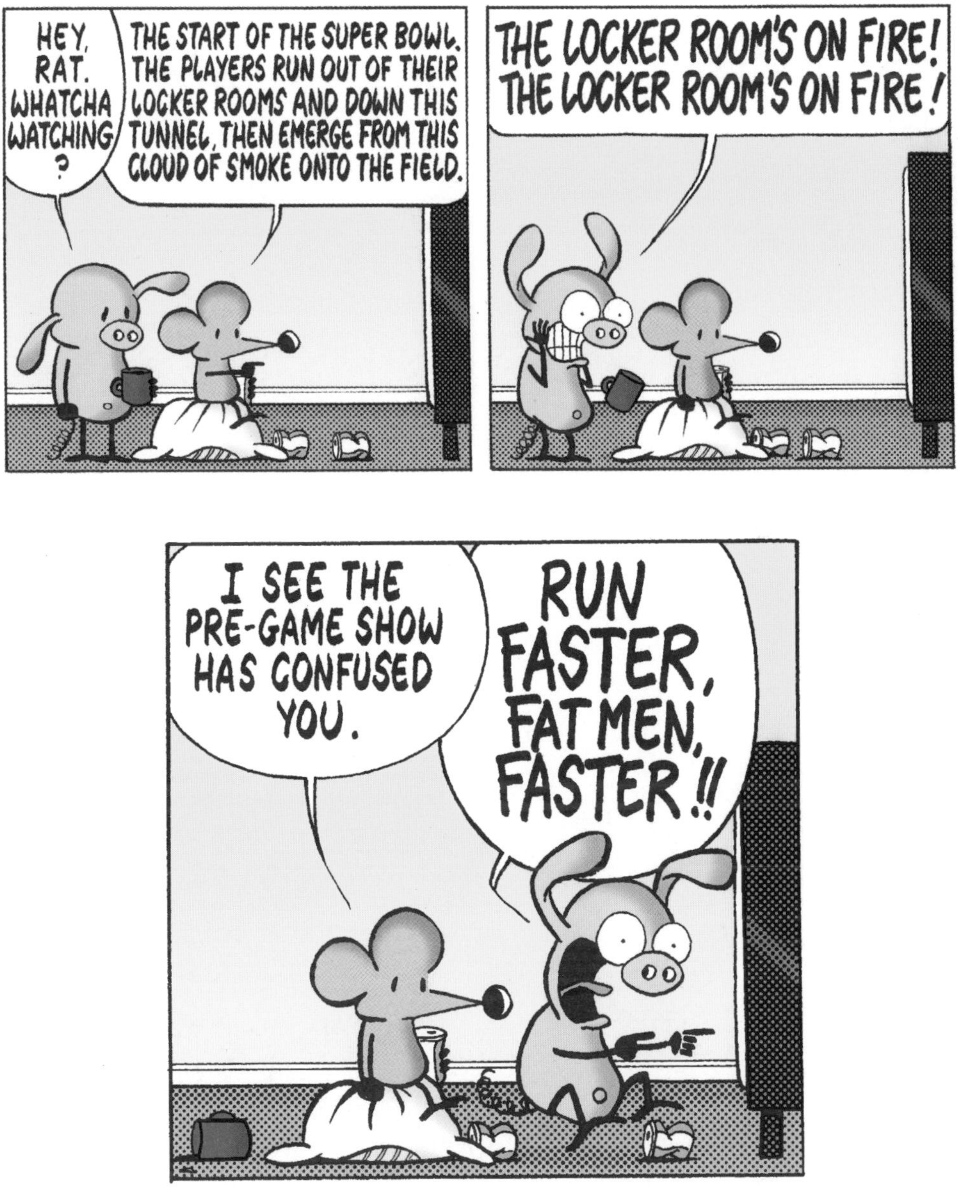
HEY, RAT. WHATCHA WATCHING?
THE START OF THE SUPER BOWL. THE PLAYERS RUN OUT OF THEIR LOCKER ROOMS AND DOWN THIS TUNNEL, THEN EMERGE FROM THIS CLOUD OF SMOKE ONTO THE FIELD.
THE LOCKER ROOM'S ON FIRE! THE LOCKER ROOM'S ON FIRE!
I SEE THE PRE-GAME SHOW HAS CONFUSED YOU.
RUN FASTER, FAT MEN, FASTER!!

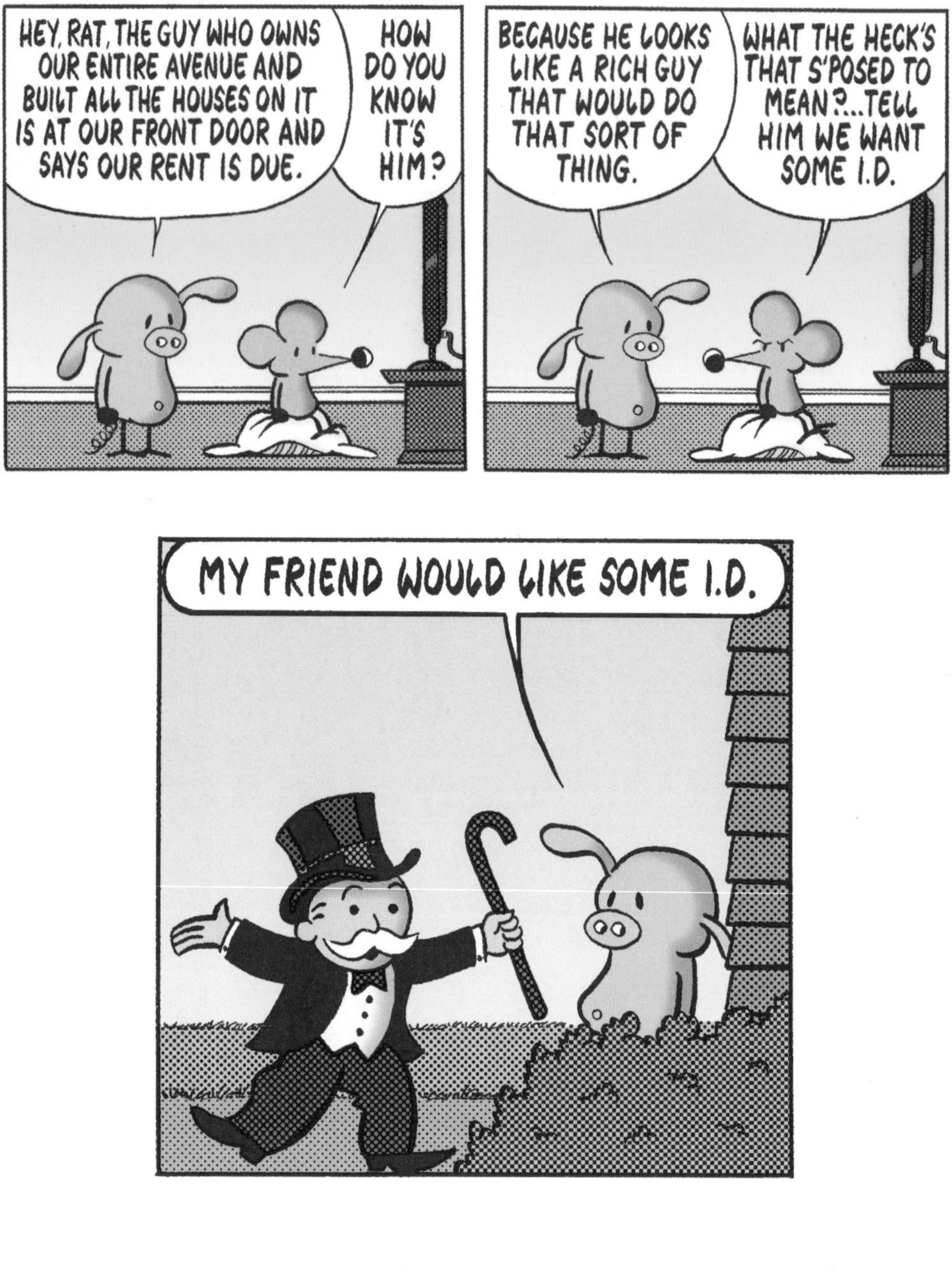
HEY, RAT, THE GUY WHO OWNS OUR ENTIRE AVENUE AND BUILT ALL THE HOUSES ON IT IS AT OUR FRONT DOOR AND SAYS OUR RENT IS DUE.
HOW DO YOU KNOW IT'S HIM?
BECAUSE HE LOOKS LIKE A RICH GUY THAT WOULD DO THAT SORT OF THING.
WHAT THE HECK'S THAT S'POSED TO MEAN?...TELL HIM WE WANT SOME I.D.
MY FRIEND WOULD LIKE SOME I.D.

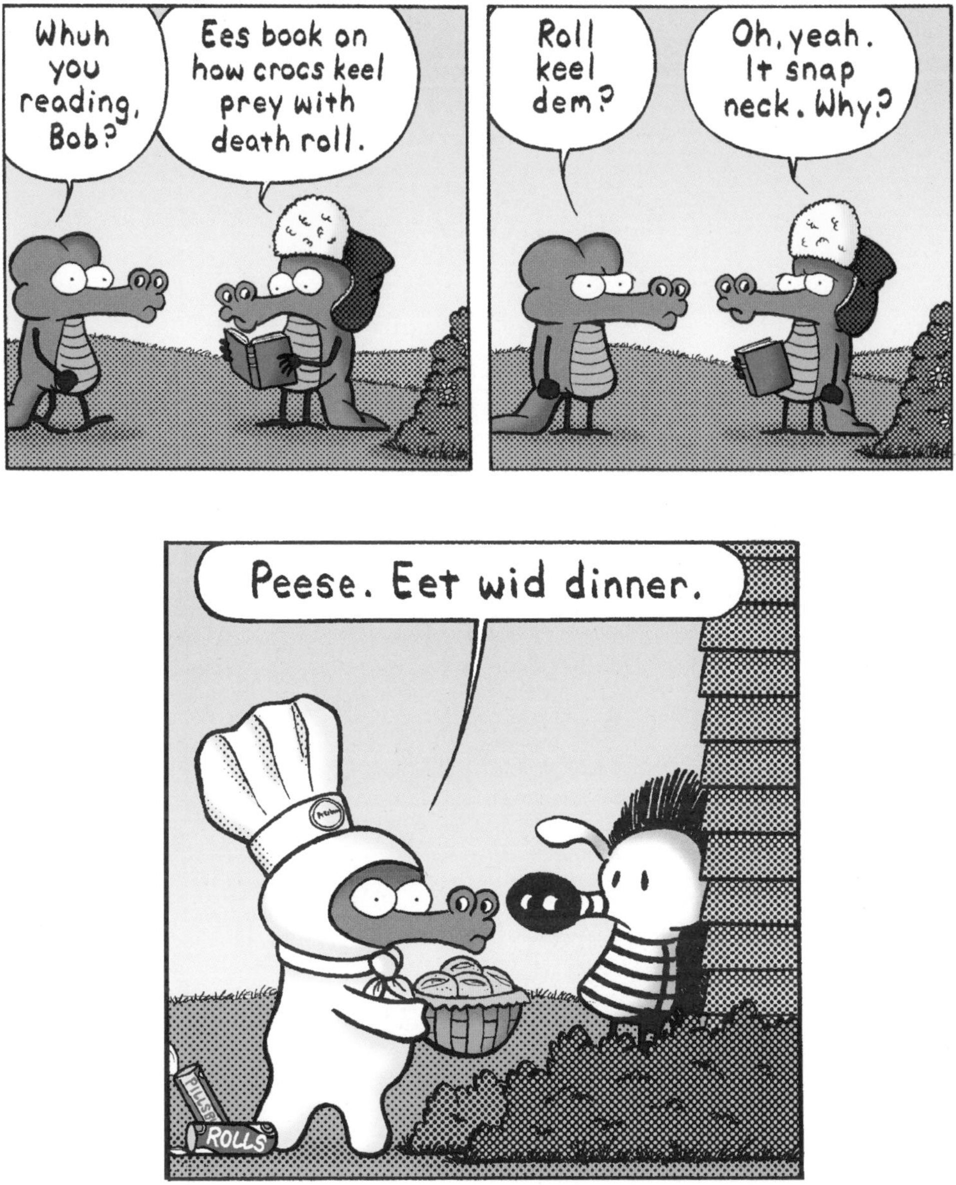
Whuh you reading, Bob?
Ees book on how crocs keel prey with death roll.
Roll keel dem?
Oh, yeah. It snap neck. Why?
Peese. Eet wid dinner.
ROLLS

WELL, SHOULD WE TRY IT?
I DON'T KNOW. LISTEN TO THIS.
'DO NOT ATTEMPT TO OPERATE BEFORE READING THIS MANUAL.'
'NEVER LEAVE THIS PRODUCT UNATTENDED WHEN IN USE.'
'ALWAYS KEEP HANDS AND HAIR AWAY FROM MOVING PARTS.'
'STEEL CUTTING METHODS USED TO MANUFACTURE PRODUCT COULD RESULT IN SHARP EDGES. TAKE CARE IN HANDLING.'
'USE EXTREME CAUTION WHEN MOVING THE PRODUCT.'

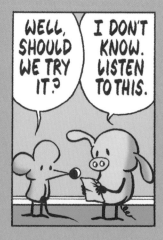

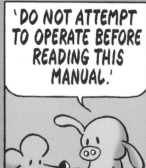

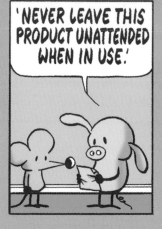

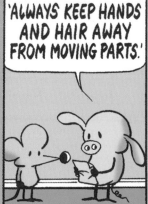

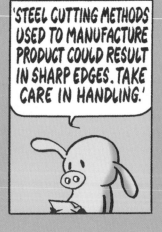

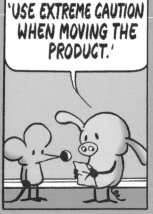

'VERY HIGH TEMPERATURES ARE REACHED DURING USE. TAKE EXTREME CARE WHEN PRODUCT IS IN USE.'
'DO NOT OPERATE NEAR DRAPES, CURTAINS, OR WALLS, AS FIRE AND SUBSTANTIAL PROPERTY DAMAGE MAY RESULT.'
'FAILURE ON THE PART OF THE USER TO ADHERE TO THESE WARNINGS COULD RESULT IN SERIOUS INJURY OR DEATH OF THE USER.'
I'VE NEVER BEEN SO AFRAID OF A TOASTER.

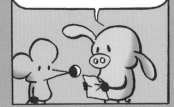

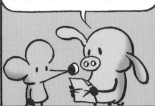

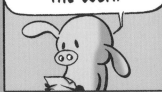

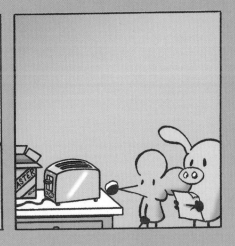

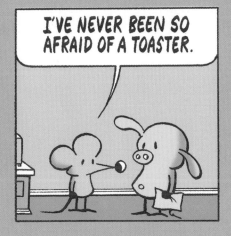

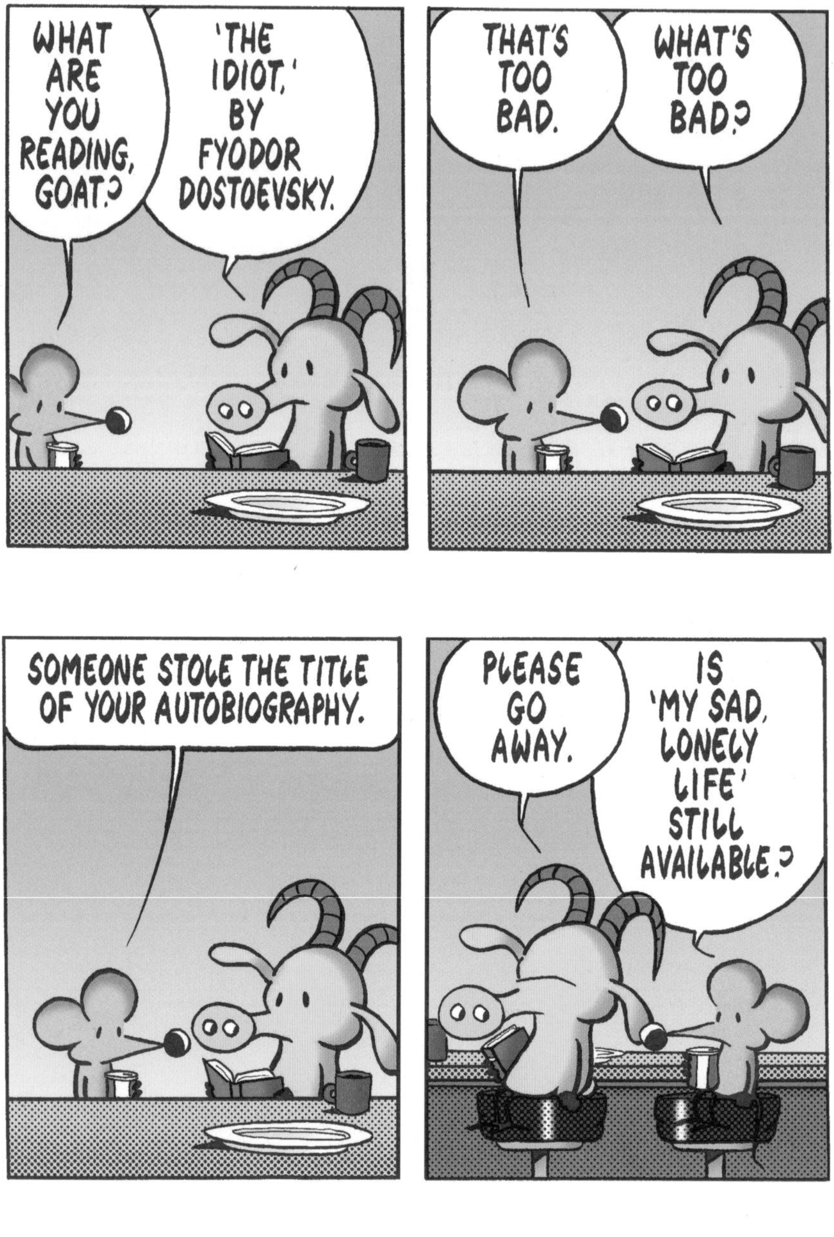
WHAT ARE YOU READING, GOAT?
'THE IDIOT,' BY FYODOR DOSTOEVSKY.
THAT'S TOO BAD.
WHAT'S TOO BAD?
SOMEONE STOLE THE TITLE OF YOUR AUTOBIOGRAPHY.
PLEASE GO AWAY.
IS 'MY SAD, LONELY LIFE' STILL AVAILABLE?

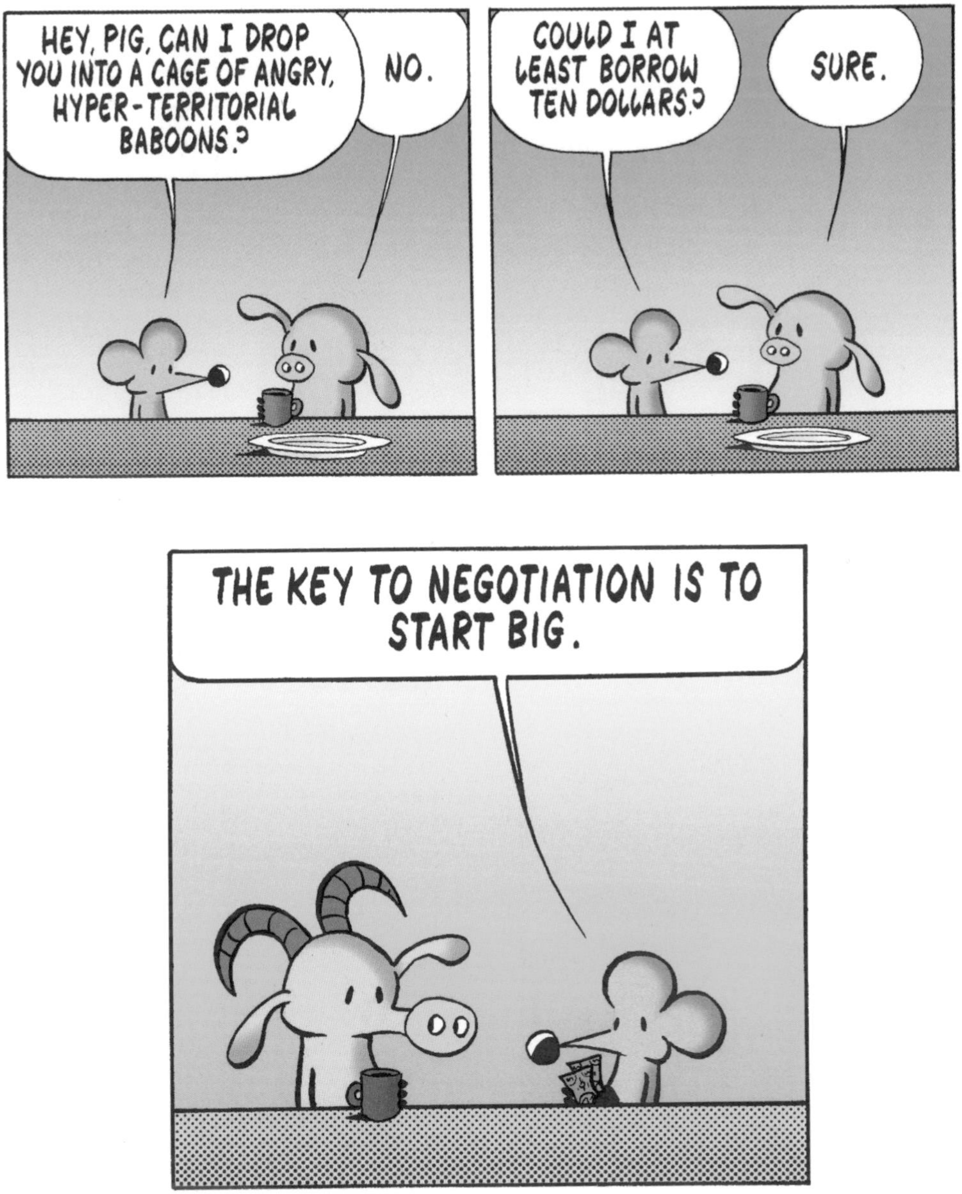
HEY, PIG, CAN I DROP YOU INTO A CAGE OF ANGRY, HYPER-TERRITORIAL BABOONS?
NO.
COULD I AT LEAST BORROW TEN DOLLARS?
SURE.
THE KEY TO NEGOTIATION IS TO START BIG.

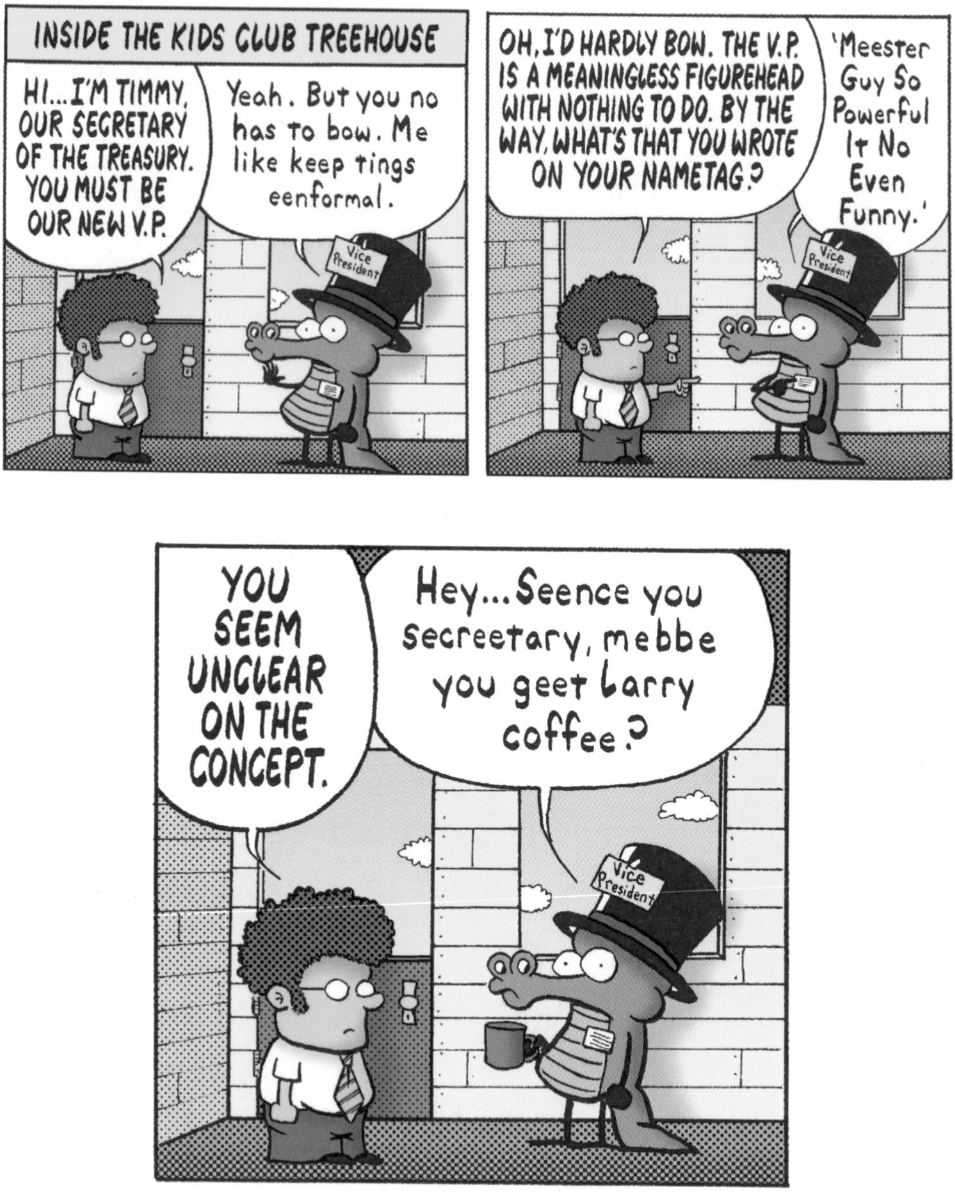
INSIDE THE KIDS CLUB TREEHOUSE
HI... I'M TIMMY, OUR SECRETARY OF THE TREASURY. YOU MUST BE OUR NEW V.P.
Yeah. But you no has to bow. Me like keep tings eenformal.
Vice President
OH, I'D HARDLY BOW. THE V.P. IS A MEANINGLESS FIGUREHEAD WITH NOTHING TO DO. BY THE WAY, WHAT'S THAT YOU WROTE ON YOUR NAMETAG?
'Meester Guy So Powerful It No Even Funny.'
Vice President
YOU SEEM UNCLEAR ON THE CONCEPT.
Hey... Seence you secreetary, mebbe you geet Larry coffee?
Vice President

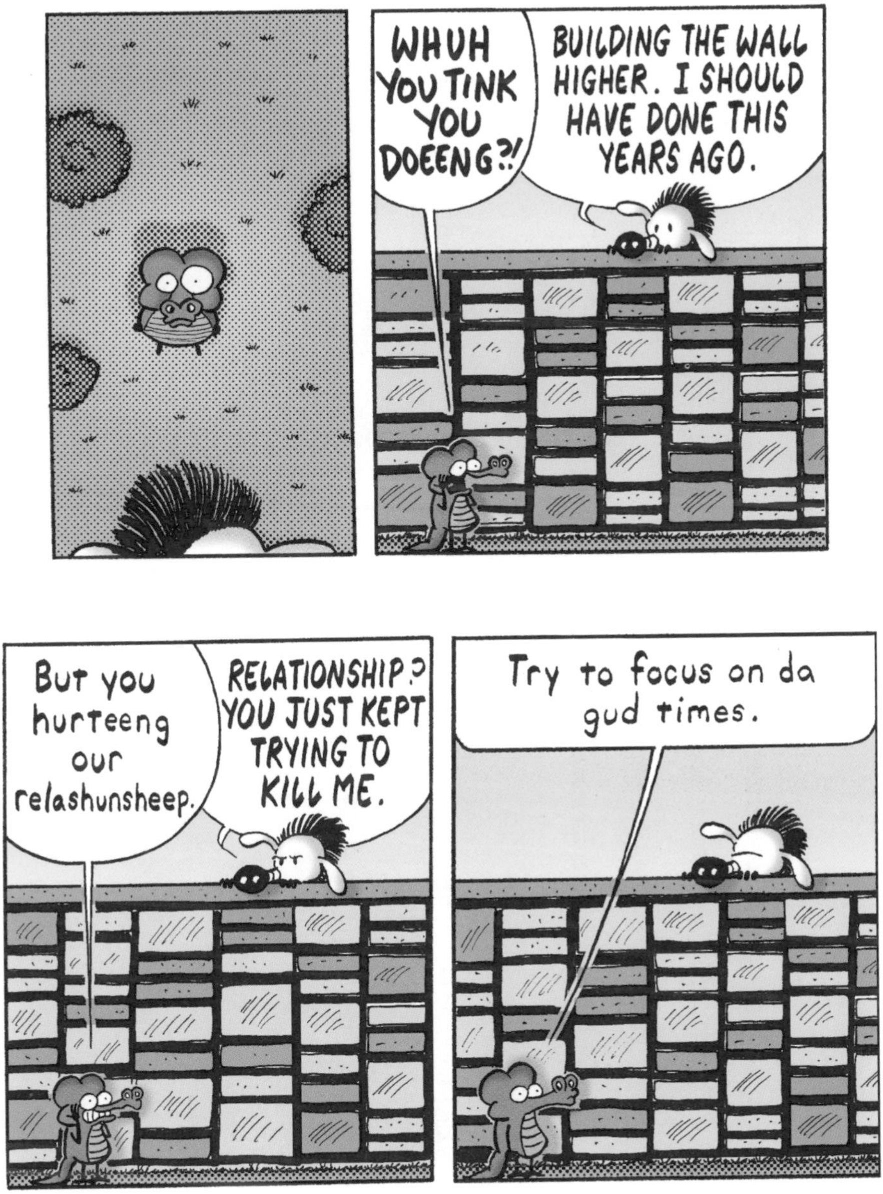
WHUH YOU TINK YOU DOEENG?!
BUILDING THE WALL HIGHER. I SHOULD HAVE DONE THIS YEARS AGO.
But you hurteeng our relashunsheep.
RELATIONSHIP? YOU JUST KEPT TRYING TO KILL ME.
Try to focus on da gud times.

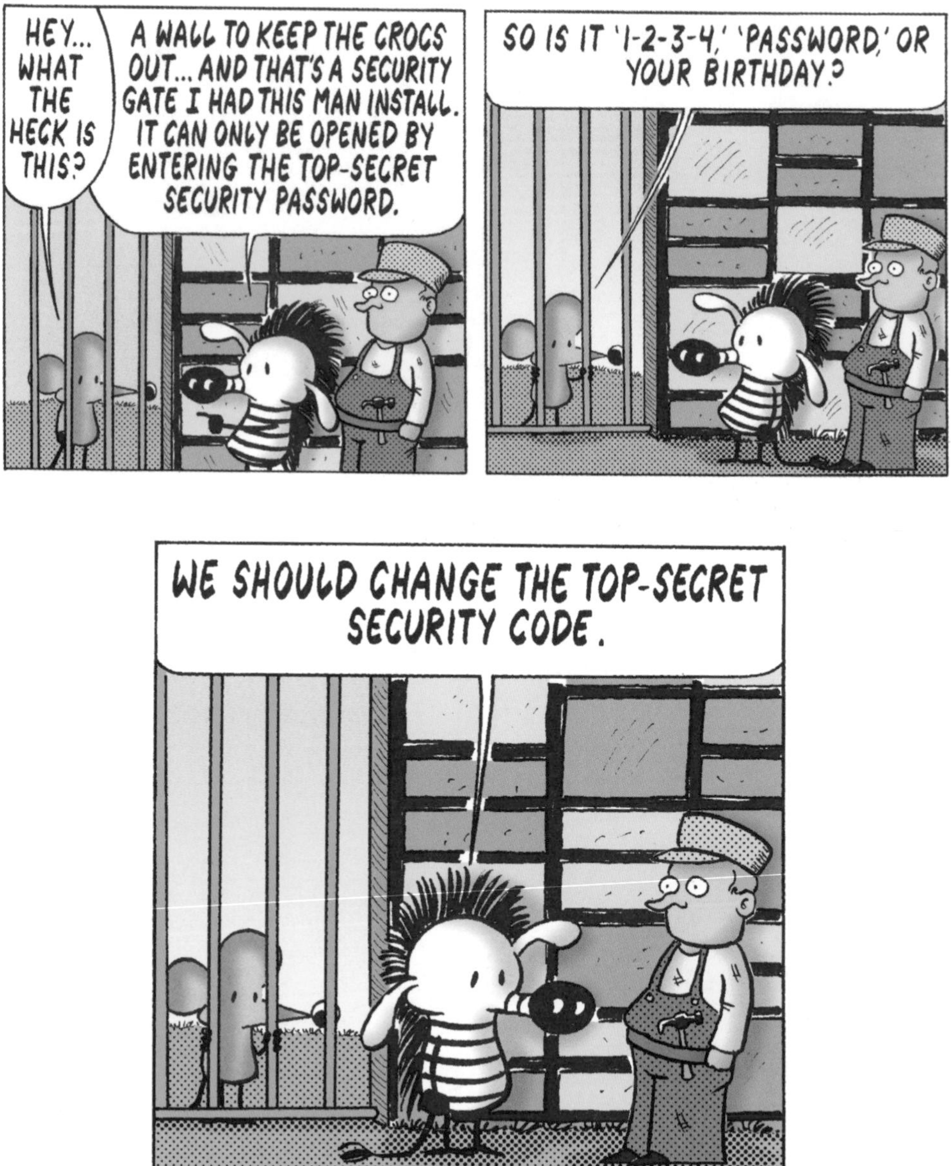
HEY... WHAT THE HECK IS THIS?
A WALL TO KEEP THE CROCS OUT... AND THAT'S A SECURITY GATE I HAD THIS MAN INSTALL. IT CAN ONLY BE OPENED BY ENTERING THE TOP-SECRET SECURITY PASSWORD.
SO IS IT '1-2-3-4,' 'PASSWORD,' OR YOUR BIRTHDAY?
WE SHOULD CHANGE THE TOP-SECRET SECURITY CODE.

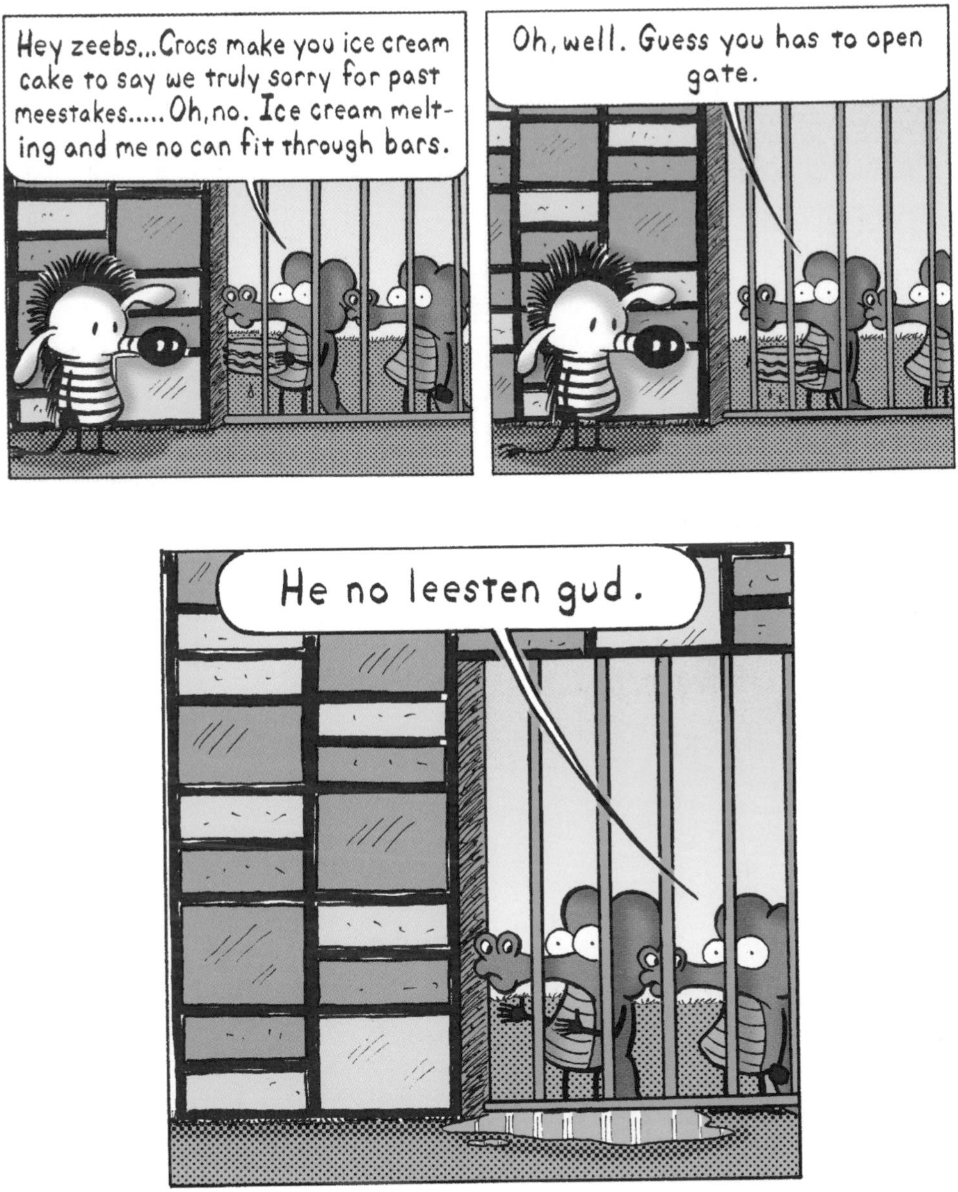
Hey zeebs...Crocs make you ice cream cake to say we truly sorry for past meestakes.....Oh, no. Ice cream melting and me no can fit through bars.
Oh, well. Guess you has to open gate.
He no leesten gud.

NOW THAT YOU HAVE THIS BIG WALL AROUND YOUR PROPERTY, AREN'T YOU WORRIED YOU COULD LOSE THE KEY TO THE GATE?
NO. I HAVE A SPARE THAT I KEEP IN A SAFE PLACE.
SAFE ENOUGH THAT YOU DON'T THINK THE CROCS CAN GET TO IT?
YEP.

Reech for it, Bob.
You reech for it, Burt.

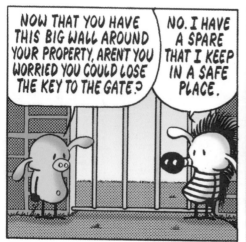

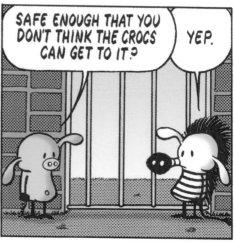

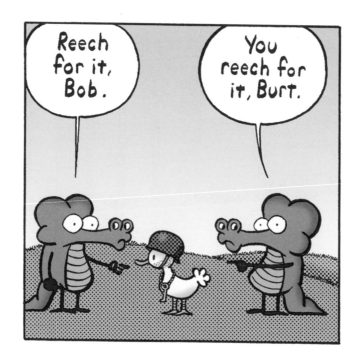

HEY, DAD, WHY'S YOUR PAL BOB IN THE BATHROOM?

He changing clothes. Gonna dress like person from City Planning Deepartment. Tell zeeba he have to tear down beeg wall around property.

DOES HE REALLY RESEMBLE A PERSON?

Peese, son. No eensult us.

Yeah. No eensult us.

Whoa. Reesemblance uncanny.

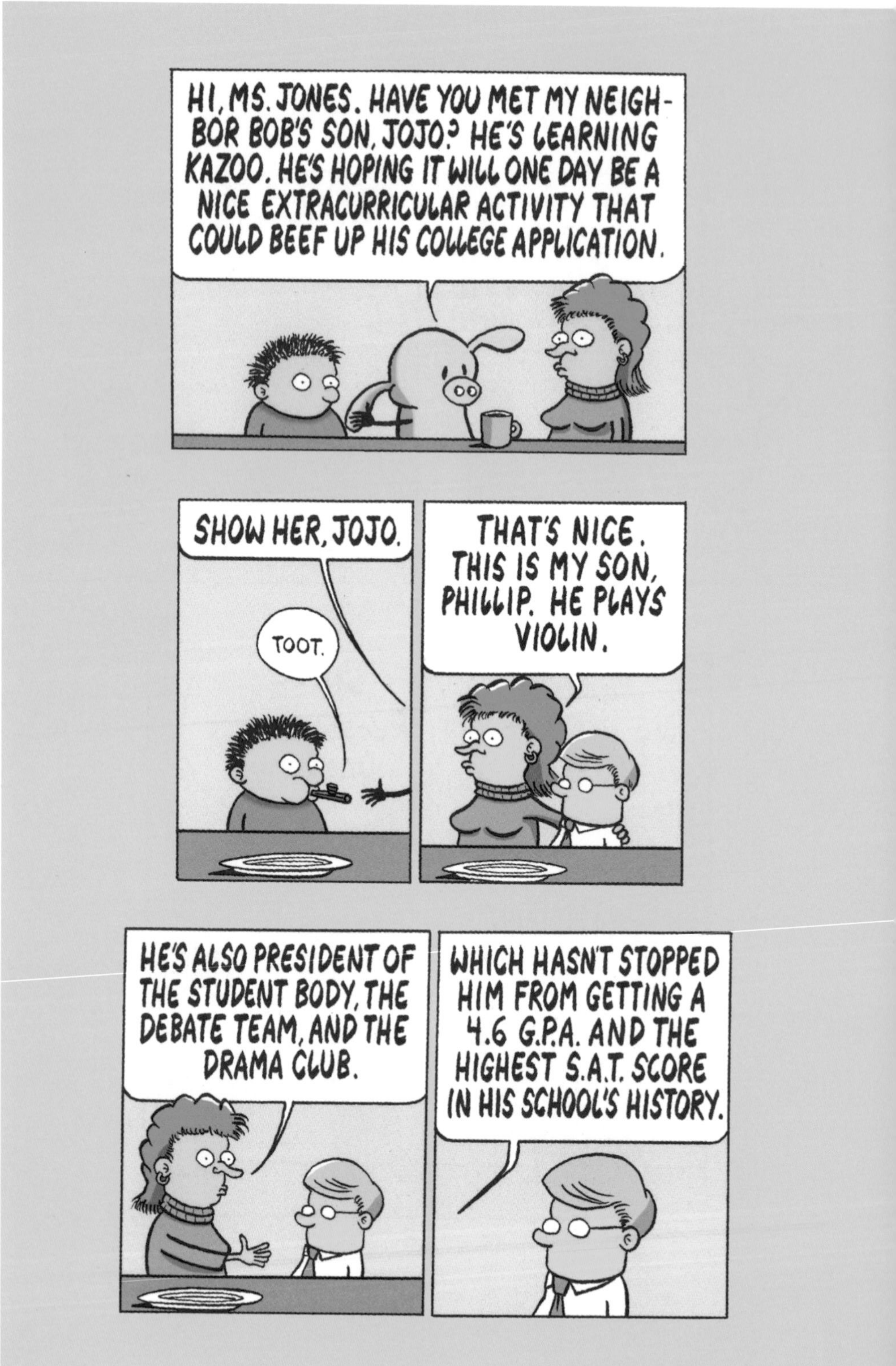
HI, MS. JONES. HAVE YOU MET MY NEIGHBOR BOB'S SON, JOJO? HE'S LEARNING KAZOO. HE'S HOPING IT WILL ONE DAY BE A NICE EXTRACURRICULAR ACTIVITY THAT COULD BEEF UP HIS COLLEGE APPLICATION.
SHOW HER, JOJO.
TOOT.
THAT'S NICE. THIS IS MY SON, PHILLIP. HE PLAYS VIOLIN.
HE'S ALSO PRESIDENT OF THE STUDENT BODY, THE DEBATE TEAM, AND THE DRAMA CLUB.
WHICH HASN'T STOPPED HIM FROM GETTING A 4.6 G.P.A. AND THE HIGHEST S.A.T. SCORE IN HIS SCHOOL'S HISTORY.

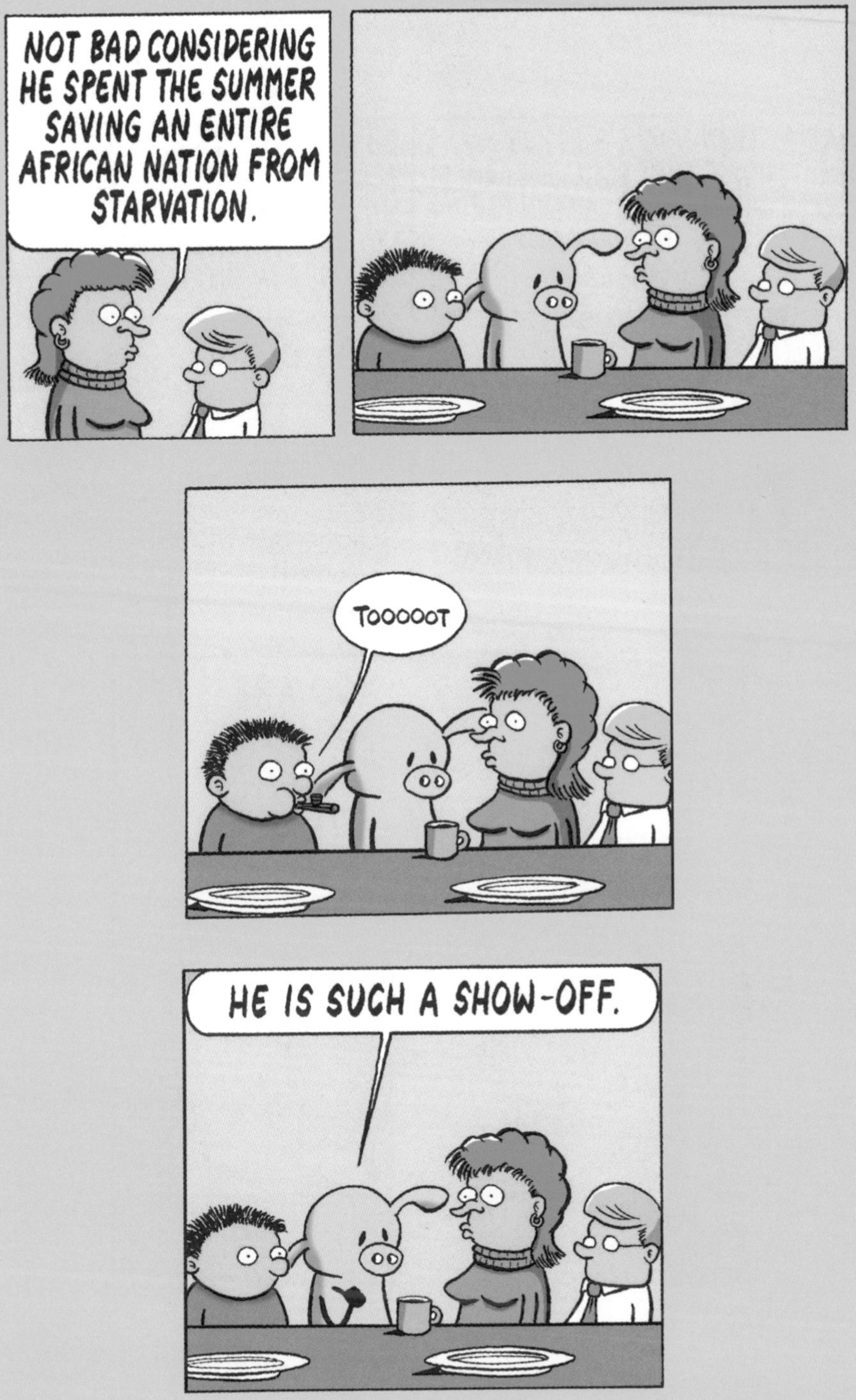
NOT BAD CONSIDERING HE SPENT THE SUMMER SAVING AN ENTIRE AFRICAN NATION FROM STARVATION.
TOOOOOT
HE IS SUCH A SHOW-OFF.

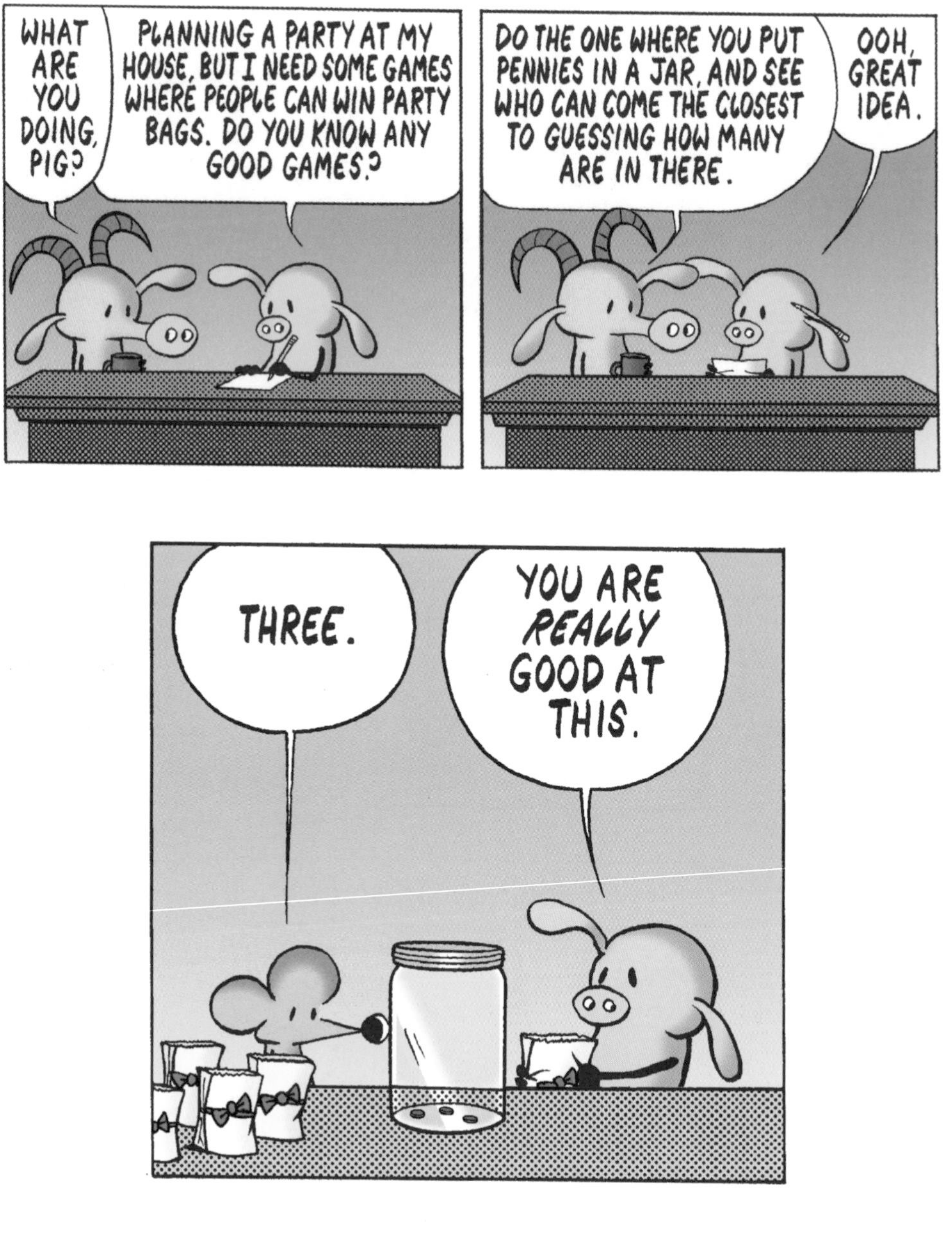
WHAT ARE YOU DOING, PIG?
PLANNING A PARTY AT MY HOUSE, BUT I NEED SOME GAMES WHERE PEOPLE CAN WIN PARTY BAGS. DO YOU KNOW ANY GOOD GAMES?
DO THE ONE WHERE YOU PUT PENNIES IN A JAR, AND SEE WHO CAN COME THE CLOSEST TO GUESSING HOW MANY ARE IN THERE.
OOH, GREAT IDEA.
THREE.
YOU ARE REALLY GOOD AT THIS.

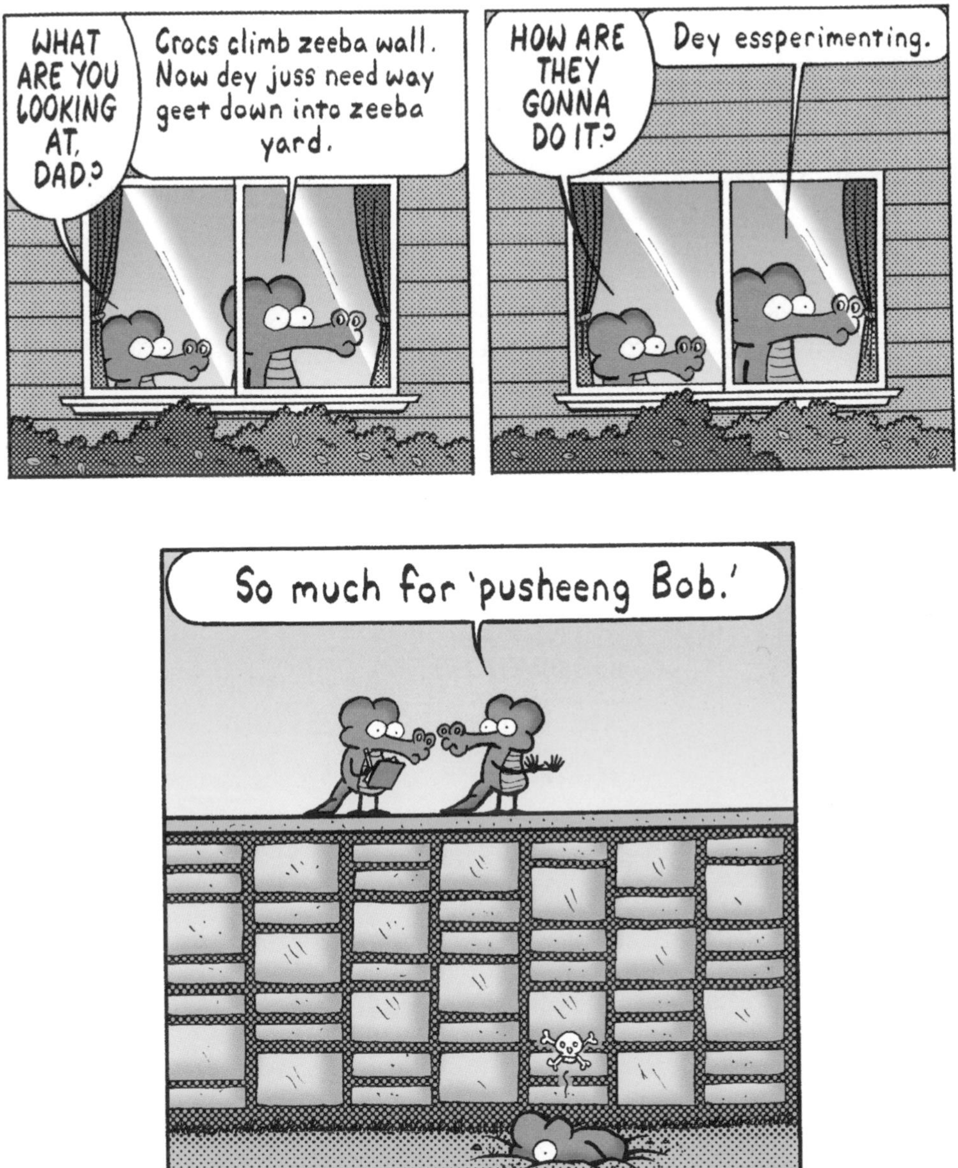
WHAT ARE YOU LOOKING AT, DAD?
Crocs climb zeeba wall. Now dey juss need way geet down into zeeba yard.
HOW ARE THEY GONNA DO IT?
Dey essperimenting.
So much for 'pusheeng Bob.'

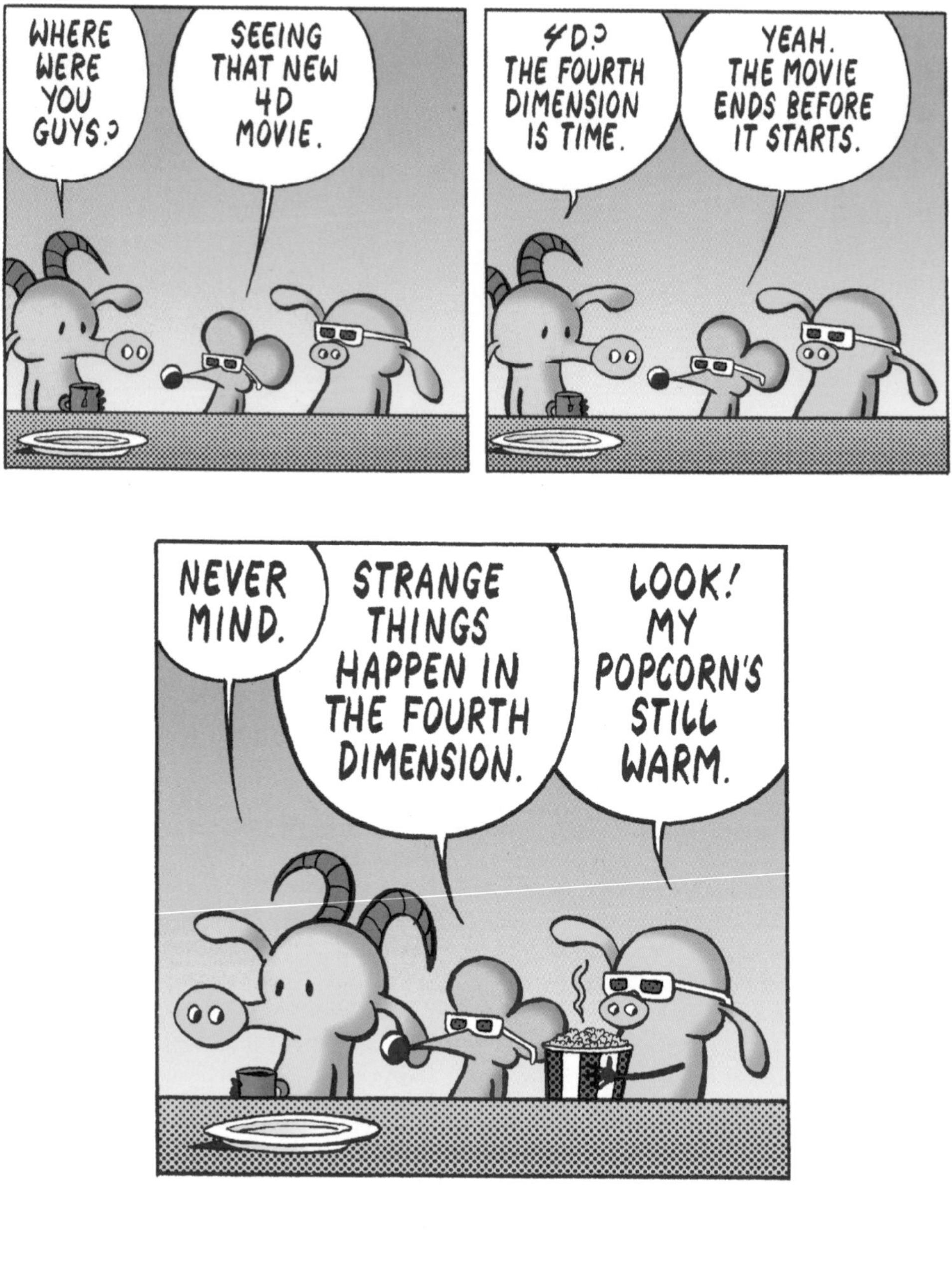
WHERE WERE YOU GUYS?
SEEING THAT NEW 4D MOVIE.
4D? THE FOURTH DIMENSION IS TIME.
YEAH. THE MOVIE ENDS BEFORE IT STARTS.
NEVER MIND.
STRANGE THINGS HAPPEN IN THE FOURTH DIMENSION.
LOOK! MY POPCORN'S STILL WARM.

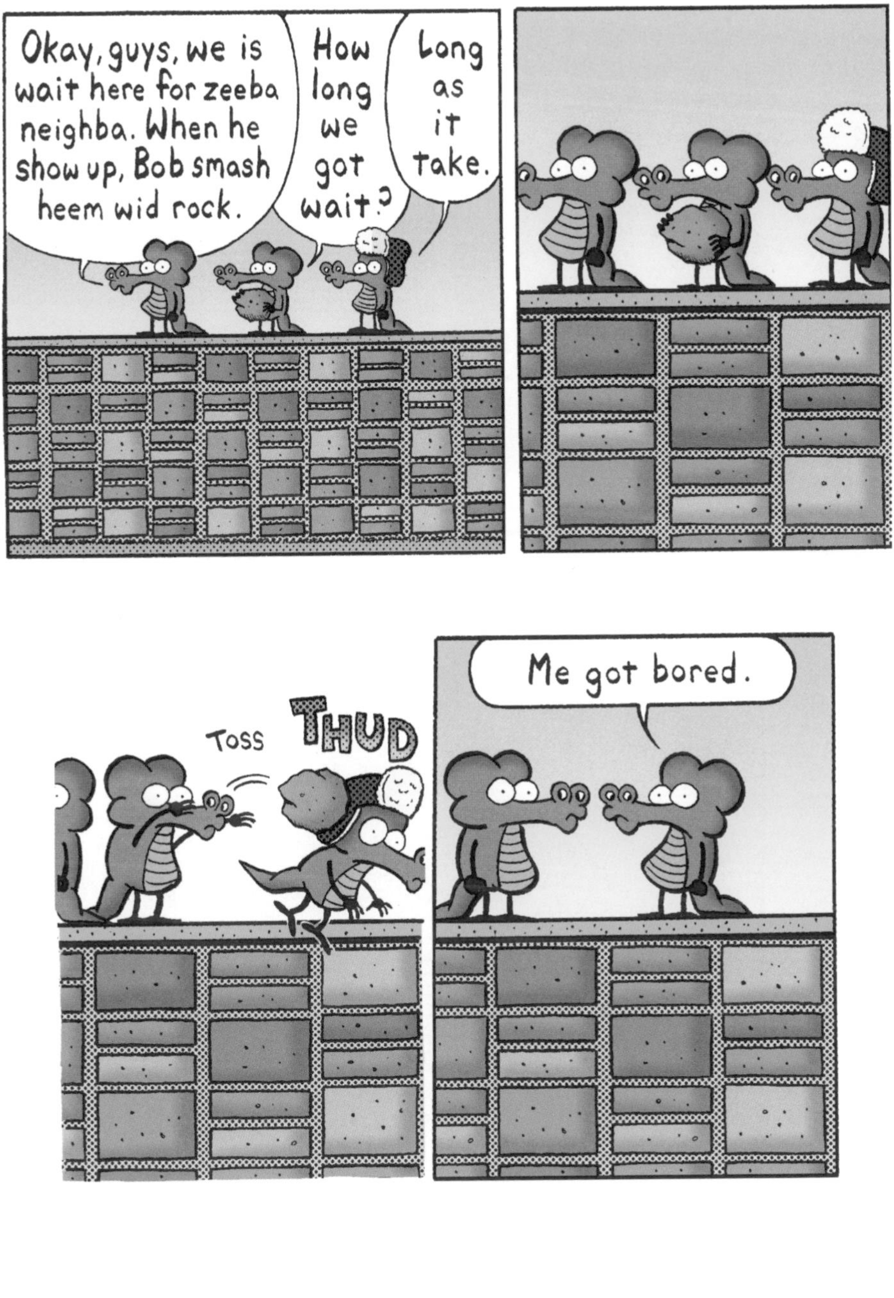
Okay, guys, we is wait here for zeeba neighba. When he show up, Bob smash heem wid rock.
How long we got wait?
Long as it take.
Toss
THUD
Me got bored.

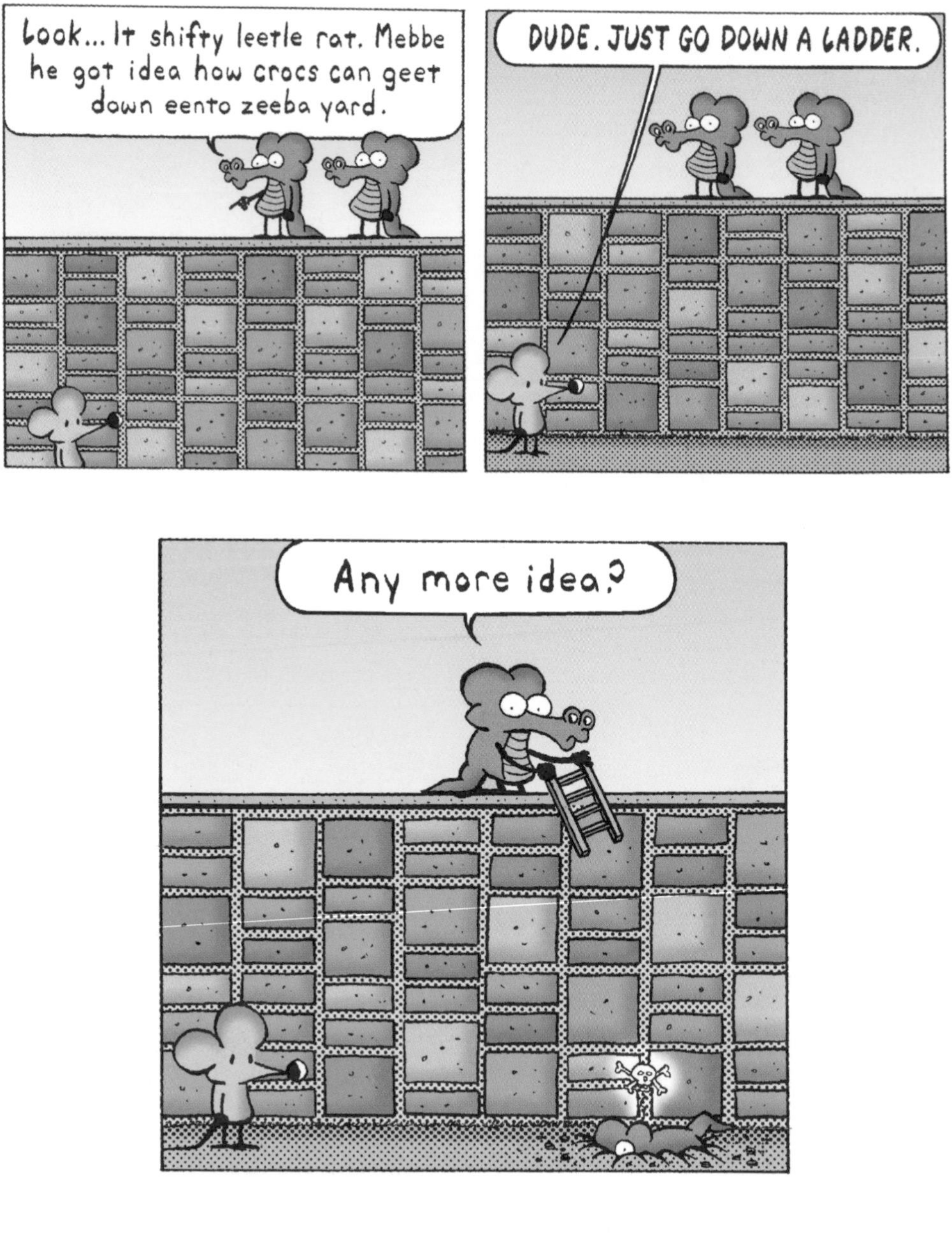
Look... It shifty leetle rat. Mebbe he got idea how crocs can geet down eento zeeba yard.
DUDE. JUST GO DOWN A LADDER.
Any more idea?

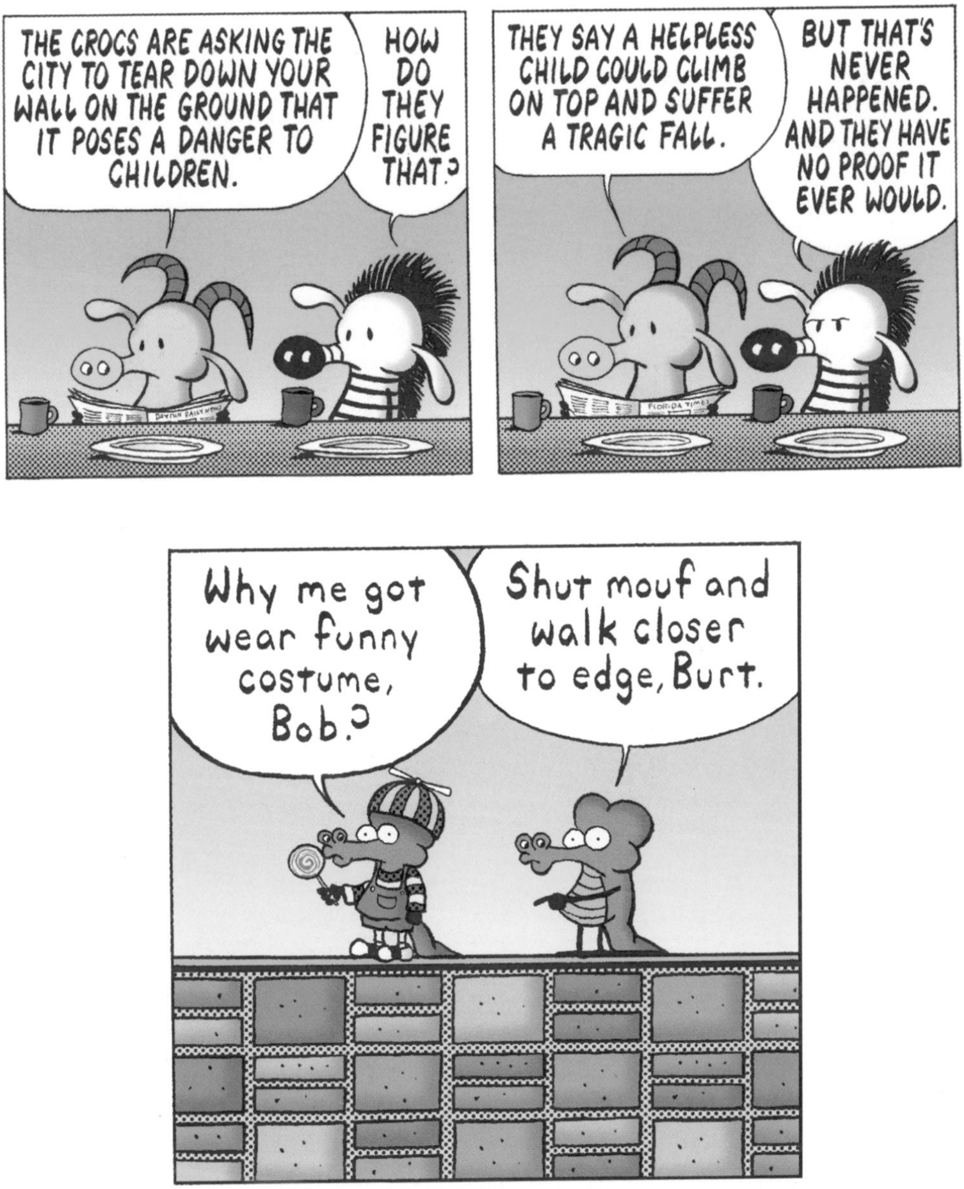
THE CROCS ARE ASKING THE CITY TO TEAR DOWN YOUR WALL ON THE GROUND THAT IT POSES A DANGER TO CHILDREN.
HOW DO THEY FIGURE THAT?
THEY SAY A HELPLESS CHILD COULD CLIMB ON TOP AND SUFFER A TRAGIC FALL.
BUT THAT'S NEVER HAPPENED. AND THEY HAVE NO PROOF IT EVER WOULD.
Why me got wear funny costume, Bob?
Shut mouf and walk closer to edge, Burt.

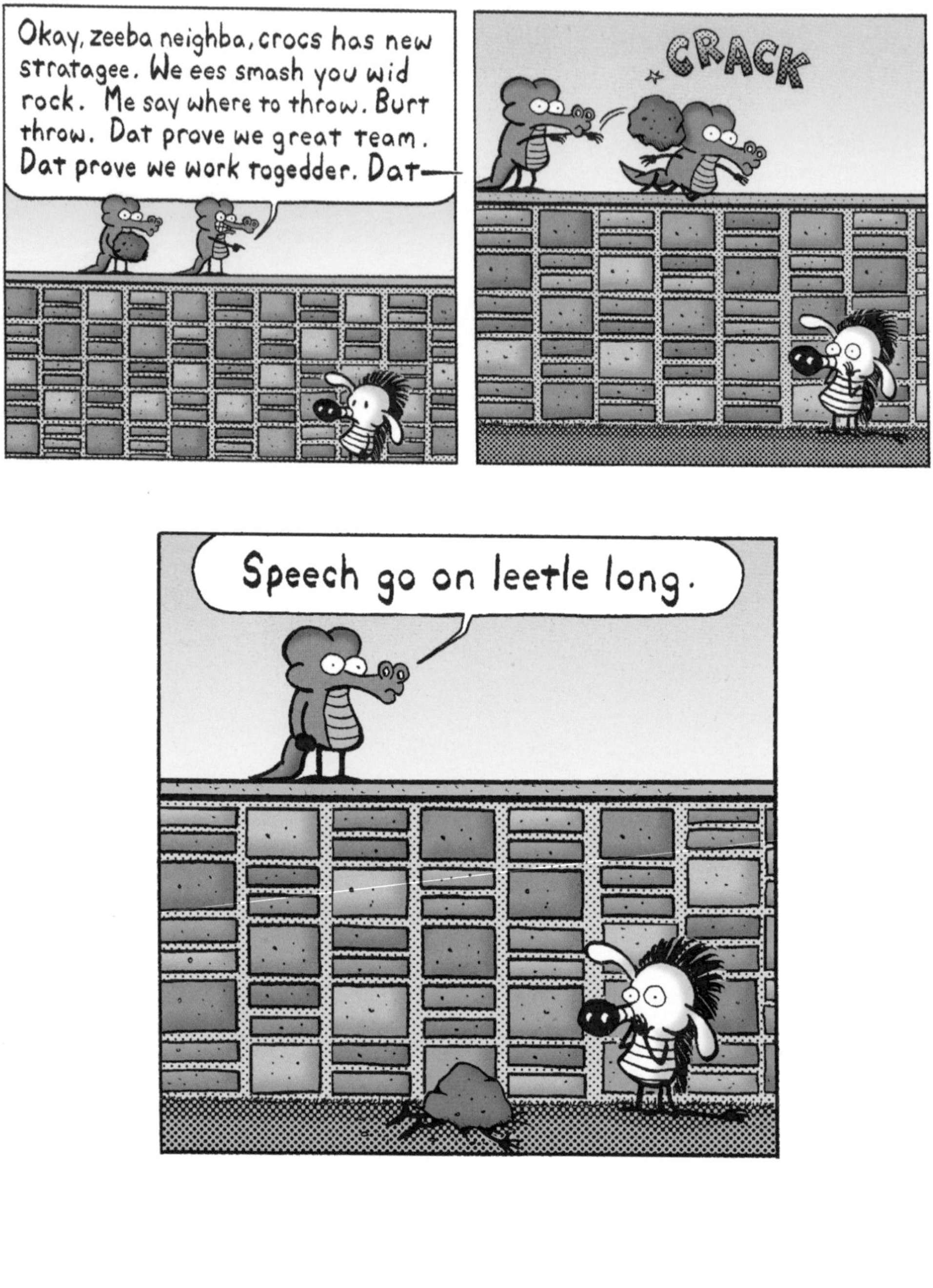
Okay, zeeba neighba, crocs has new stratagee. We ees smash you wid rock. Me say where to throw. Burt throw. Dat prove we great team. Dat prove we work togedder. Dat—
CRACK
Speech go on leetle long.

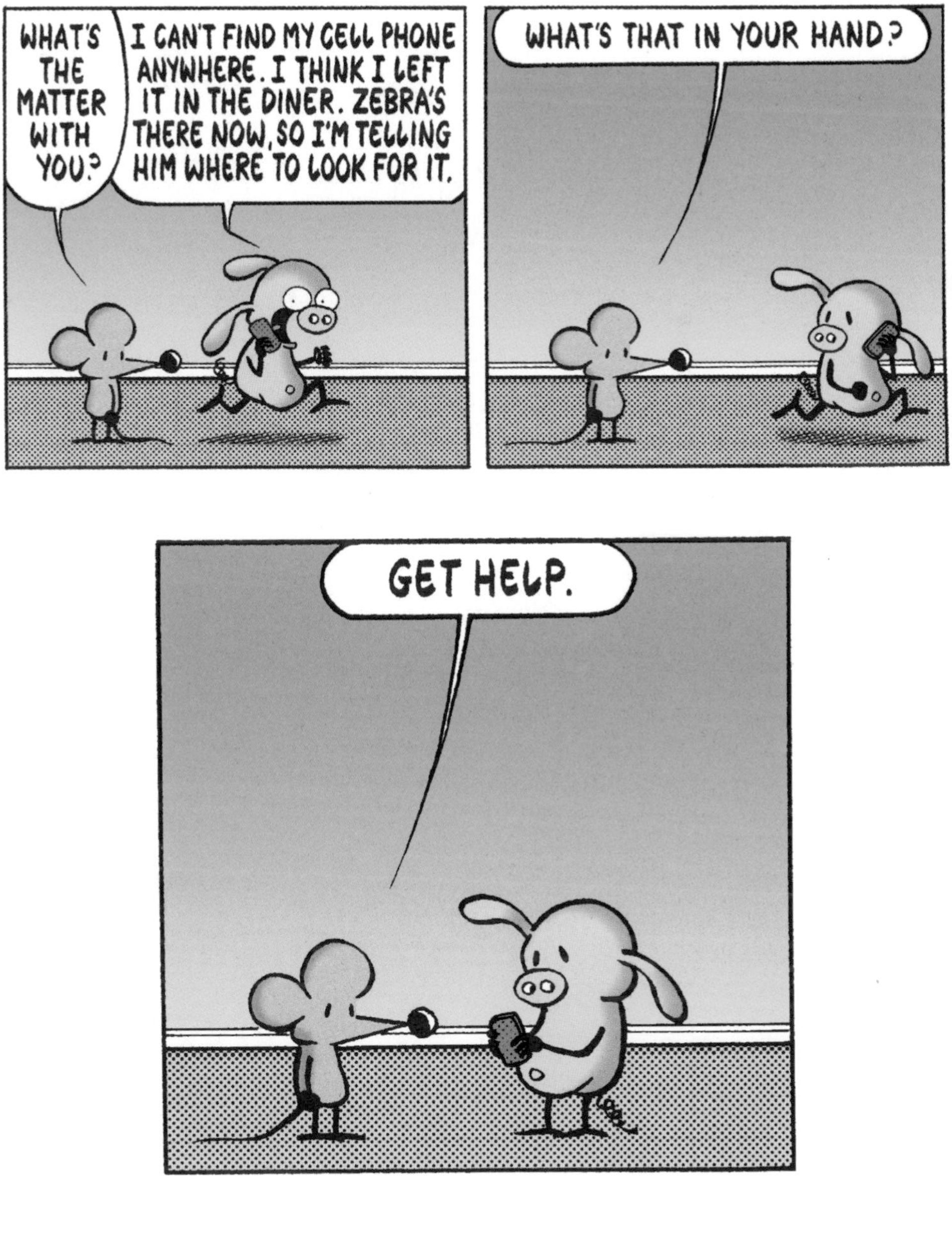
WHAT'S THE MATTER WITH YOU?
I CAN'T FIND MY CELL PHONE ANYWHERE. I THINK I LEFT IT IN THE DINER. ZEBRA'S THERE NOW, SO I'M TELLING HIM WHERE TO LOOK FOR IT.
WHAT'S THAT IN YOUR HAND?
GET HELP.

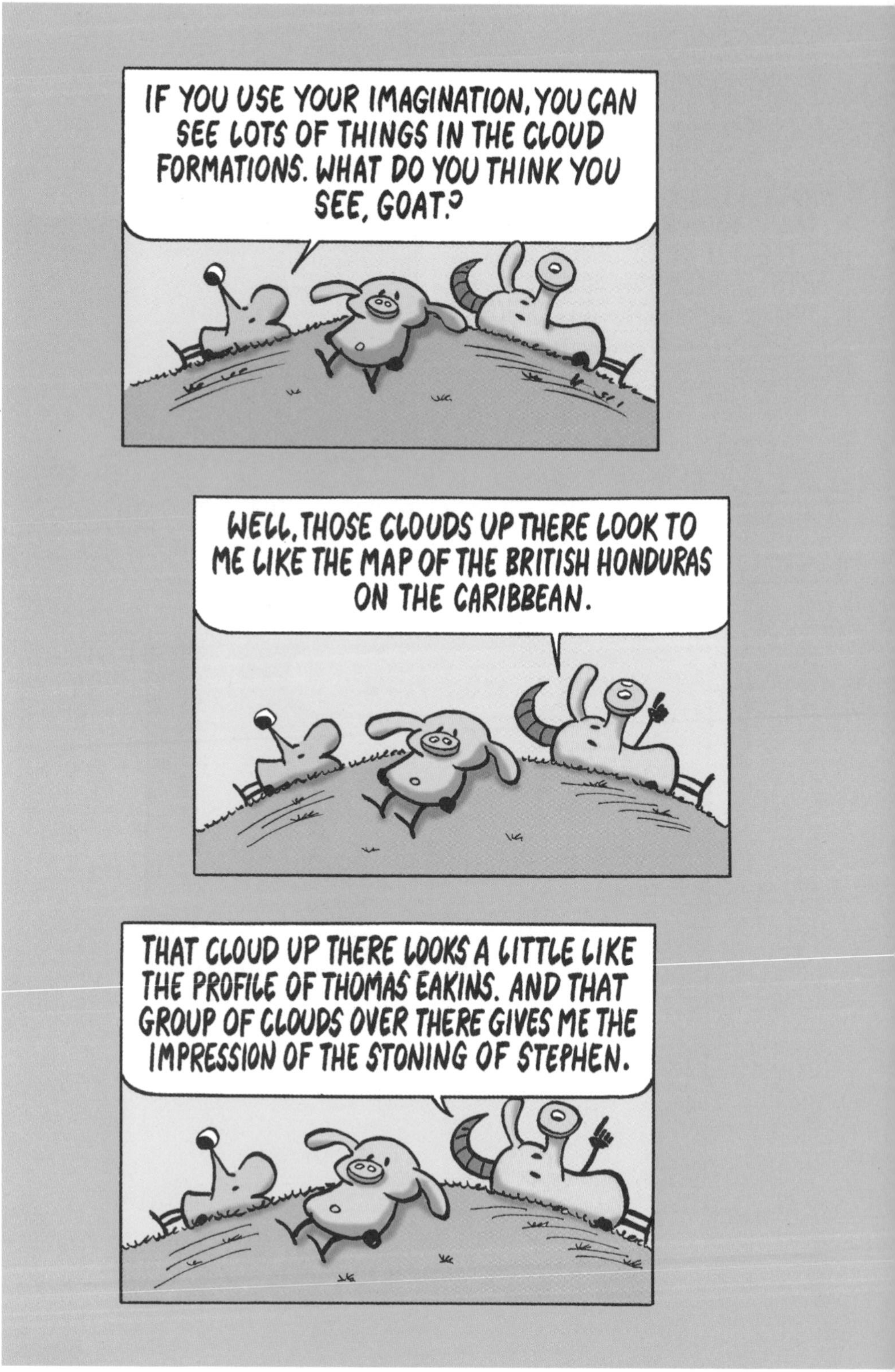
IF YOU USE YOUR IMAGINATION, YOU CAN SEE LOTS OF THINGS IN THE CLOUD FORMATIONS. WHAT DO YOU THINK YOU SEE, GOAT?
WELL, THOSE CLOUDS UP THERE LOOK TO ME LIKE THE MAP OF THE BRITISH HONDURAS ON THE CARIBBEAN.
THAT CLOUD UP THERE LOOKS A LITTLE LIKE THE PROFILE OF THOMAS EAKINS. AND THAT GROUP OF CLOUDS OVER THERE GIVES ME THE IMPRESSION OF THE STONING OF STEPHEN.

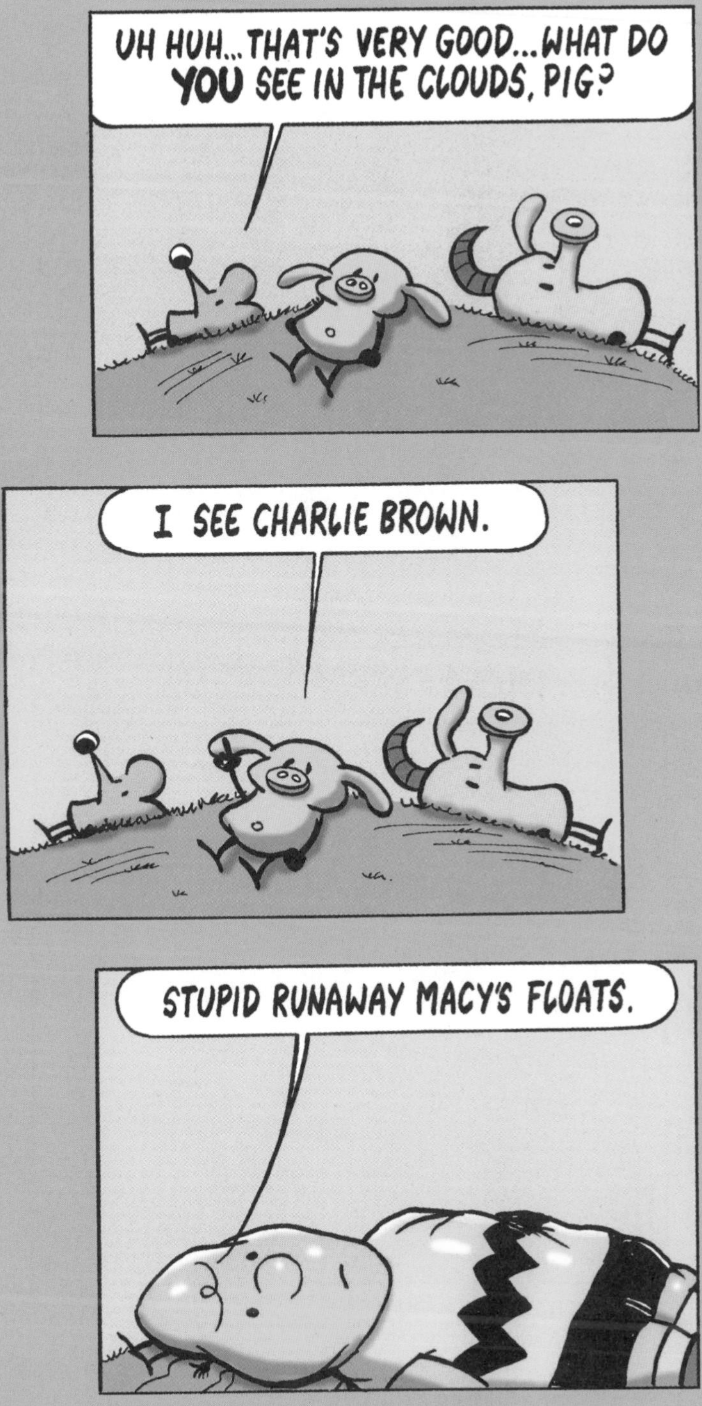
UH HUH... THAT'S VERY GOOD... WHAT DO YOU SEE IN THE CLOUDS, PIG?
I SEE CHARLIE BROWN.
STUPID RUNAWAY MACY'S FLOATS.

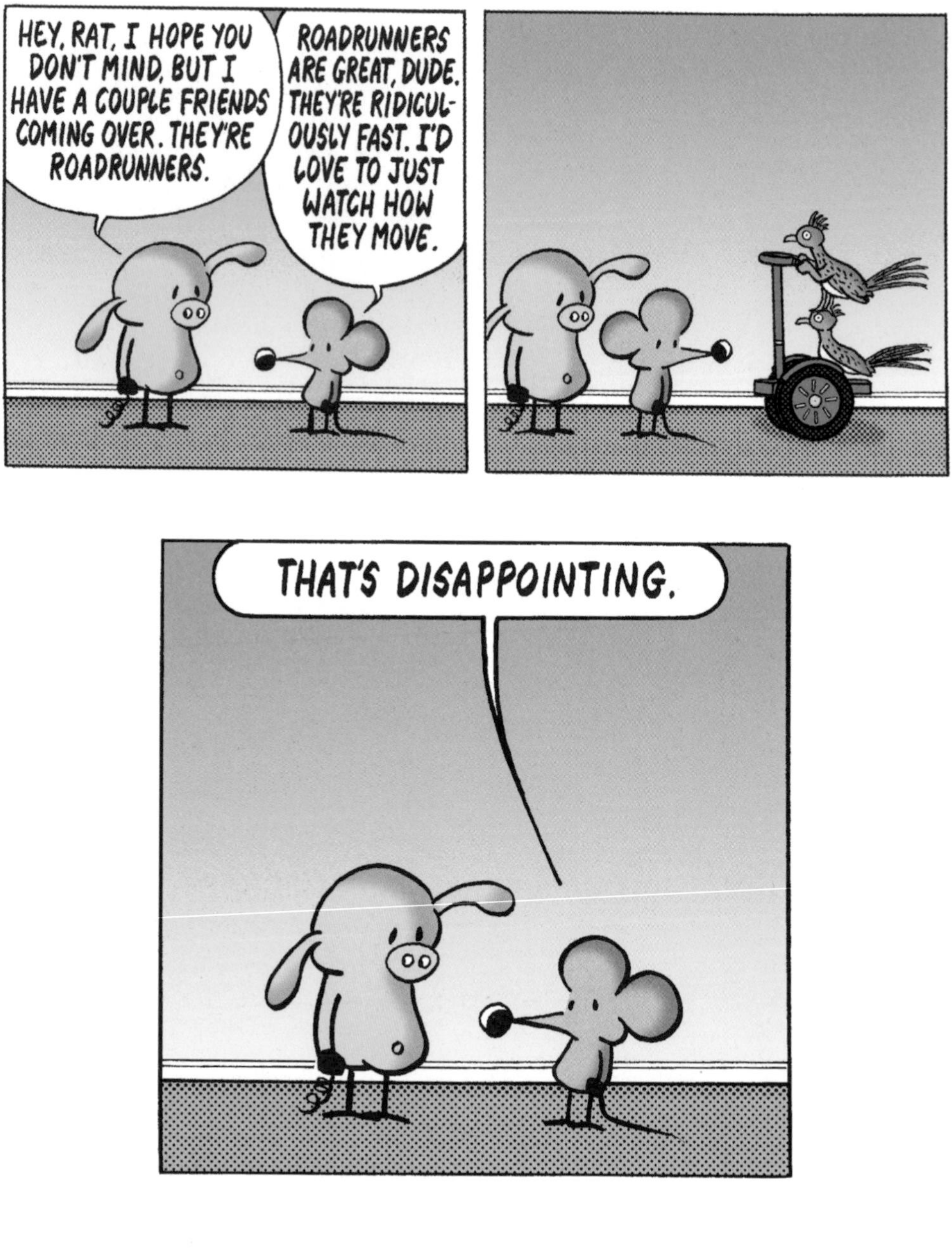
HEY, RAT, I HOPE YOU DON'T MIND, BUT I HAVE A COUPLE FRIENDS COMING OVER. THEY'RE ROADRUNNERS.
ROADRUNNERS ARE GREAT, DUDE. THEY'RE RIDICULOUSLY FAST. I'D LOVE TO JUST WATCH HOW THEY MOVE.
THAT'S DISAPPOINTING.

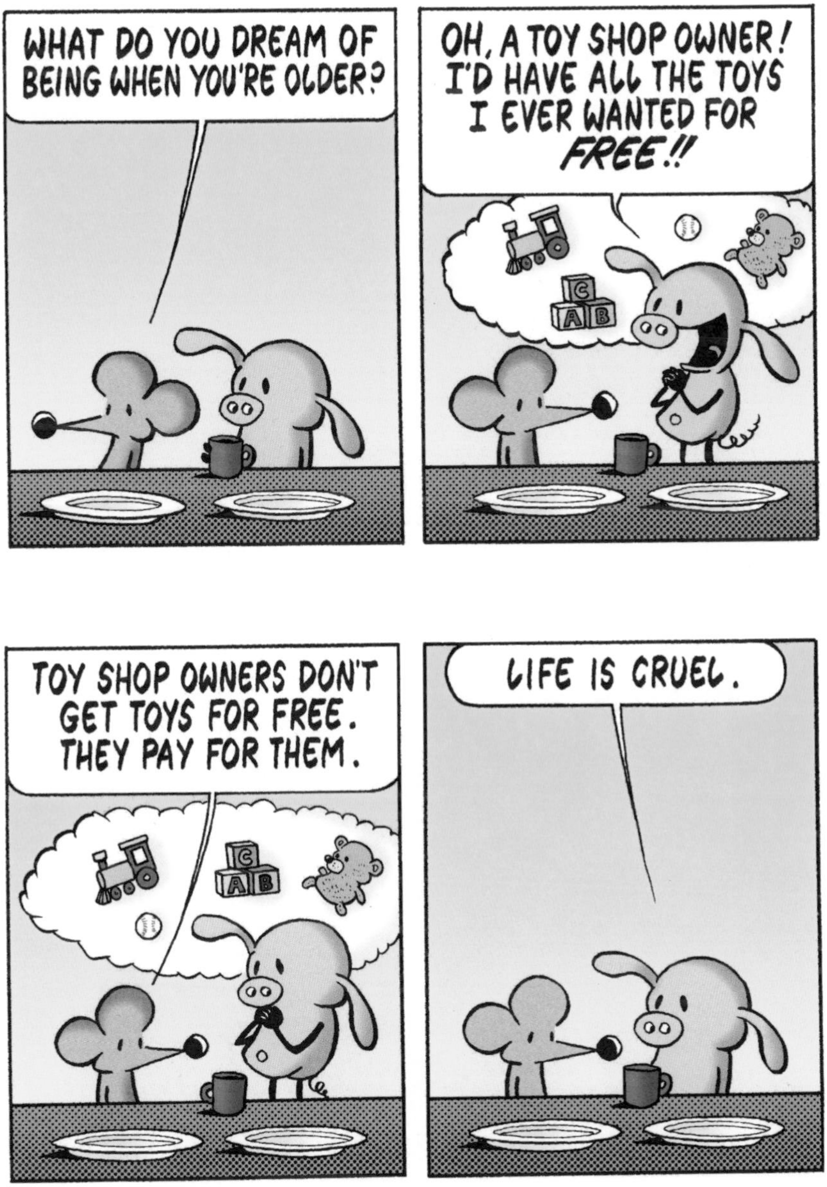
WHAT DO YOU DREAM OF BEING WHEN YOU'RE OLDER?
OH, A TOY SHOP OWNER! I'D HAVE ALL THE TOYS I EVER WANTED FOR FREE!!
TOY SHOP OWNERS DON'T GET TOYS FOR FREE. THEY PAY FOR THEM.
LIFE IS CRUEL.

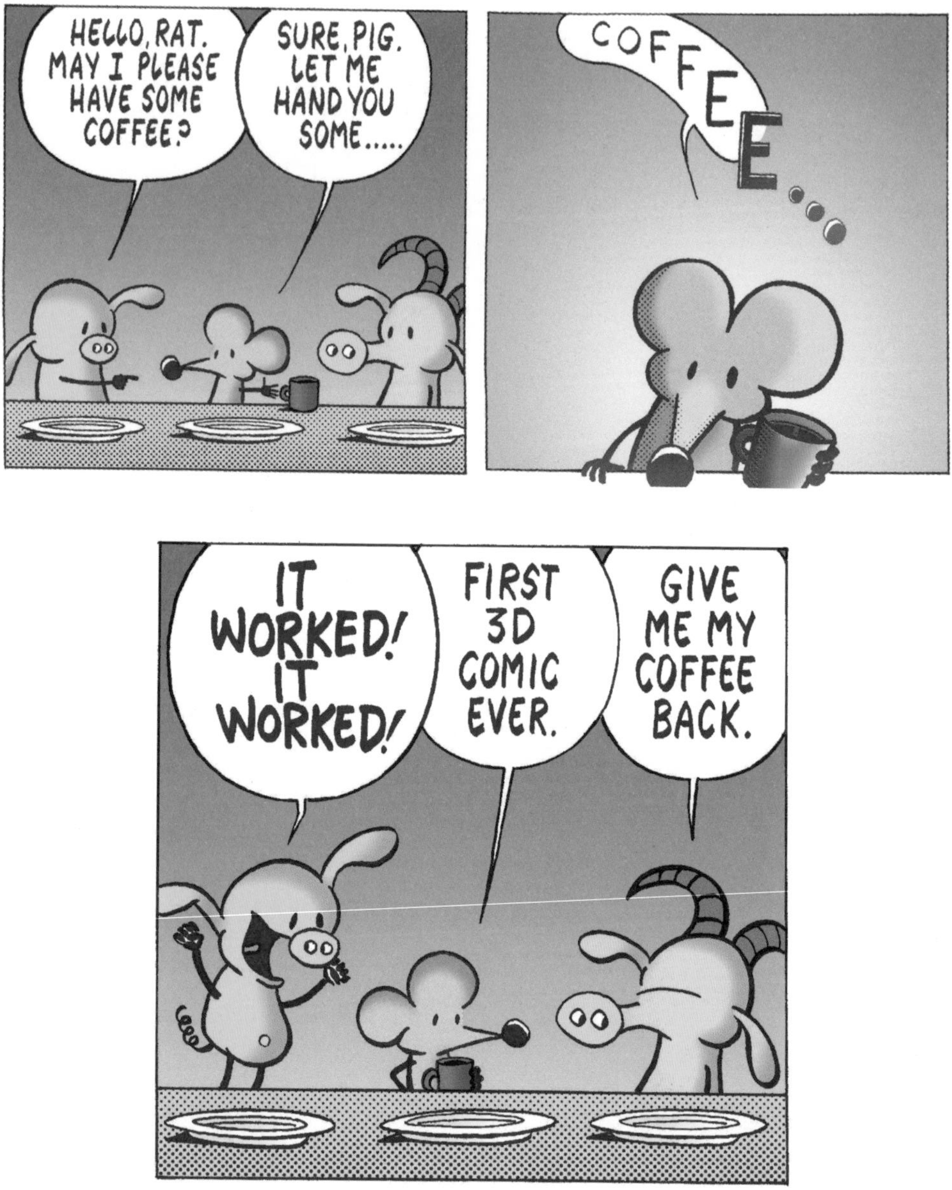
HELLO, RAT. MAY I PLEASE HAVE SOME COFFEE?
SURE, PIG. LET ME HAND YOU SOME.....
COFFEE...
IT WORKED! IT WORKED!
FIRST 3D COMIC EVER.
GIVE ME MY COFFEE BACK.

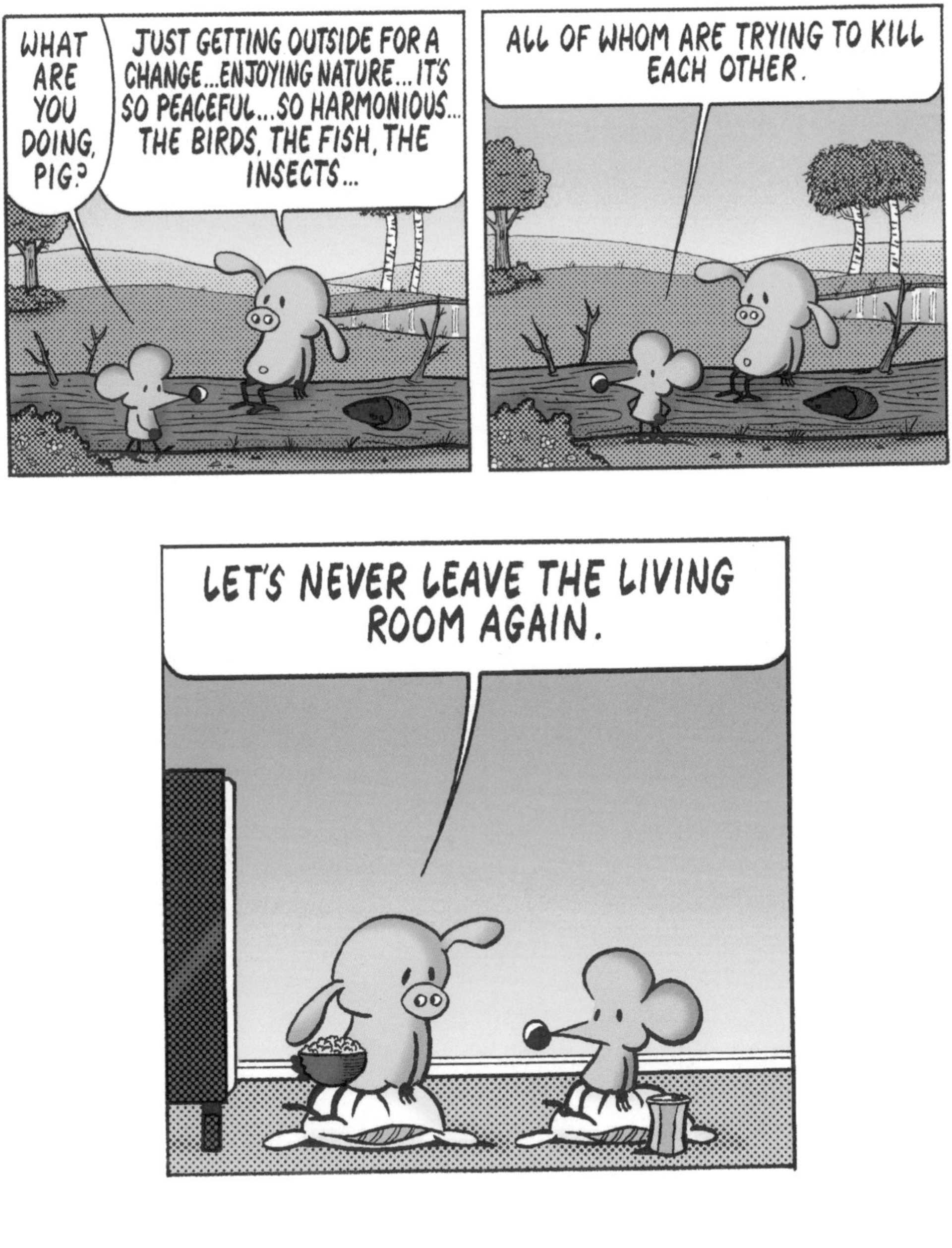
WHAT ARE YOU DOING, PIG?
JUST GETTING OUTSIDE FOR A CHANGE...ENJOYING NATURE...IT'S SO PEACEFUL...SO HARMONIOUS... THE BIRDS, THE FISH, THE INSECTS...
ALL OF WHOM ARE TRYING TO KILL EACH OTHER.
LET'S NEVER LEAVE THE LIVING ROOM AGAIN.

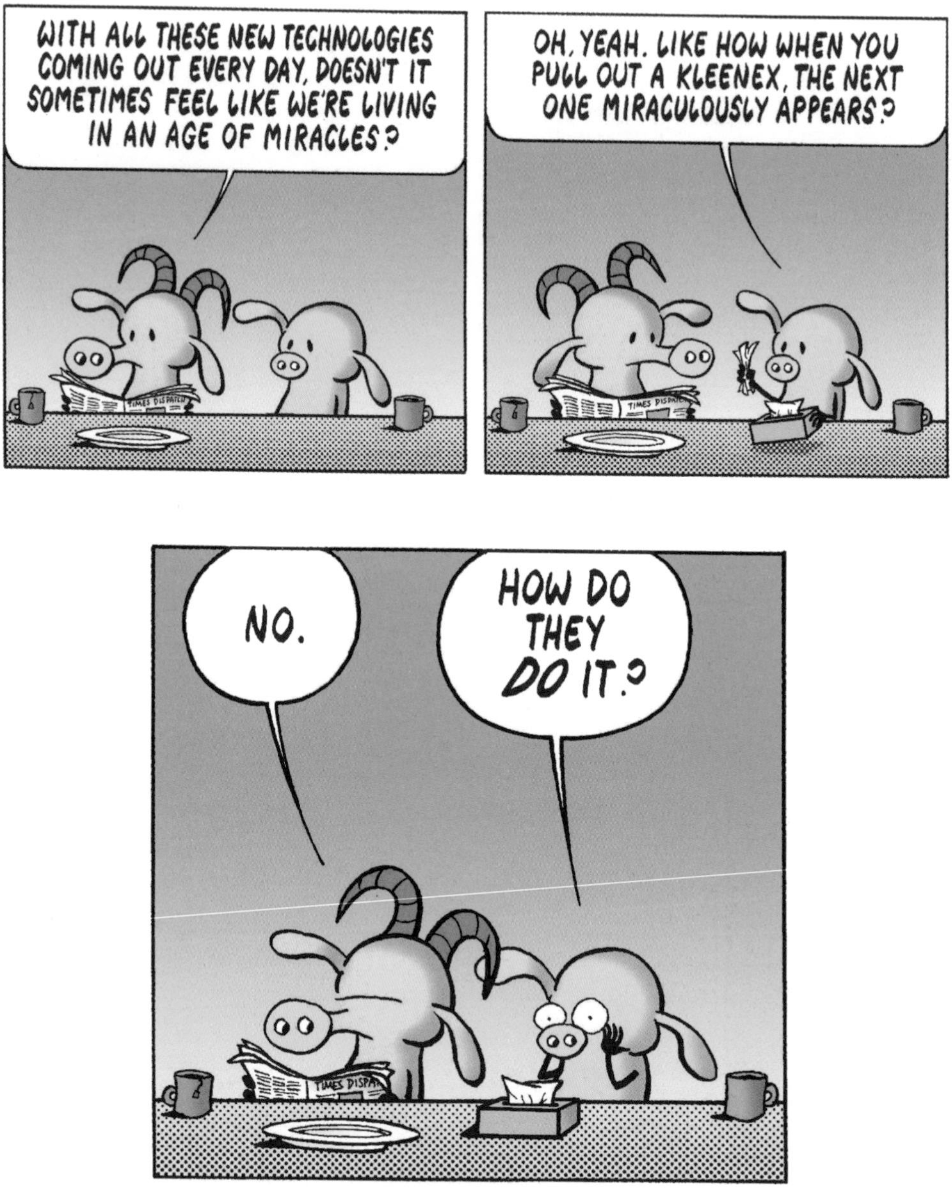
WITH ALL THESE NEW TECHNOLOGIES COMING OUT EVERY DAY, DOESN'T IT SOMETIMES FEEL LIKE WE'RE LIVING IN AN AGE OF MIRACLES?
TIMES DISPATCH
OH, YEAH. LIKE HOW WHEN YOU PULL OUT A KLEENEX, THE NEXT ONE MIRACULOUSLY APPEARS?
NO.
HOW DO THEY DO IT?

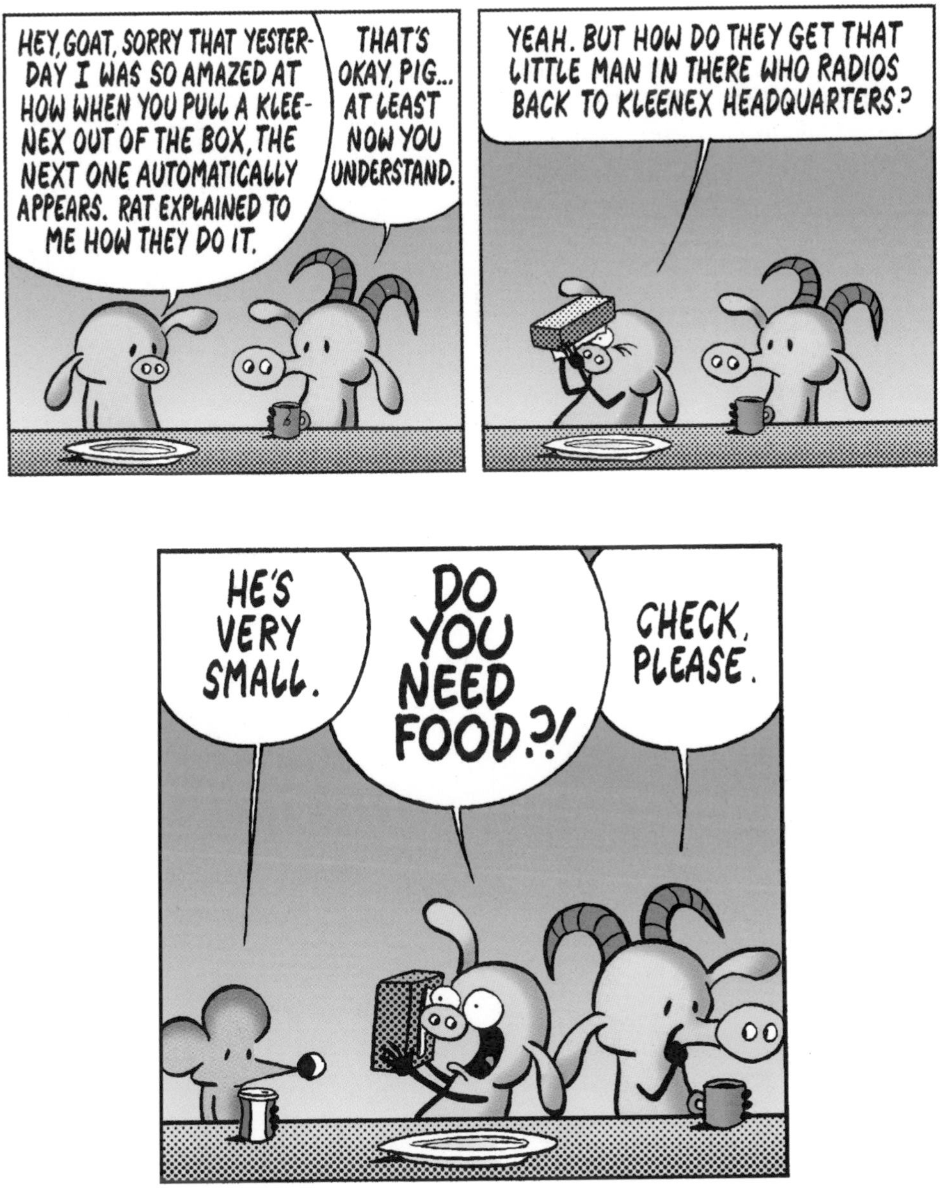
HEY, GOAT, SORRY THAT YESTERDAY I WAS SO AMAZED AT HOW WHEN YOU PULL A KLEENEX OUT OF THE BOX, THE NEXT ONE AUTOMATICALLY APPEARS. RAT EXPLAINED TO ME HOW THEY DO IT.
THAT'S OKAY, PIG... AT LEAST NOW YOU UNDERSTAND.
YEAH. BUT HOW DO THEY GET THAT LITTLE MAN IN THERE WHO RADIOS BACK TO KLEENEX HEADQUARTERS?
HE'S VERY SMALL.
DO YOU NEED FOOD?!
CHECK, PLEASE.

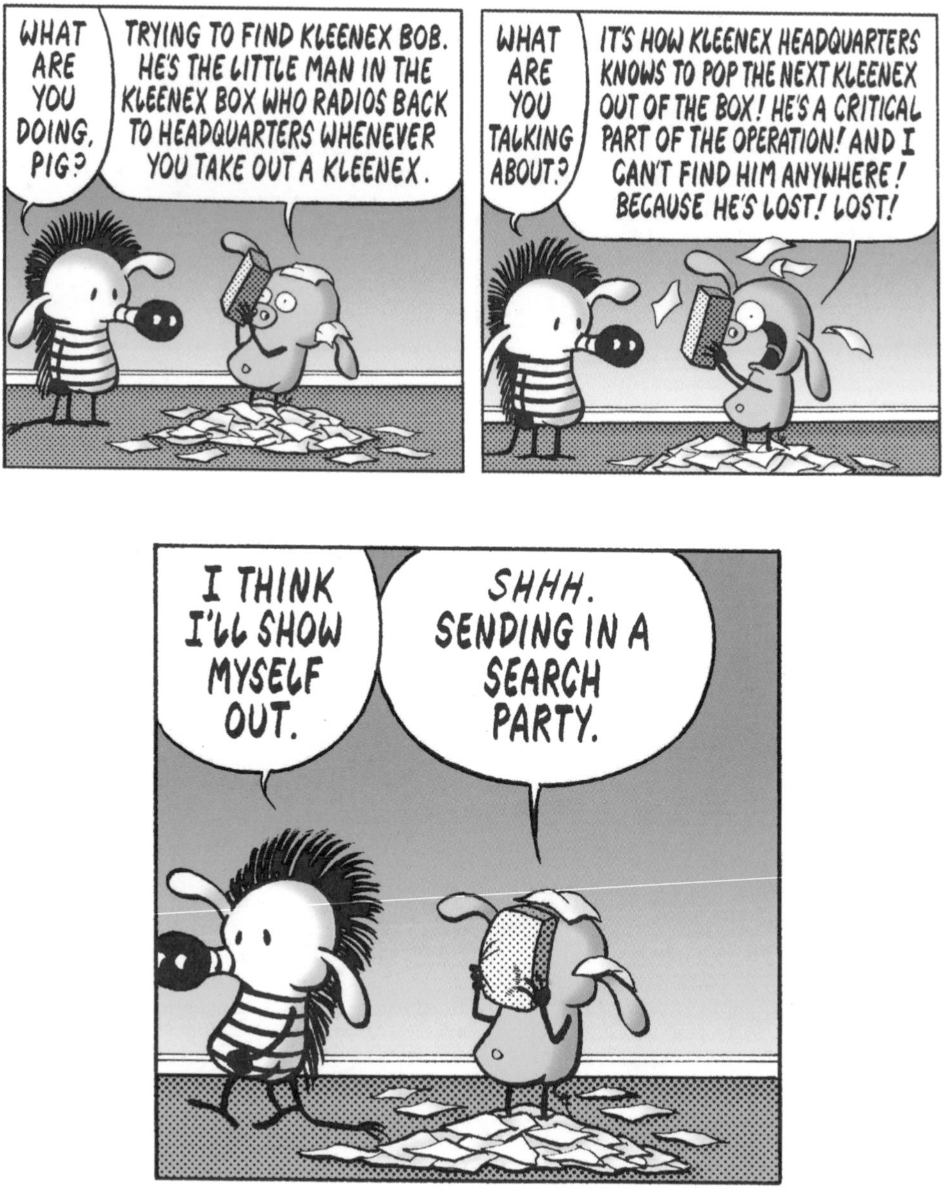
WHAT ARE YOU DOING, PIG?
TRYING TO FIND KLEENEX BOB. HE'S THE LITTLE MAN IN THE KLEENEX BOX WHO RADIOS BACK TO HEADQUARTERS WHENEVER YOU TAKE OUT A KLEENEX.
WHAT ARE YOU TALKING ABOUT?
IT'S HOW KLEENEX HEADQUARTERS KNOWS TO POP THE NEXT KLEENEX OUT OF THE BOX! HE'S A CRITICAL PART OF THE OPERATION! AND I CAN'T FIND HIM ANYWHERE! BECAUSE HE'S LOST! LOST!
I THINK I'LL SHOW MYSELF OUT.
SHHH. SENDING IN A SEARCH PARTY.

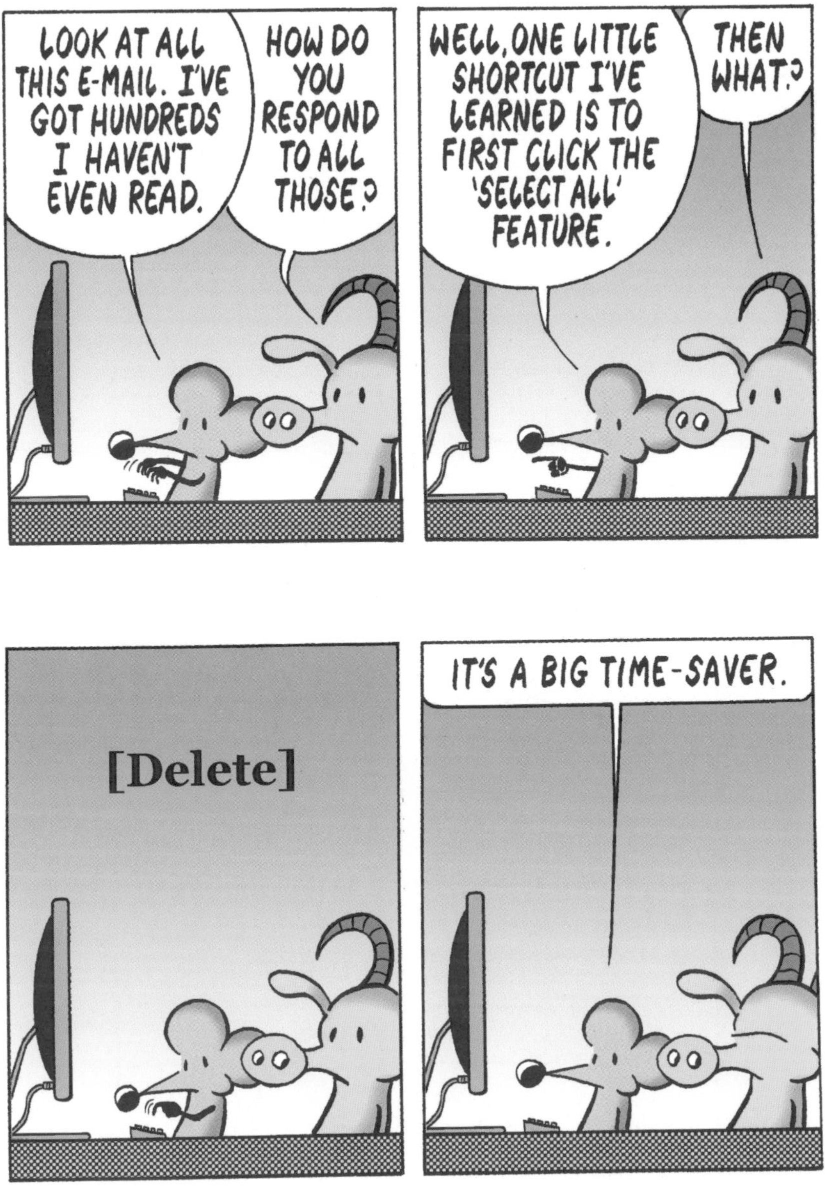
LOOK AT ALL THIS E-MAIL. I'VE GOT HUNDREDS I HAVEN'T EVEN READ.
HOW DO YOU RESPOND TO ALL THOSE?
WELL, ONE LITTLE SHORTCUT I'VE LEARNED IS TO FIRST CLICK THE 'SELECT ALL' FEATURE.
THEN WHAT?
[Delete]
IT'S A BIG TIME-SAVER.

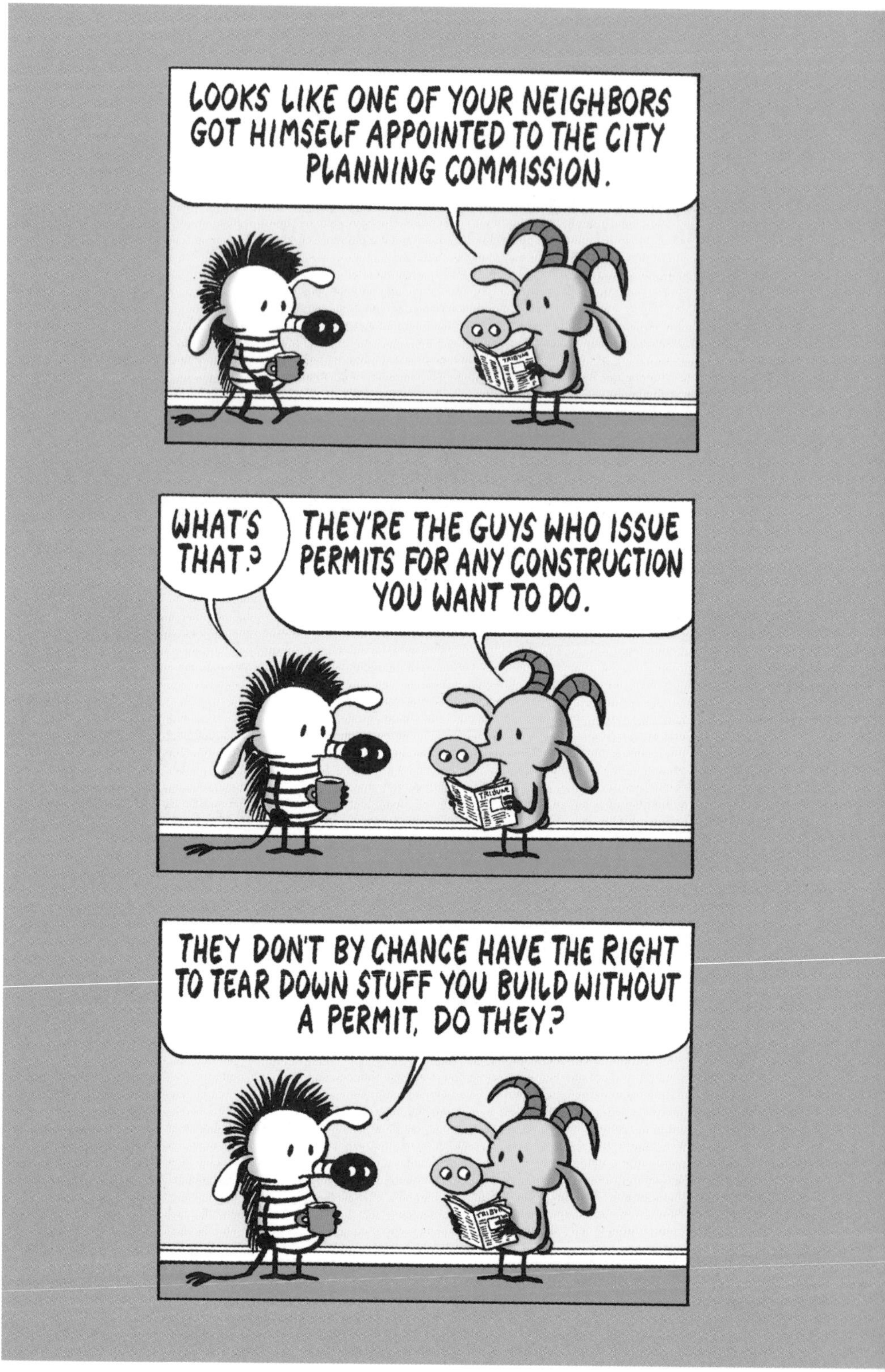
LOOKS LIKE ONE OF YOUR NEIGHBORS GOT HIMSELF APPOINTED TO THE CITY PLANNING COMMISSION.
WHAT'S THAT?
THEY'RE THE GUYS WHO ISSUE PERMITS FOR ANY CONSTRUCTION YOU WANT TO DO.
THEY DON'T BY CHANCE HAVE THE RIGHT TO TEAR DOWN STUFF YOU BUILD WITHOUT A PERMIT, DO THEY?

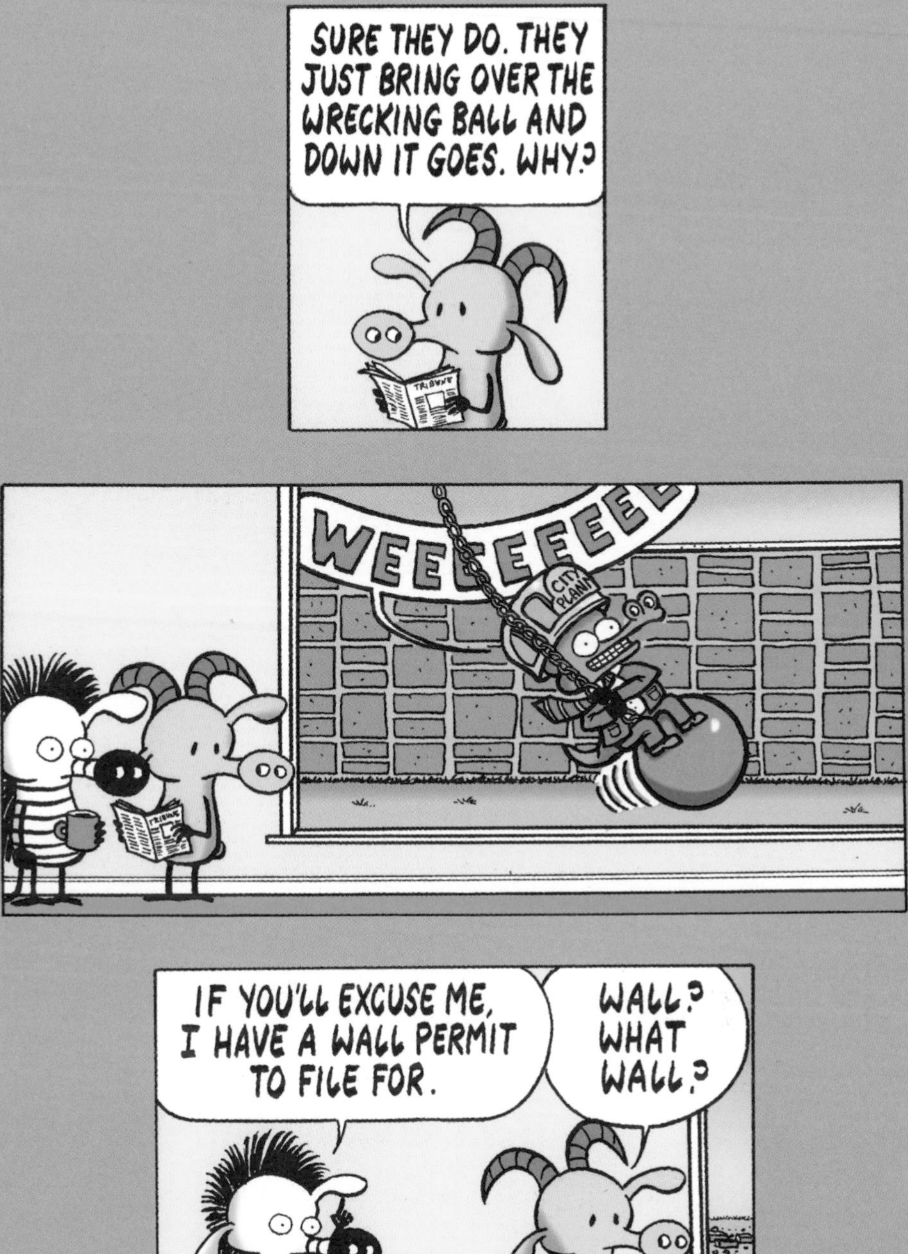
SURE THEY DO. THEY JUST BRING OVER THE WRECKING BALL AND DOWN IT GOES. WHY?
WEEEEEEEE
CITY PLANN
TRIBUNE
IF YOU'LL EXCUSE ME, I HAVE A WALL PERMIT TO FILE FOR.
WALL? WHAT WALL?

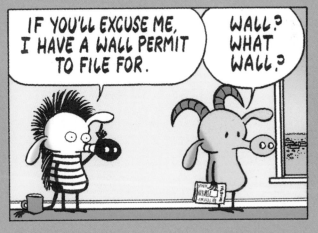

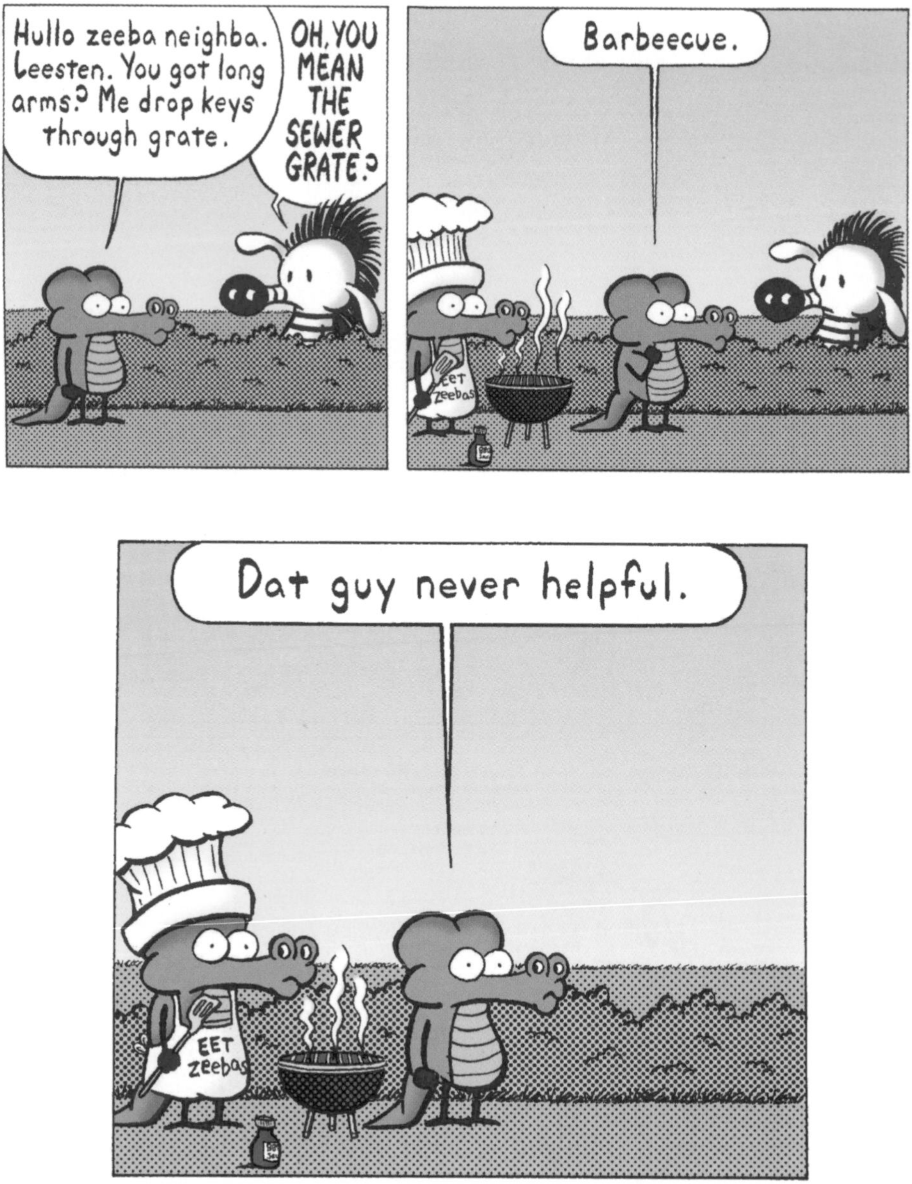
Hullo zeeba neighba. Leesten. You got long arms? Me drop keys through grate.
OH, YOU MEAN THE SEWER GRATE?
Barbeecue.
EET Zeebas
Dat guy never helpful.
EET Zeebas

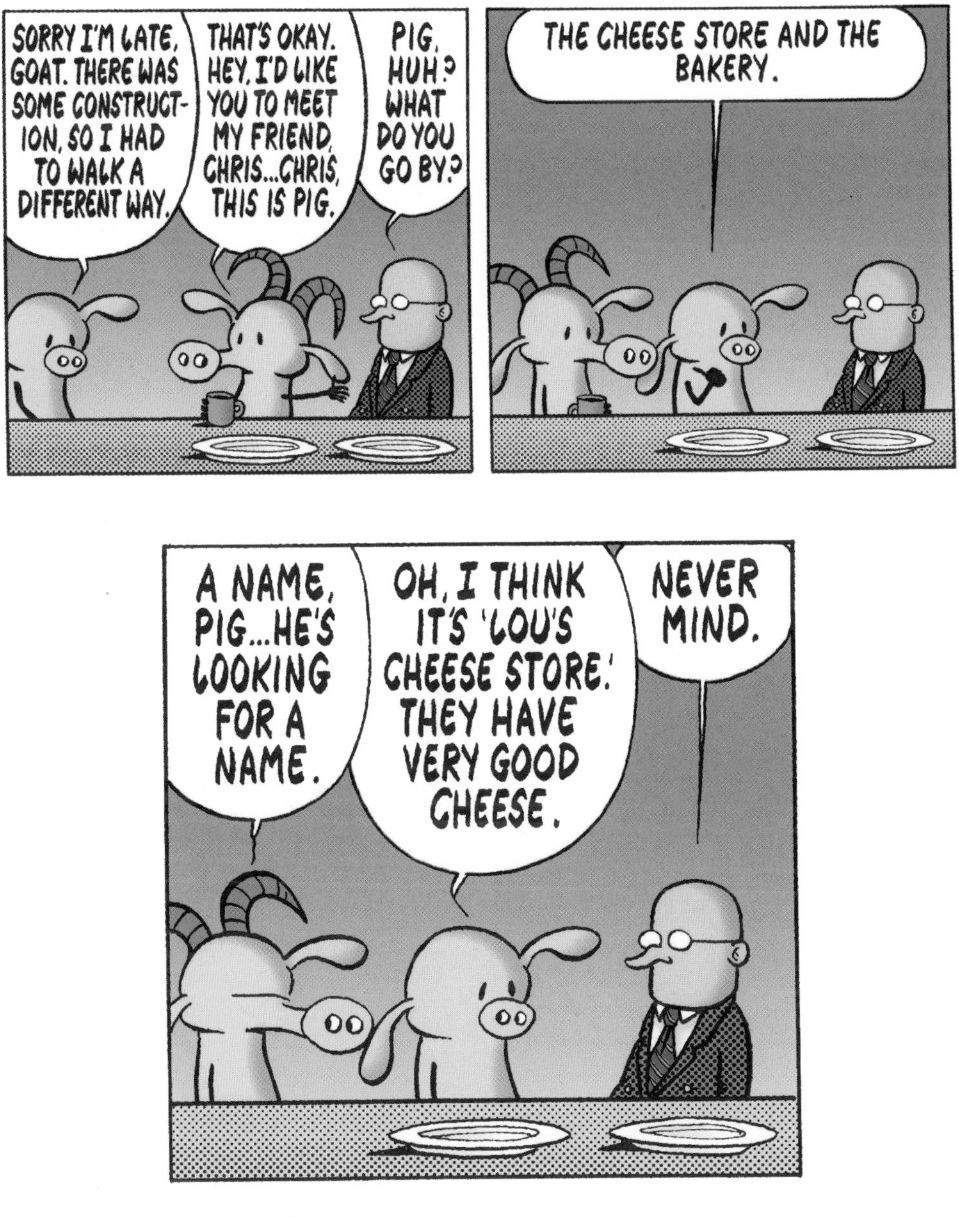
SORRY I'M LATE, GOAT. THERE WAS SOME CONSTRUCTION, SO I HAD TO WALK A DIFFERENT WAY.
THAT'S OKAY. HEY, I'D LIKE YOU TO MEET MY FRIEND, CHRIS...CHRIS, THIS IS PIG.
PIG, HUH? WHAT DO YOU GO BY?
THE CHEESE STORE AND THE BAKERY.
A NAME, PIG...HE'S LOOKING FOR A NAME.
OH, I THINK IT'S 'LOU'S CHEESE STORE.' THEY HAVE VERY GOOD CHEESE.
NEVER MIND.

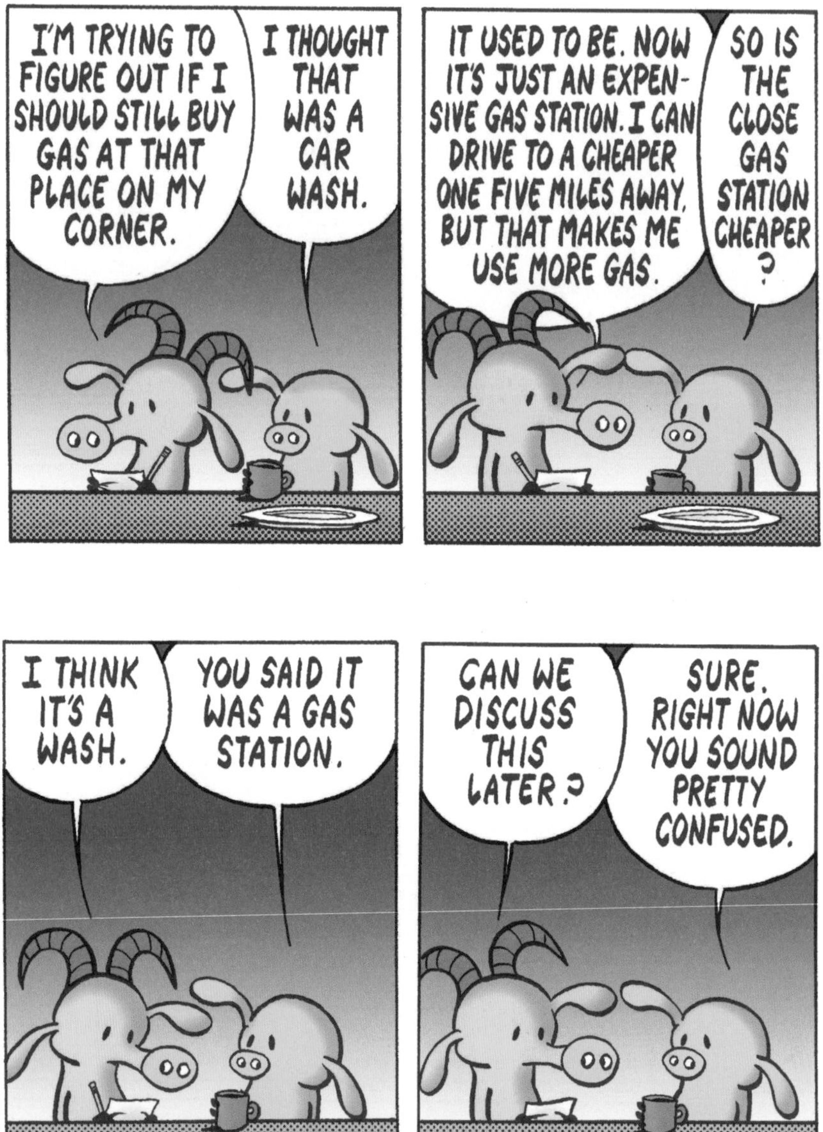
I'M TRYING TO FIGURE OUT IF I SHOULD STILL BUY GAS AT THAT PLACE ON MY CORNER.
I THOUGHT THAT WAS A CAR WASH.
IT USED TO BE. NOW IT'S JUST AN EXPENSIVE GAS STATION. I CAN DRIVE TO A CHEAPER ONE FIVE MILES AWAY, BUT THAT MAKES ME USE MORE GAS.
SO IS THE CLOSE GAS STATION CHEAPER?
I THINK IT'S A WASH.
YOU SAID IT WAS A GAS STATION.
CAN WE DISCUSS THIS LATER?
SURE. RIGHT NOW YOU SOUND PRETTY CONFUSED.

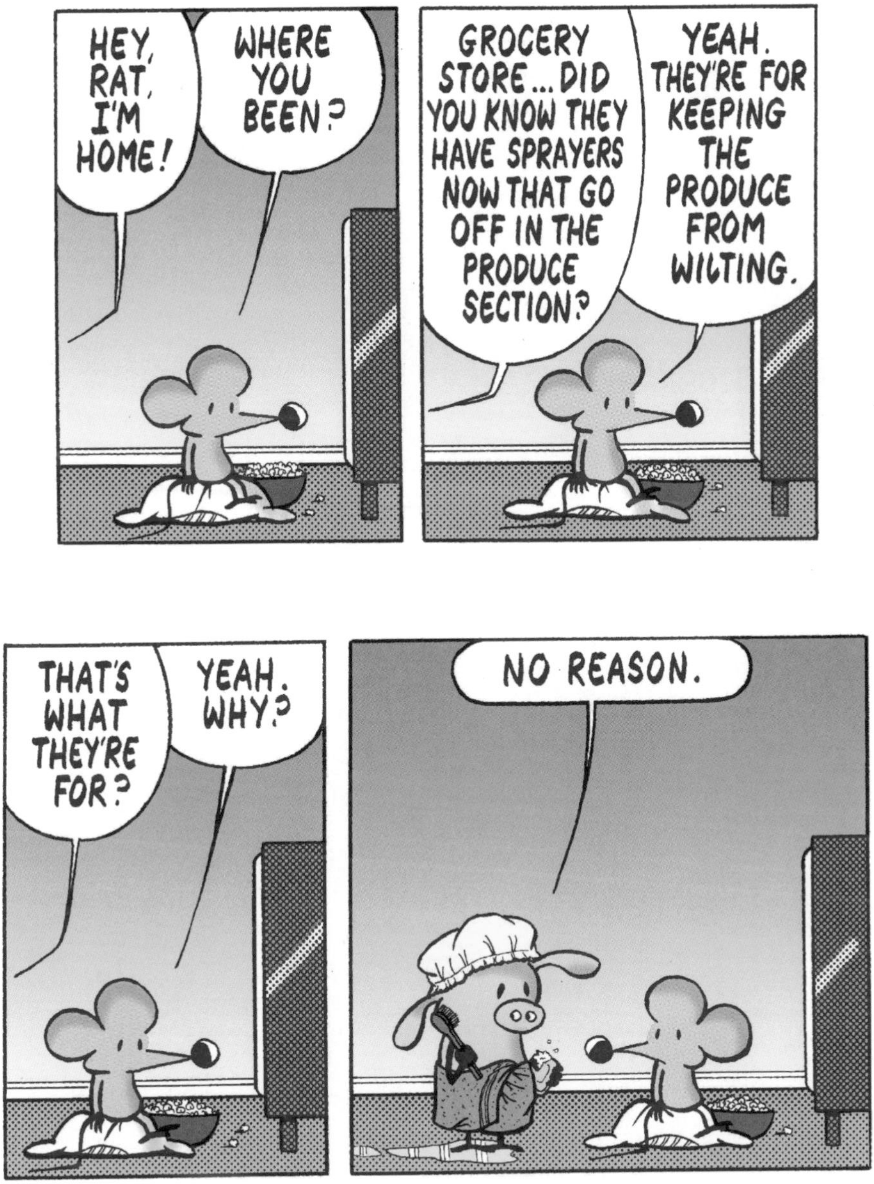
HEY, RAT, I'M HOME!
WHERE YOU BEEN?
GROCERY STORE... DID YOU KNOW THEY HAVE SPRAYERS NOW THAT GO OFF IN THE PRODUCE SECTION?
YEAH. THEY'RE FOR KEEPING THE PRODUCE FROM WILTING.
THAT'S WHAT THEY'RE FOR?
YEAH. WHY?
NO REASON.

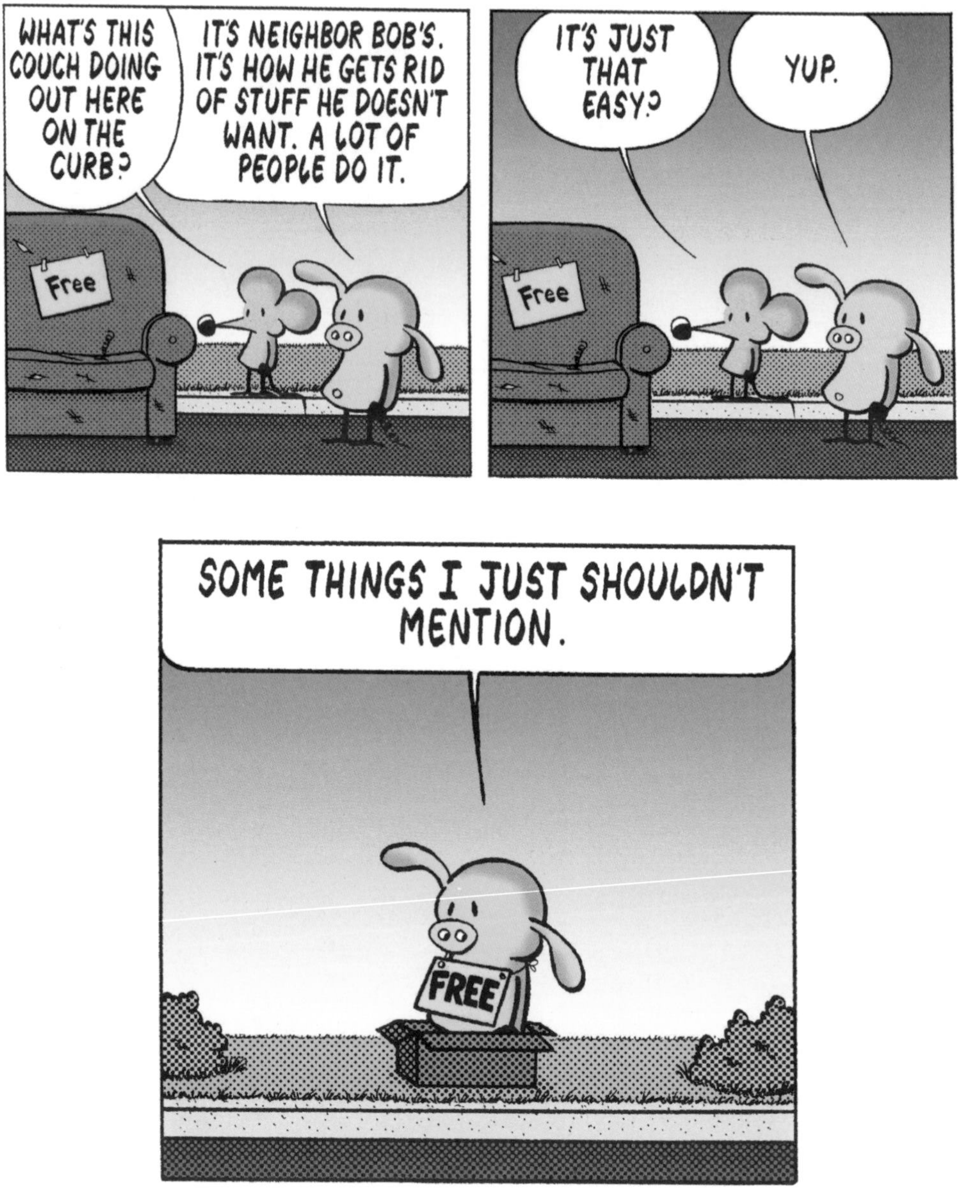
WHAT'S THIS COUCH DOING OUT HERE ON THE CURB?
IT'S NEIGHBOR BOB'S. IT'S HOW HE GETS RID OF STUFF HE DOESN'T WANT. A LOT OF PEOPLE DO IT.
Free
IT'S JUST THAT EASY?
YUP.
Free
SOME THINGS I JUST SHOULDN'T MENTION.
FREE

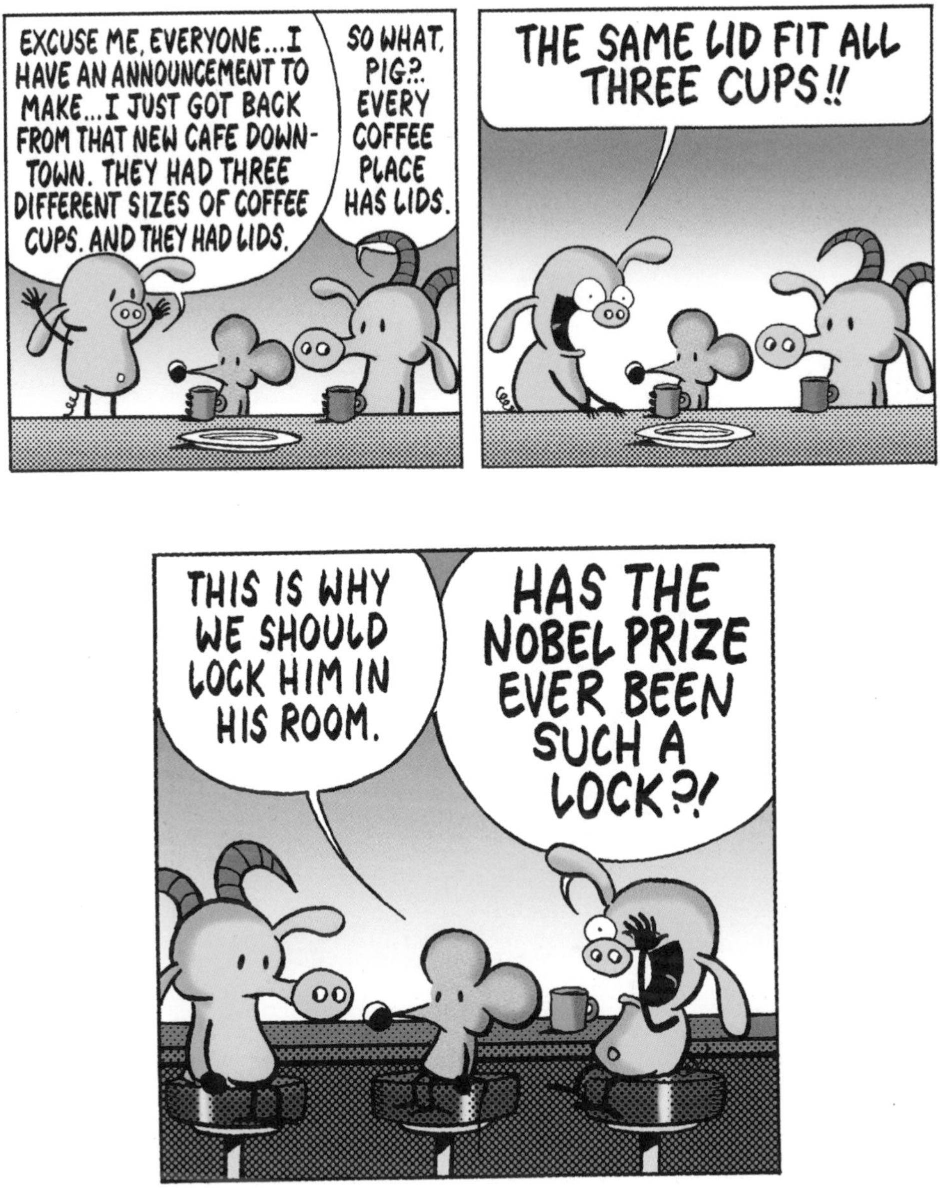
EXCUSE ME, EVERYONE...I HAVE AN ANNOUNCEMENT TO MAKE...I JUST GOT BACK FROM THAT NEW CAFE DOWN-TOWN. THEY HAD THREE DIFFERENT SIZES OF COFFEE CUPS. AND THEY HAD LIDS.
SO WHAT, PIG?. EVERY COFFEE PLACE HAS LIDS.
THE SAME LID FIT ALL THREE CUPS!!
THIS IS WHY WE SHOULD LOCK HIM IN HIS ROOM.
HAS THE NOBEL PRIZE EVER BEEN SUCH A LOCK?!

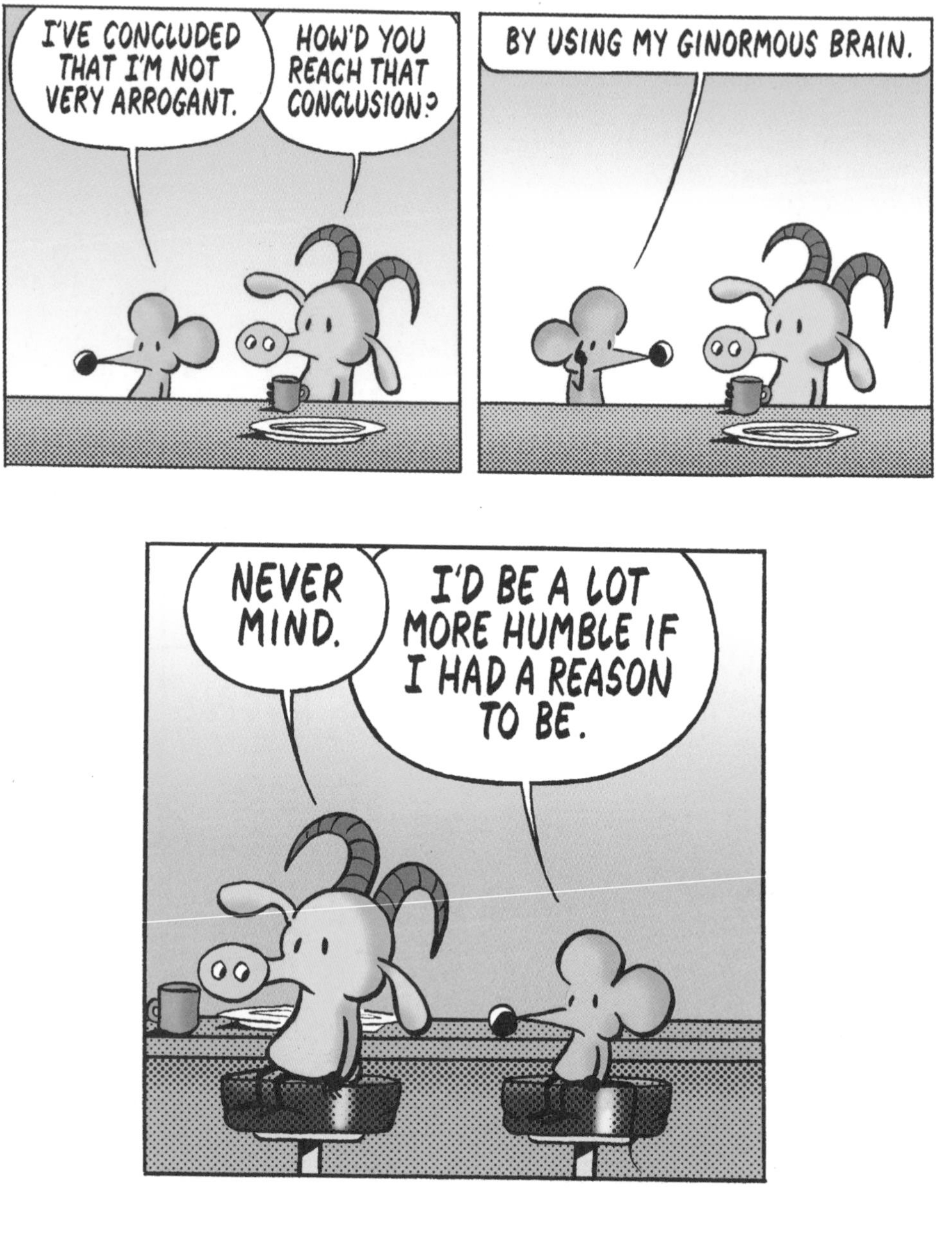
I'VE CONCLUDED THAT I'M NOT VERY ARROGANT.
HOW'D YOU REACH THAT CONCLUSION?
BY USING MY GINORMOUS BRAIN.
NEVER MIND.
I'D BE A LOT MORE HUMBLE IF I HAD A REASON TO BE.

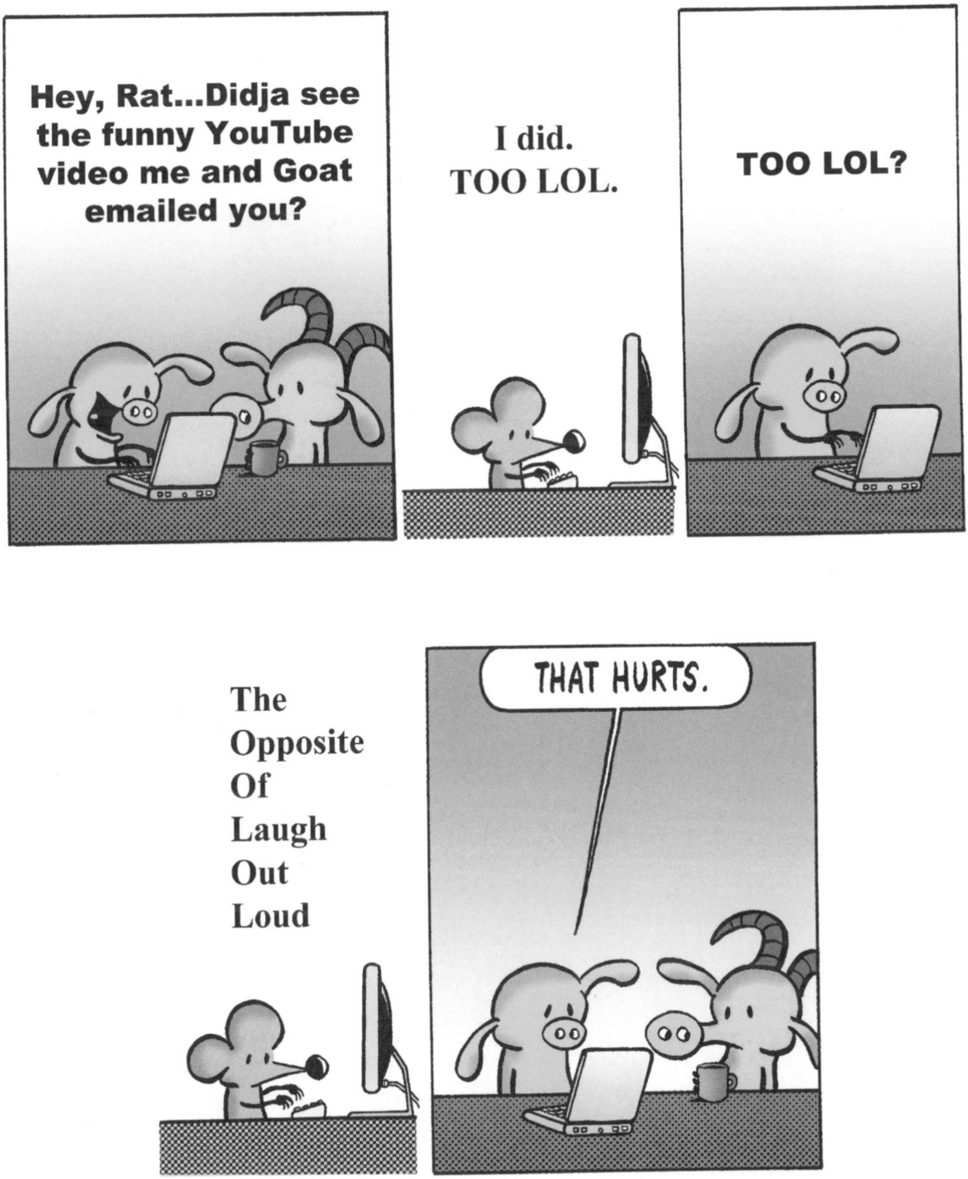
Hey, Rat...Didja see the funny YouTube video me and Goat emailed you?
I did. TOO LOL.
TOO LOL?
The Opposite Of Laugh Out Loud
THAT HURTS.

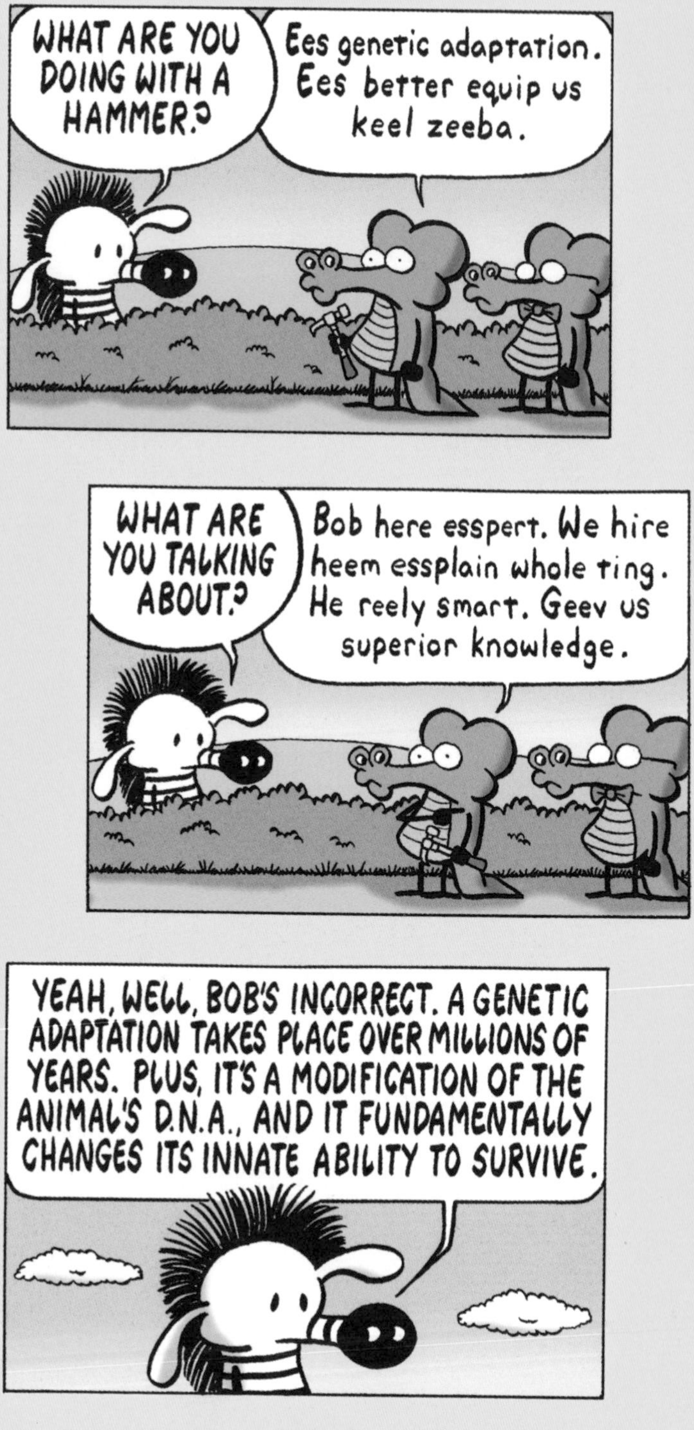
WHAT ARE YOU DOING WITH A HAMMER?
Ees genetic adaptation. Ees better equip us keel zeeba.
WHAT ARE YOU TALKING ABOUT?
Bob here esspert. We hire heem essplain whole ting. He reely smart. Geev us superior knowledge.
YEAH, WELL, BOB'S INCORRECT. A GENETIC ADAPTATION TAKES PLACE OVER MILLIONS OF YEARS. PLUS, IT'S A MODIFICATION OF THE ANIMAL'S D.N.A., AND IT FUNDAMENTALLY CHANGES ITS INNATE ABILITY TO SURVIVE.

CRACK
Me fundamentally change Bob.

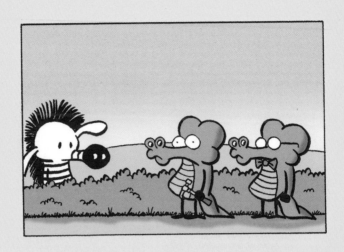

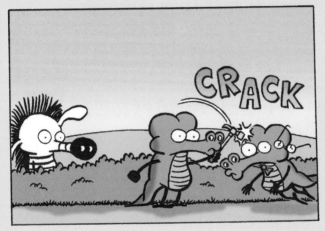

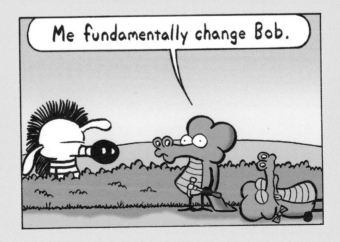

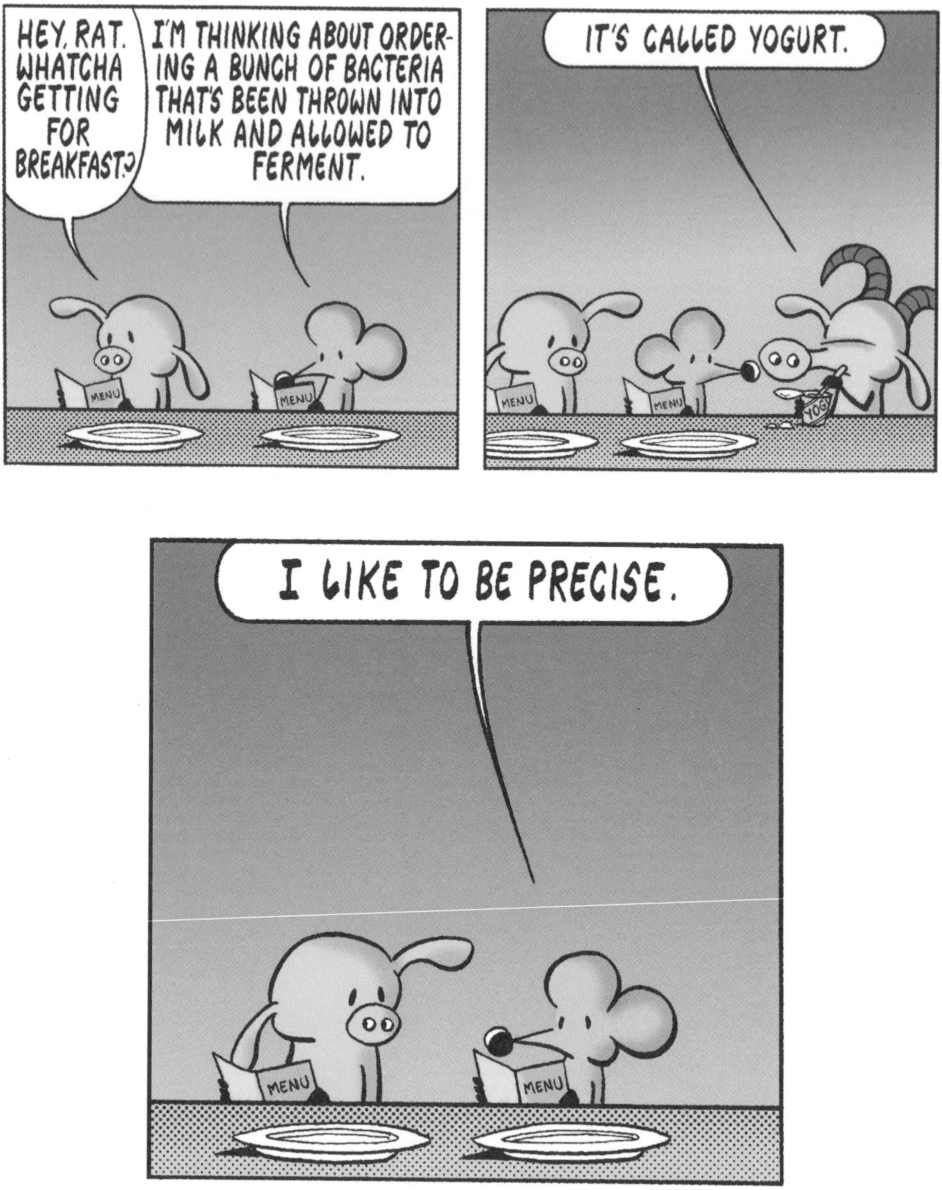
HEY, RAT. WHATCHA GETTING FOR BREAKFAST?
I'M THINKING ABOUT ORDERING A BUNCH OF BACTERIA THAT'S BEEN THROWN INTO MILK AND ALLOWED TO FERMENT.
MENU
MENU
IT'S CALLED YOGURT.
YOG
I LIKE TO BE PRECISE.

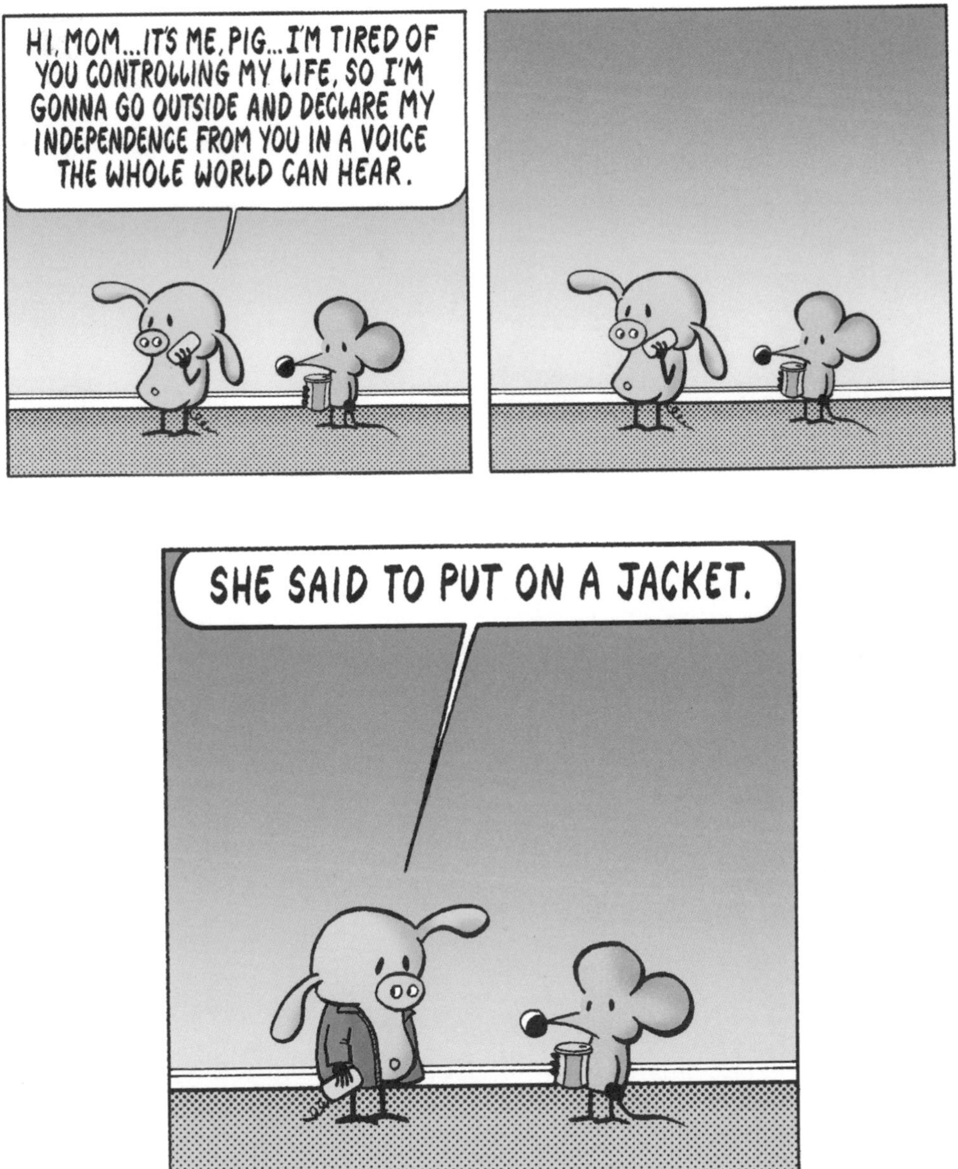
HI, MOM...IT'S ME, PIG...I'M TIRED OF YOU CONTROLLING MY LIFE, SO I'M GONNA GO OUTSIDE AND DECLARE MY INDEPENDENCE FROM YOU IN A VOICE THE WHOLE WORLD CAN HEAR.
SHE SAID TO PUT ON A JACKET.

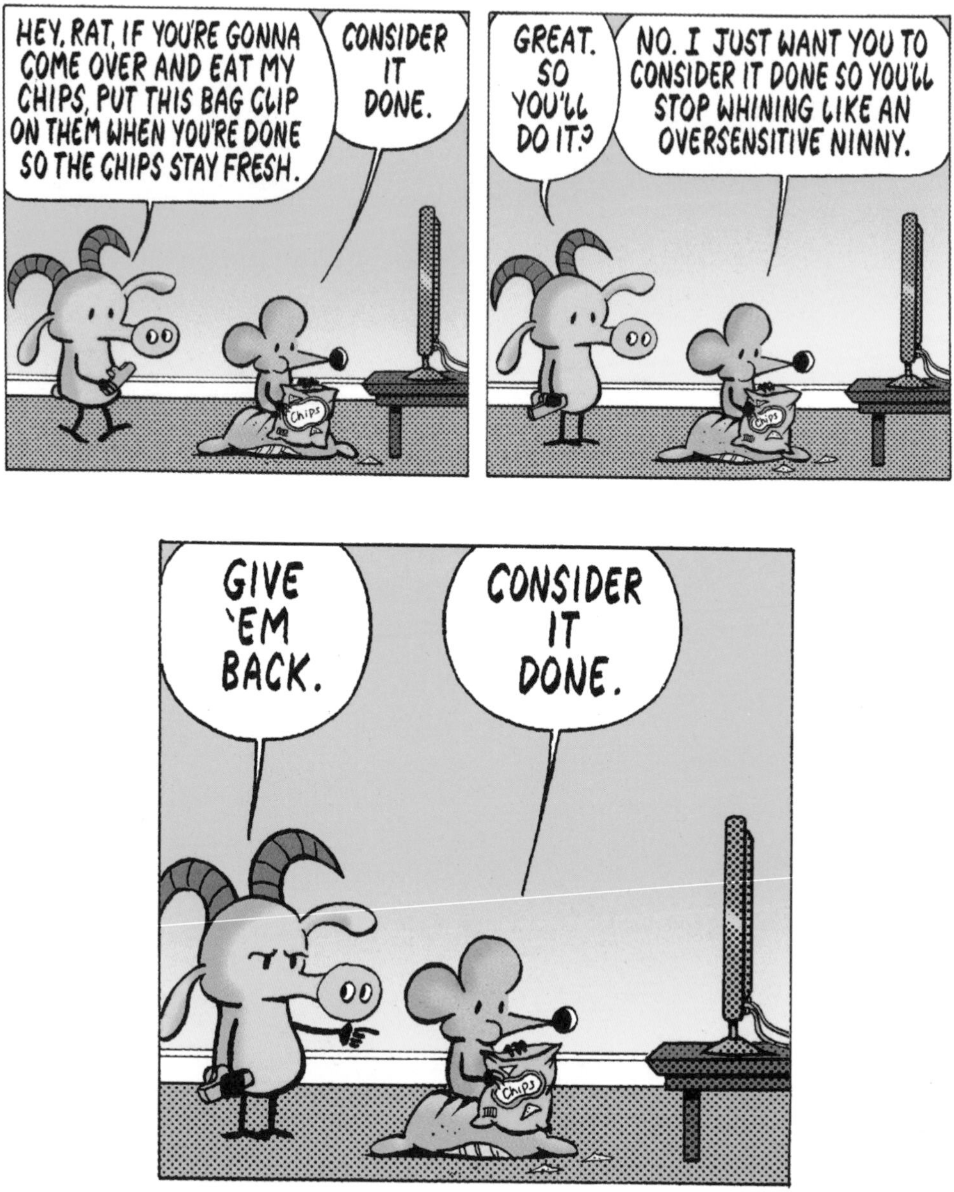
HEY, RAT, IF YOU'RE GONNA COME OVER AND EAT MY CHIPS, PUT THIS BAG CLIP ON THEM WHEN YOU'RE DONE SO THE CHIPS STAY FRESH.
CONSIDER IT DONE.
GREAT. SO YOU'LL DO IT?
NO. I JUST WANT YOU TO CONSIDER IT DONE SO YOU'LL STOP WHINING LIKE AN OVERSENSITIVE NINNY.
GIVE 'EM BACK.
CONSIDER IT DONE.

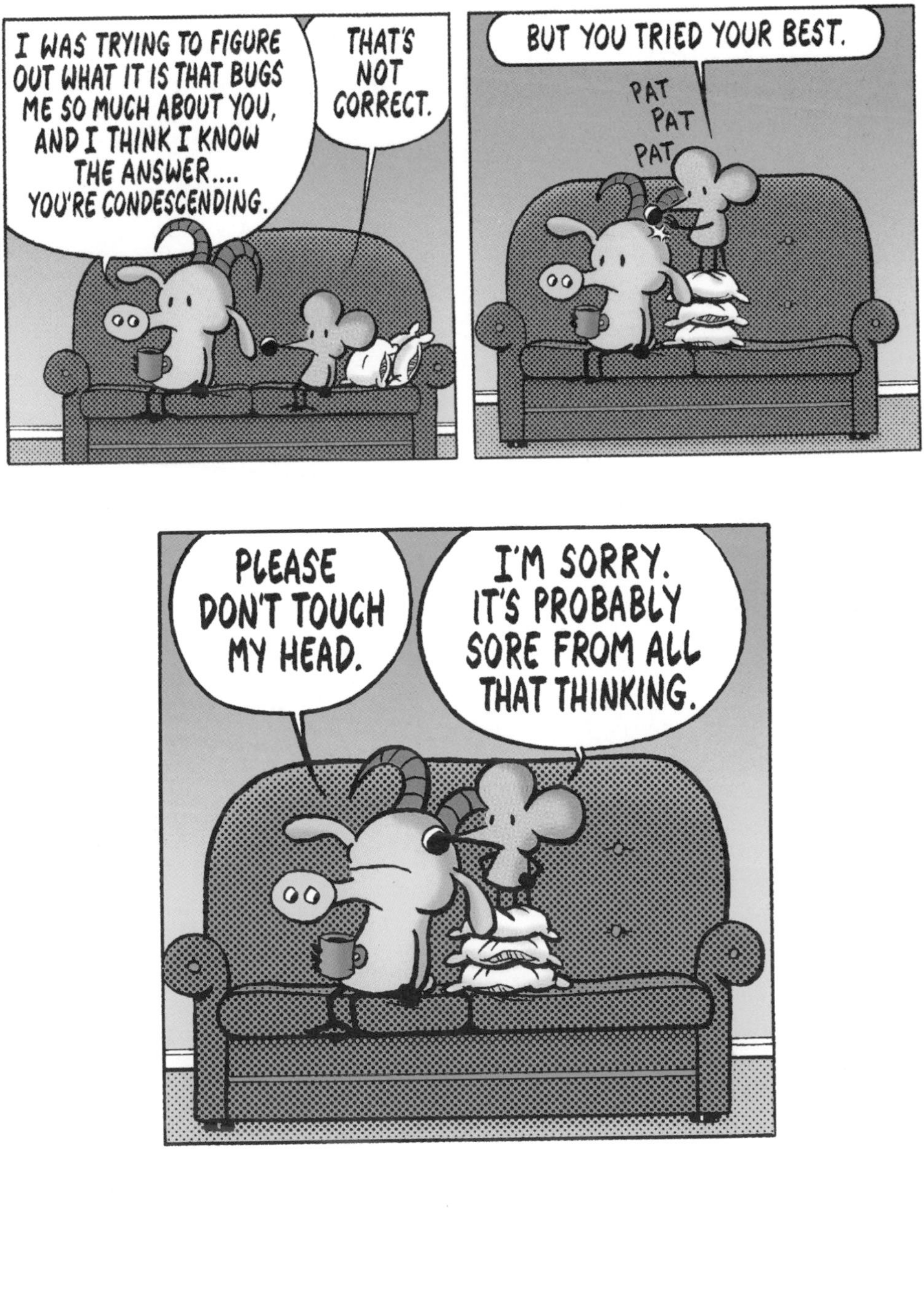
I WAS TRYING TO FIGURE OUT WHAT IT IS THAT BUGS ME SO MUCH ABOUT YOU, AND I THINK I KNOW THE ANSWER.... YOU'RE CONDESCENDING.
THAT'S NOT CORRECT.
BUT YOU TRIED YOUR BEST.
PAT PAT PAT
PLEASE DON'T TOUCH MY HEAD.
I'M SORRY. IT'S PROBABLY SORE FROM ALL THAT THINKING.

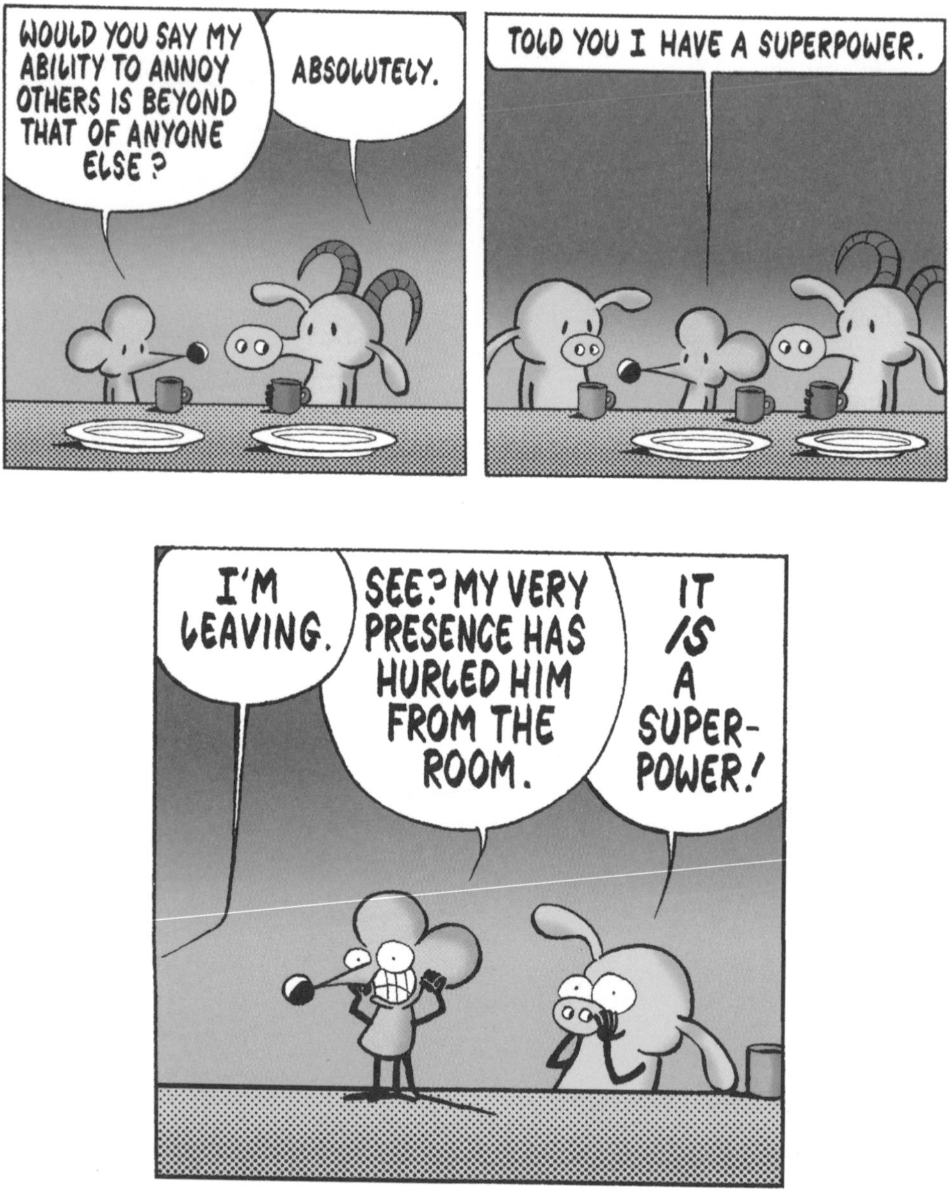
WOULD YOU SAY MY ABILITY TO ANNOY OTHERS IS BEYOND THAT OF ANYONE ELSE?
ABSOLUTELY.
TOLD YOU I HAVE A SUPERPOWER.
I'M LEAVING.
SEE? MY VERY PRESENCE HAS HURLED HIM FROM THE ROOM.
IT *IS* A SUPER-POWER!

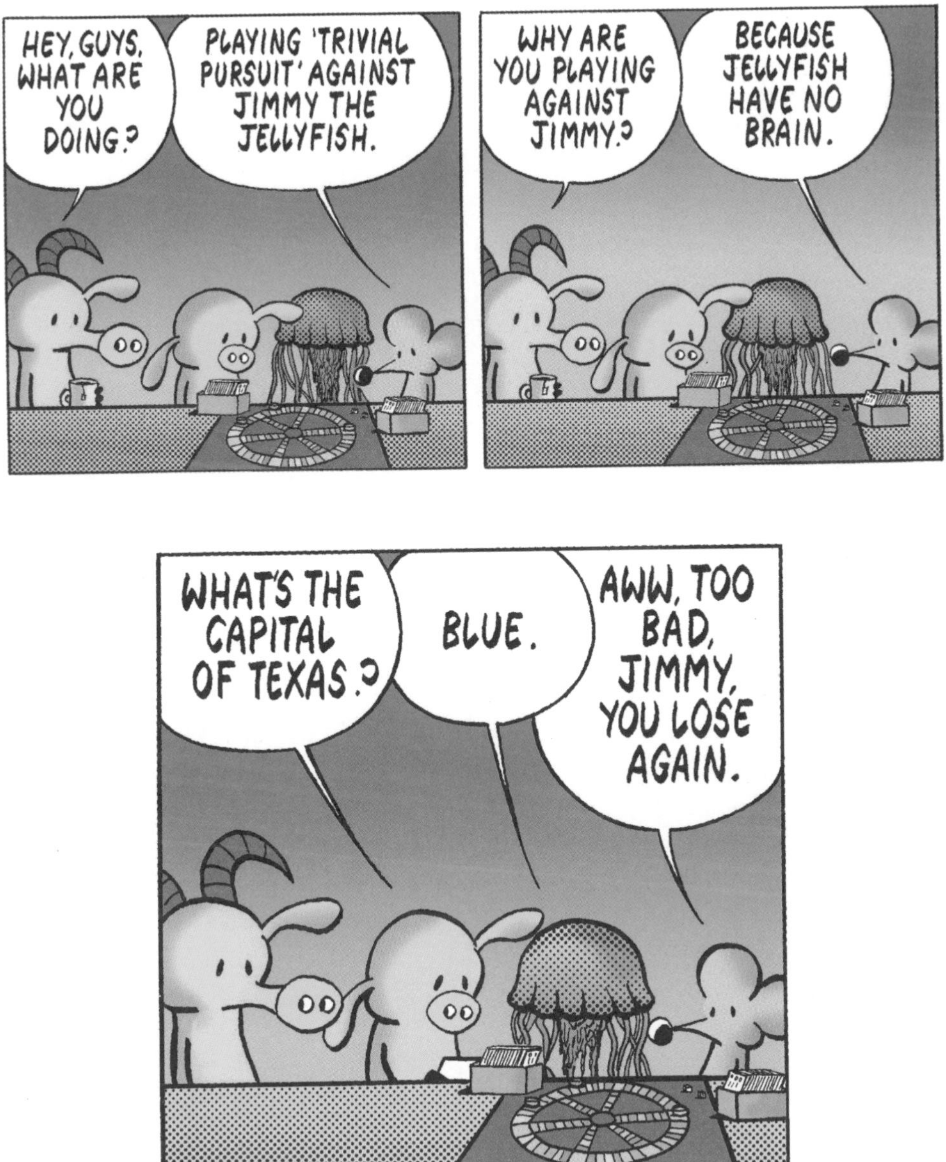
HEY, GUYS, WHAT ARE YOU DOING?
PLAYING 'TRIVIAL PURSUIT' AGAINST JIMMY THE JELLYFISH.
WHY ARE YOU PLAYING AGAINST JIMMY?
BECAUSE JELLYFISH HAVE NO BRAIN.
WHAT'S THE CAPITAL OF TEXAS?
BLUE.
AWW, TOO BAD, JIMMY, YOU LOSE AGAIN.

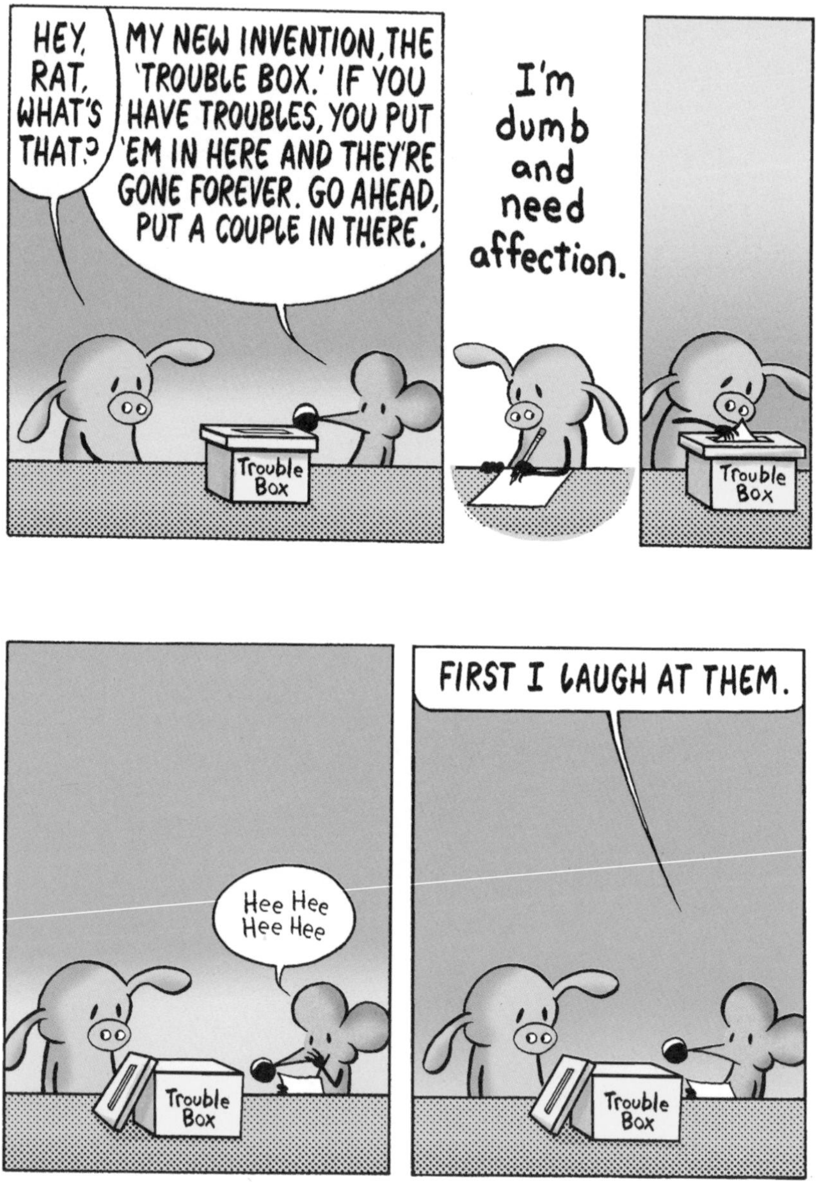
HEY, RAT, WHAT'S THAT?
MY NEW INVENTION, THE 'TROUBLE BOX.' IF YOU HAVE TROUBLES, YOU PUT 'EM IN HERE AND THEY'RE GONE FOREVER. GO AHEAD, PUT A COUPLE IN THERE.
Trouble Box
I'm dumb and need affection.
Trouble Box
Hee Hee Hee Hee
Trouble Box
FIRST I LAUGH AT THEM.
Trouble Box

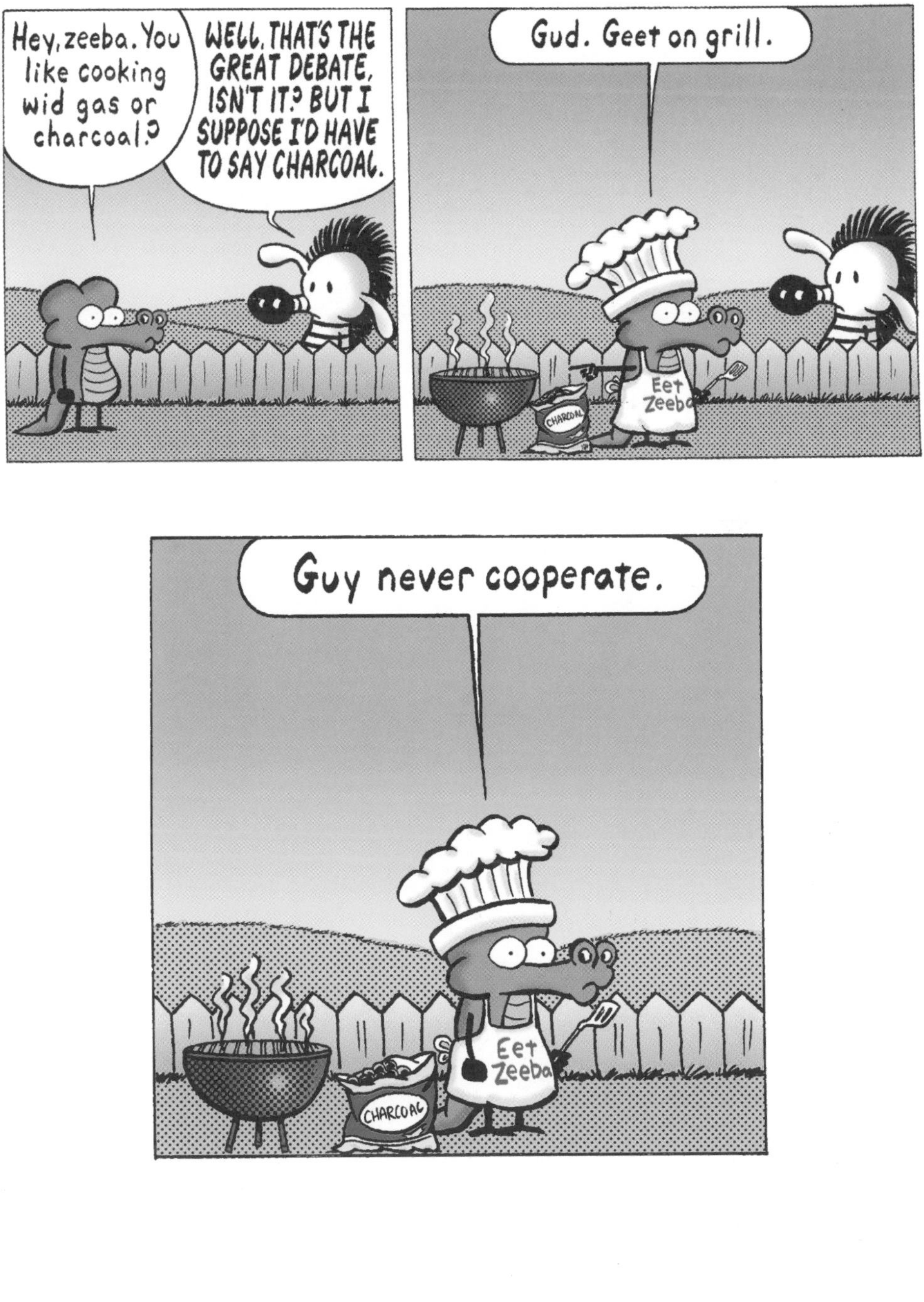
Hey, zeeba. You like cooking wid gas or charcoal?
WELL, THAT'S THE GREAT DEBATE, ISN'T IT? BUT I SUPPOSE I'D HAVE TO SAY CHARCOAL.
Gud. Geet on grill.
Eet Zeeba
CHARCOAL
Guy never cooperate.
Eet Zeeba
CHARCOAL

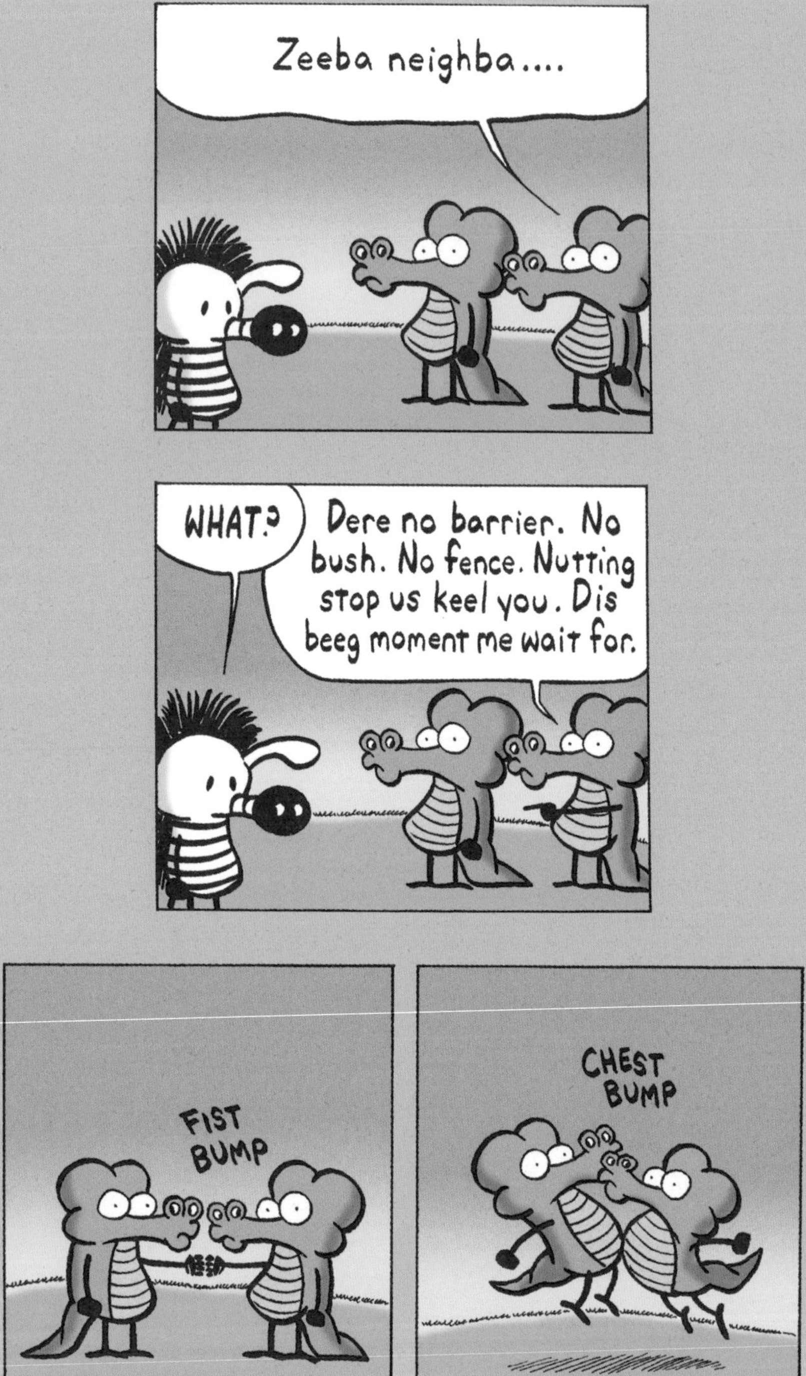
Zeeba neighba....
WHAT?
Dere no barrier. No bush. No fence. Nutting stop us keel you. Dis beeg moment me wait for.
FIST BUMP
CHEST BUMP

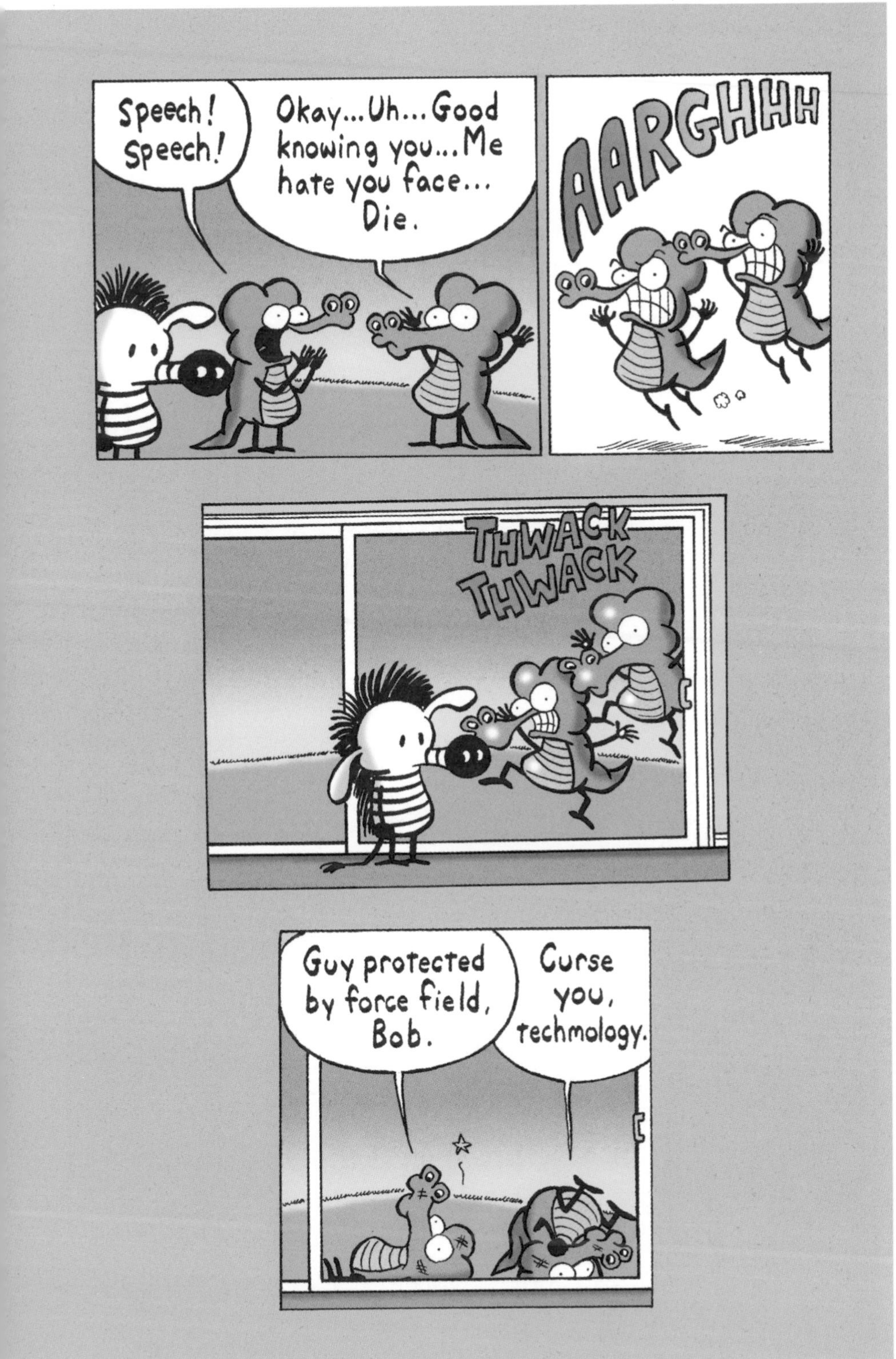
Speech! Speech!
Okay...Uh...Good knowing you...Me hate you face... Die.
AARGHHH
THWACK THWACK
Guy protected by force field, Bob.
Curse you, techmology.

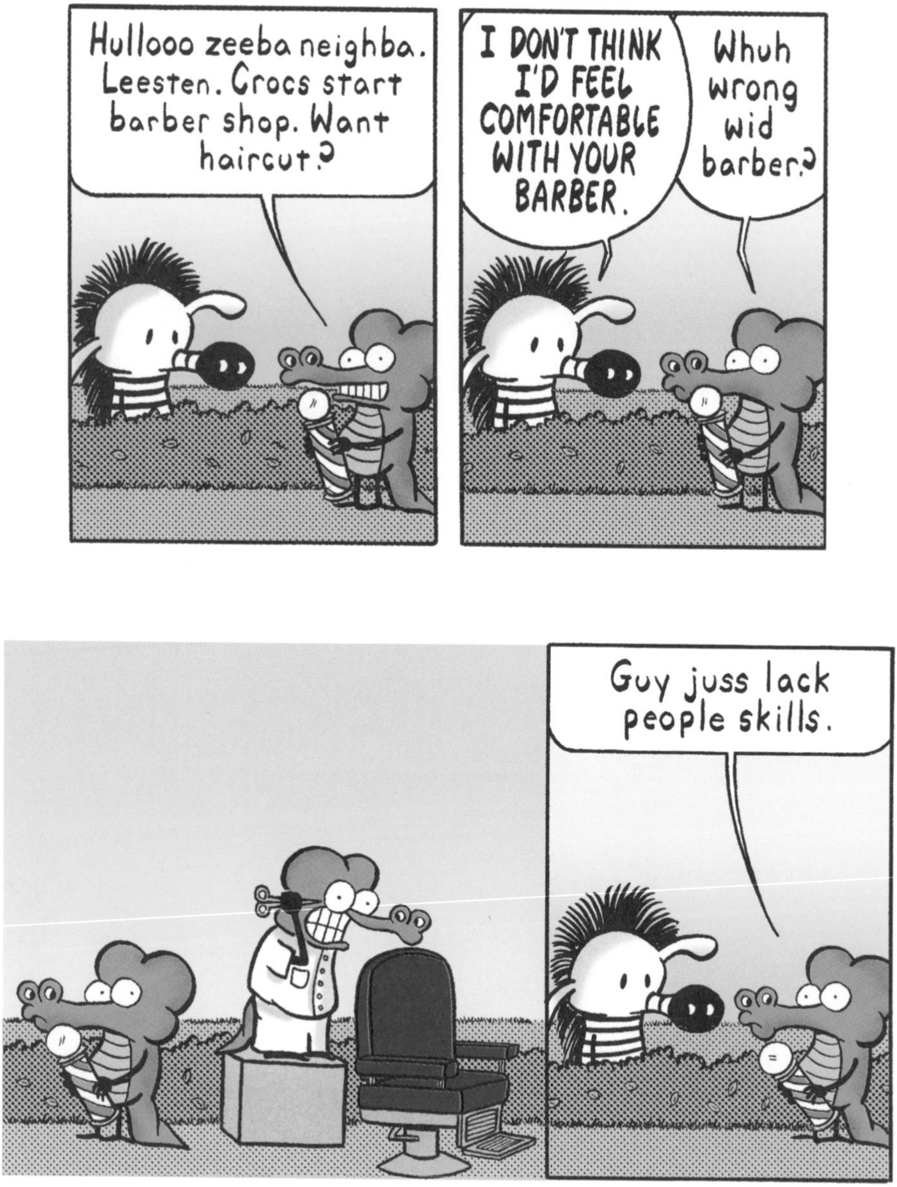
Hullooo zeeba neighba. Leesten. Crocs start barber shop. Want haircut?
I DON'T THINK I'D FEEL COMFORTABLE WITH YOUR BARBER.
Whuh wrong wid barber?
Guy juss lack people skills.

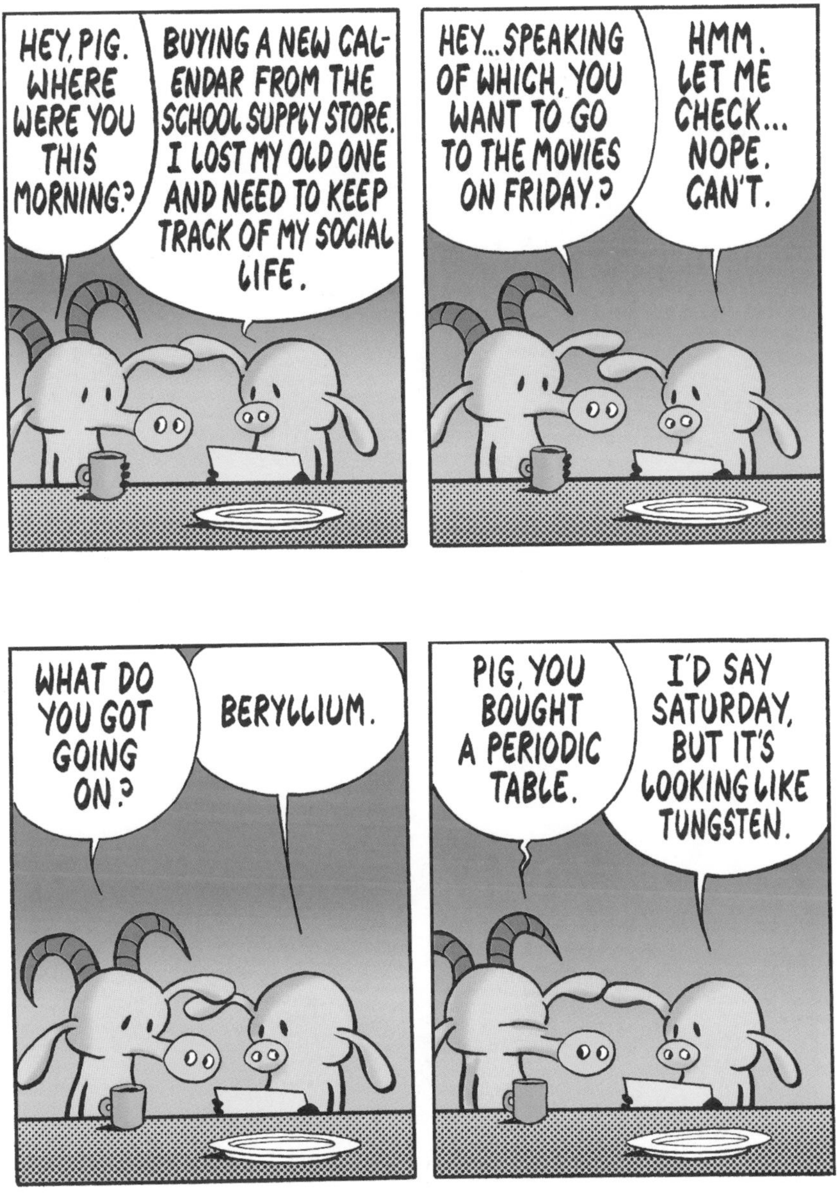
HEY, PIG. WHERE WERE YOU THIS MORNING?
BUYING A NEW CALENDAR FROM THE SCHOOL SUPPLY STORE. I LOST MY OLD ONE AND NEED TO KEEP TRACK OF MY SOCIAL LIFE.
HEY... SPEAKING OF WHICH, YOU WANT TO GO TO THE MOVIES ON FRIDAY?
HMM. LET ME CHECK... NOPE. CAN'T.
WHAT DO YOU GOT GOING ON?
BERYLLIUM.
PIG, YOU BOUGHT A PERIODIC TABLE.
I'D SAY SATURDAY, BUT IT'S LOOKING LIKE TUNGSTEN.

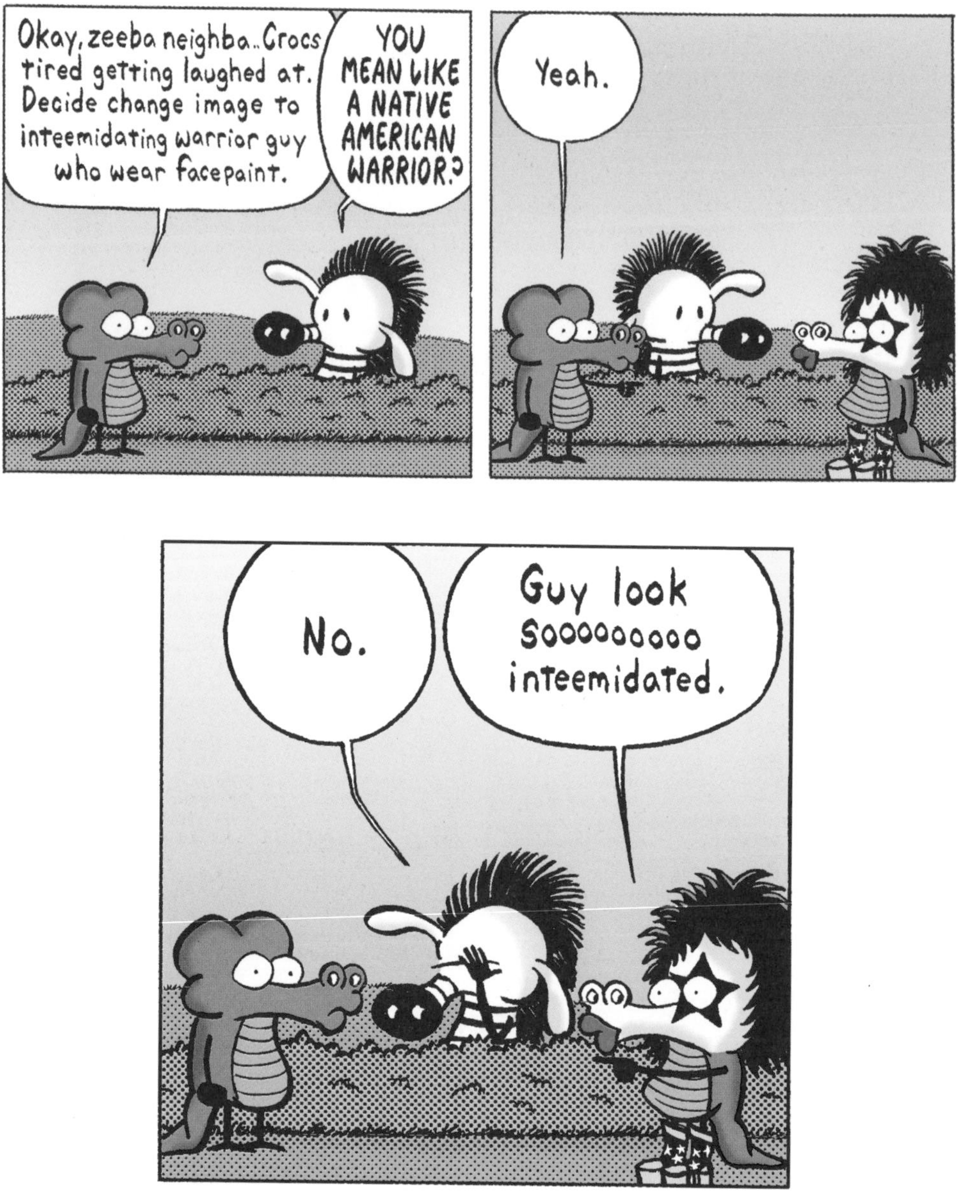
Okay, zeeba neighba.. Crocs tired getting laughed at. Decide change image to inteemidating warrior guy who wear facepaint.
YOU MEAN LIKE A NATIVE AMERICAN WARRIOR?
Yeah.
No.
Guy look sooooooooo inteemidated.

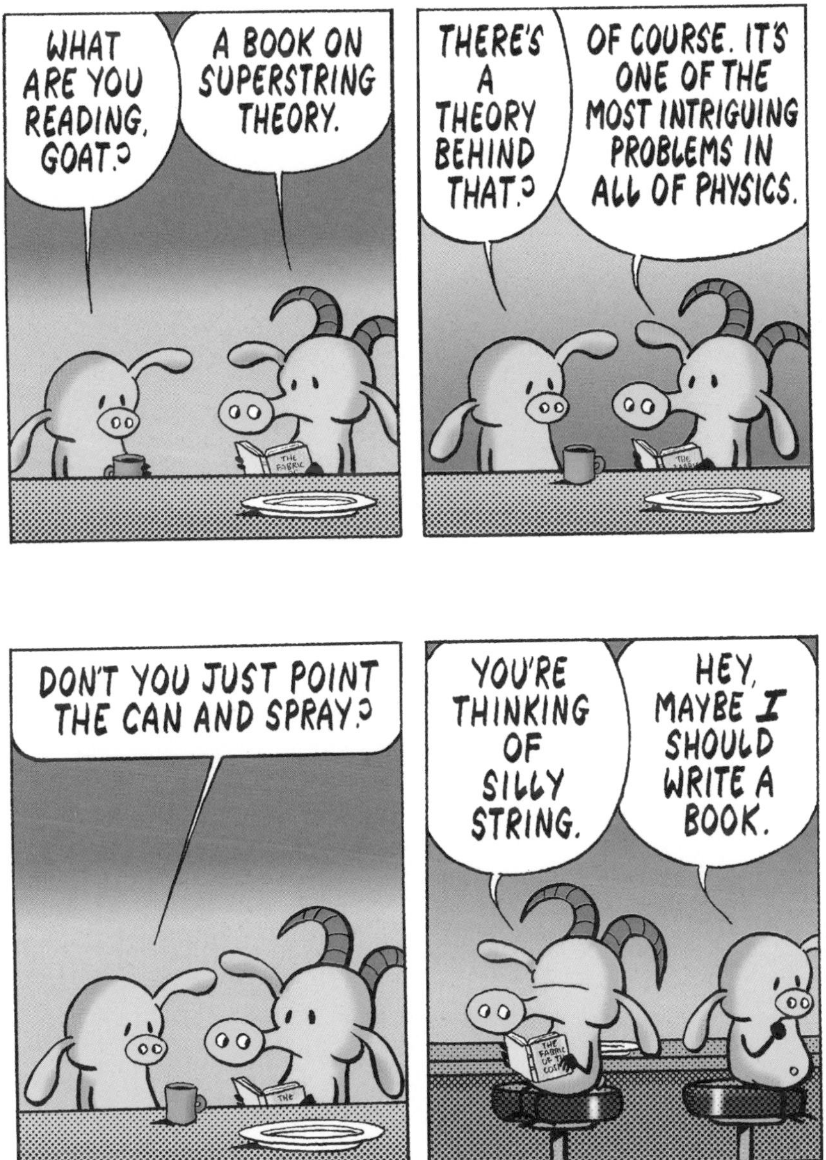
WHAT ARE YOU READING, GOAT?
A BOOK ON SUPERSTRING THEORY.
THERE'S A THEORY BEHIND THAT?
OF COURSE. IT'S ONE OF THE MOST INTRIGUING PROBLEMS IN ALL OF PHYSICS.
DON'T YOU JUST POINT THE CAN AND SPRAY?
YOU'RE THINKING OF SILLY STRING.
HEY, MAYBE I SHOULD WRITE A BOOK.

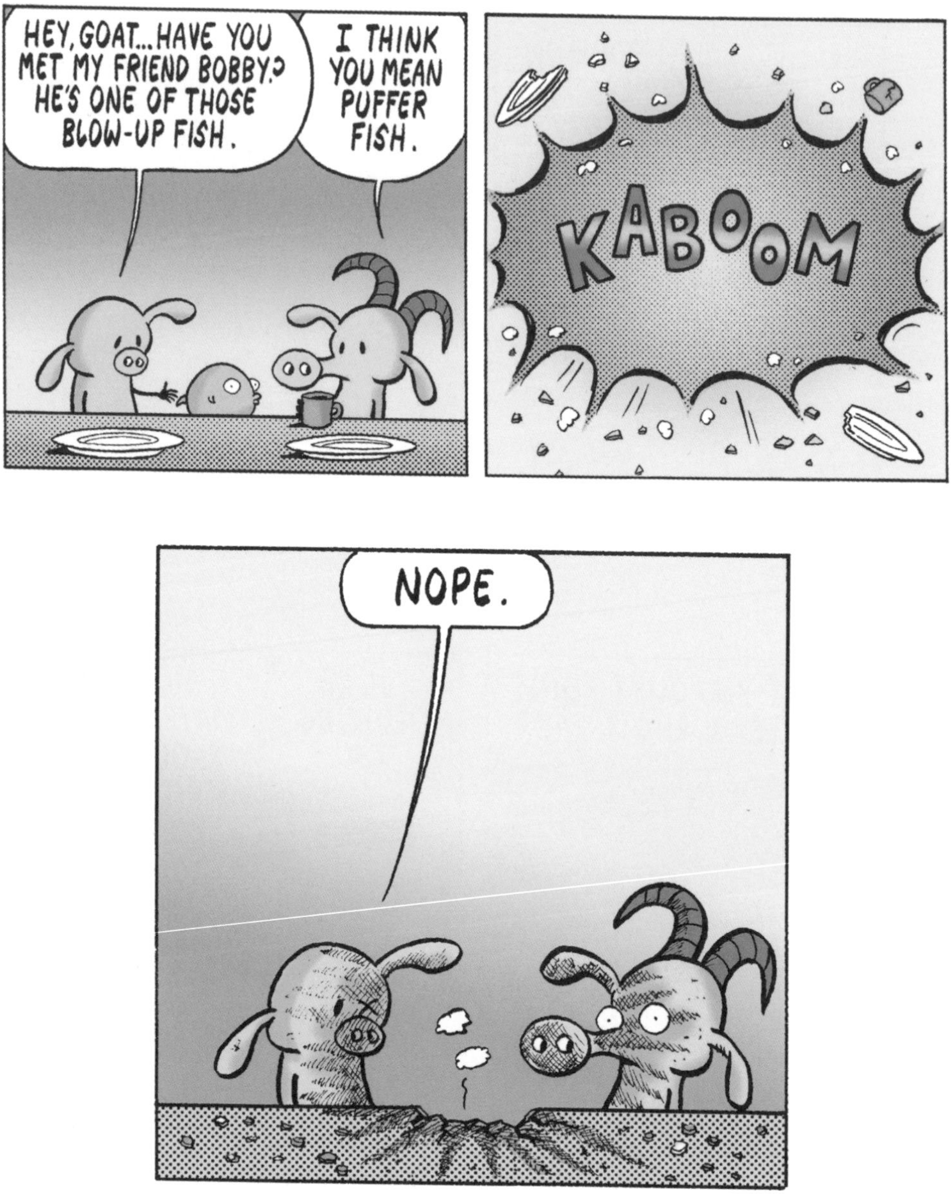
HEY, GOAT...HAVE YOU MET MY FRIEND BOBBY? HE'S ONE OF THOSE BLOW-UP FISH.
I THINK YOU MEAN PUFFER FISH.
KABOOM
NOPE.

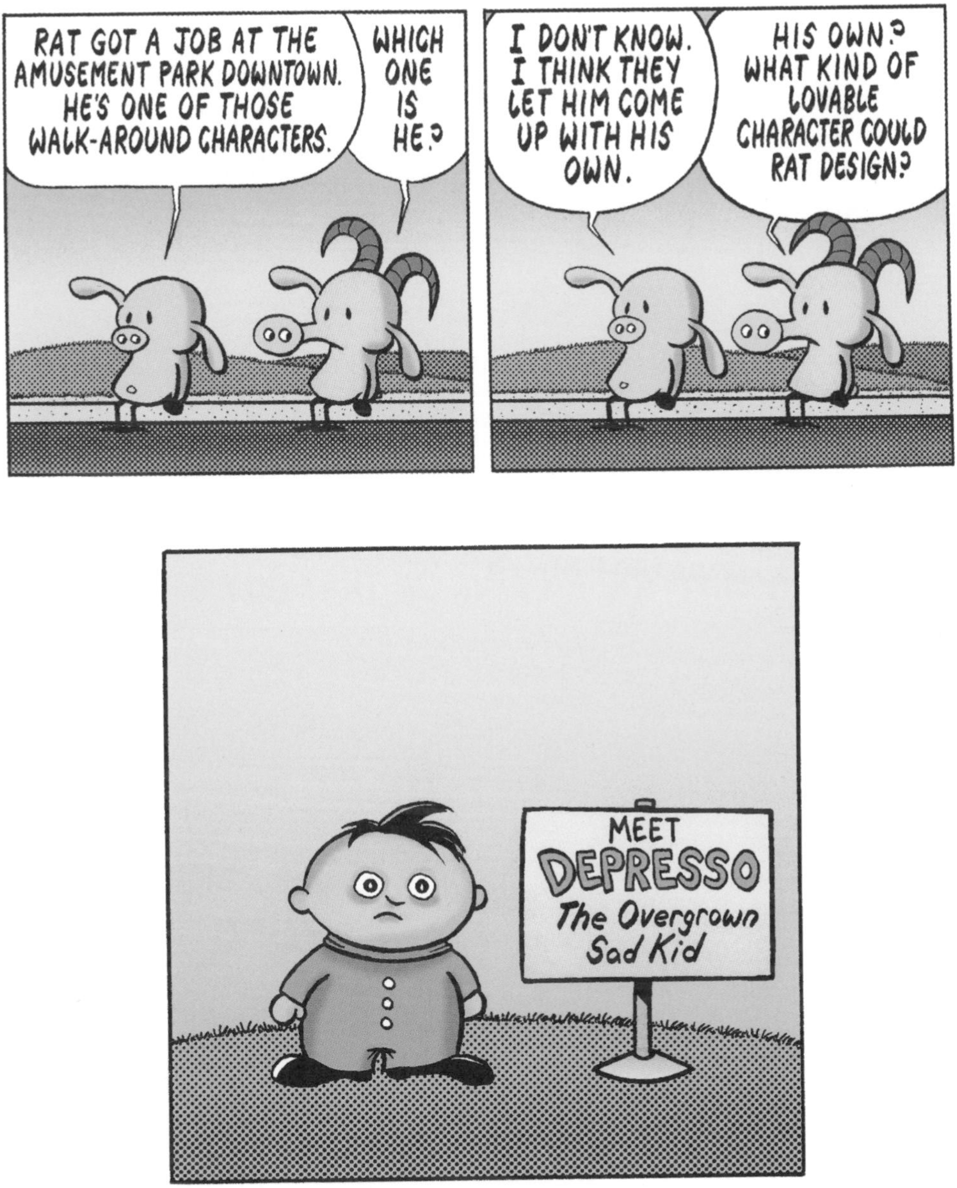
RAT GOT A JOB AT THE AMUSEMENT PARK DOWNTOWN. HE'S ONE OF THOSE WALK-AROUND CHARACTERS.
WHICH ONE IS HE?
I DON'T KNOW. I THINK THEY LET HIM COME UP WITH HIS OWN.
HIS OWN? WHAT KIND OF LOVABLE CHARACTER COULD RAT DESIGN?
MEET
DEPRESSO
The Overgrown Sad Kid

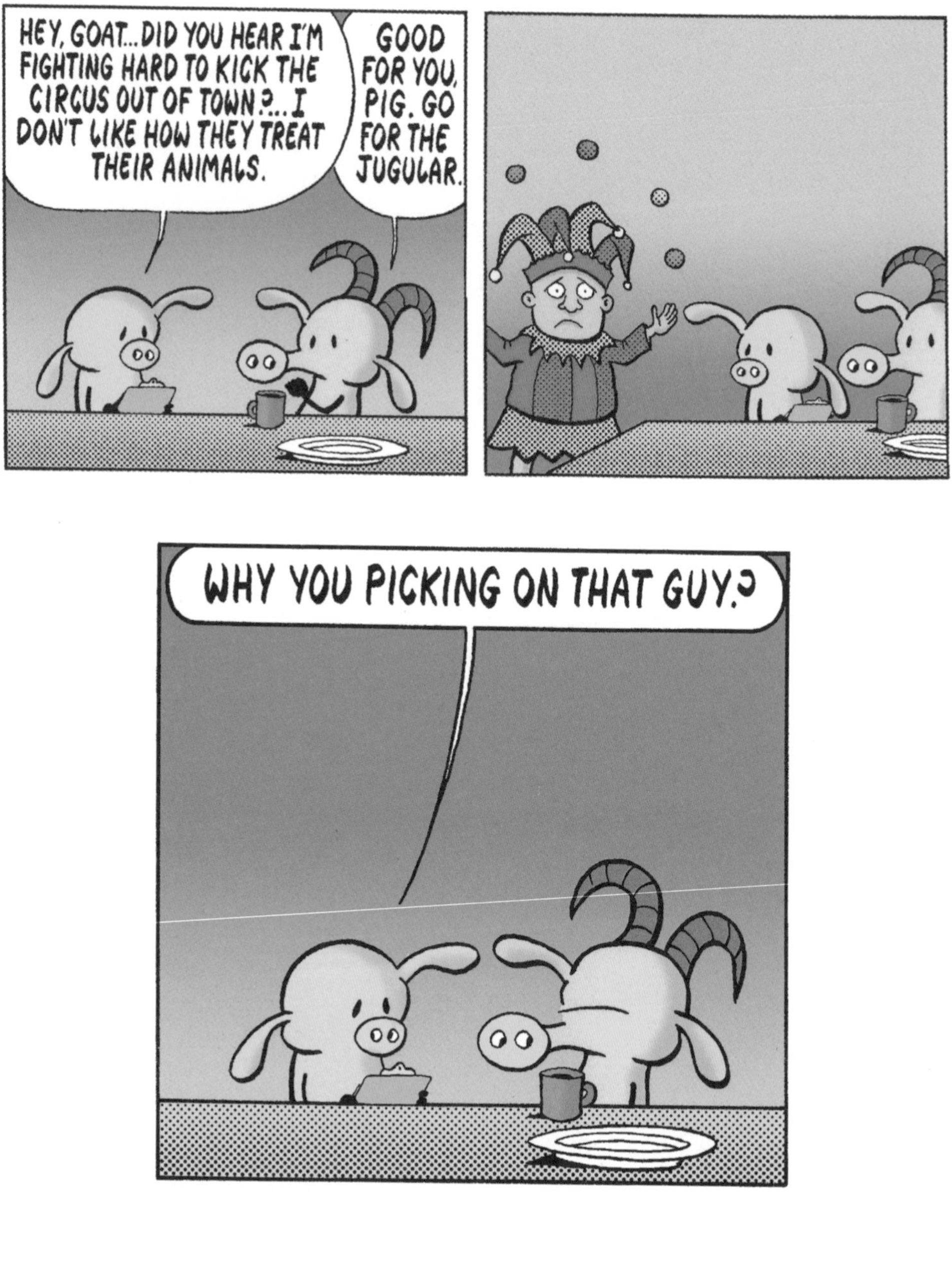
HEY, GOAT...DID YOU HEAR I'M FIGHTING HARD TO KICK THE CIRCUS OUT OF TOWN?...I DON'T LIKE HOW THEY TREAT THEIR ANIMALS.
GOOD FOR YOU, PIG. GO FOR THE JUGULAR.
WHY YOU PICKING ON THAT GUY?

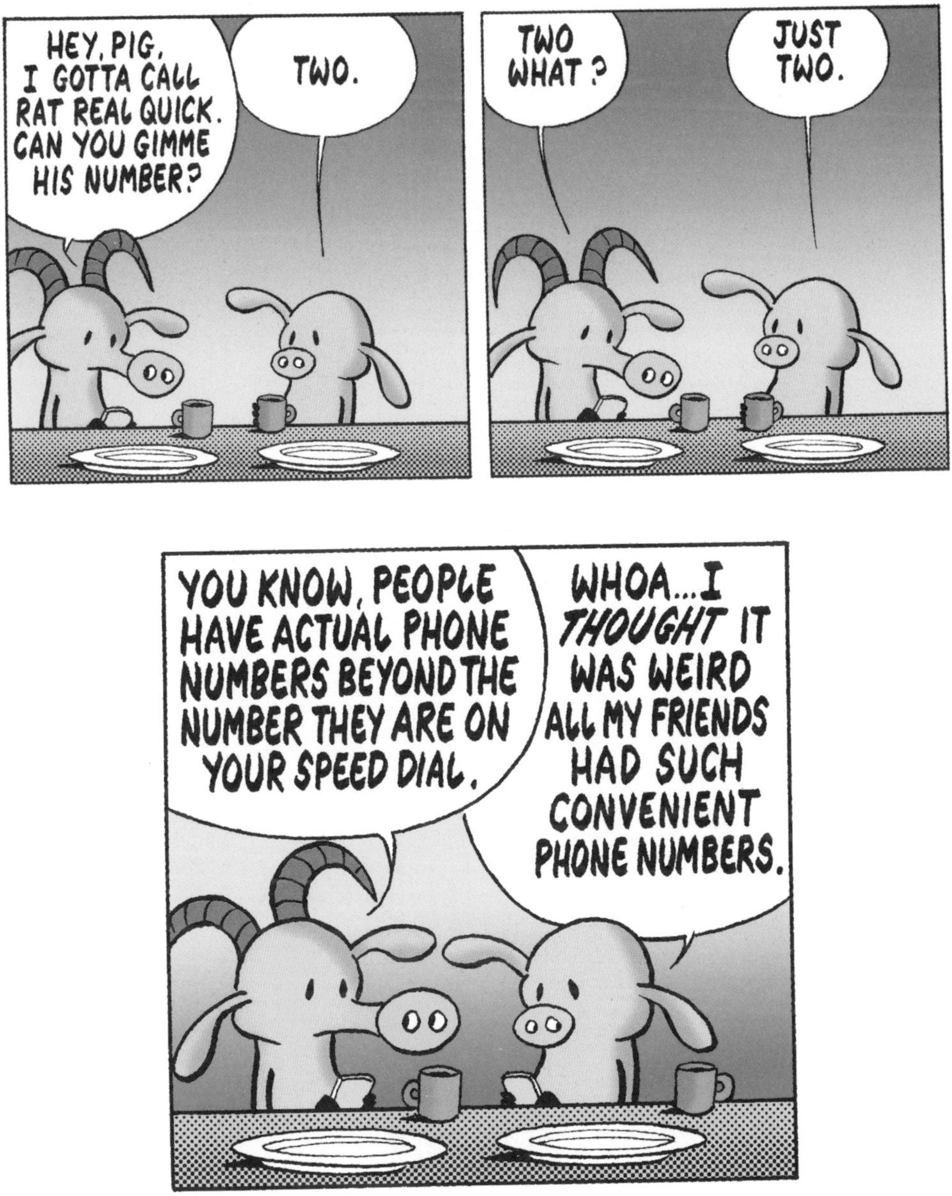
HEY, PIG, I GOTTA CALL RAT REAL QUICK. CAN YOU GIMME HIS NUMBER?
TWO.
TWO WHAT?
JUST TWO.
YOU KNOW, PEOPLE HAVE ACTUAL PHONE NUMBERS BEYOND THE NUMBER THEY ARE ON YOUR SPEED DIAL.
WHOA...I *THOUGHT* IT WAS WEIRD ALL MY FRIENDS HAD SUCH CONVENIENT PHONE NUMBERS.

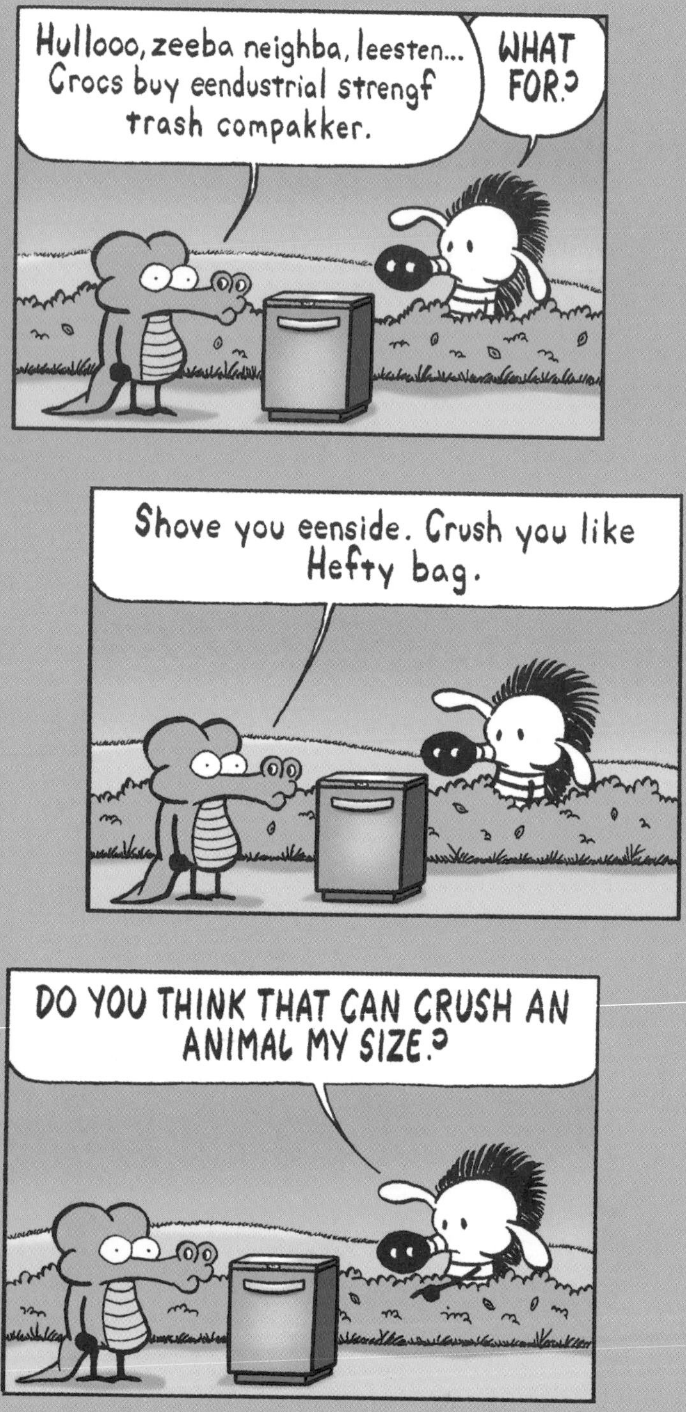
Hullooo, zeeba neighba, leesten... Crocs buy eendustrial strengf trash compakker.
WHAT FOR?
Shove you eenside. Crush you like Hefty bag.
DO YOU THINK THAT CAN CRUSH AN ANIMAL MY SIZE?

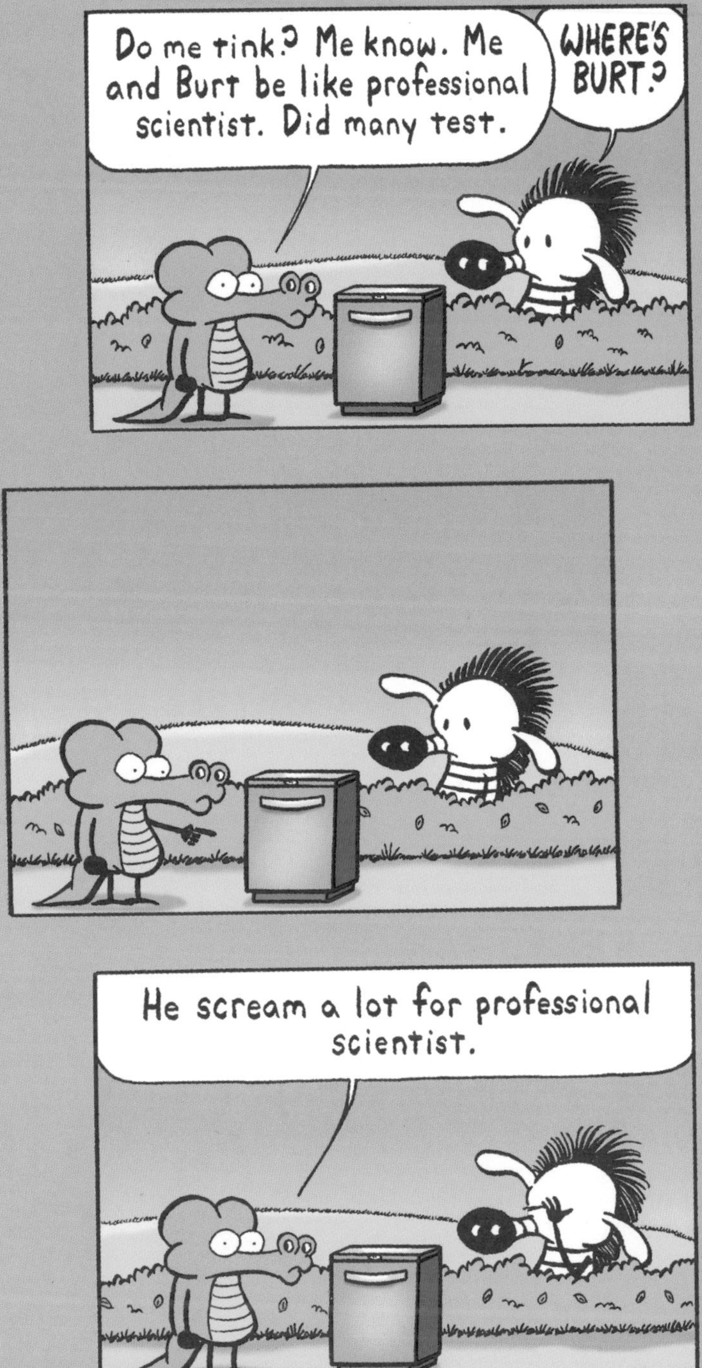
Do me tink? Me know. Me and Burt be like professional scientist. Did many test.
WHERE'S BURT?
He scream a lot for professional scientist.

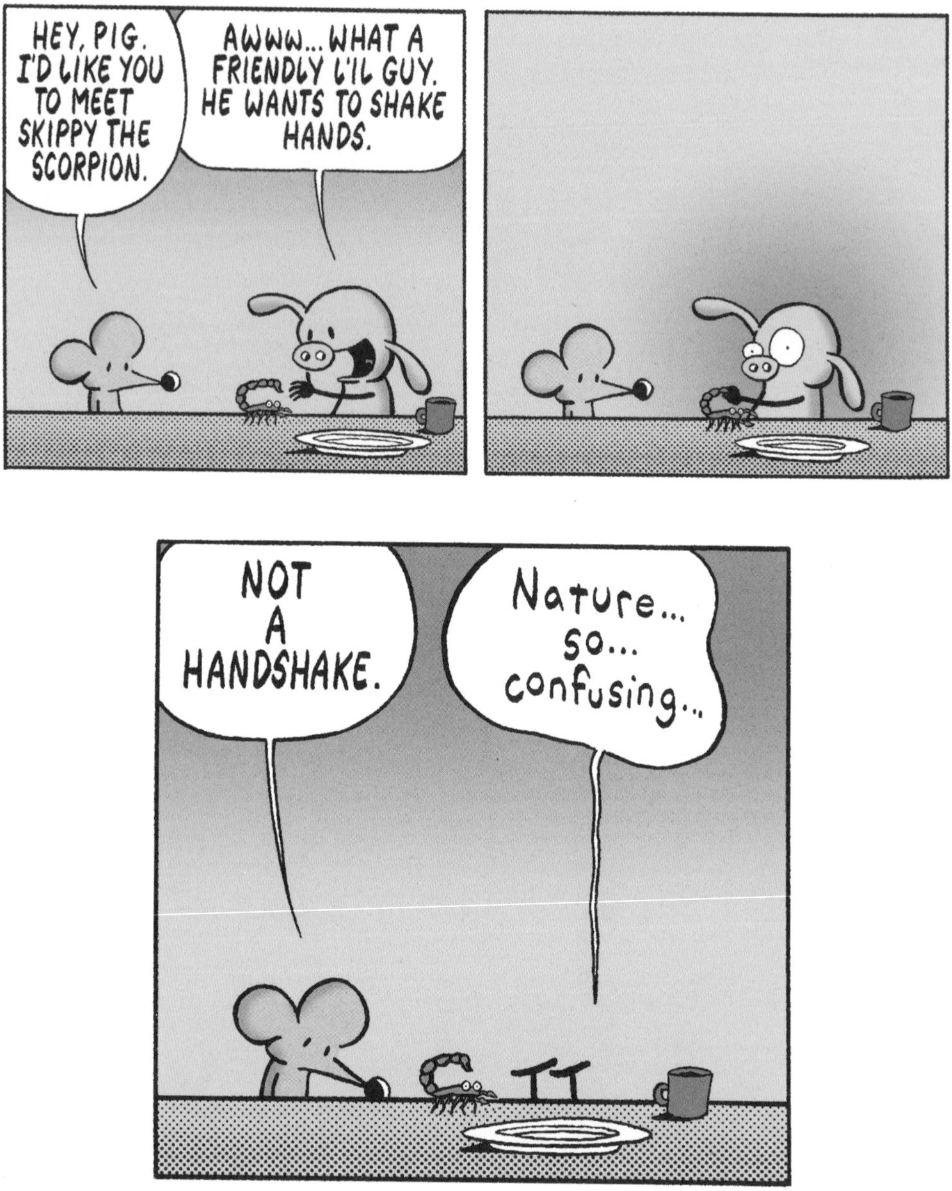
HEY, PIG. I'D LIKE YOU TO MEET SKIPPY THE SCORPION.
AWWW... WHAT A FRIENDLY L'IL GUY. HE WANTS TO SHAKE HANDS.
NOT A HANDSHAKE.
Nature... so... confusing...

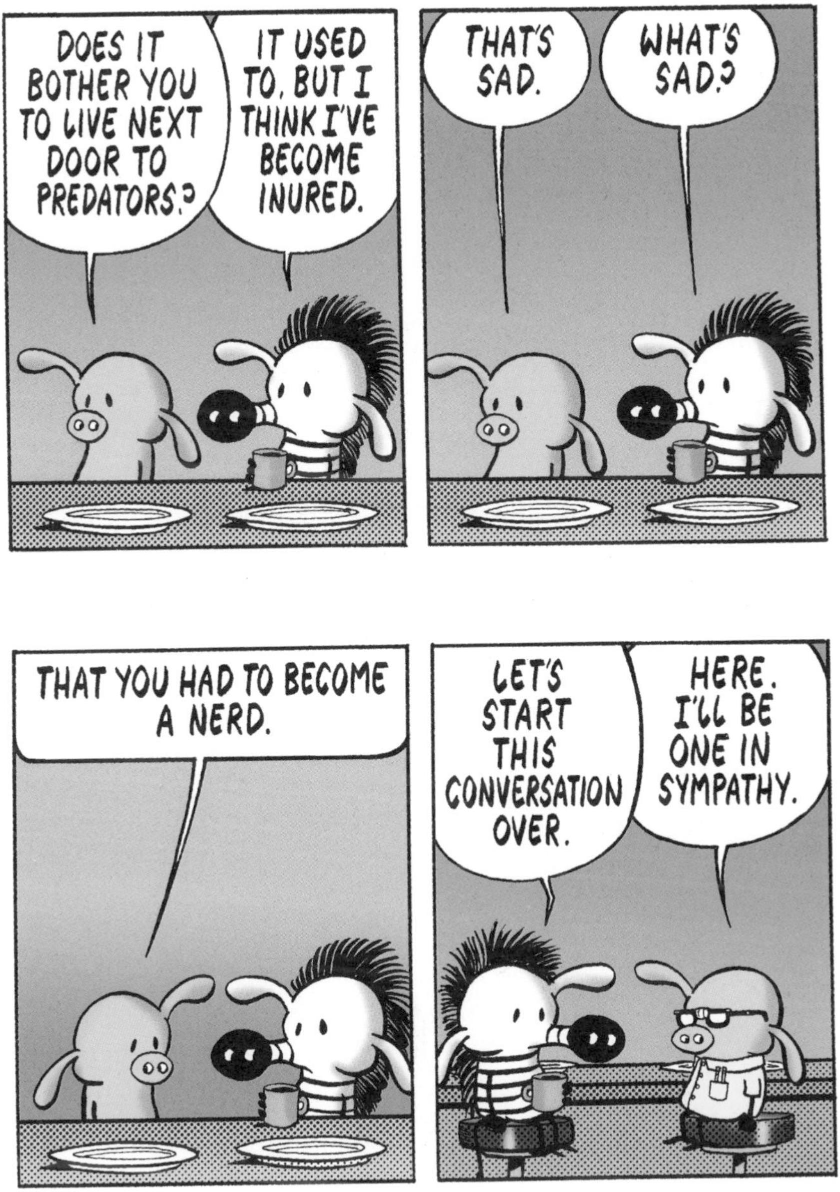
DOES IT BOTHER YOU TO LIVE NEXT DOOR TO PREDATORS?
IT USED TO, BUT I THINK I'VE BECOME INURED.
THAT'S SAD.
WHAT'S SAD?
THAT YOU HAD TO BECOME A NERD.
LET'S START THIS CONVERSATION OVER.
HERE. I'LL BE ONE IN SYMPATHY.

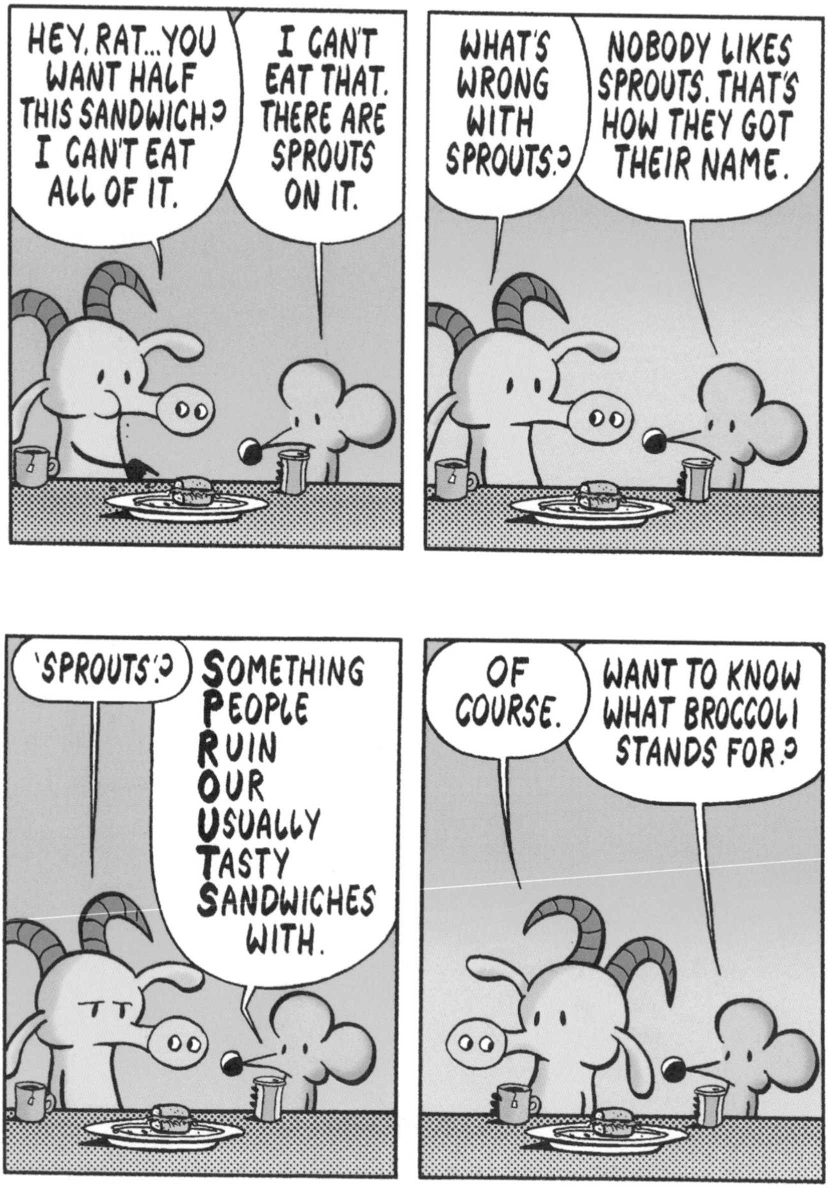
HEY, RAT...YOU WANT HALF THIS SANDWICH? I CAN'T EAT ALL OF IT.
I CAN'T EAT THAT. THERE ARE SPROUTS ON IT.
WHAT'S WRONG WITH SPROUTS?
NOBODY LIKES SPROUTS. THAT'S HOW THEY GOT THEIR NAME.
'SPROUTS'?
SOMETHING PEOPLE RUIN OUR USUALLY TASTY SANDWICHES WITH.
OF COURSE.
WANT TO KNOW WHAT BROCCOLI STANDS FOR?

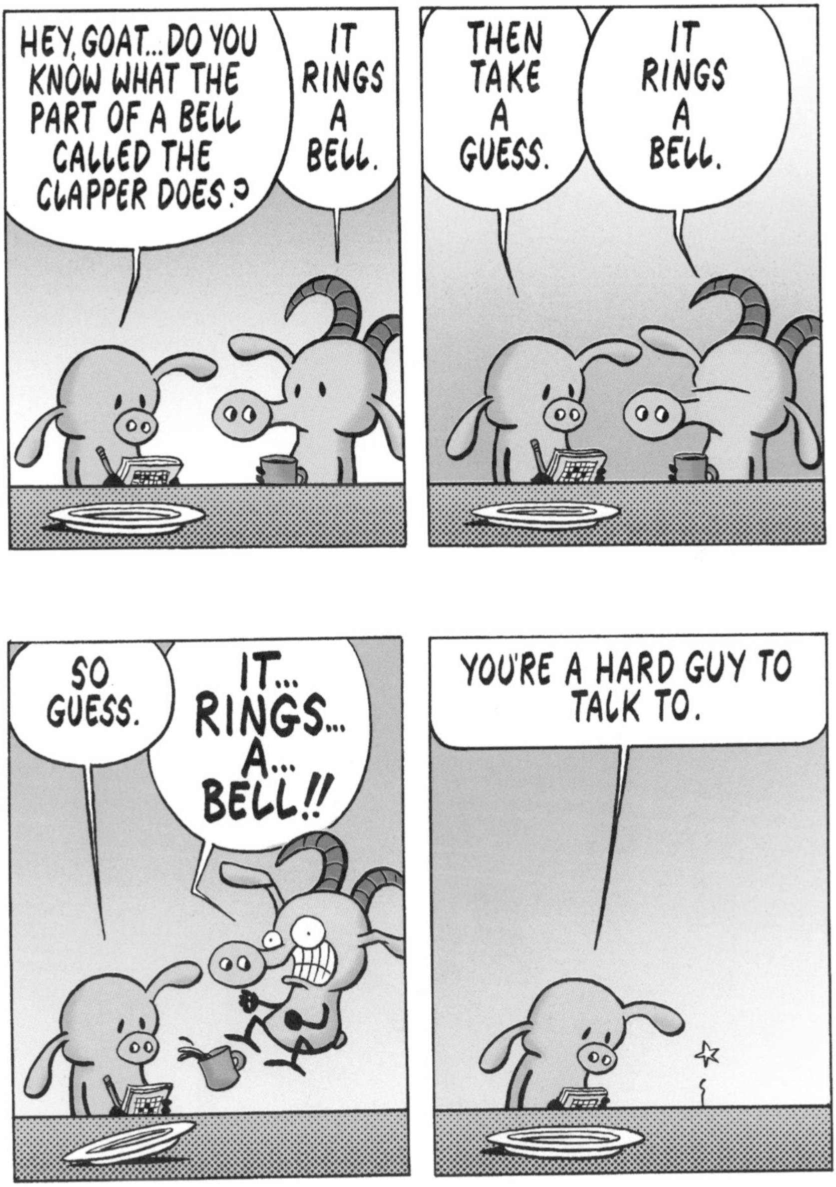
HEY, GOAT...DO YOU KNOW WHAT THE PART OF A BELL CALLED THE CLAPPER DOES?
IT RINGS A BELL.
THEN TAKE A GUESS.
IT RINGS A BELL.
SO GUESS.
IT... RINGS... A... BELL!!
YOU'RE A HARD GUY TO TALK TO.

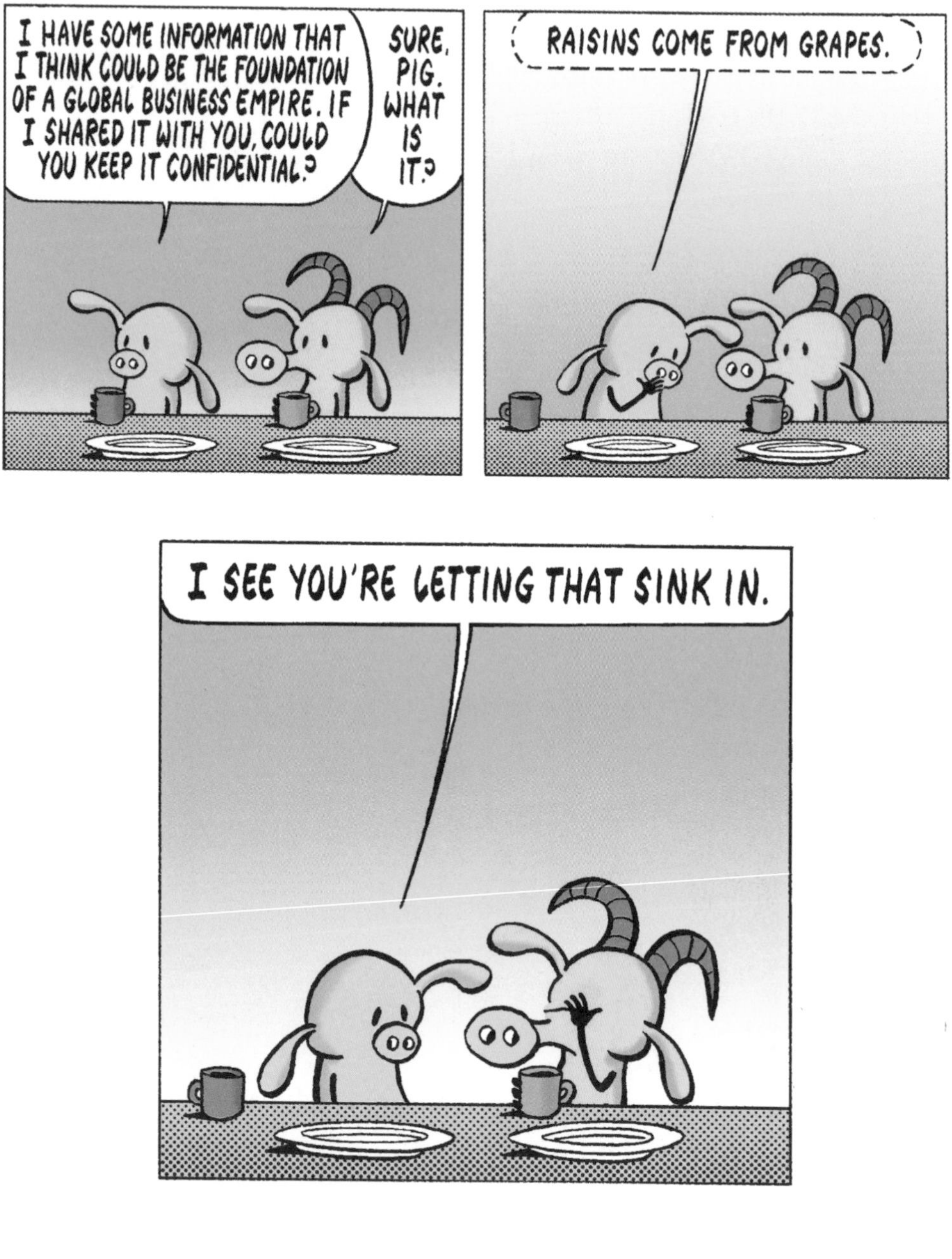
I HAVE SOME INFORMATION THAT I THINK COULD BE THE FOUNDATION OF A GLOBAL BUSINESS EMPIRE. IF I SHARED IT WITH YOU, COULD YOU KEEP IT CONFIDENTIAL?
SURE, PIG. WHAT IS IT?
RAISINS COME FROM GRAPES.
I SEE YOU'RE LETTING THAT SINK IN.

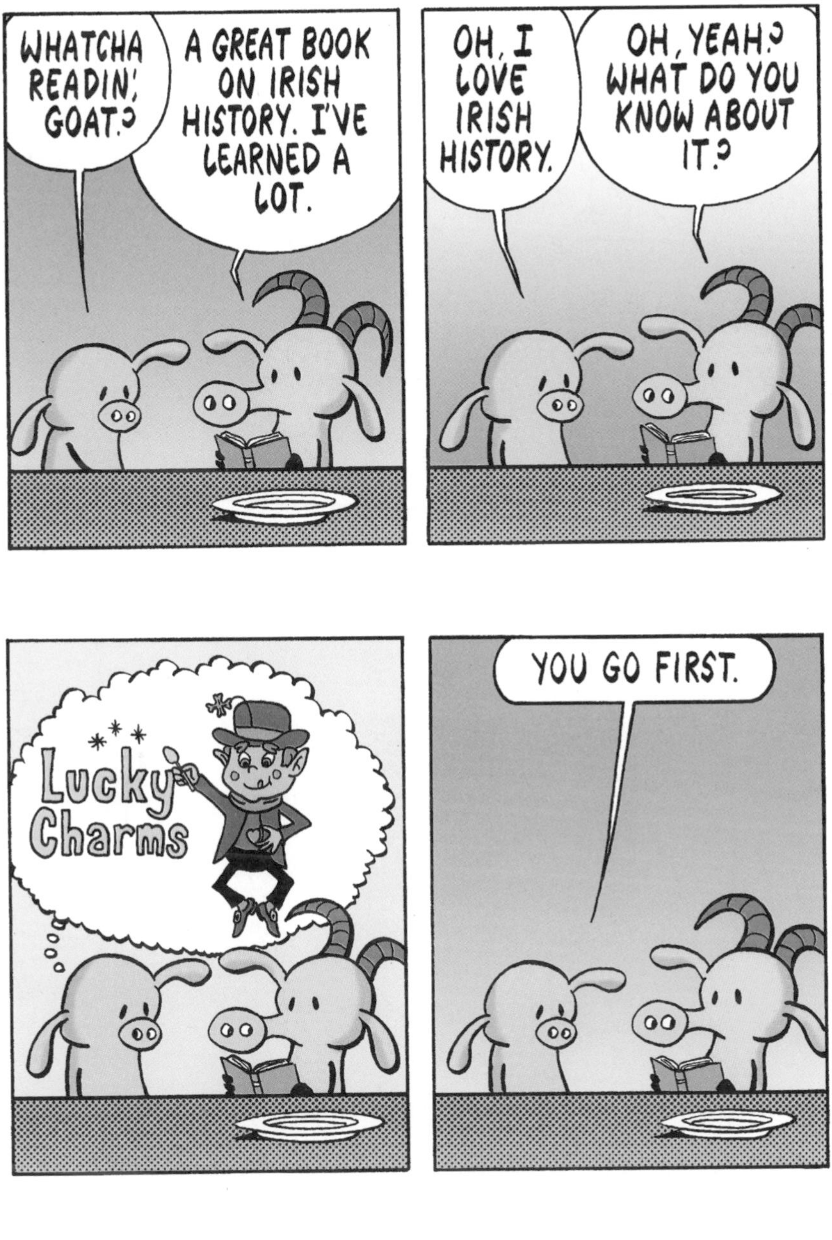
WHATCHA READIN', GOAT?
A GREAT BOOK ON IRISH HISTORY. I'VE LEARNED A LOT.
OH, I LOVE IRISH HISTORY.
OH, YEAH? WHAT DO YOU KNOW ABOUT IT?
Lucky Charms
YOU GO FIRST.

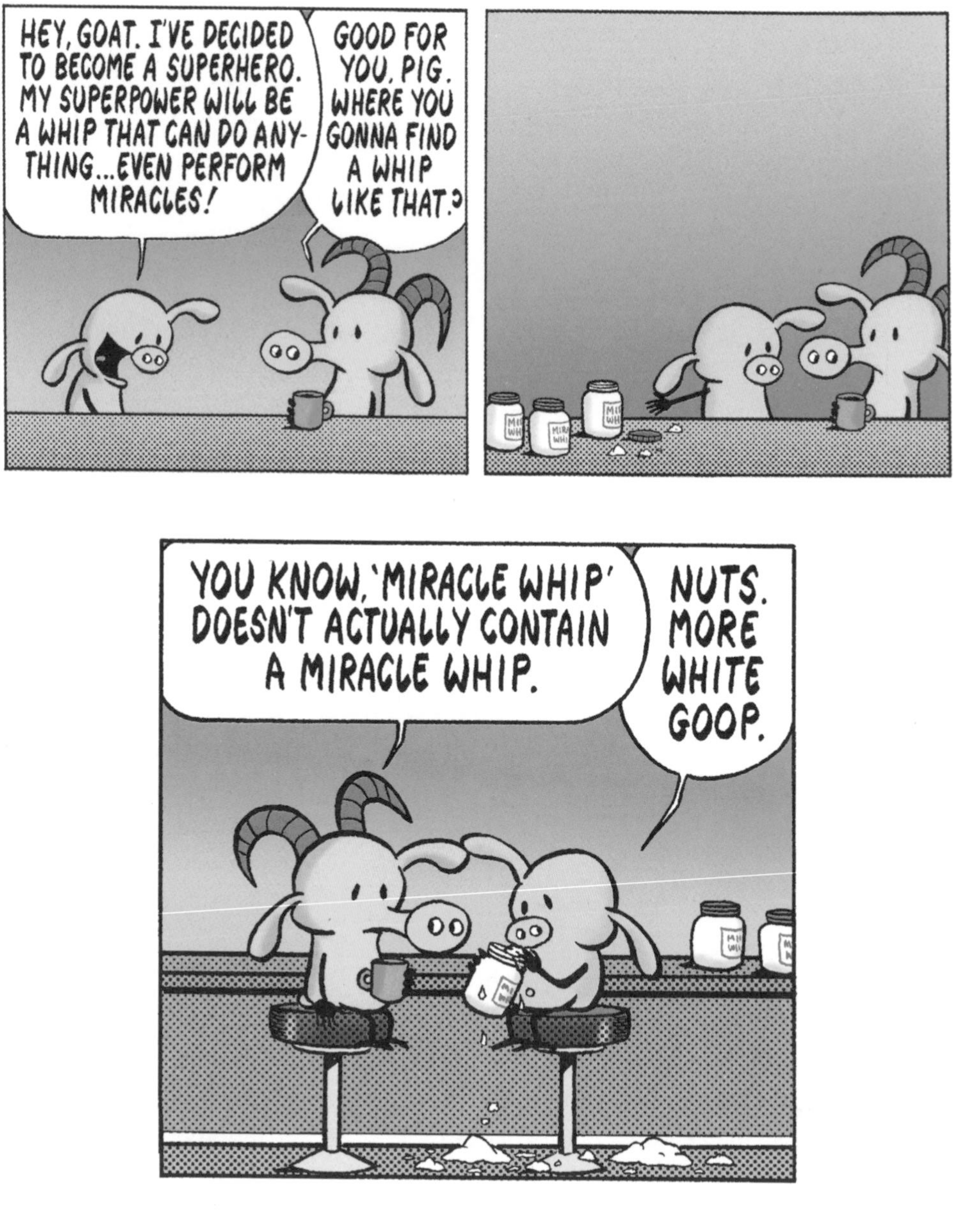
HEY, GOAT. I'VE DECIDED TO BECOME A SUPERHERO. MY SUPERPOWER WILL BE A WHIP THAT CAN DO ANY-THING...EVEN PERFORM MIRACLES!
GOOD FOR YOU, PIG. WHERE YOU GONNA FIND A WHIP LIKE THAT?
YOU KNOW, 'MIRACLE WHIP' DOESN'T ACTUALLY CONTAIN A MIRACLE WHIP.
NUTS. MORE WHITE GOOP.

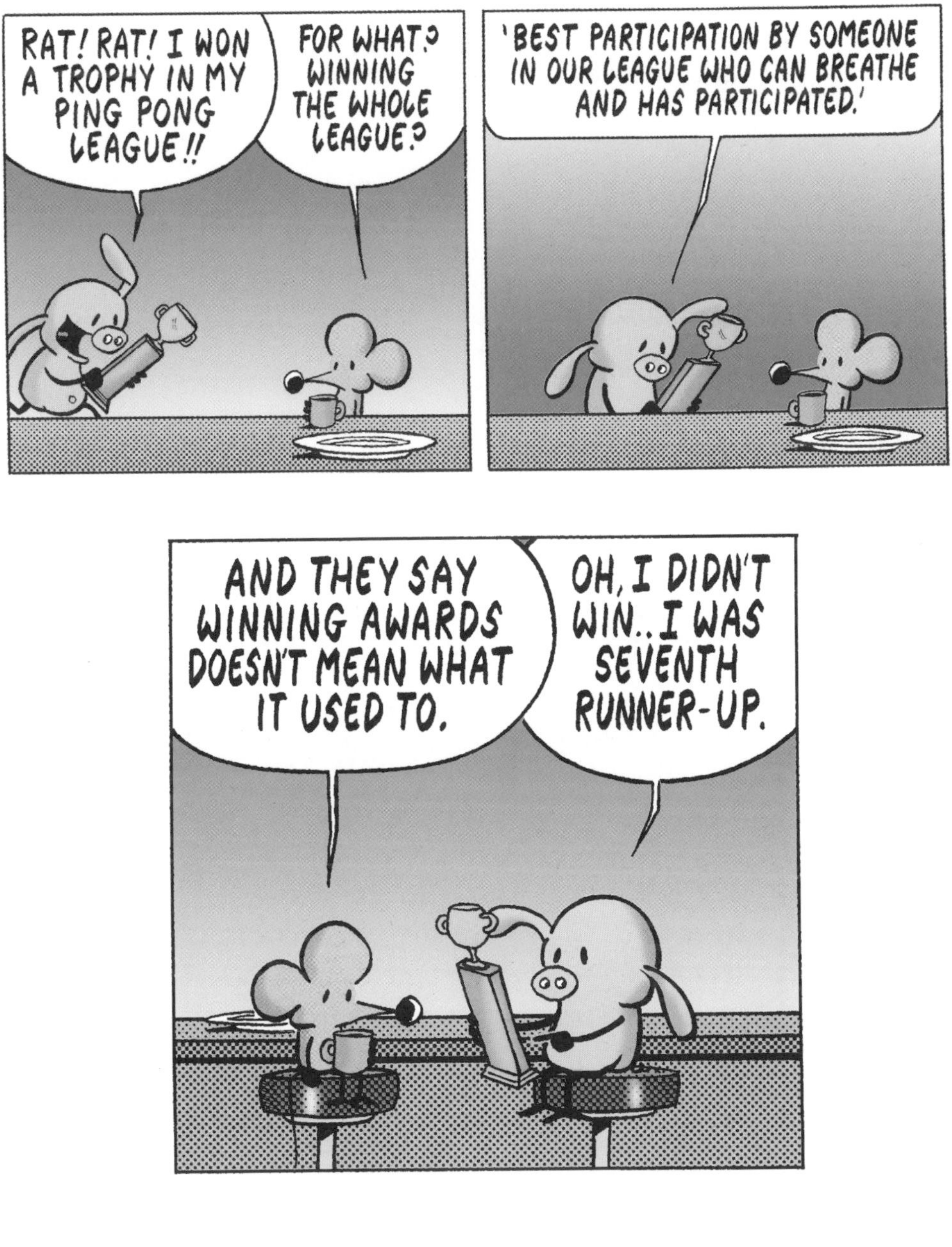
RAT! RAT! I WON A TROPHY IN MY PING PONG LEAGUE!!
FOR WHAT? WINNING THE WHOLE LEAGUE?
'BEST PARTICIPATION BY SOMEONE IN OUR LEAGUE WHO CAN BREATHE AND HAS PARTICIPATED.'
AND THEY SAY WINNING AWARDS DOESN'T MEAN WHAT IT USED TO.
OH, I DIDN'T WIN.. I WAS SEVENTH RUNNER-UP.

BOB! BOB! Guess whuh me see.
Whuh?
Dead deer. On highway. Stoopid tings try run across. Geet hit.
Dead deer taste gud.
Me know dat, Bob. So go steal beegest truck possible. We zoom down highway. Run over everyting.

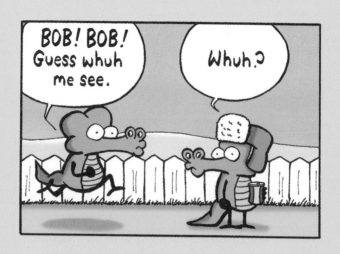

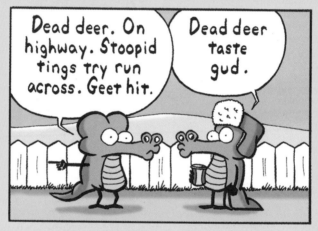

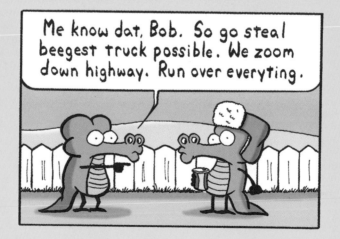

How 'bout YOU go run across highway, Bob?
GIMME BACK THE CART, PAL.
Peese no hit me, Man-Een-Funny-Pants.

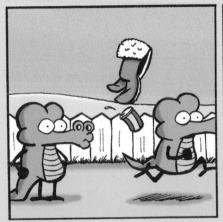

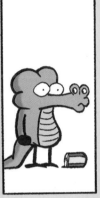

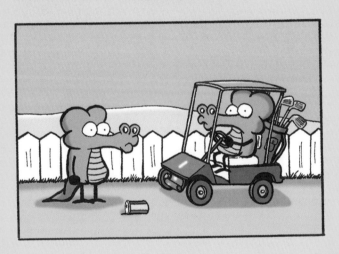

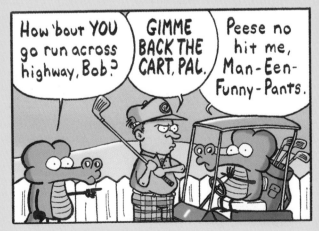

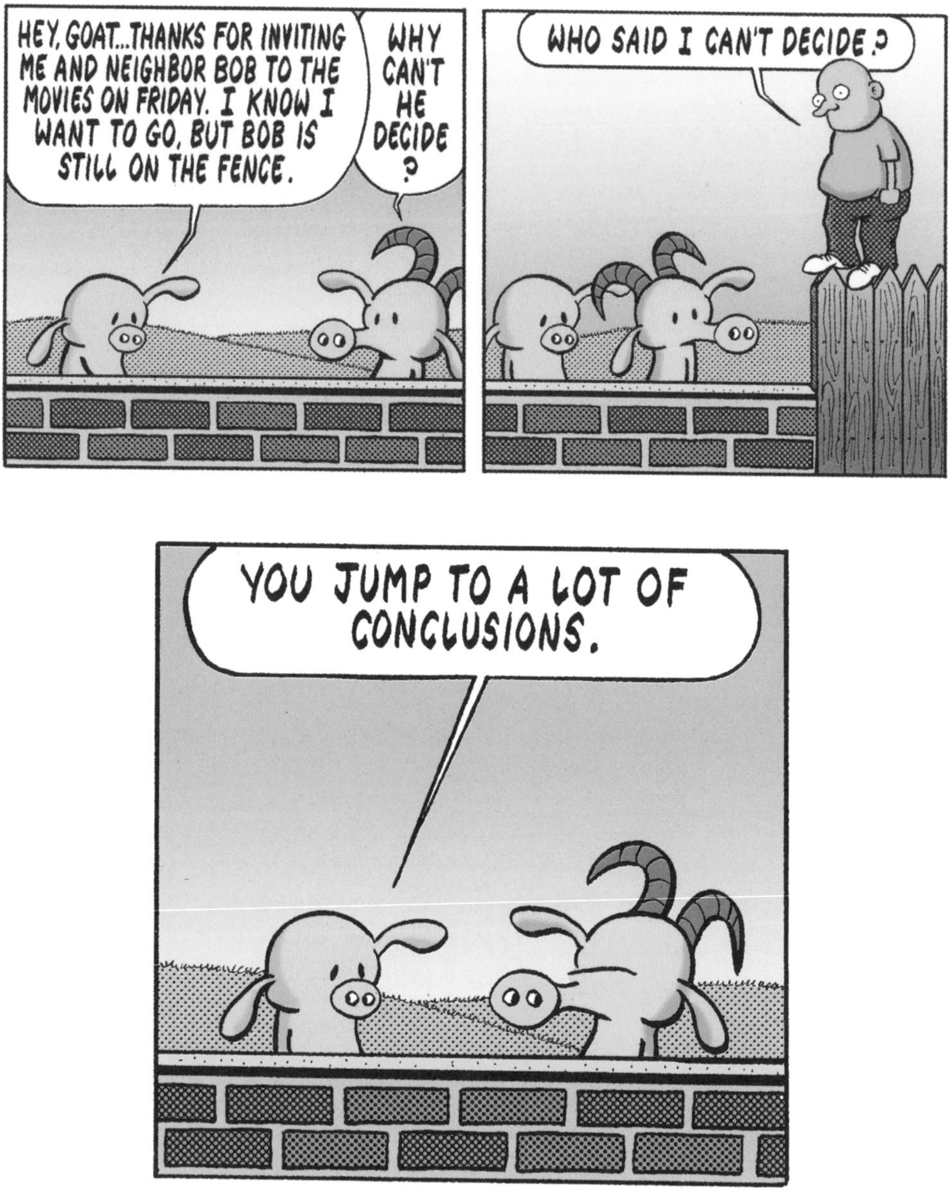
HEY, GOAT...THANKS FOR INVITING ME AND NEIGHBOR BOB TO THE MOVIES ON FRIDAY. I KNOW I WANT TO GO, BUT BOB IS STILL ON THE FENCE.
WHY CAN'T HE DECIDE?
WHO SAID I CAN'T DECIDE?
YOU JUMP TO A LOT OF CONCLUSIONS.

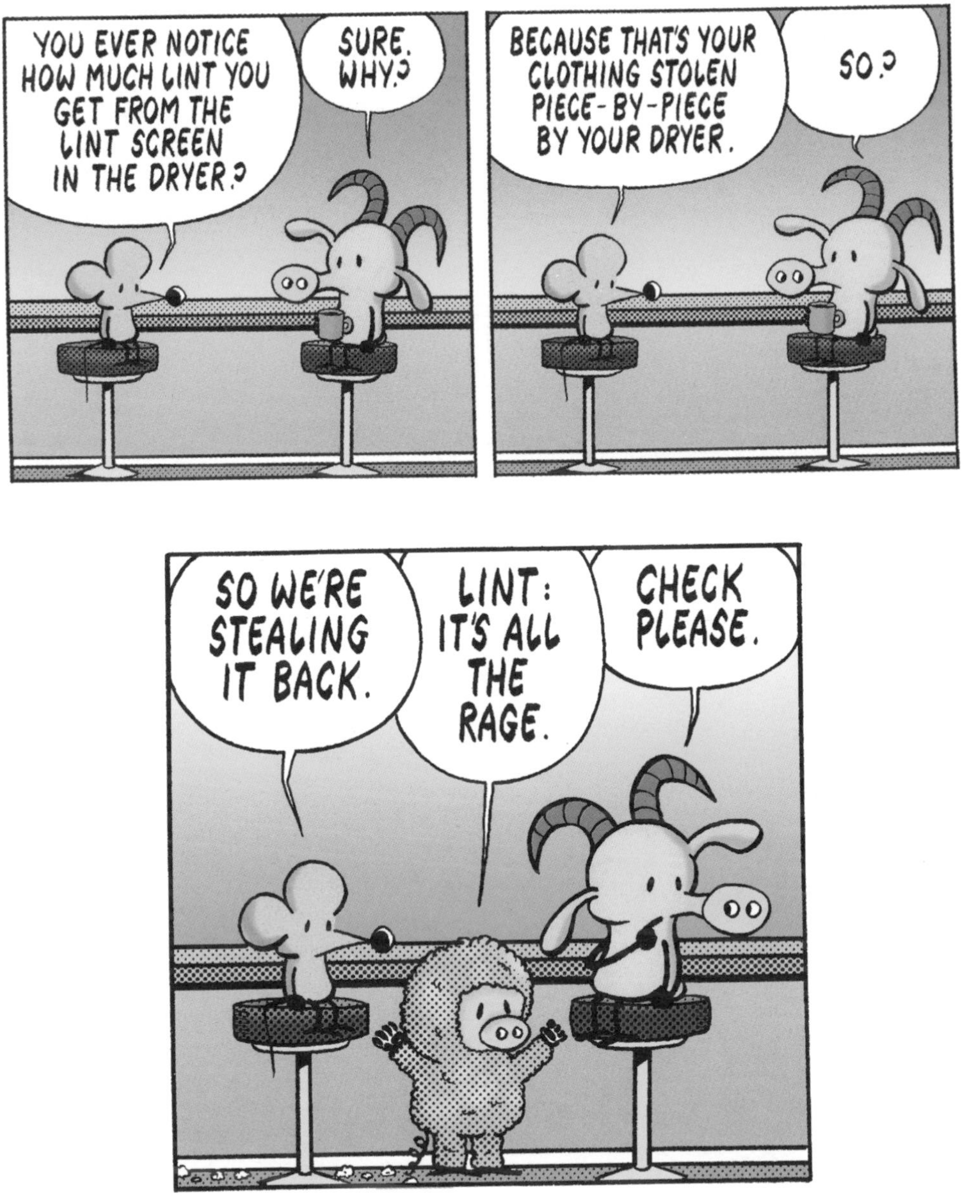

YOU EVER NOTICE HOW MUCH LINT YOU GET FROM THE LINT SCREEN IN THE DRYER?
SURE. WHY?
BECAUSE THAT'S YOUR CLOTHING STOLEN PIECE-BY-PIECE BY YOUR DRYER.
SO?
SO WE'RE STEALING IT BACK.
LINT: IT'S ALL THE RAGE.
CHECK PLEASE.

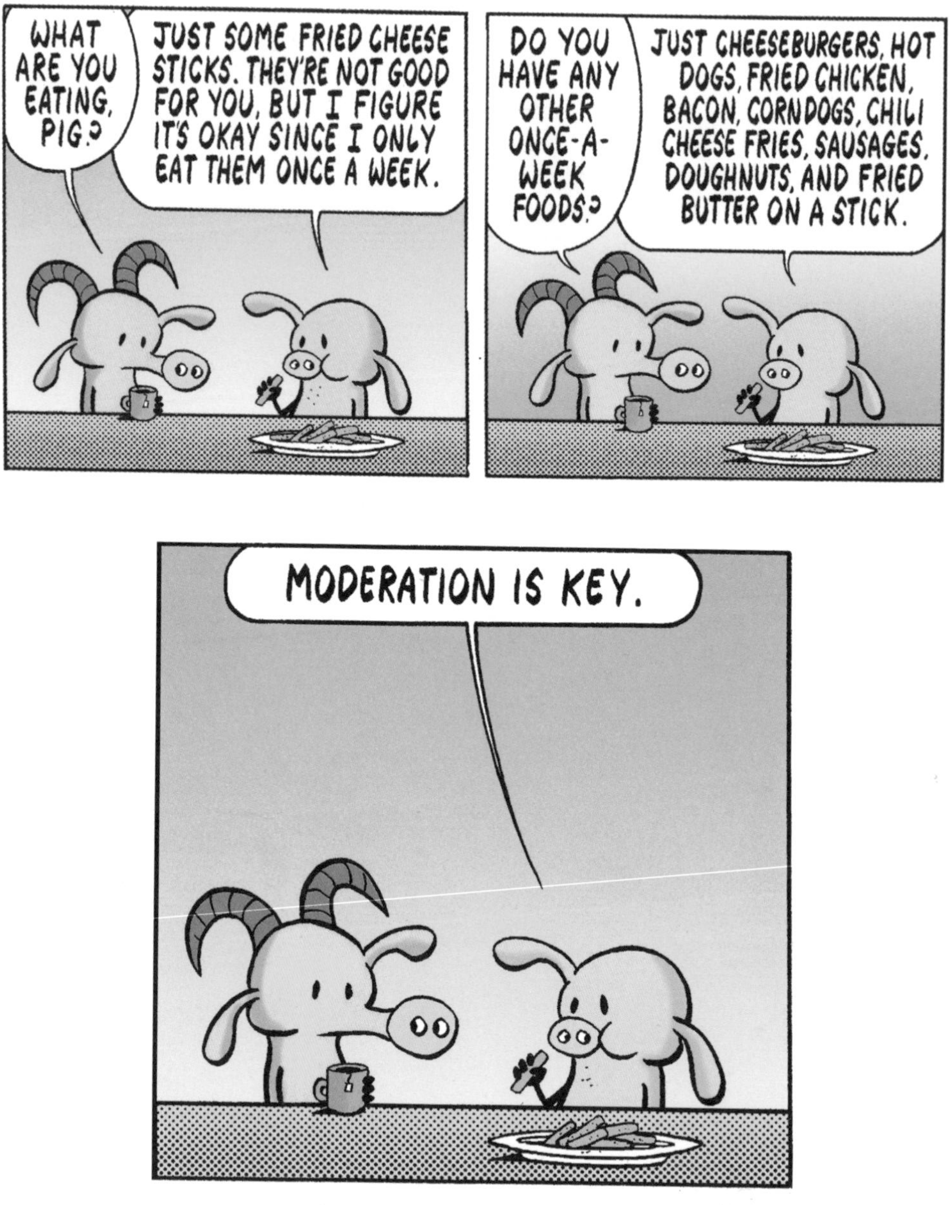
WHAT ARE YOU EATING, PIG?
JUST SOME FRIED CHEESE STICKS. THEY'RE NOT GOOD FOR YOU, BUT I FIGURE IT'S OKAY SINCE I ONLY EAT THEM ONCE A WEEK.
DO YOU HAVE ANY OTHER ONCE-A-WEEK FOODS?
JUST CHEESEBURGERS, HOT DOGS, FRIED CHICKEN, BACON, CORNDOGS, CHILI CHEESE FRIES, SAUSAGES, DOUGHNUTS, AND FRIED BUTTER ON A STICK.
MODERATION IS KEY.

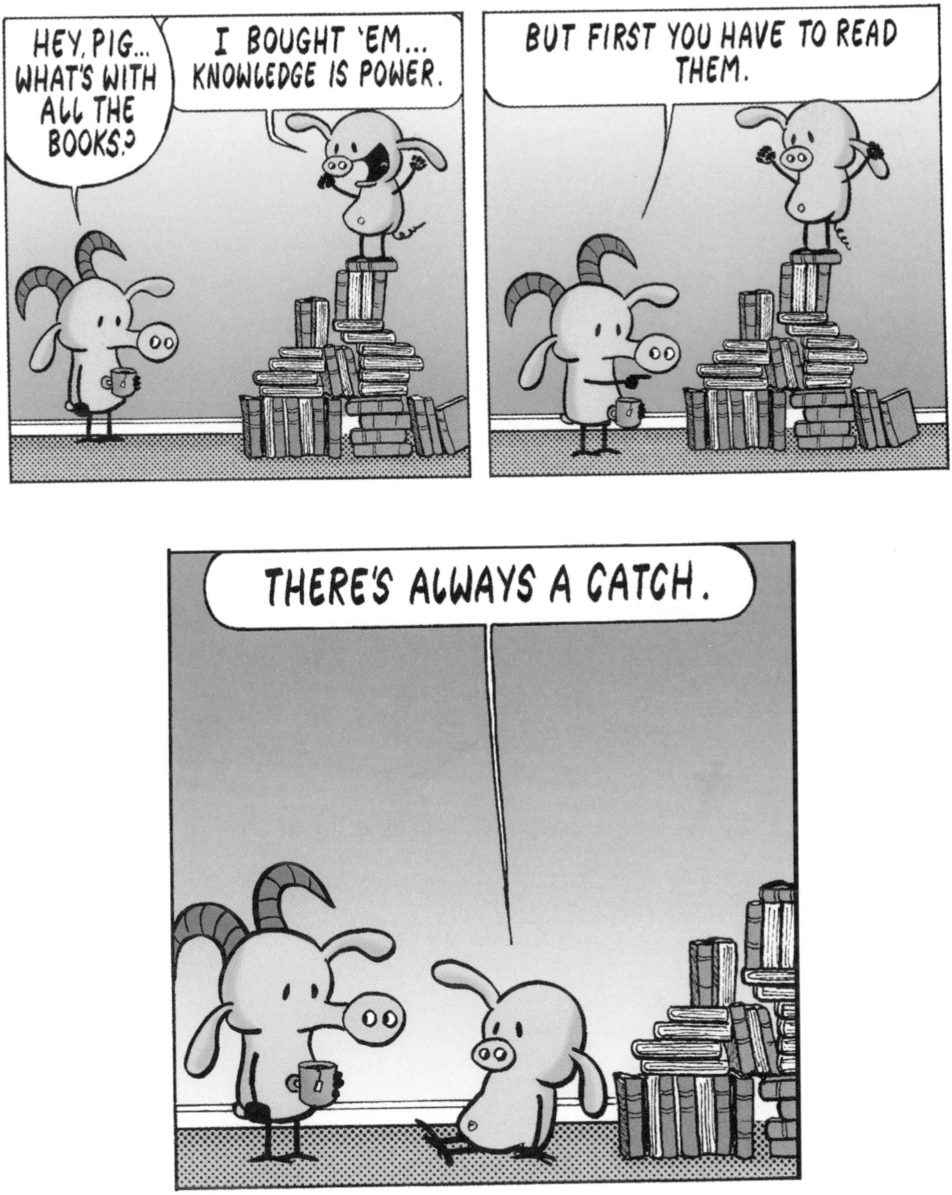
HEY, PIG... WHAT'S WITH ALL THE BOOKS?
I BOUGHT 'EM... KNOWLEDGE IS POWER.
BUT FIRST YOU HAVE TO READ THEM.
THERE'S ALWAYS A CATCH.

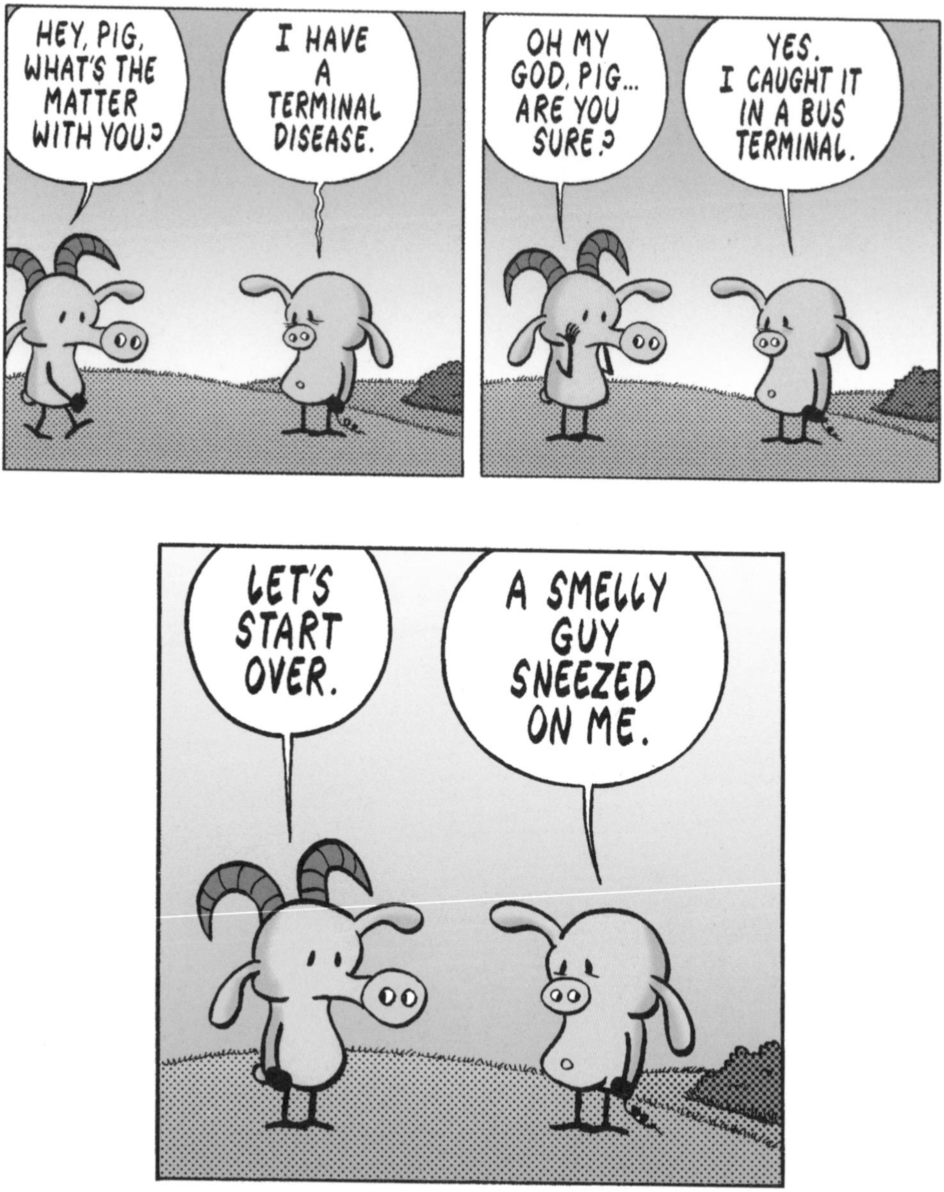
HEY, PIG, WHAT'S THE MATTER WITH YOU?
I HAVE A TERMINAL DISEASE.
OH MY GOD, PIG... ARE YOU SURE?
YES. I CAUGHT IT IN A BUS TERMINAL.
LET'S START OVER.
A SMELLY GUY SNEEZED ON ME.

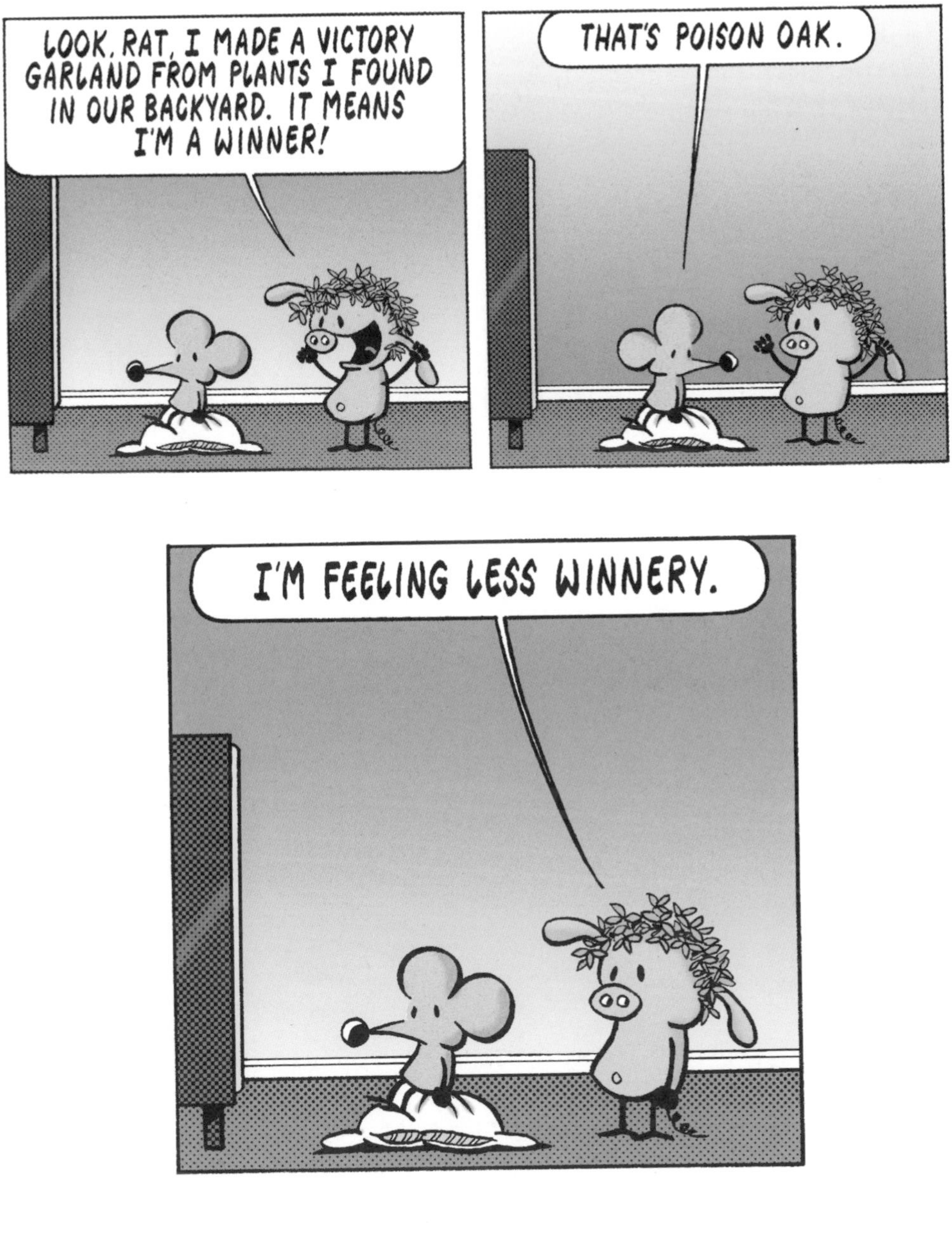
LOOK, RAT, I MADE A VICTORY GARLAND FROM PLANTS I FOUND IN OUR BACKYARD. IT MEANS I'M A WINNER!
THAT'S POISON OAK.
I'M FEELING LESS WINNERY.

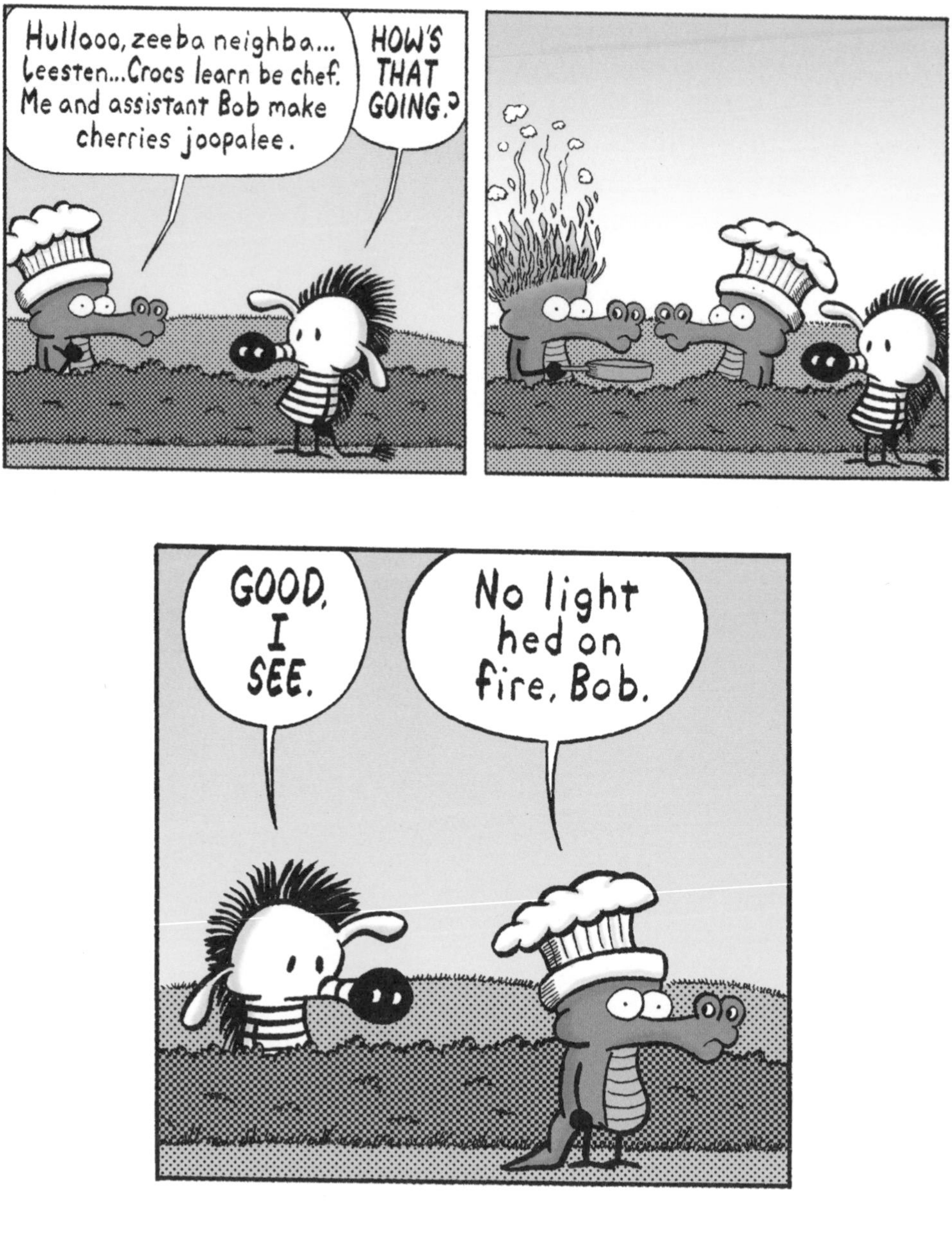
Hullooo, zeeba neighba... Leesten...Crocs learn be chef. Me and assistant Bob make cherries joopalee.
HOW'S THAT GOING?
GOOD, I SEE.
No light hed on fire, Bob.

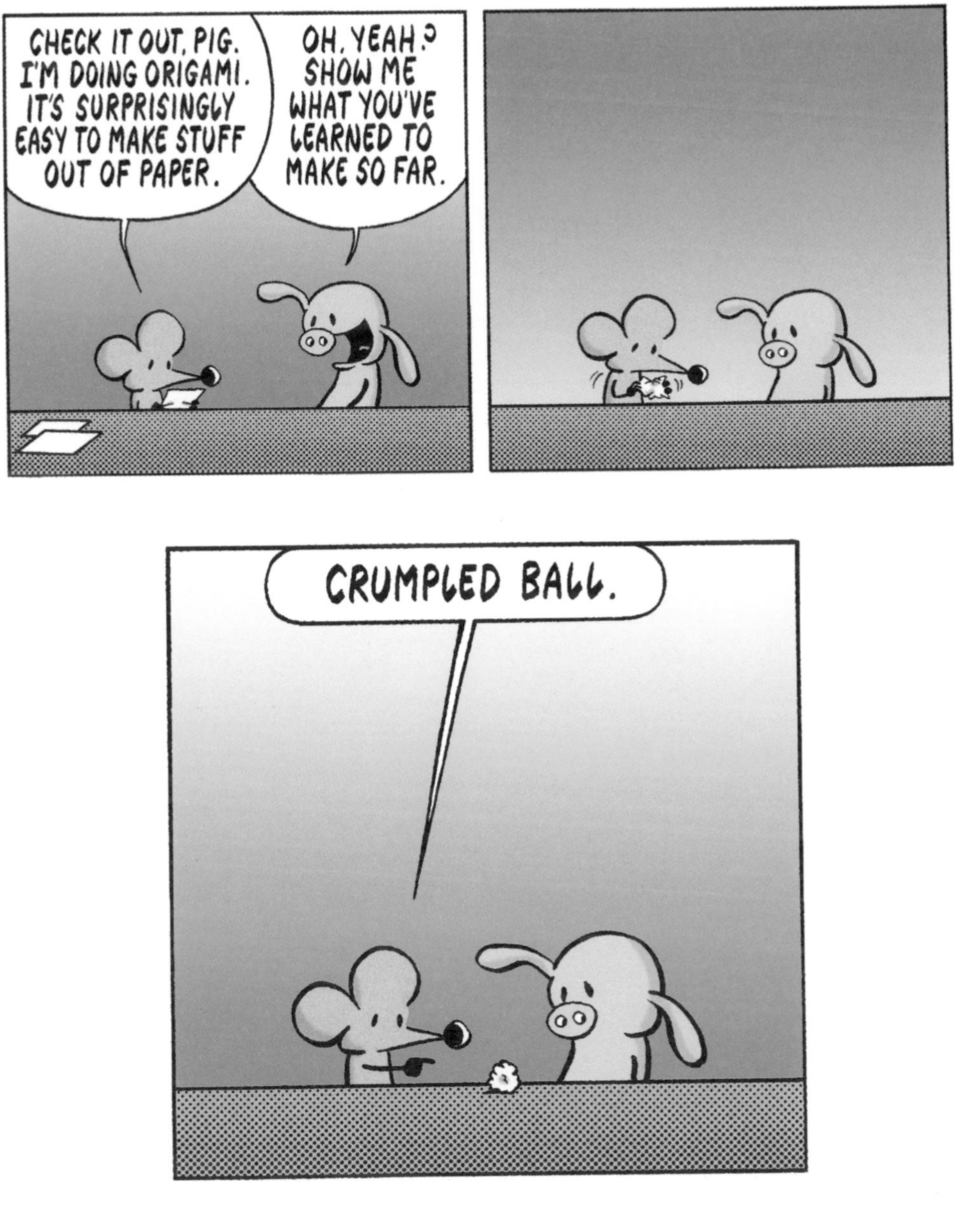
CHECK IT OUT, PIG. I'M DOING ORIGAMI. IT'S SURPRISINGLY EASY TO MAKE STUFF OUT OF PAPER.
OH, YEAH? SHOW ME WHAT YOU'VE LEARNED TO MAKE SO FAR.
CRUMPLED BALL.

HEY THERE, PIG...YOU LOOK HAPPY.
I AM! I JUST MEASURED MYSELF. I'M FIVE FEET, NINE INCHES TALL!
GEE, PIG...THAT SOUNDS A LITTLE HIGH.
WELL, I DID MEASURE MYSELF WITH SHOES.
EVEN WITH SHOES, THAT SOUNDS HIGH.
HERE, MEASURE FOR YOURSELF. I'LL STAND AGAINST THAT FENCE.

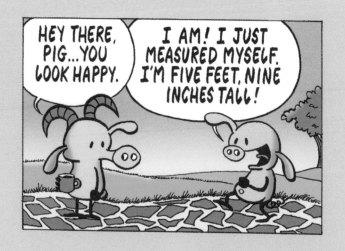

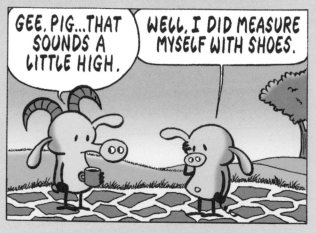

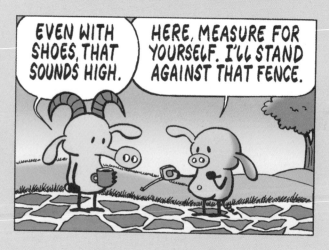

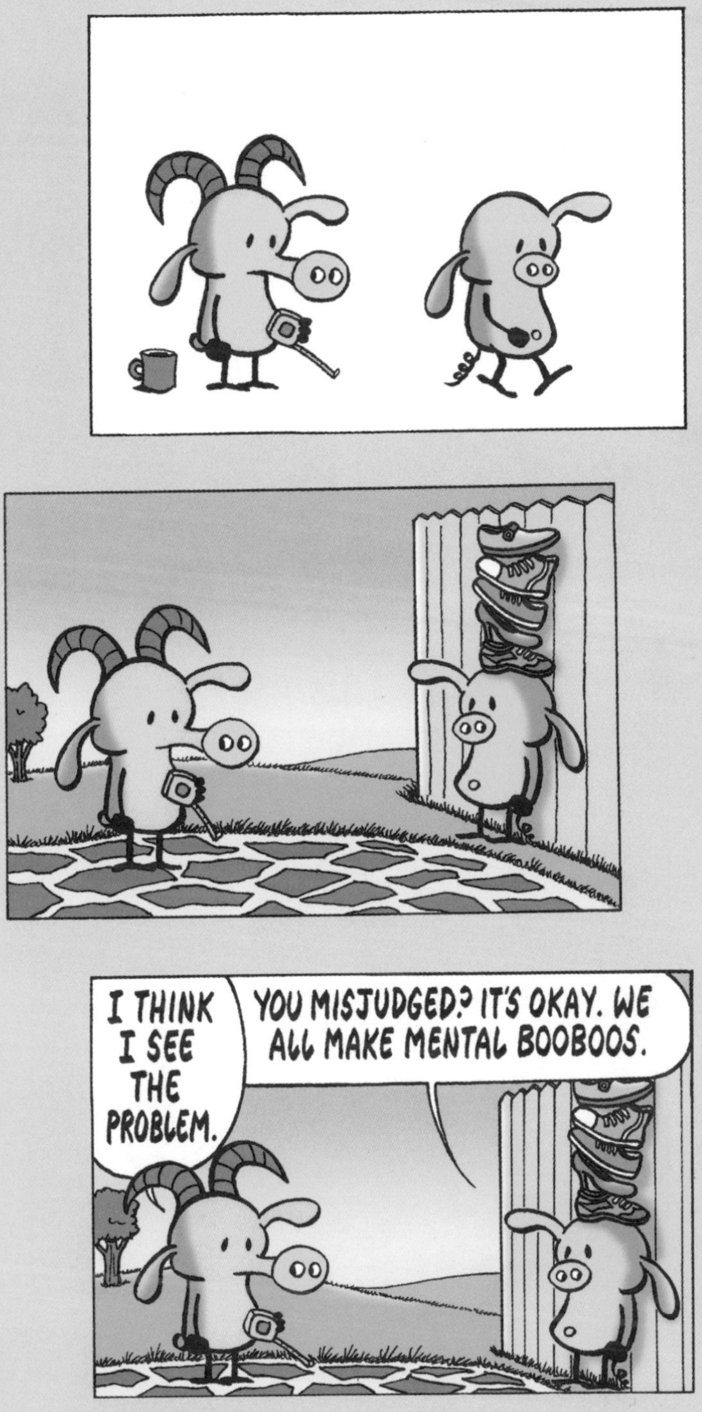
I THINK I SEE THE PROBLEM.
YOU MISJUDGED? IT'S OKAY. WE ALL MAKE MENTAL BOOBOOS.

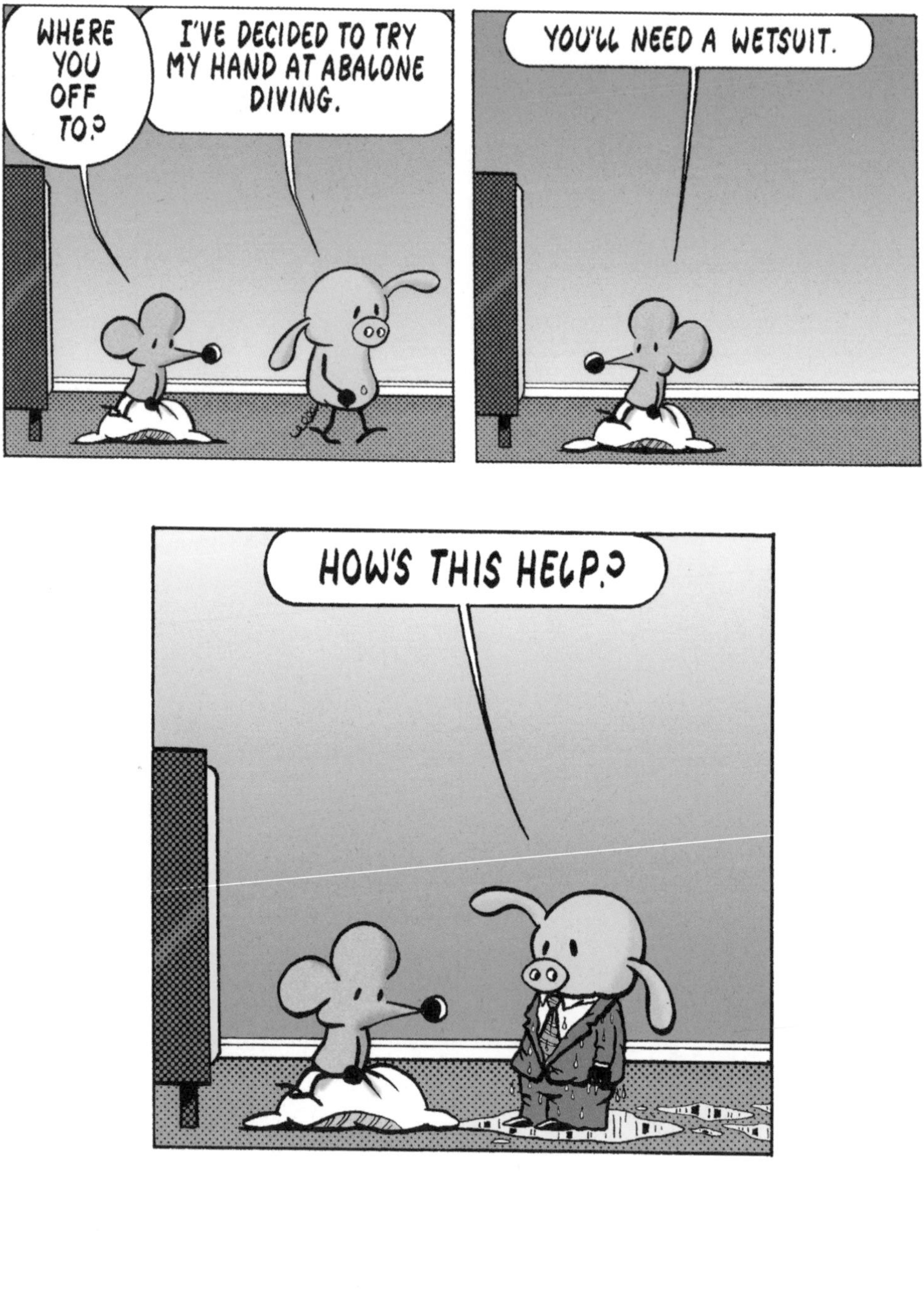
WHERE YOU OFF TO?
I'VE DECIDED TO TRY MY HAND AT ABALONE DIVING.
YOU'LL NEED A WETSUIT.
HOW'S THIS HELP?

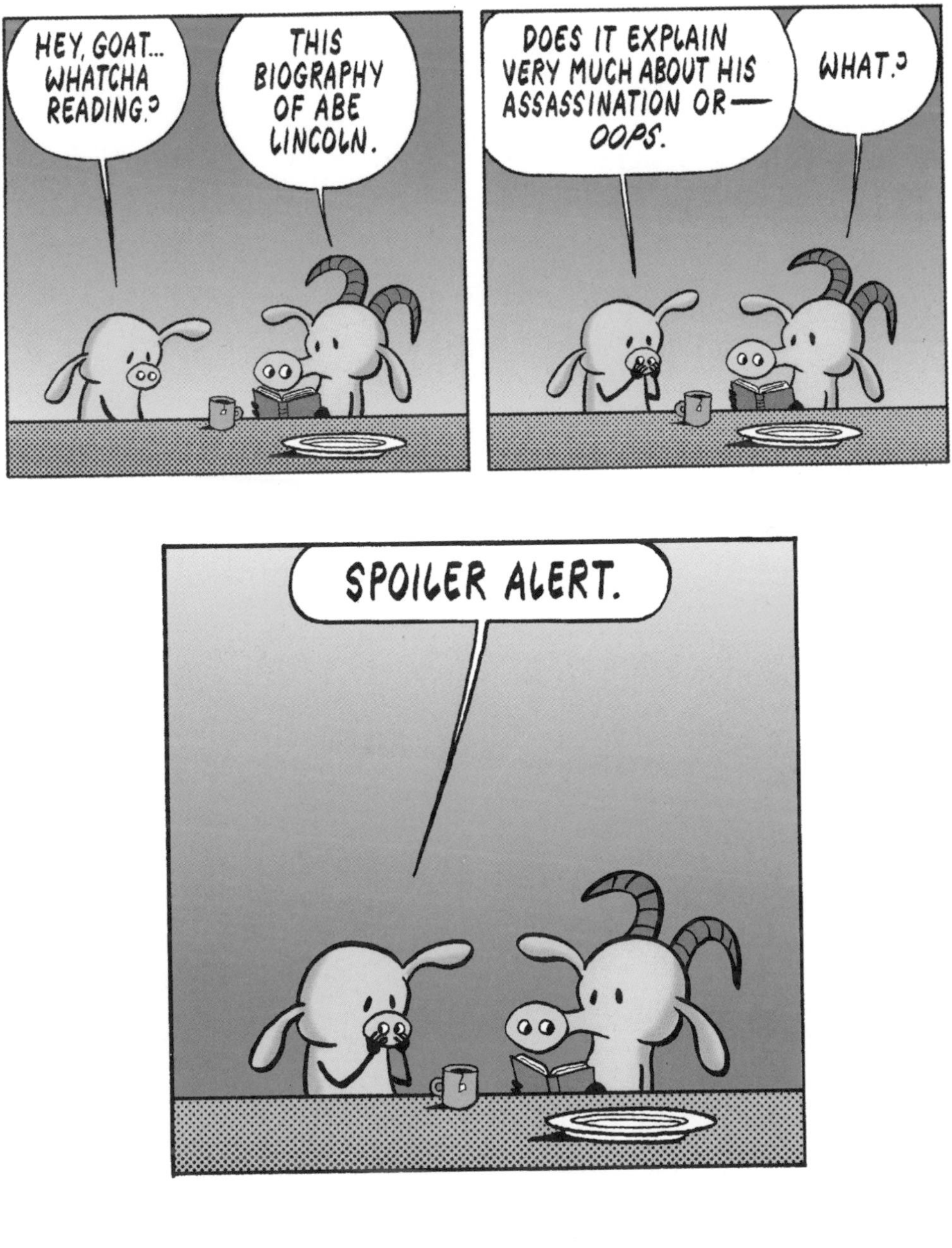
HEY, GOAT... WHATCHA READING?
THIS BIOGRAPHY OF ABE LINCOLN.
DOES IT EXPLAIN VERY MUCH ABOUT HIS ASSASSINATION OR— OOPS.
WHAT?
SPOILER ALERT.

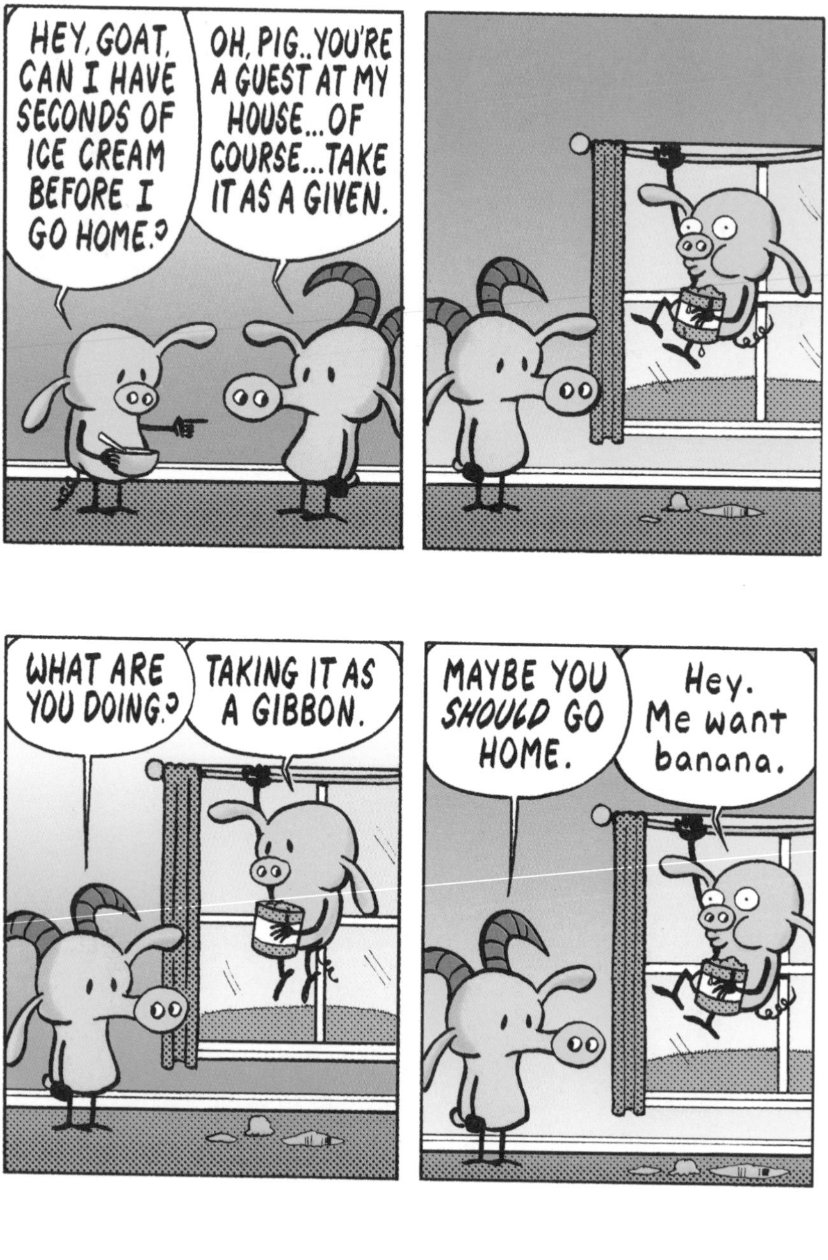
HEY, GOAT, CAN I HAVE SECONDS OF ICE CREAM BEFORE I GO HOME?
OH, PIG.. YOU'RE A GUEST AT MY HOUSE...OF COURSE...TAKE IT AS A GIVEN.
WHAT ARE YOU DOING?
TAKING IT AS A GIBBON.
MAYBE YOU SHOULD GO HOME.
Hey. Me want banana.

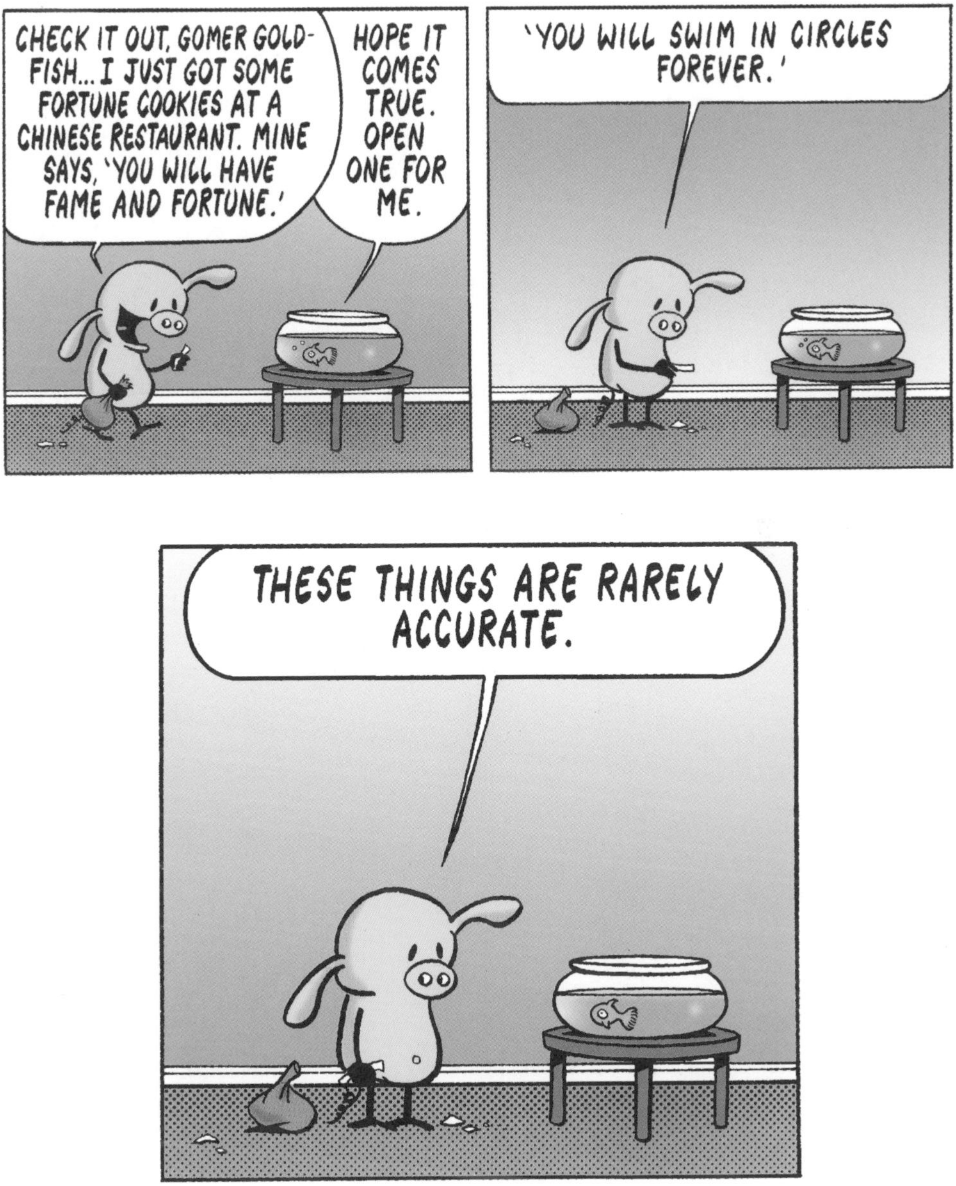
CHECK IT OUT, GOMER GOLD-FISH... I JUST GOT SOME FORTUNE COOKIES AT A CHINESE RESTAURANT. MINE SAYS, 'YOU WILL HAVE FAME AND FORTUNE.'
HOPE IT COMES TRUE. OPEN ONE FOR ME.
'YOU WILL SWIM IN CIRCLES FOREVER.'
THESE THINGS ARE RARELY ACCURATE.

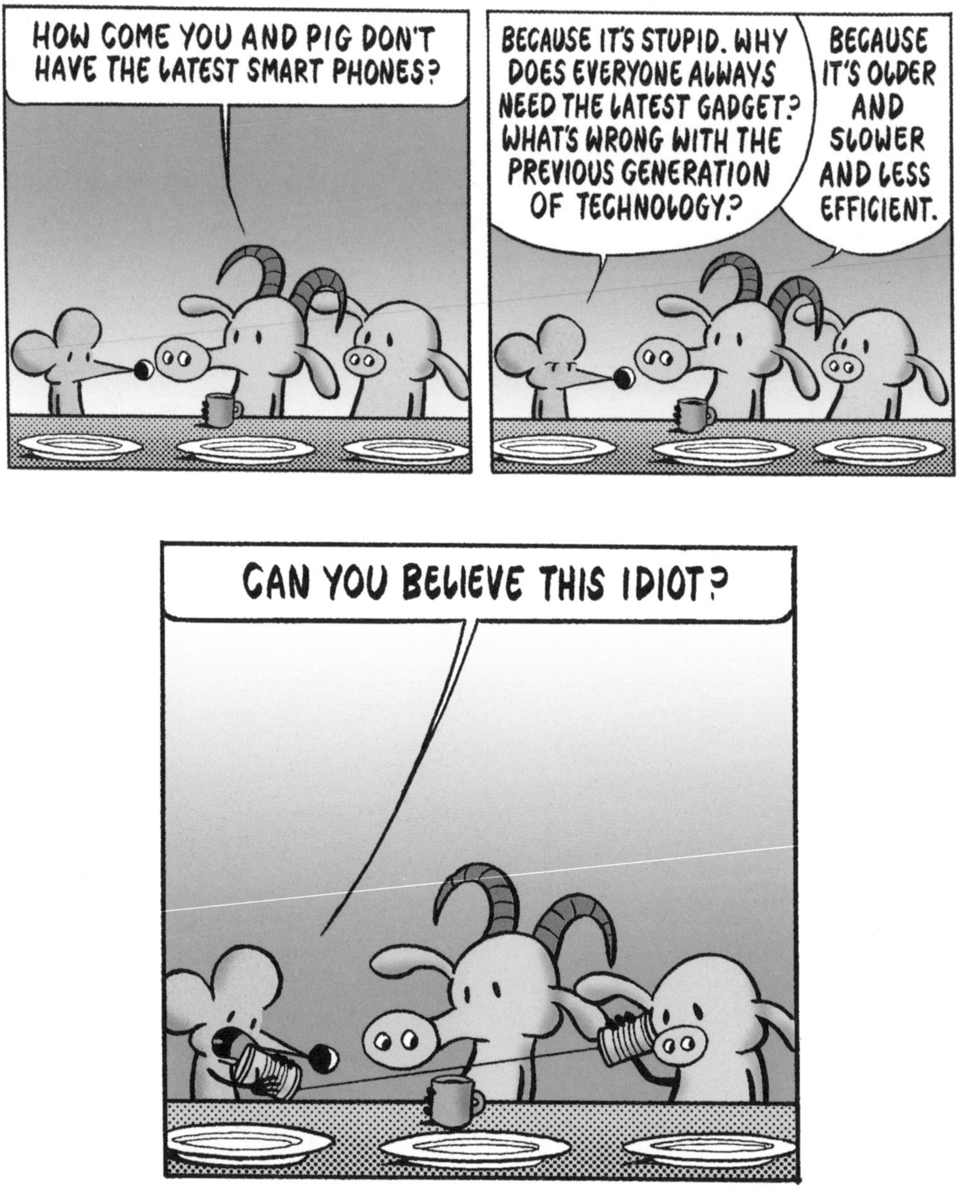
HOW COME YOU AND PIG DON'T HAVE THE LATEST SMART PHONES?
BECAUSE IT'S STUPID. WHY DOES EVERYONE ALWAYS NEED THE LATEST GADGET? WHAT'S WRONG WITH THE PREVIOUS GENERATION OF TECHNOLOGY?
BECAUSE IT'S OLDER AND SLOWER AND LESS EFFICIENT.
CAN YOU BELIEVE THIS IDIOT?

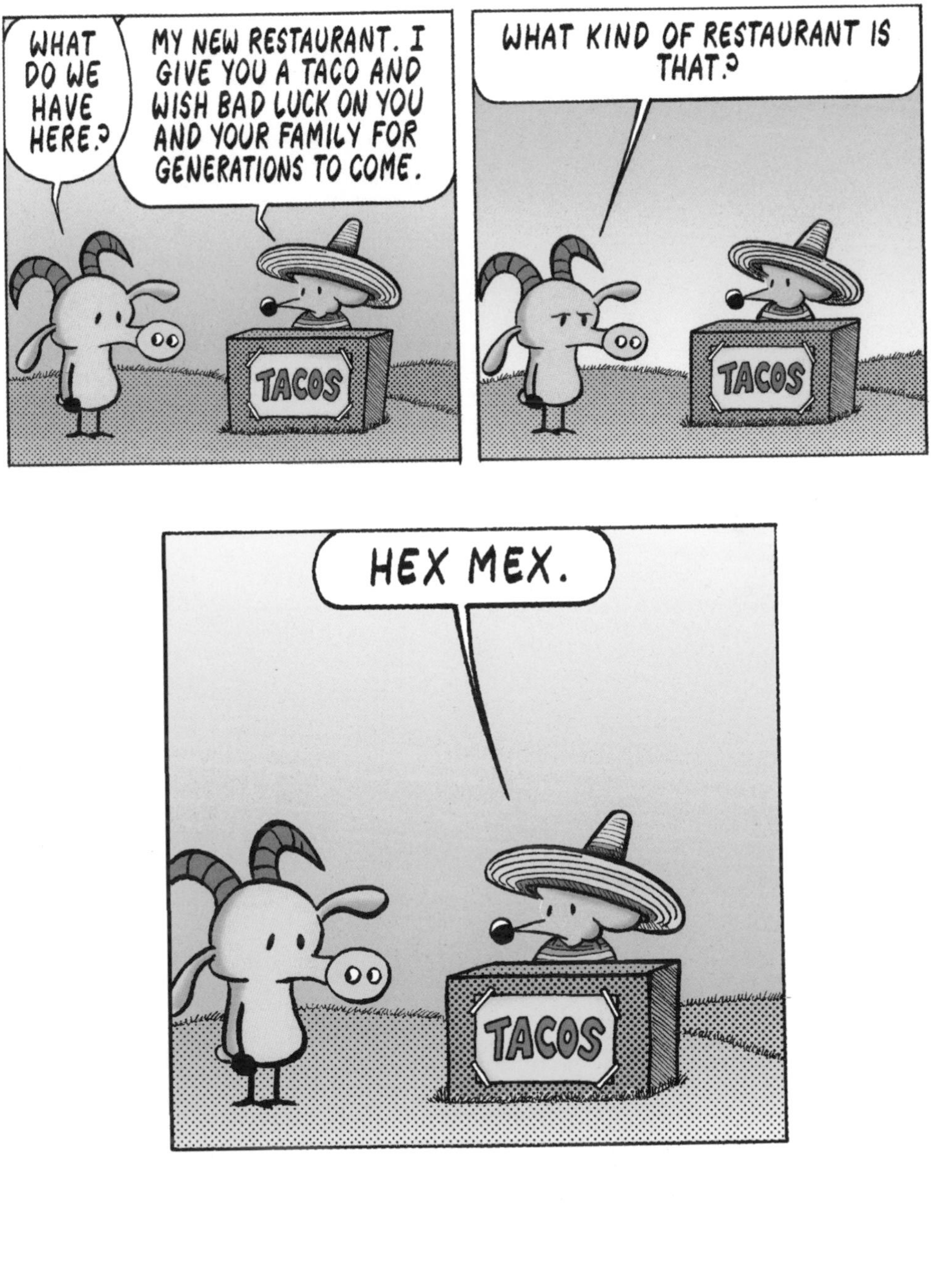
WHAT DO WE HAVE HERE?
MY NEW RESTAURANT. I GIVE YOU A TACO AND WISH BAD LUCK ON YOU AND YOUR FAMILY FOR GENERATIONS TO COME.
TACOS
WHAT KIND OF RESTAURANT IS THAT?
TACOS
HEX MEX.
TACOS

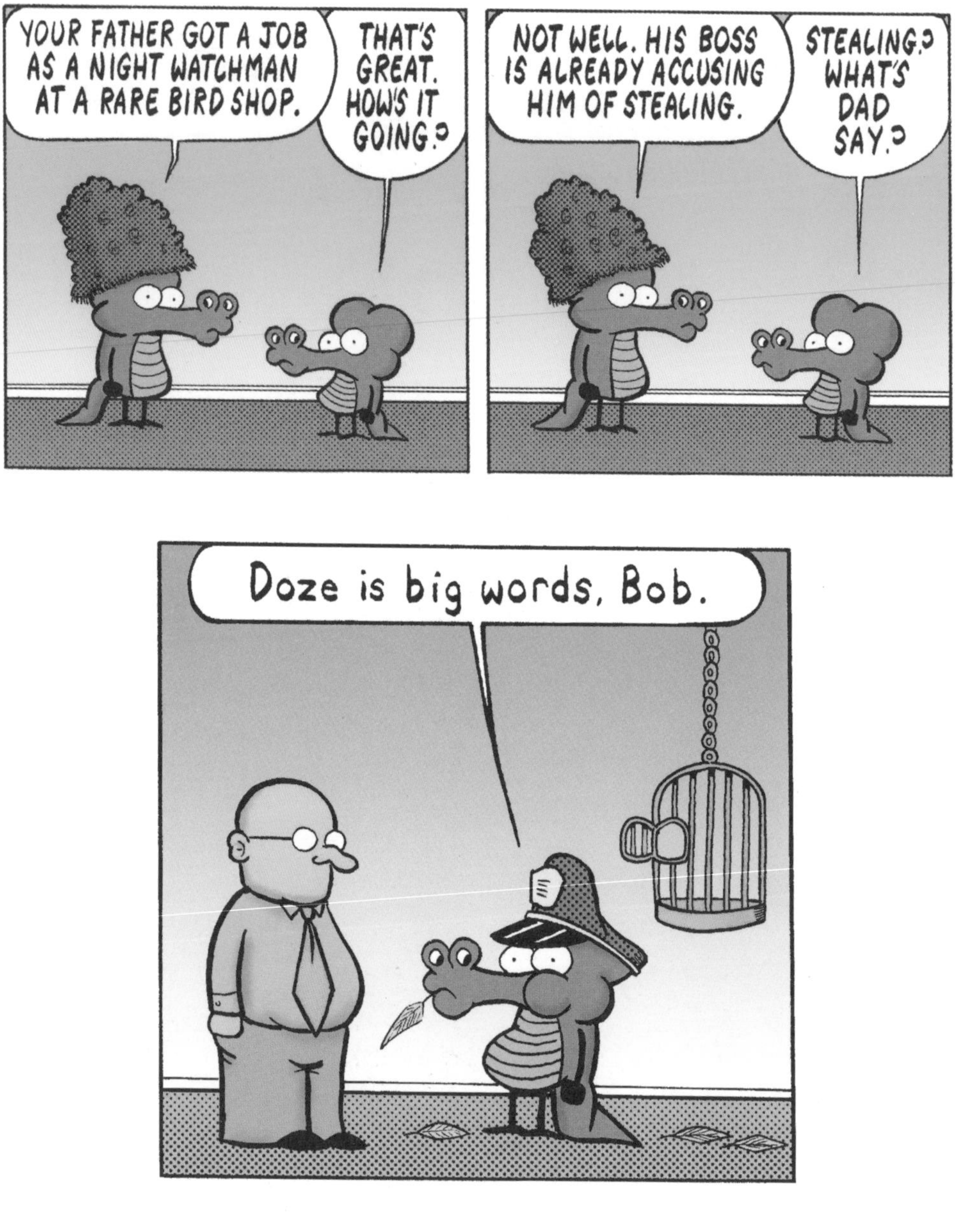
YOUR FATHER GOT A JOB AS A NIGHT WATCHMAN AT A RARE BIRD SHOP.
THAT'S GREAT. HOW'S IT GOING?
NOT WELL. HIS BOSS IS ALREADY ACCUSING HIM OF STEALING.
STEALING? WHAT'S DAD SAY?
Doze is big words, Bob.

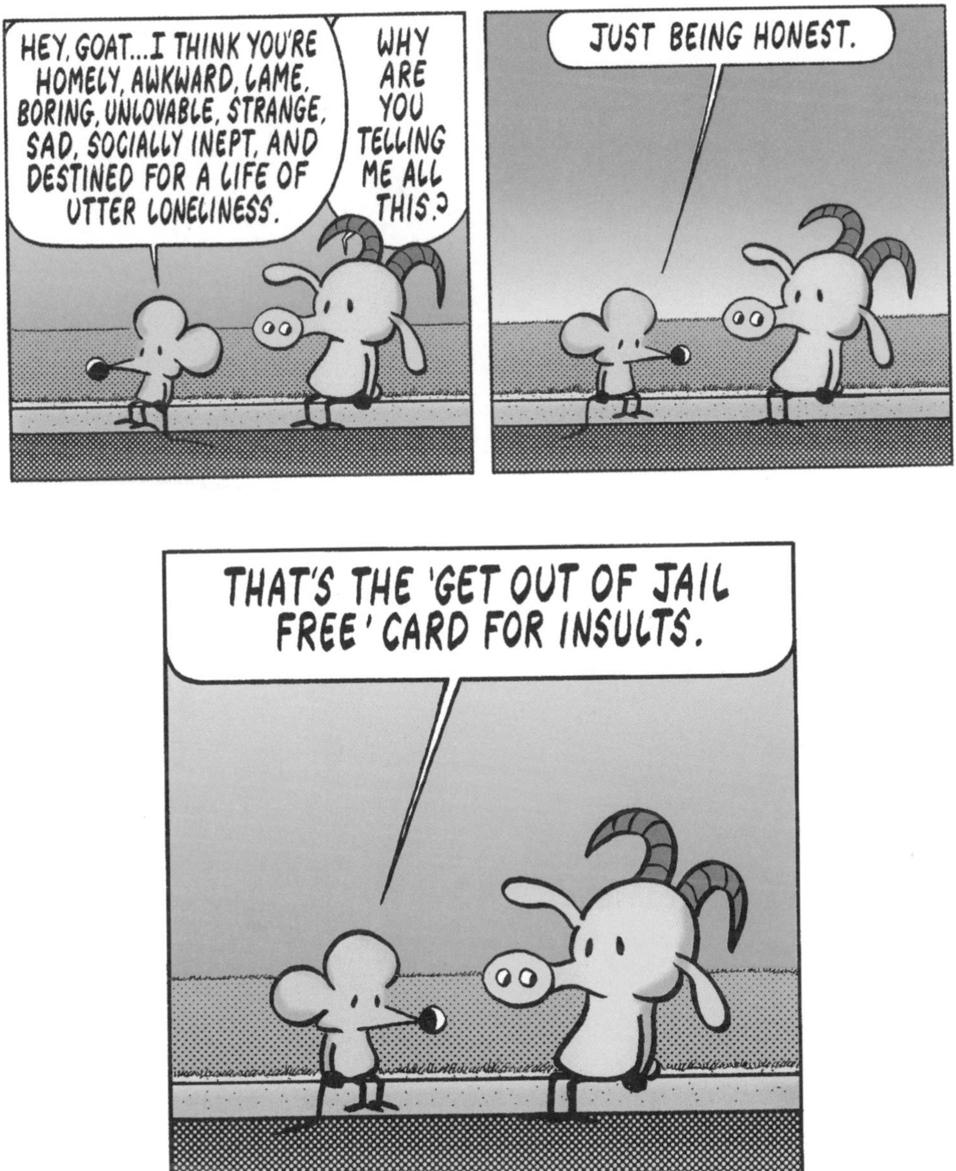
HEY, GOAT...I THINK YOU'RE HOMELY, AWKWARD, LAME, BORING, UNLOVABLE, STRANGE, SAD, SOCIALLY INEPT, AND DESTINED FOR A LIFE OF UTTER LONELINESS.
WHY ARE YOU TELLING ME ALL THIS?
JUST BEING HONEST.
THAT'S THE 'GET OUT OF JAIL FREE' CARD FOR INSULTS.

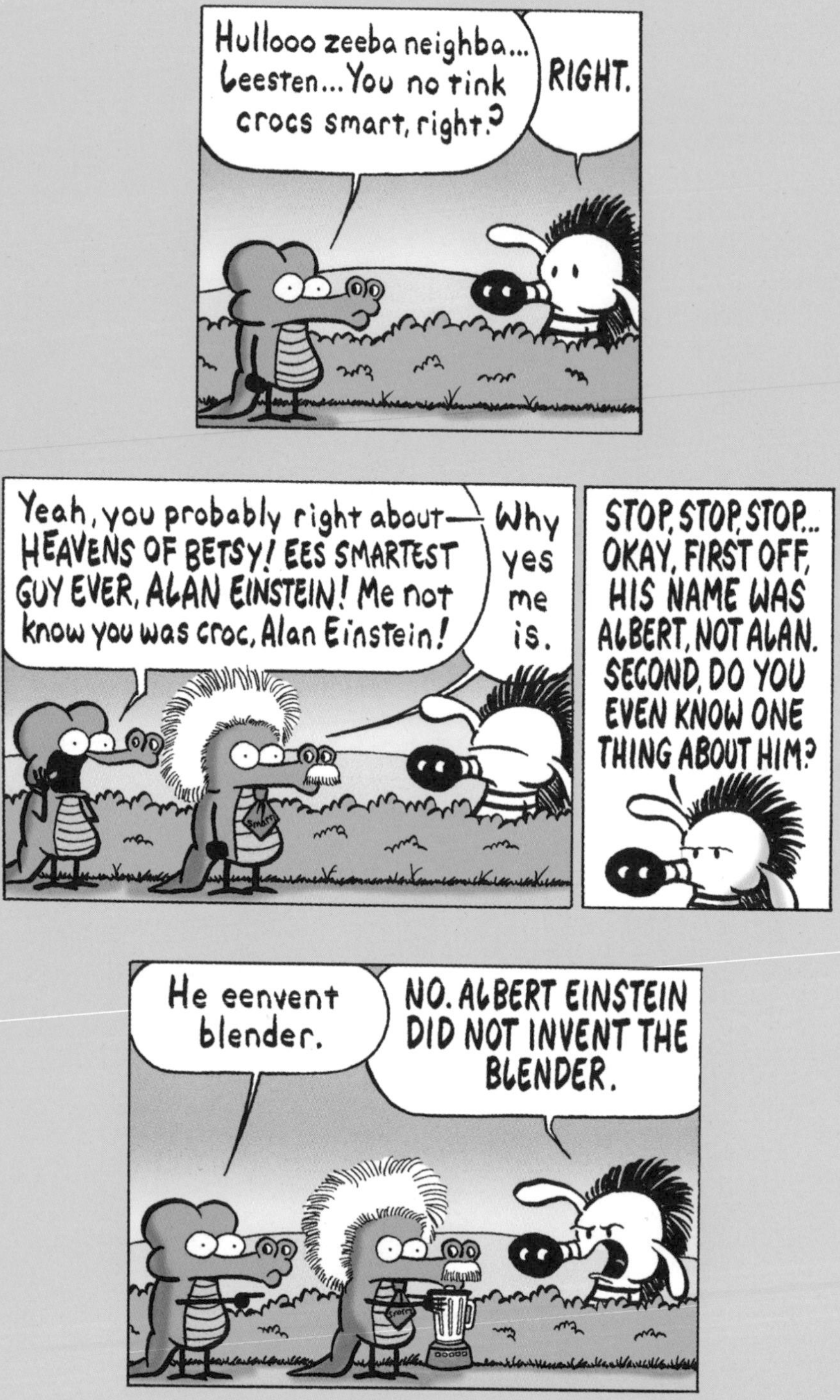

Hullooo zeeba neighba... Leesten... You no tink crocs smart, right?
RIGHT.
Yeah, you probably right about— HEAVENS OF BETSY! EES SMARTEST GUY EVER, ALAN EINSTEIN! Me not know you was croc, Alan Einstein!
Why yes me is.
STOP, STOP, STOP... OKAY, FIRST OFF, HIS NAME WAS ALBERT, NOT ALAN. SECOND, DO YOU EVEN KNOW ONE THING ABOUT HIM?
He eenvent blender.
NO. ALBERT EINSTEIN DID NOT INVENT THE BLENDER.

Toaster?
Sticky notes?
HAM??
NO! NO! NO! ALBERT EINSTEIN FORMULATED THE THEORY OF RELATIVITY! E=MC²! AND YOU KNOW WHAT ELSE ABOUT ALBERT EINSTEIN? HE'S DEAD! DEAD! SO WHAT ARE YOU GONNA SAY NOW?!
Ack.
Great... Now you keel Alan Einstein.
ALBERT
Inventing ham took lot out of me.

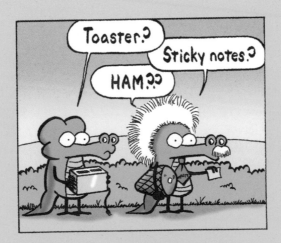

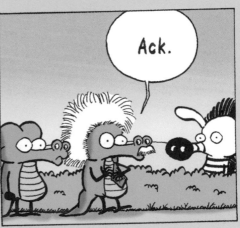

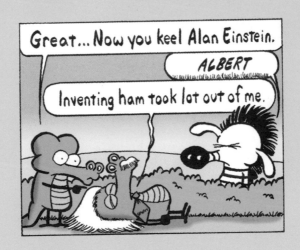

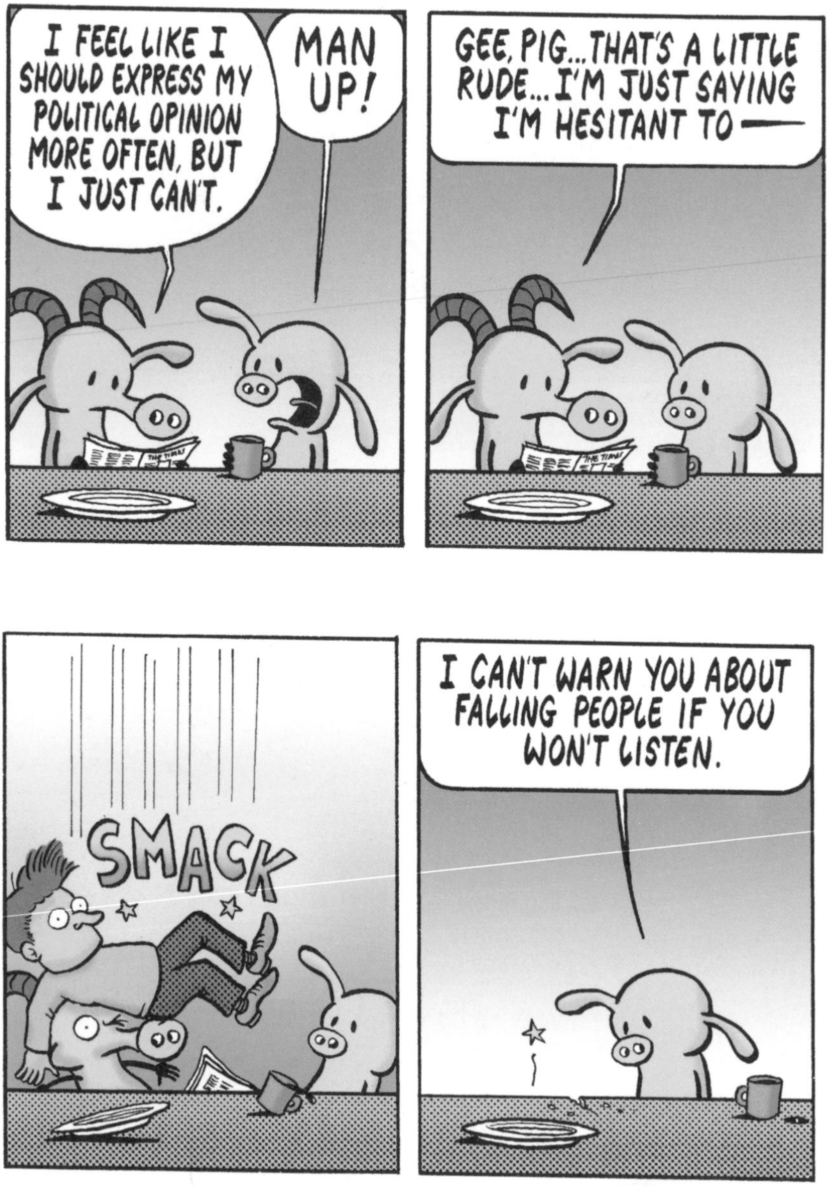
I FEEL LIKE I SHOULD EXPRESS MY POLITICAL OPINION MORE OFTEN, BUT I JUST CAN'T.
MAN UP!
GEE, PIG...THAT'S A LITTLE RUDE...I'M JUST SAYING I'M HESITANT TO—
THE TIMES
SMACK
I CAN'T WARN YOU ABOUT FALLING PEOPLE IF YOU WON'T LISTEN.

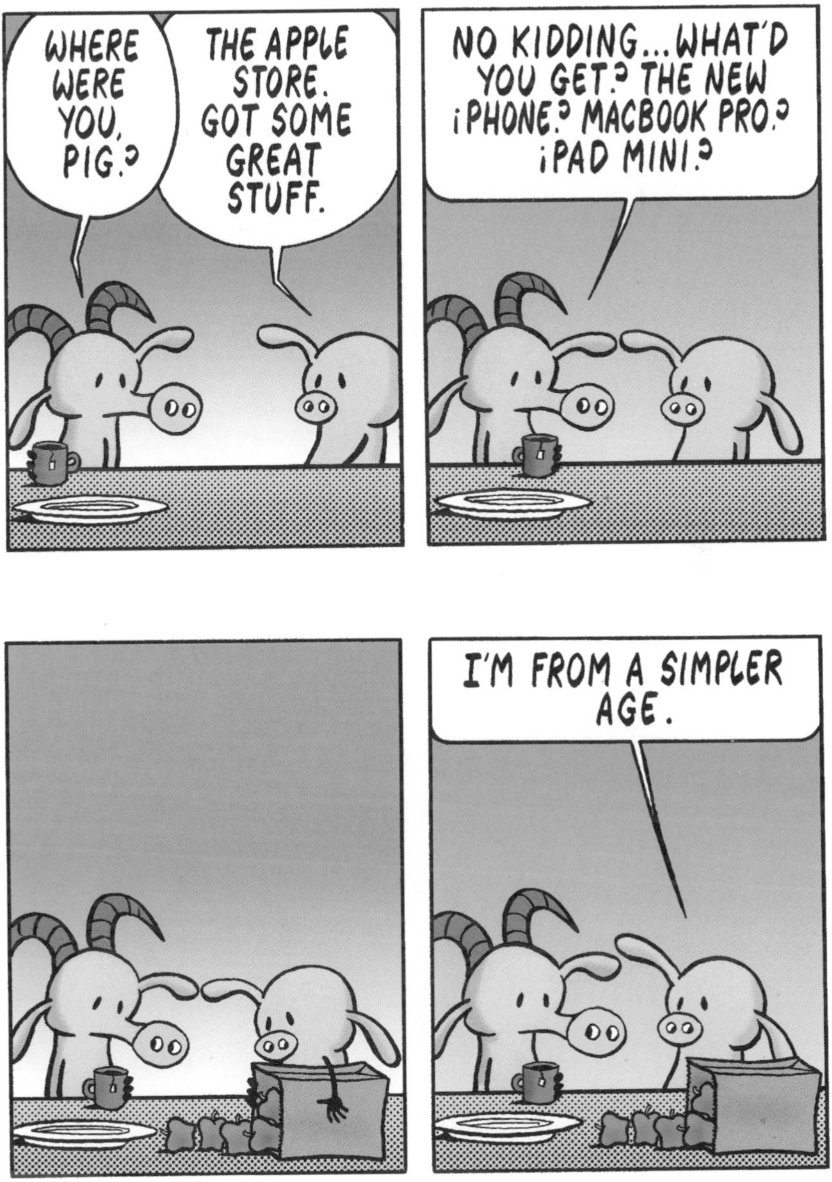
WHERE WERE YOU, PIG?
THE APPLE STORE. GOT SOME GREAT STUFF.
NO KIDDING...WHAT'D YOU GET? THE NEW iPHONE? MACBOOK PRO? iPAD MINI?
I'M FROM A SIMPLER AGE.

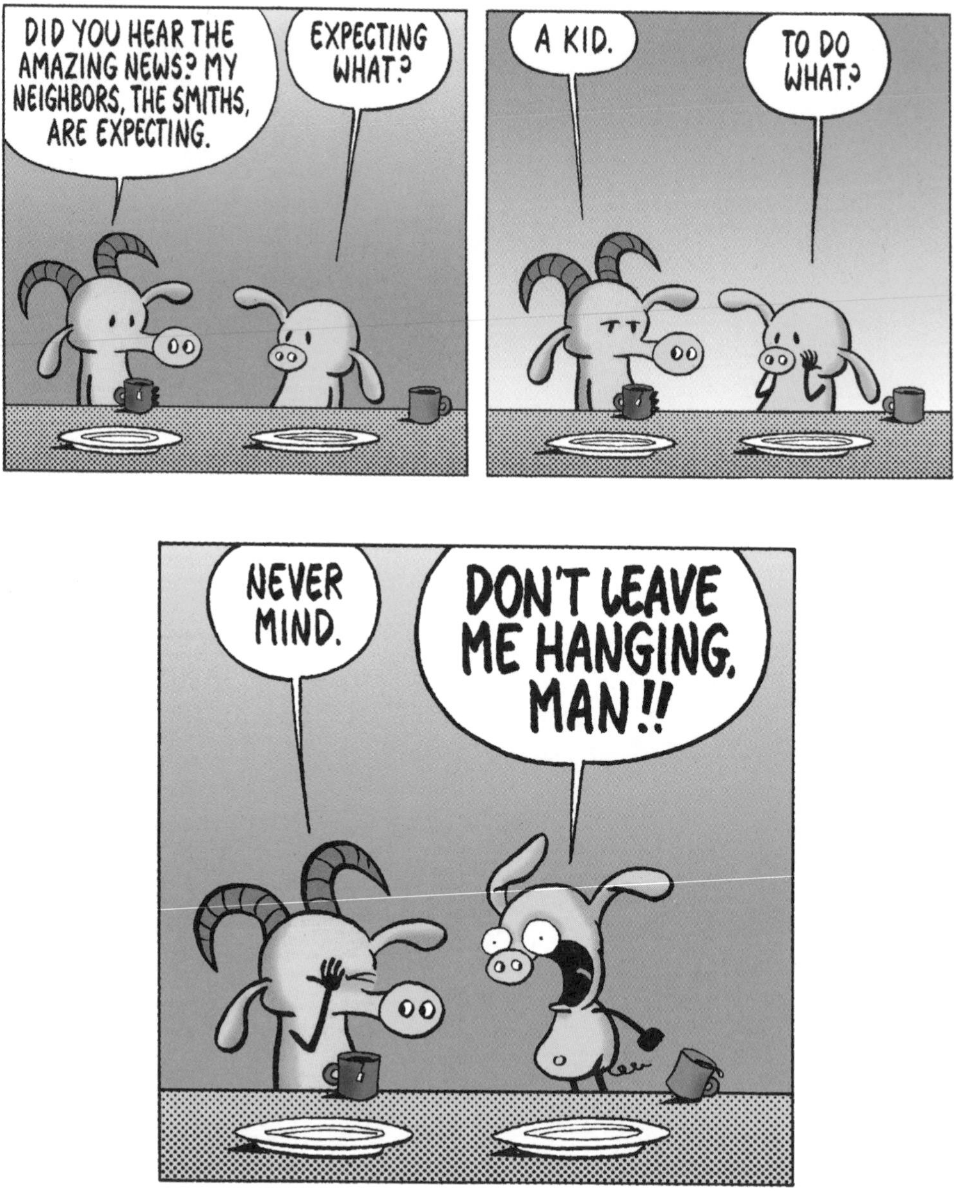
DID YOU HEAR THE AMAZING NEWS? MY NEIGHBORS, THE SMITHS, ARE EXPECTING.
EXPECTING WHAT?
A KID.
TO DO WHAT?
NEVER MIND.
DON'T LEAVE ME HANGING, MAN!!

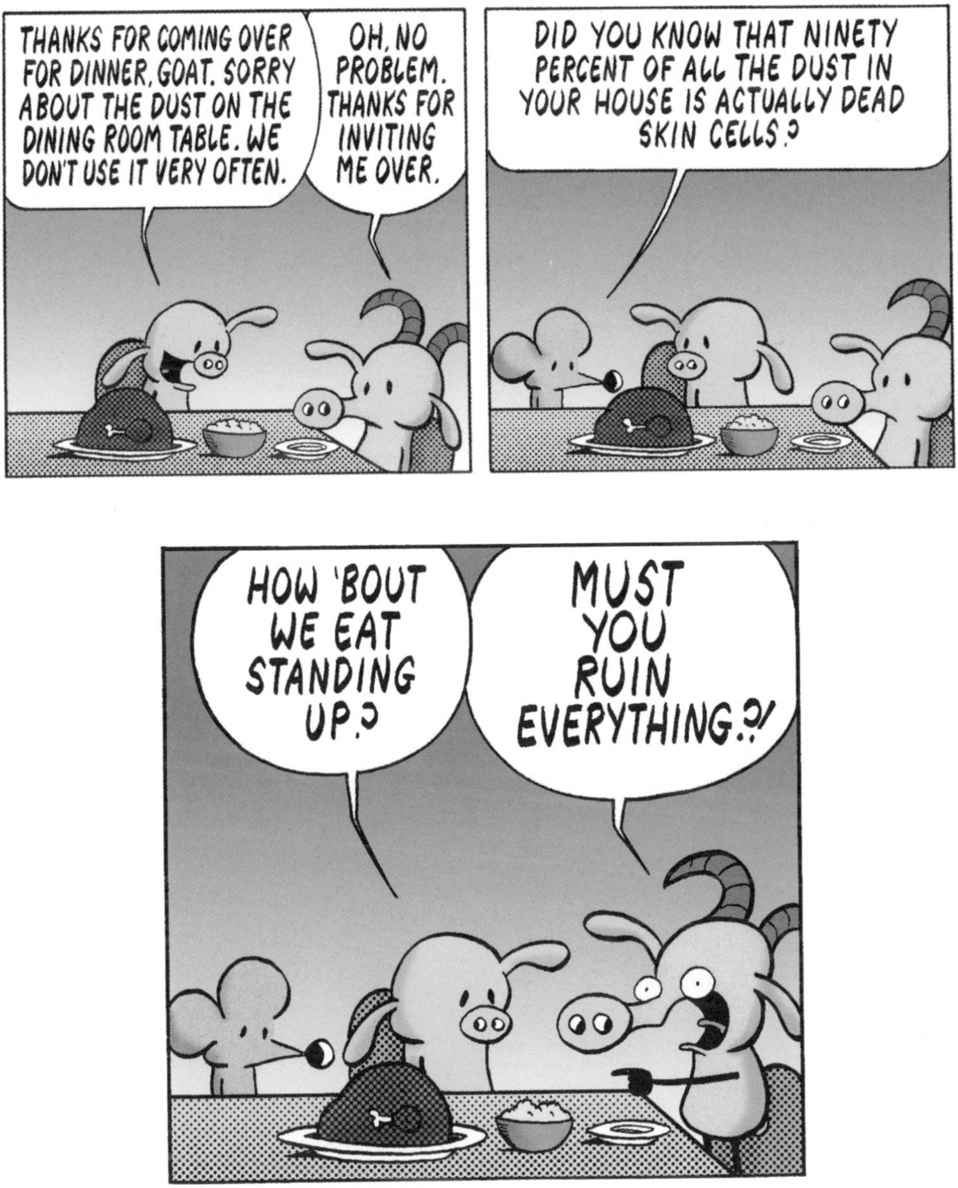
THANKS FOR COMING OVER FOR DINNER, GOAT. SORRY ABOUT THE DUST ON THE DINING ROOM TABLE. WE DON'T USE IT VERY OFTEN.
OH, NO PROBLEM. THANKS FOR INVITING ME OVER.
DID YOU KNOW THAT NINETY PERCENT OF ALL THE DUST IN YOUR HOUSE IS ACTUALLY DEAD SKIN CELLS?
HOW 'BOUT WE EAT STANDING UP?
MUST YOU RUIN EVERYTHING?!

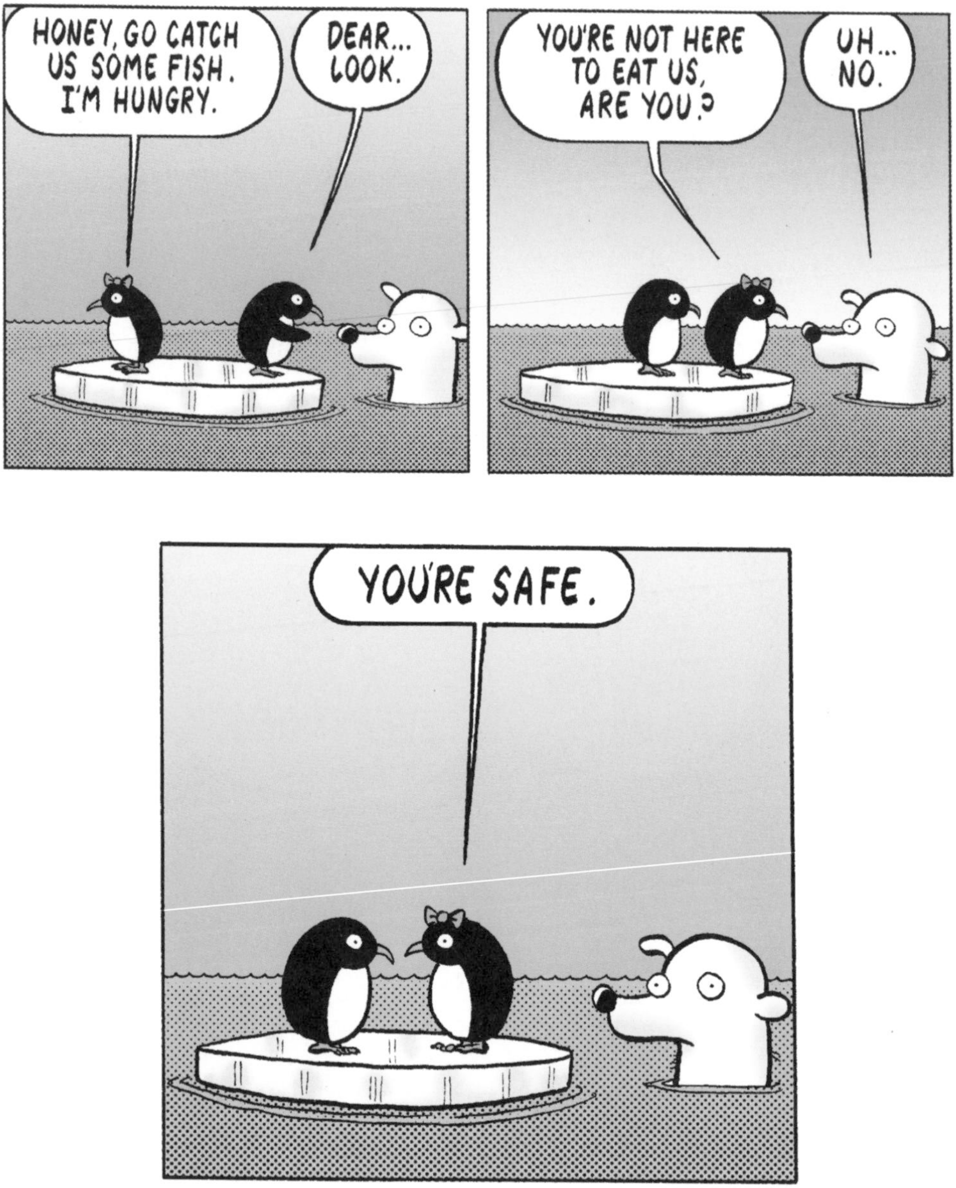
HONEY, GO CATCH US SOME FISH. I'M HUNGRY.
DEAR... LOOK.
YOU'RE NOT HERE TO EAT US, ARE YOU?
UH... NO.
YOU'RE SAFE.

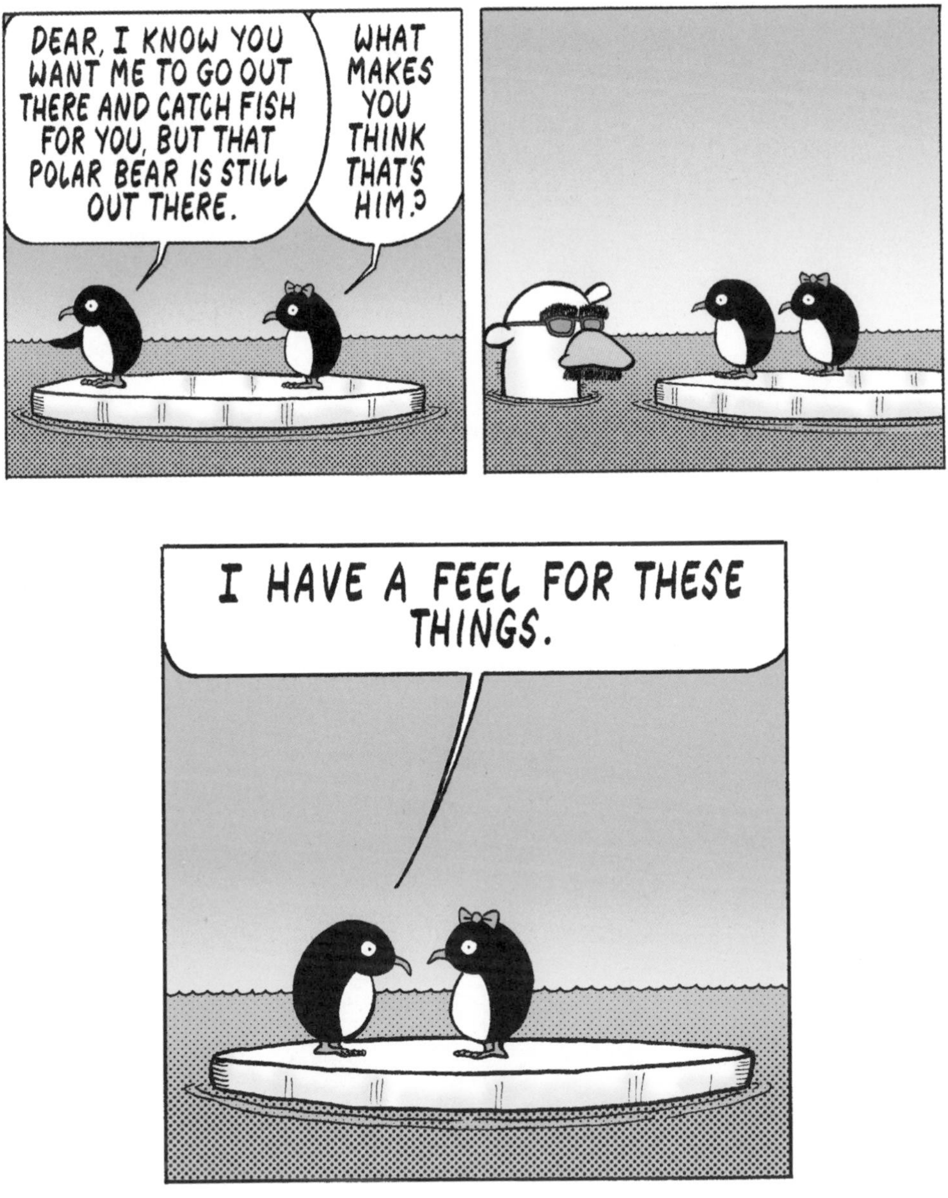
DEAR, I KNOW YOU WANT ME TO GO OUT THERE AND CATCH FISH FOR YOU, BUT THAT POLAR BEAR IS STILL OUT THERE.
WHAT MAKES YOU THINK THAT'S HIM?
I HAVE A FEEL FOR THESE THINGS.

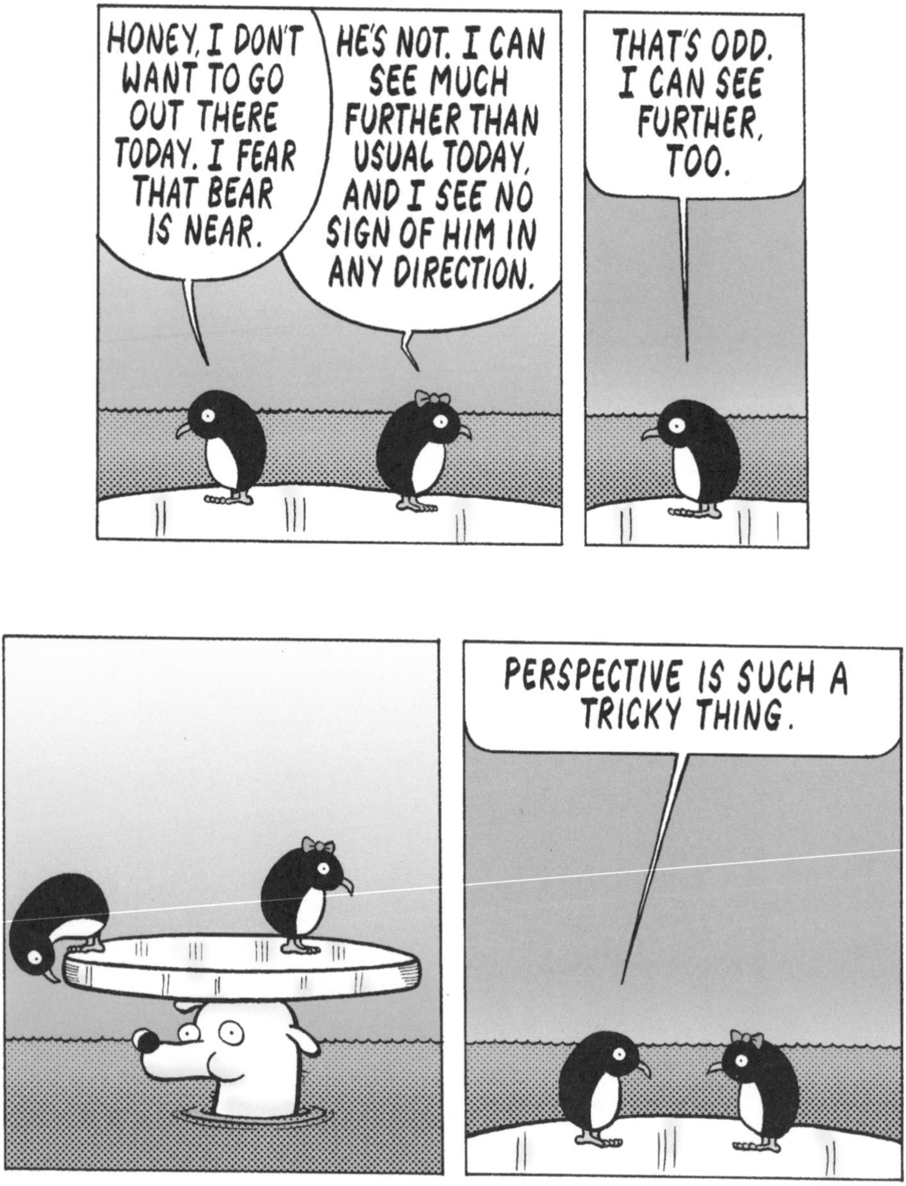
HONEY, I DON'T WANT TO GO OUT THERE TODAY. I FEAR THAT BEAR IS NEAR.
HE'S NOT. I CAN SEE MUCH FURTHER THAN USUAL TODAY, AND I SEE NO SIGN OF HIM IN ANY DIRECTION.
THAT'S ODD. I CAN SEE FURTHER, TOO.
PERSPECTIVE IS SUCH A TRICKY THING.

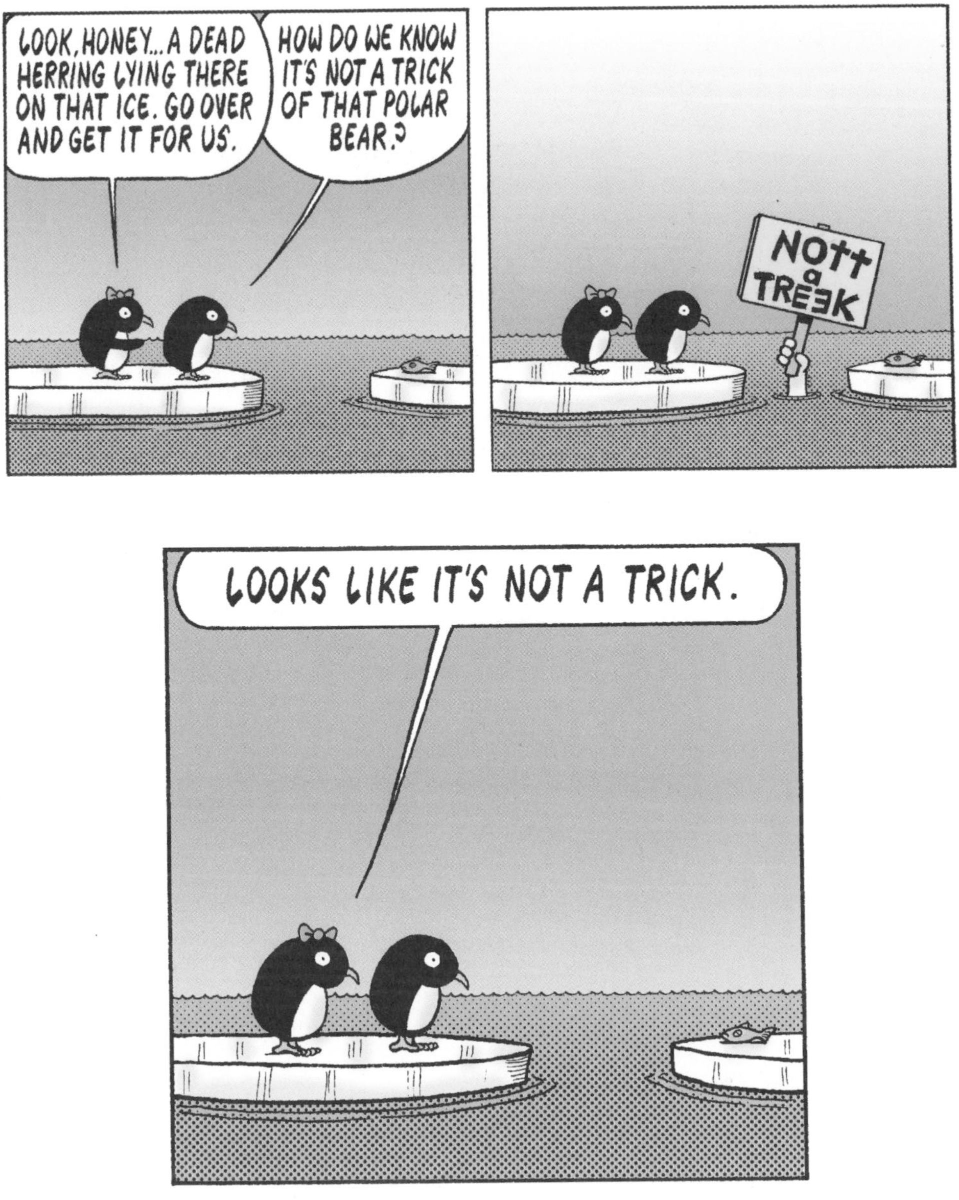
LOOK, HONEY... A DEAD HERRING LYING THERE ON THAT ICE. GO OVER AND GET IT FOR US.
HOW DO WE KNOW IT'S NOT A TRICK OF THAT POLAR BEAR?
NOTT a TREƎK
LOOKS LIKE IT'S NOT A TRICK.

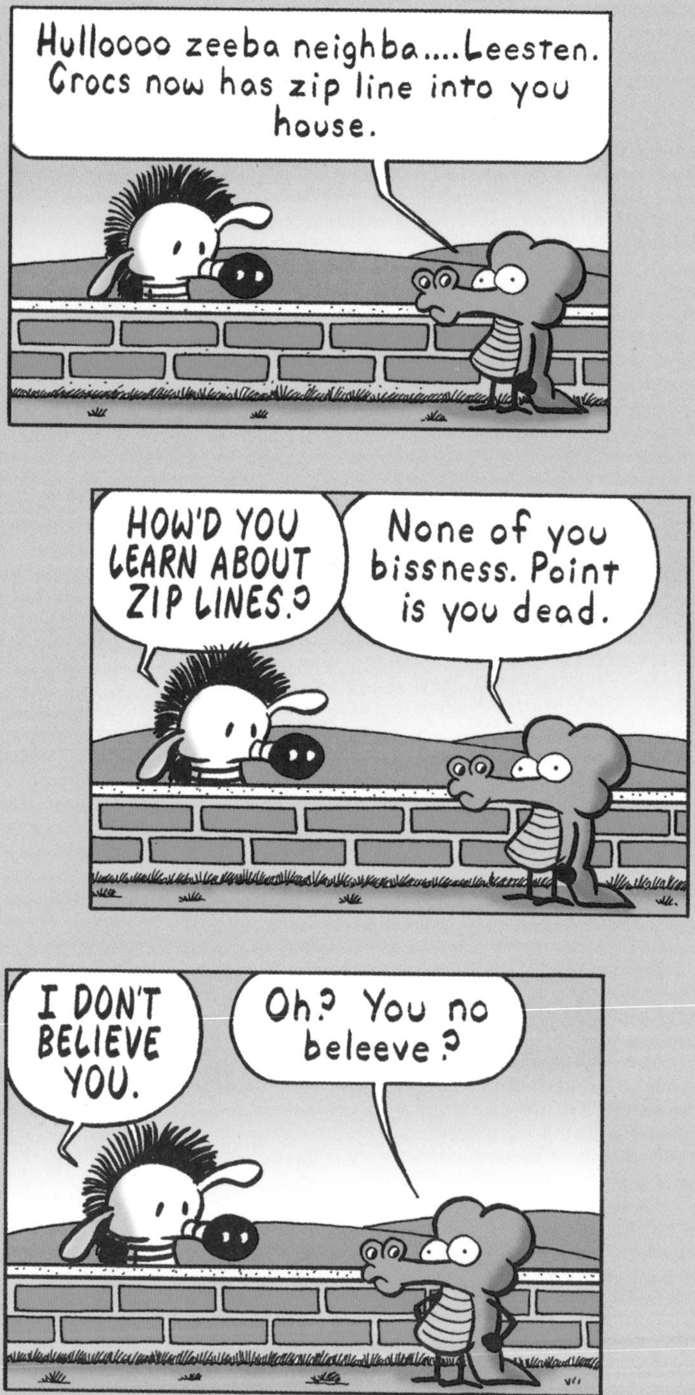
Hulloooo zeeba neighba....Leesten. Crocs now has zip line into you house.
HOW'D YOU LEARN ABOUT ZIP LINES?
None of you bissness. Point is you dead.
I DON'T BELIEVE YOU.
Oh? You no beleeve?

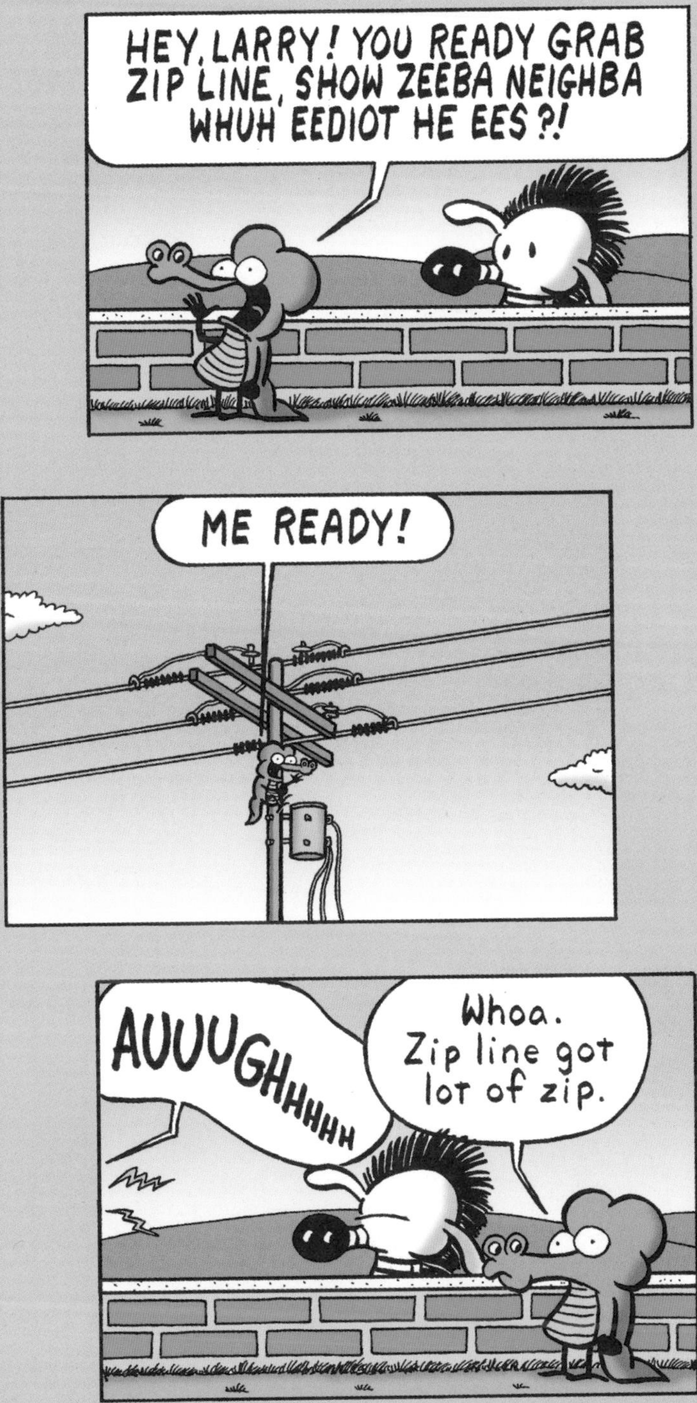
HEY, LARRY! YOU READY GRAB ZIP LINE, SHOW ZEEBA NEIGHBA WHUH EEDIOT HE EES?!
ME READY!
AUUUGHHHHH
Whoa. Zip line got lot of zip.

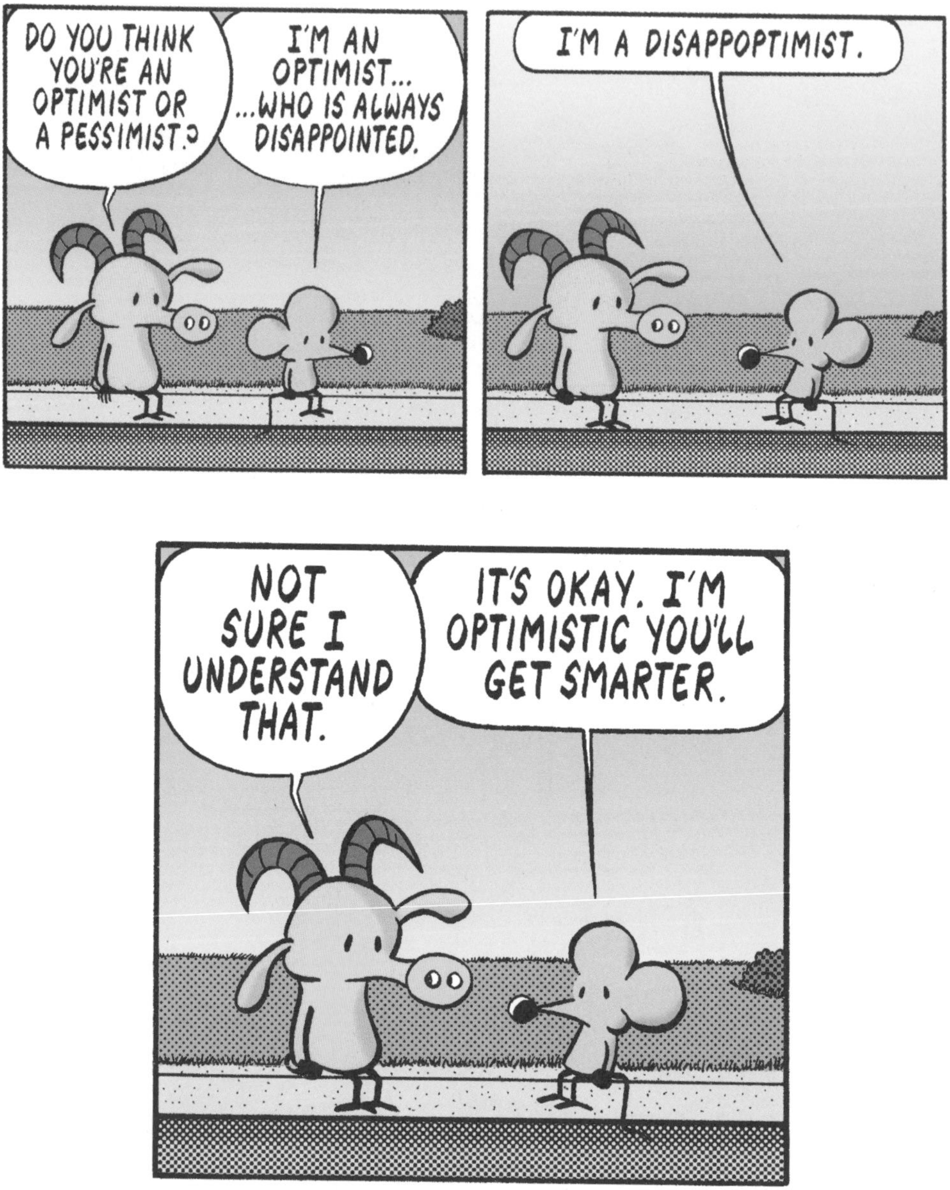

DO YOU THINK YOU'RE AN OPTIMIST OR A PESSIMIST?
I'M AN OPTIMIST... ...WHO IS ALWAYS DISAPPOINTED.
I'M A DISAPPOPTIMIST.
NOT SURE I UNDERSTAND THAT.
IT'S OKAY. I'M OPTIMISTIC YOU'LL GET SMARTER.

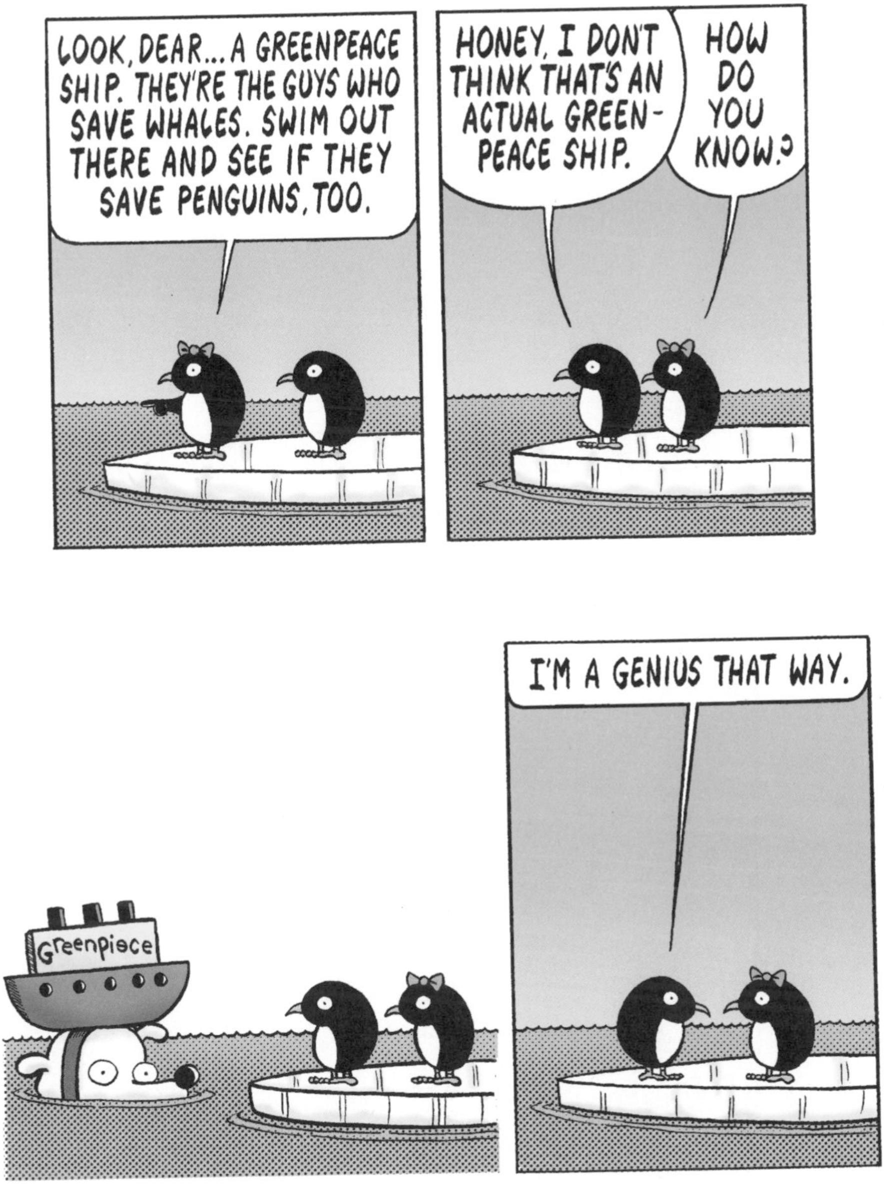
LOOK, DEAR... A GREENPEACE SHIP. THEY'RE THE GUYS WHO SAVE WHALES. SWIM OUT THERE AND SEE IF THEY SAVE PENGUINS, TOO.
HONEY, I DON'T THINK THAT'S AN ACTUAL GREEN-PEACE SHIP.
HOW DO YOU KNOW?
Greenpiece
I'M A GENIUS THAT WAY.

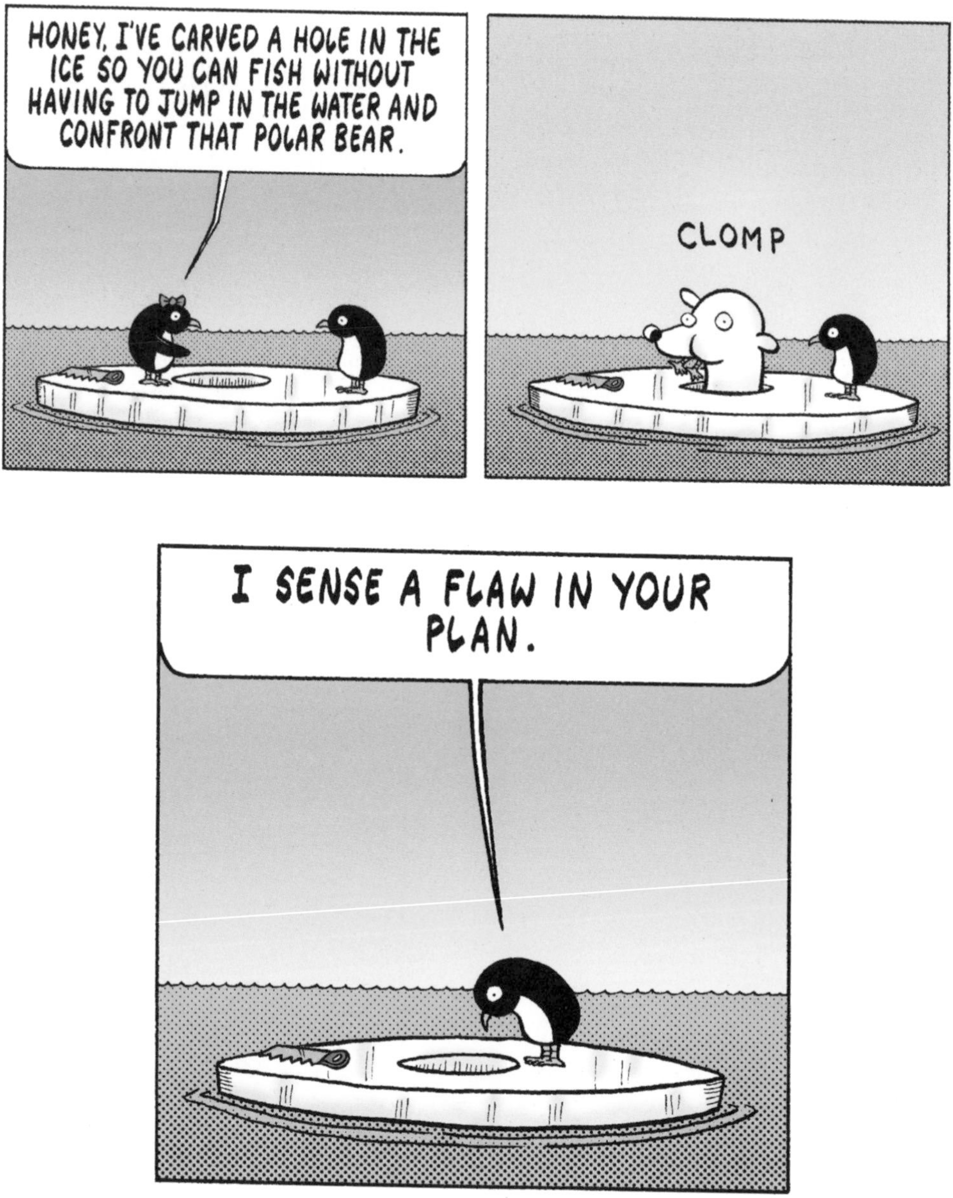
HONEY, I'VE CARVED A HOLE IN THE ICE SO YOU CAN FISH WITHOUT HAVING TO JUMP IN THE WATER AND CONFRONT THAT POLAR BEAR.
CLOMP
I SENSE A FLAW IN YOUR PLAN.

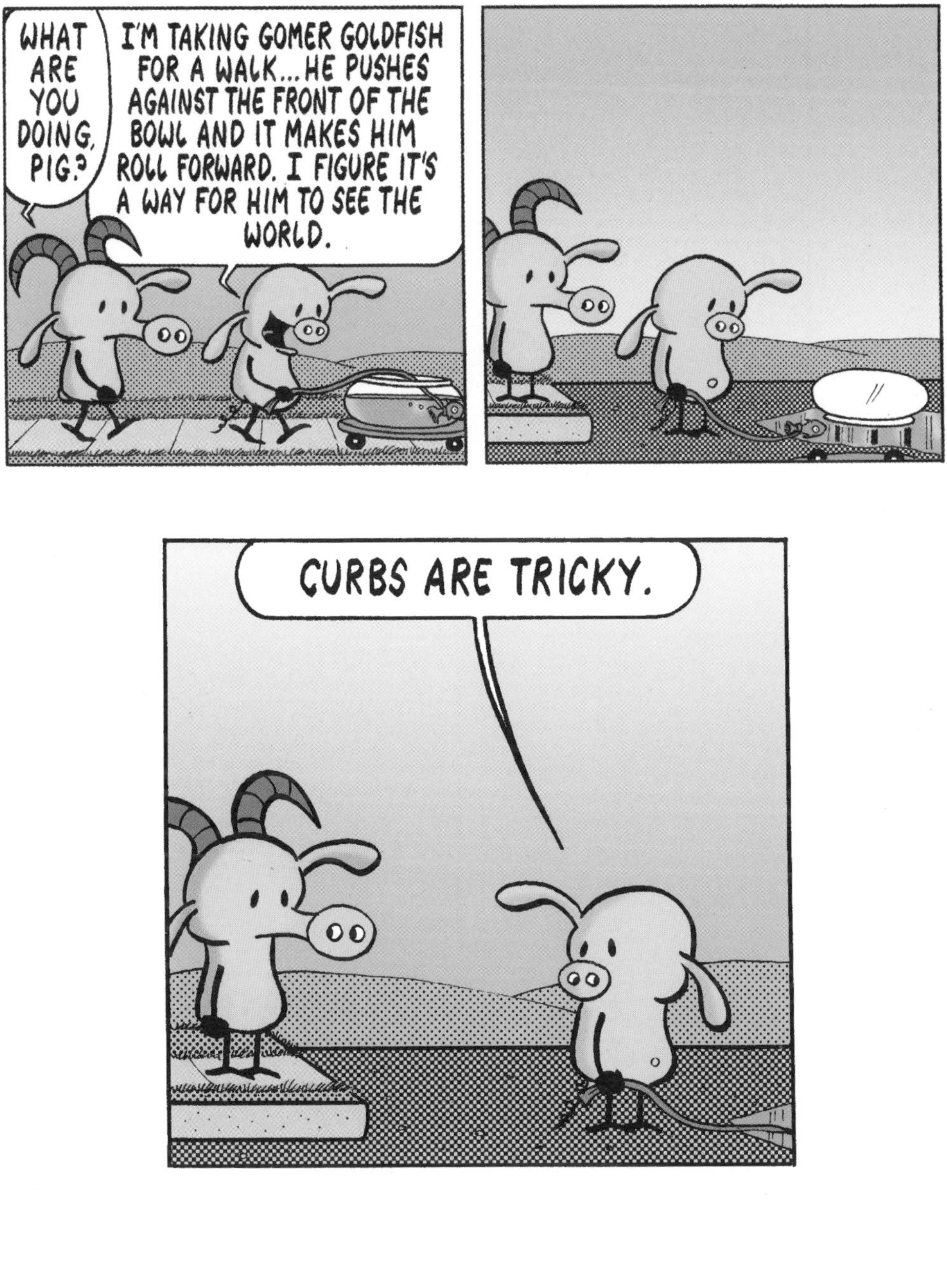
WHAT ARE YOU DOING, PIG?
I'M TAKING GOMER GOLDFISH FOR A WALK... HE PUSHES AGAINST THE FRONT OF THE BOWL AND IT MAKES HIM ROLL FORWARD. I FIGURE IT'S A WAY FOR HIM TO SEE THE WORLD.
CURBS ARE TRICKY.

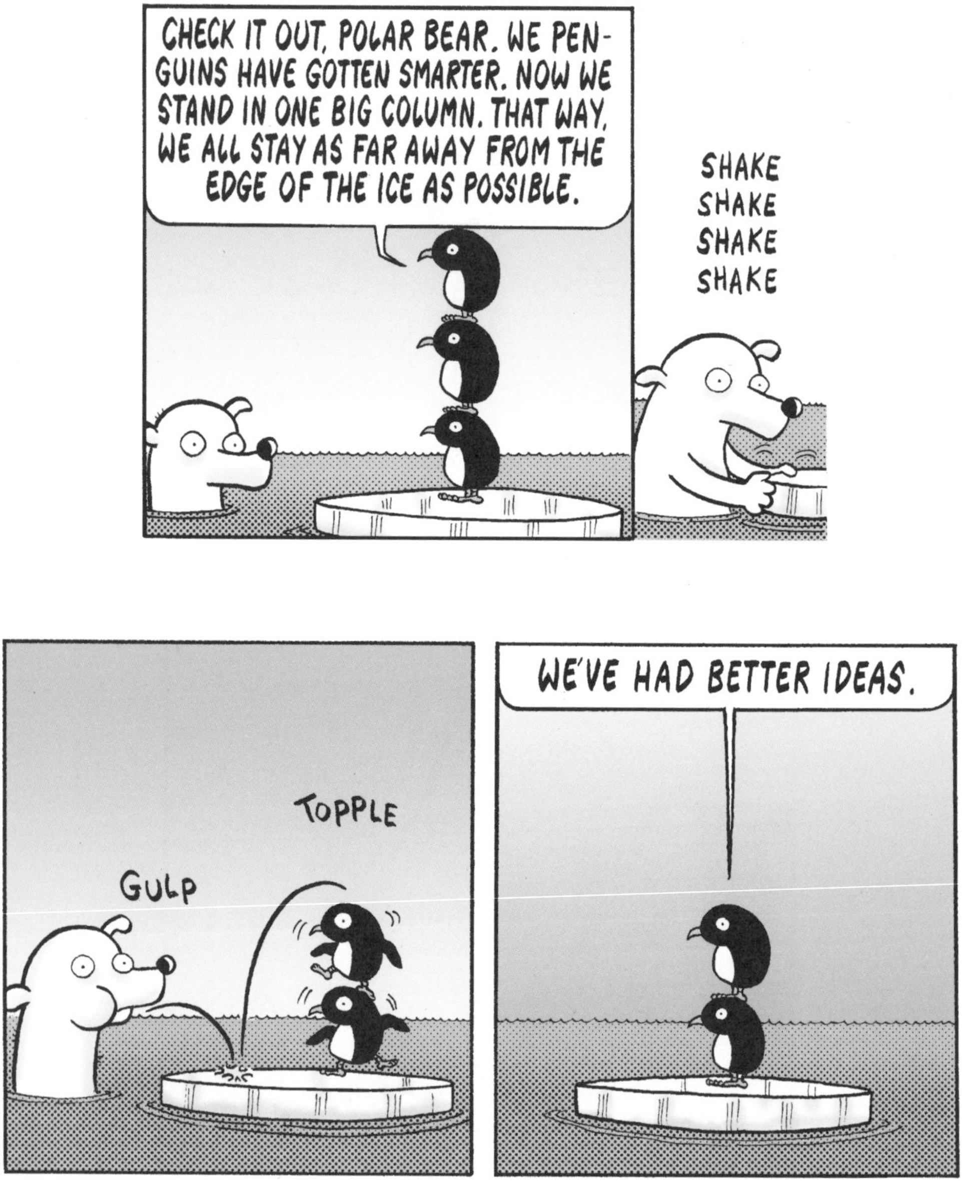
CHECK IT OUT, POLAR BEAR. WE PENGUINS HAVE GOTTEN SMARTER. NOW WE STAND IN ONE BIG COLUMN. THAT WAY, WE ALL STAY AS FAR AWAY FROM THE EDGE OF THE ICE AS POSSIBLE.
SHAKE SHAKE SHAKE SHAKE
TOPPLE
GULP
WE'VE HAD BETTER IDEAS.

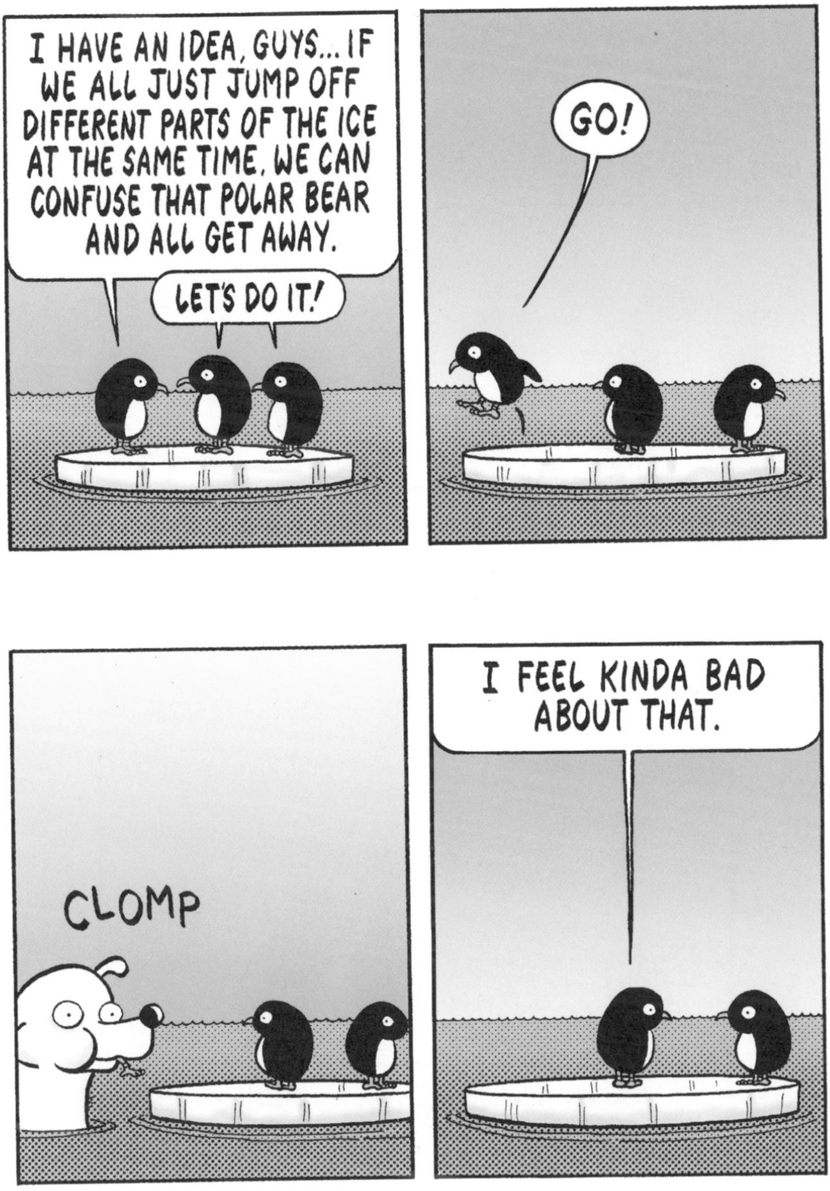

I HAVE AN IDEA, GUYS... IF WE ALL JUST JUMP OFF DIFFERENT PARTS OF THE ICE AT THE SAME TIME, WE CAN CONFUSE THAT POLAR BEAR AND ALL GET AWAY.
LET'S DO IT!
GO!
CLOMP
I FEEL KINDA BAD ABOUT THAT.

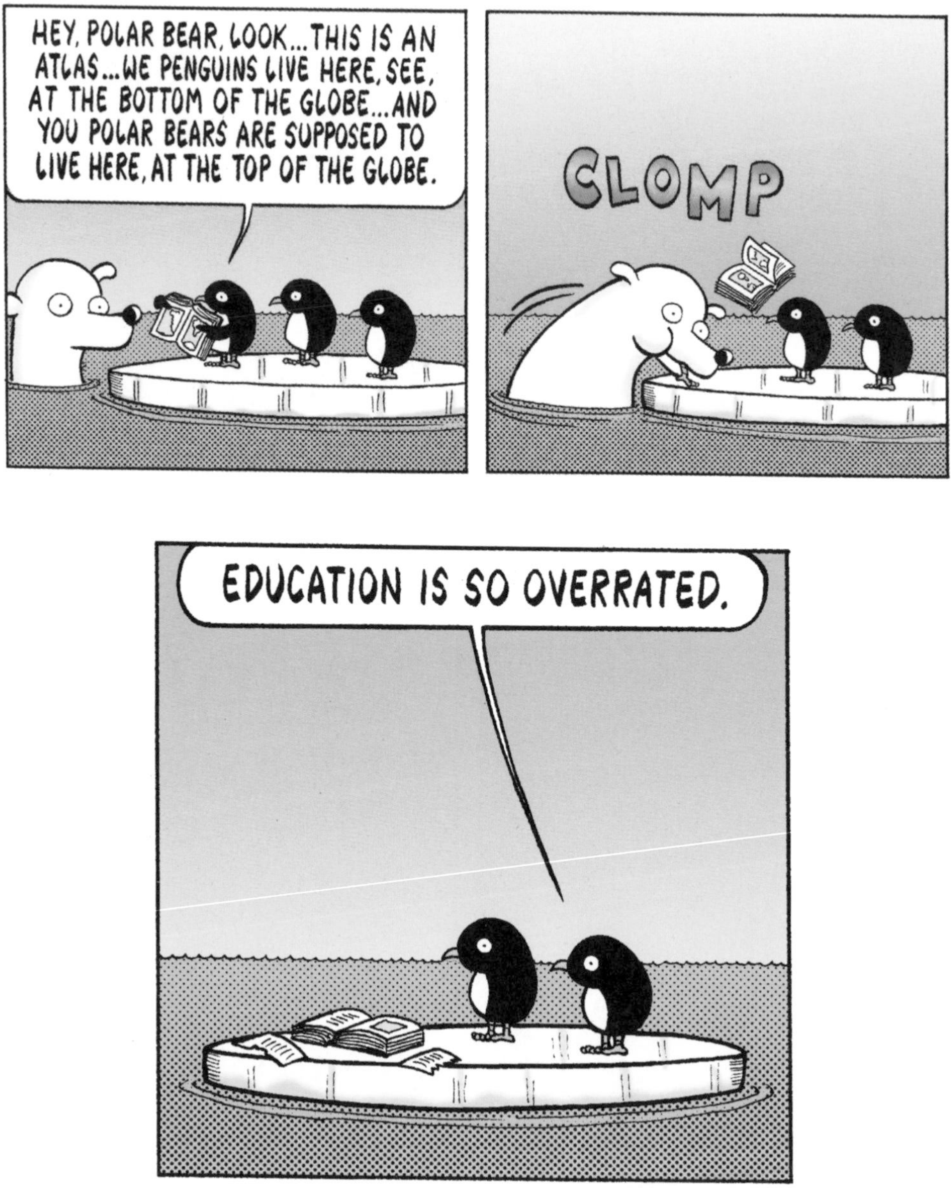
HEY, POLAR BEAR, LOOK...THIS IS AN ATLAS...WE PENGUINS LIVE HERE, SEE, AT THE BOTTOM OF THE GLOBE...AND YOU POLAR BEARS ARE SUPPOSED TO LIVE HERE, AT THE TOP OF THE GLOBE.
CLOMP
EDUCATION IS SO OVERRATED.

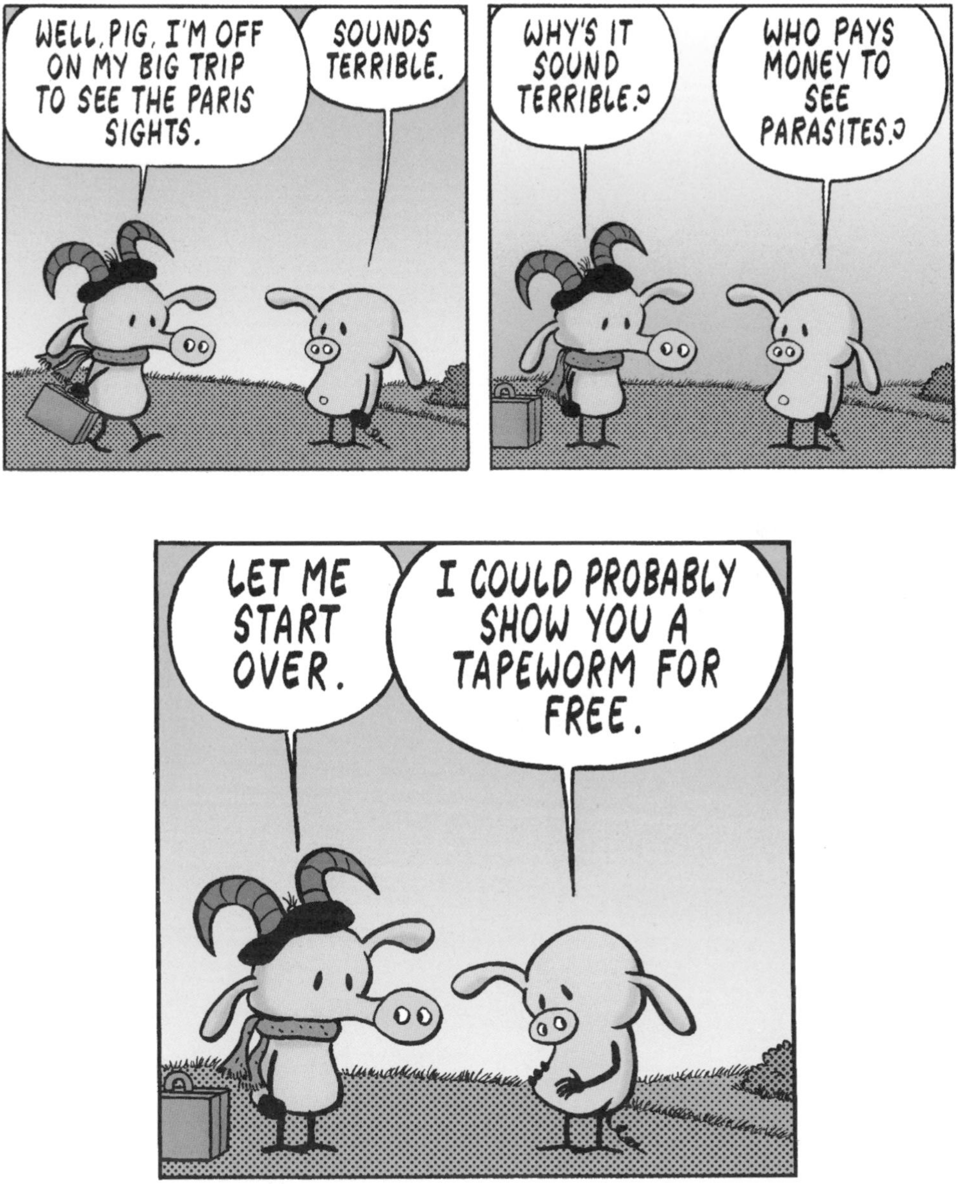
WELL, PIG, I'M OFF ON MY BIG TRIP TO SEE THE PARIS SIGHTS.
SOUNDS TERRIBLE.
WHY'S IT SOUND TERRIBLE?
WHO PAYS MONEY TO SEE PARASITES?
LET ME START OVER.
I COULD PROBABLY SHOW YOU A TAPEWORM FOR FREE.

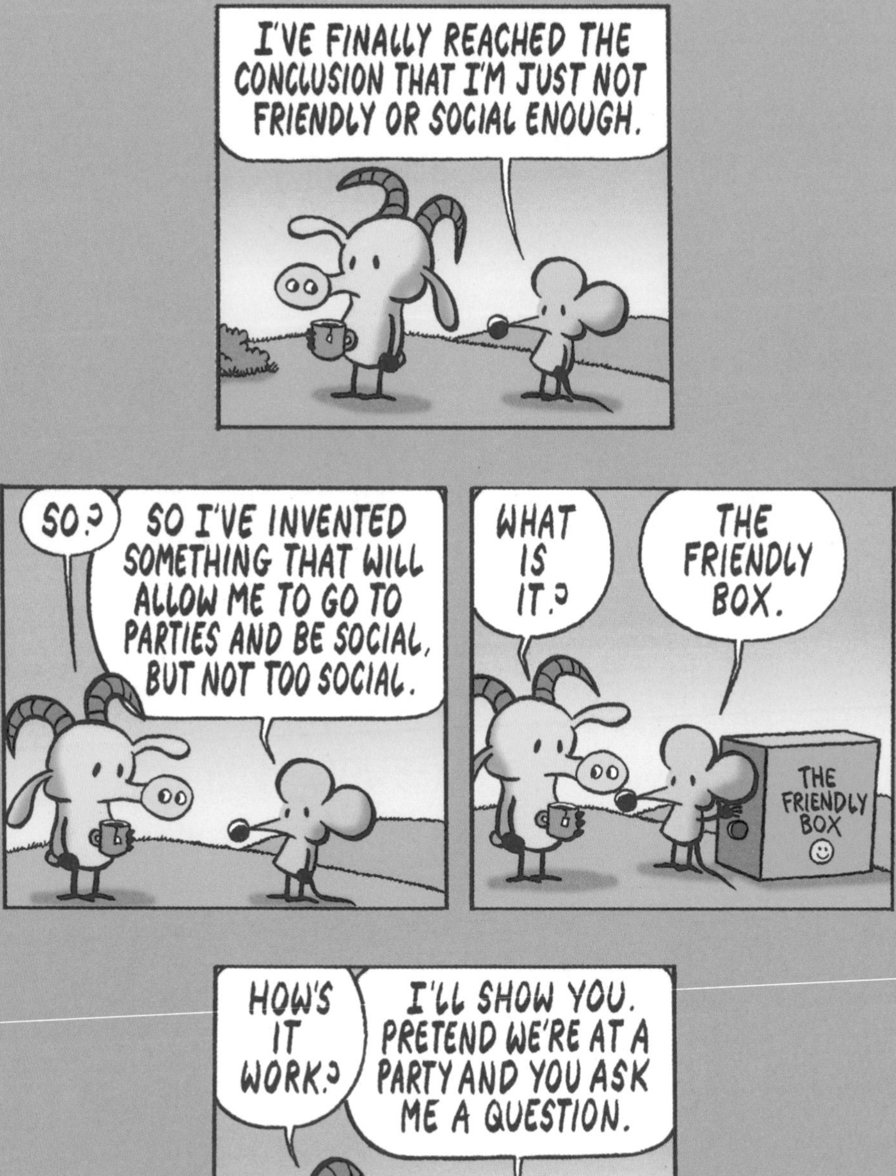
I'VE FINALLY REACHED THE CONCLUSION THAT I'M JUST NOT FRIENDLY OR SOCIAL ENOUGH.
SO?
SO I'VE INVENTED SOMETHING THAT WILL ALLOW ME TO GO TO PARTIES AND BE SOCIAL, BUT NOT TOO SOCIAL.
WHAT IS IT?
THE FRIENDLY BOX.
THE FRIENDLY BOX
HOW'S IT WORK?
I'LL SHOW YOU. PRETEND WE'RE AT A PARTY AND YOU ASK ME A QUESTION.

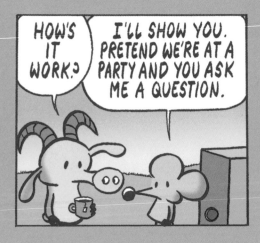

HEY... UH... HAVE YOU TRIED THE DIP?
NO. NO I HAVE NOT.
THE FRIENDLY BOX
WHAT ARE YOU DOING?
I'M STICKING OUT MY LEG. IT'S WHAT I CALL 'LIMITED SOCIAL INTERACTION.'
THE FRIENDLY BOX
IT'S WHAT I CALL SOMEONE WHO WON'T BE INVITED TO A LOT OF PARTIES.
COME A LITTLE CLOSER TO THE FRIENDLY BOX AND SAY THAT.
WELL, LOOK WHO'S BEING SOCIAL!
THE FRIENDLY BOX

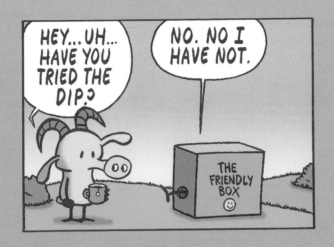

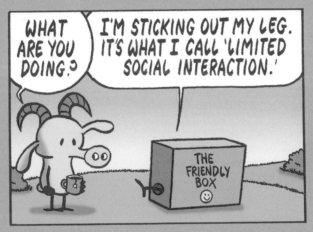

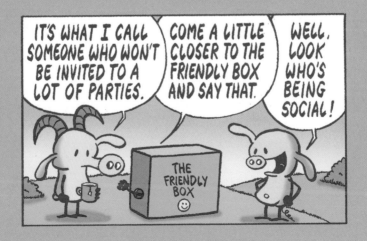

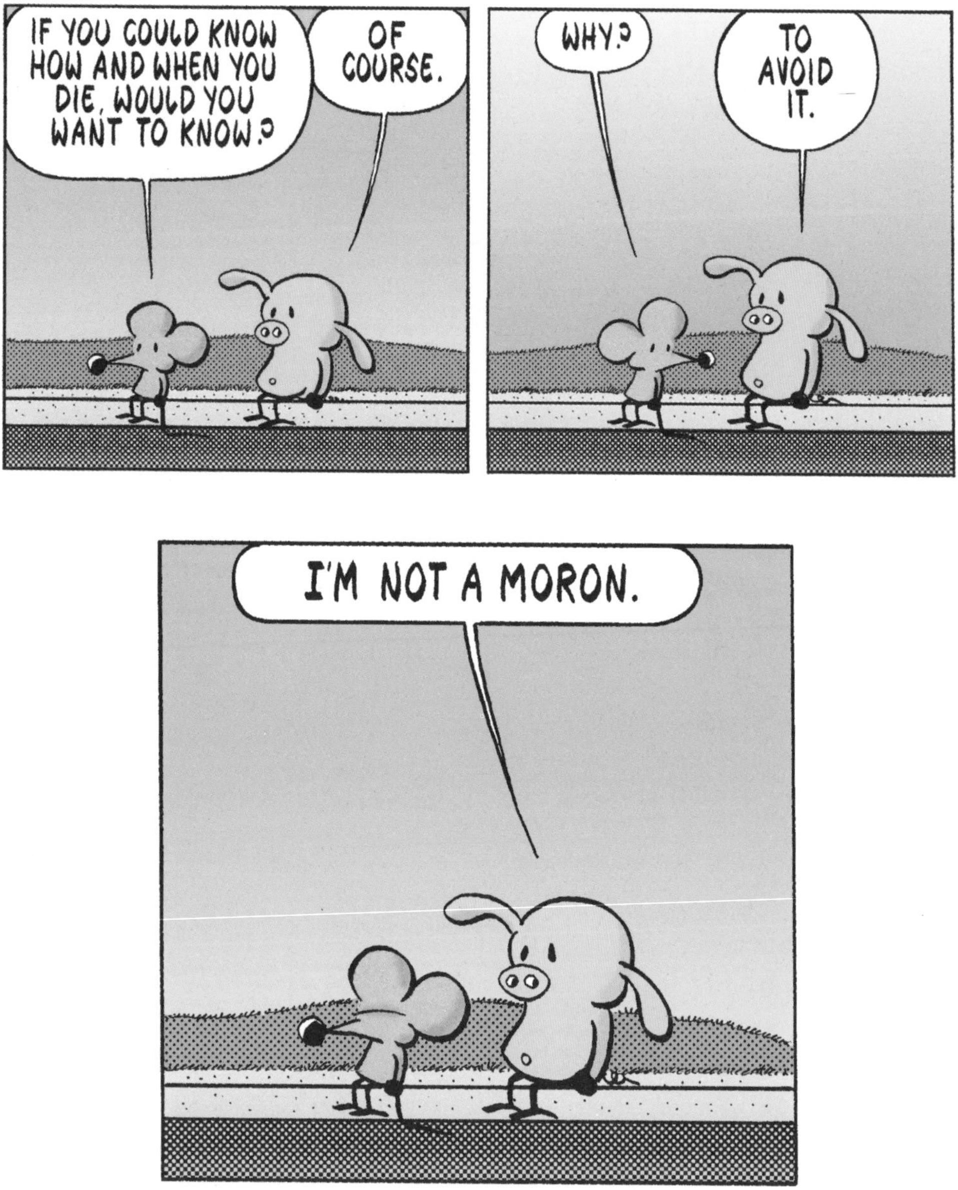
IF YOU COULD KNOW HOW AND WHEN YOU DIE, WOULD YOU WANT TO KNOW?
OF COURSE.
WHY?
TO AVOID IT.
I'M NOT A MORON.

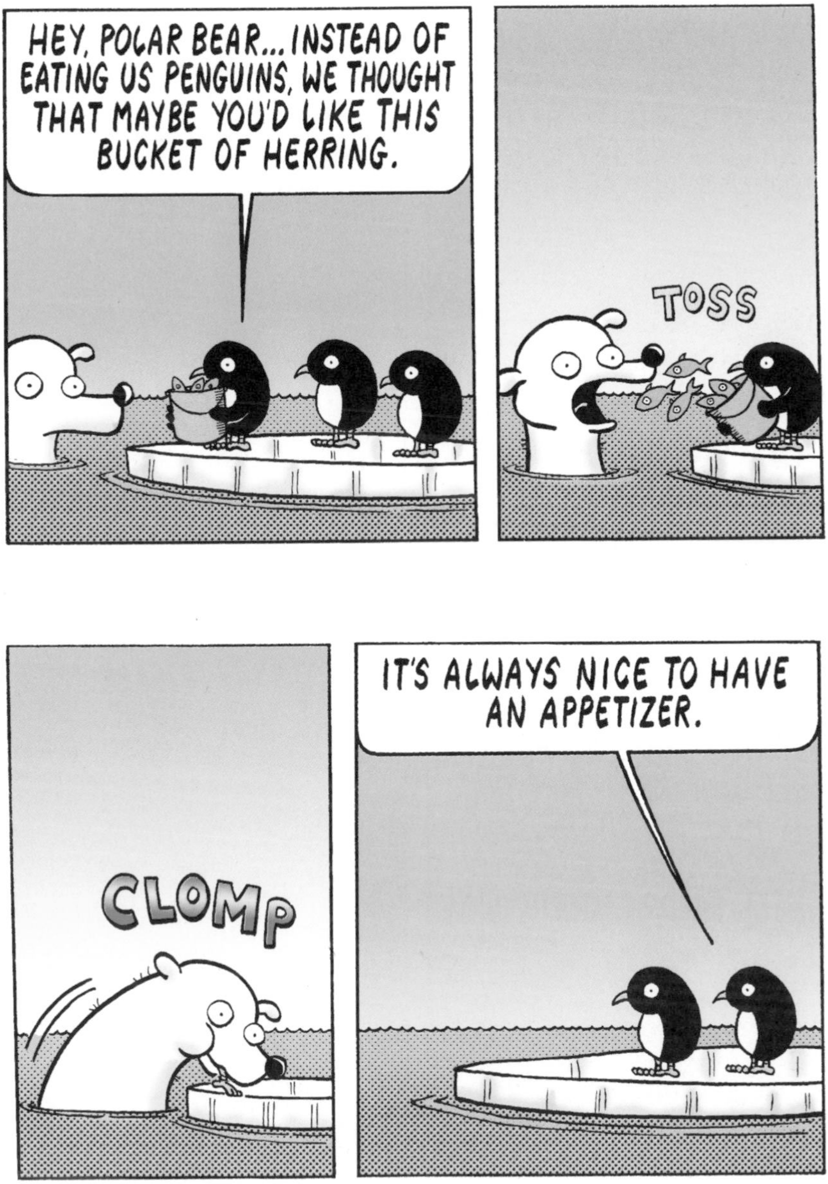
HEY, POLAR BEAR... INSTEAD OF EATING US PENGUINS, WE THOUGHT THAT MAYBE YOU'D LIKE THIS BUCKET OF HERRING.
TOSS
CLOMP
IT'S ALWAYS NICE TO HAVE AN APPETIZER.

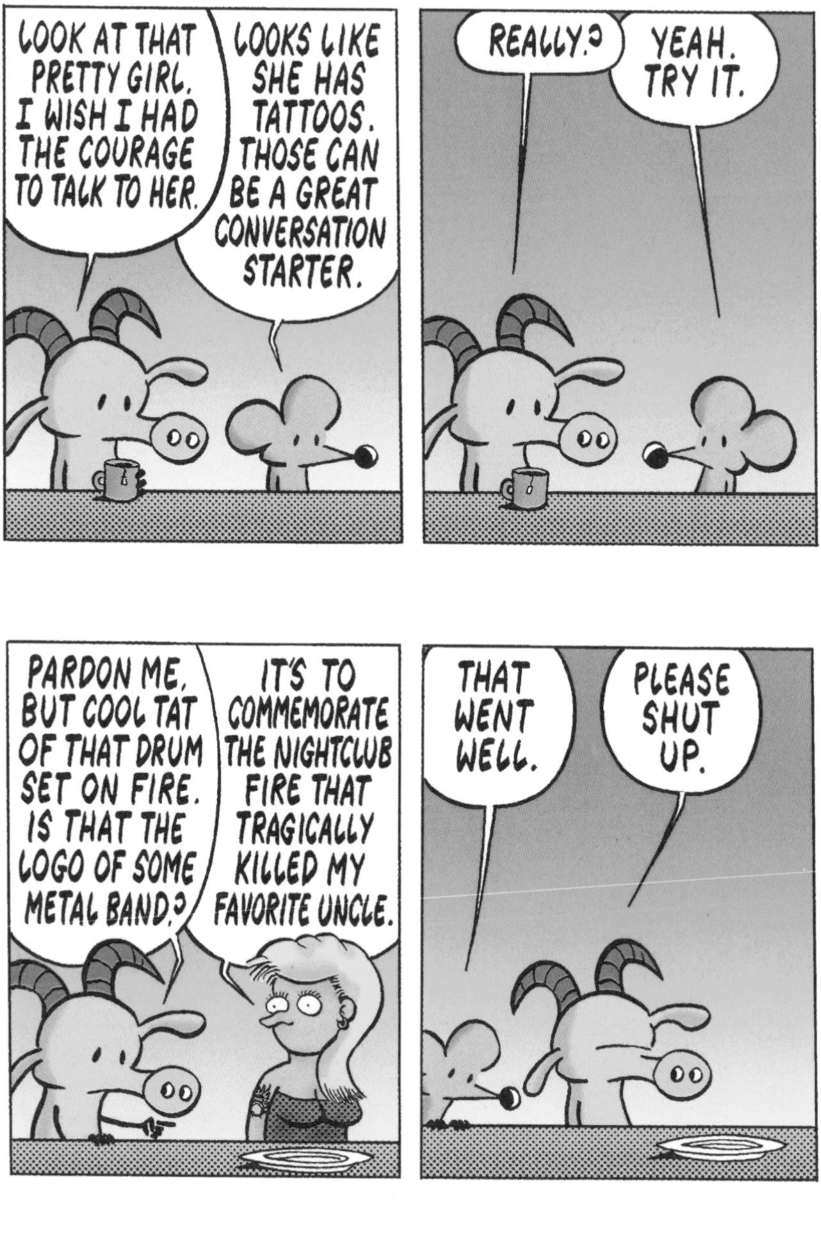
LOOK AT THAT PRETTY GIRL. I WISH I HAD THE COURAGE TO TALK TO HER.
LOOKS LIKE SHE HAS TATTOOS. THOSE CAN BE A GREAT CONVERSATION STARTER.
REALLY?
YEAH. TRY IT.
PARDON ME, BUT COOL TAT OF THAT DRUM SET ON FIRE. IS THAT THE LOGO OF SOME METAL BAND?
IT'S TO COMMEMORATE THE NIGHTCLUB FIRE THAT TRAGICALLY KILLED MY FAVORITE UNCLE.
THAT WENT WELL.
PLEASE SHUT UP.

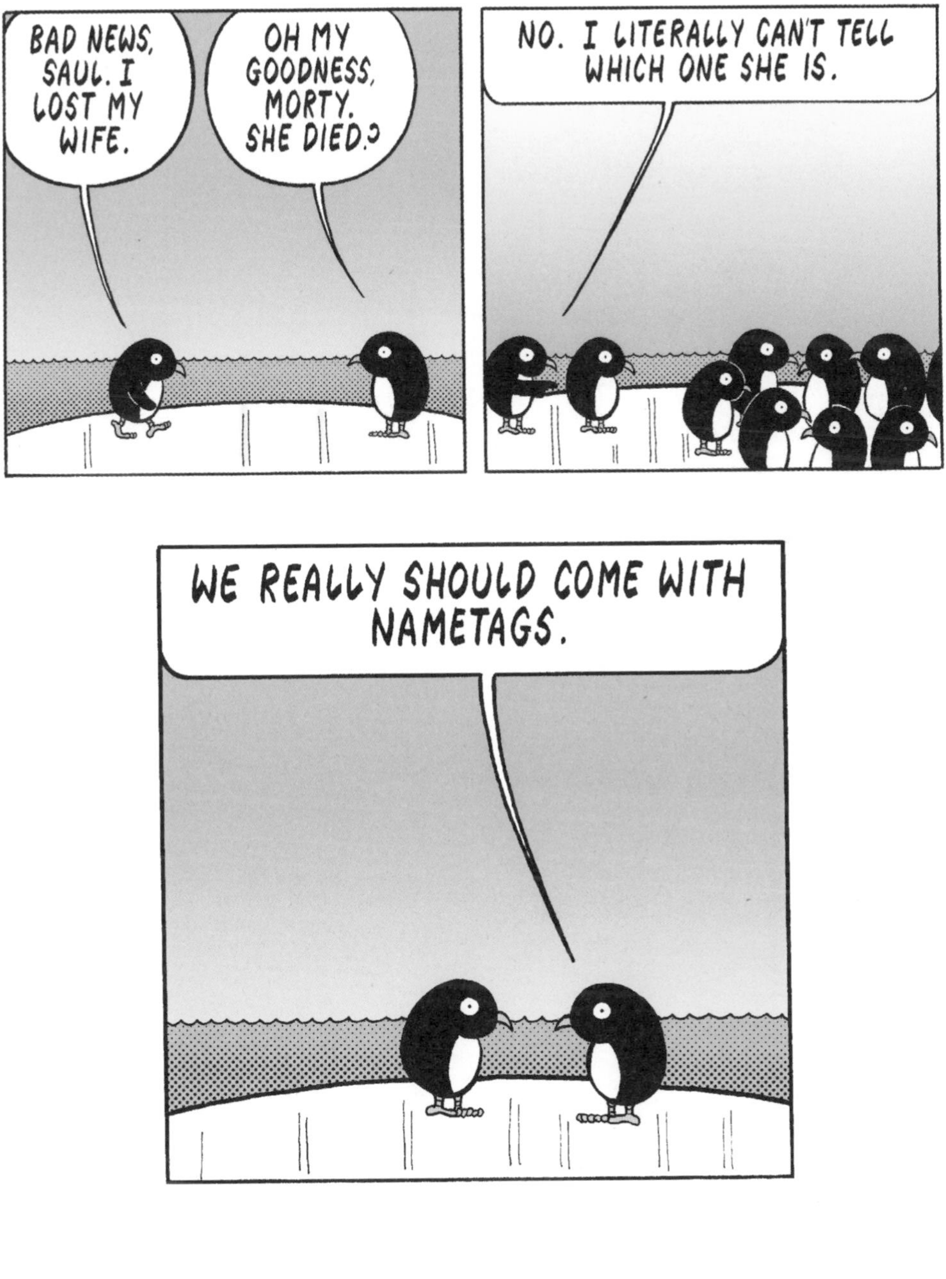
BAD NEWS, SAUL. I LOST MY WIFE.
OH MY GOODNESS, MORTY. SHE DIED?
NO. I LITERALLY CAN'T TELL WHICH ONE SHE IS.
WE REALLY SHOULD COME WITH NAMETAGS.

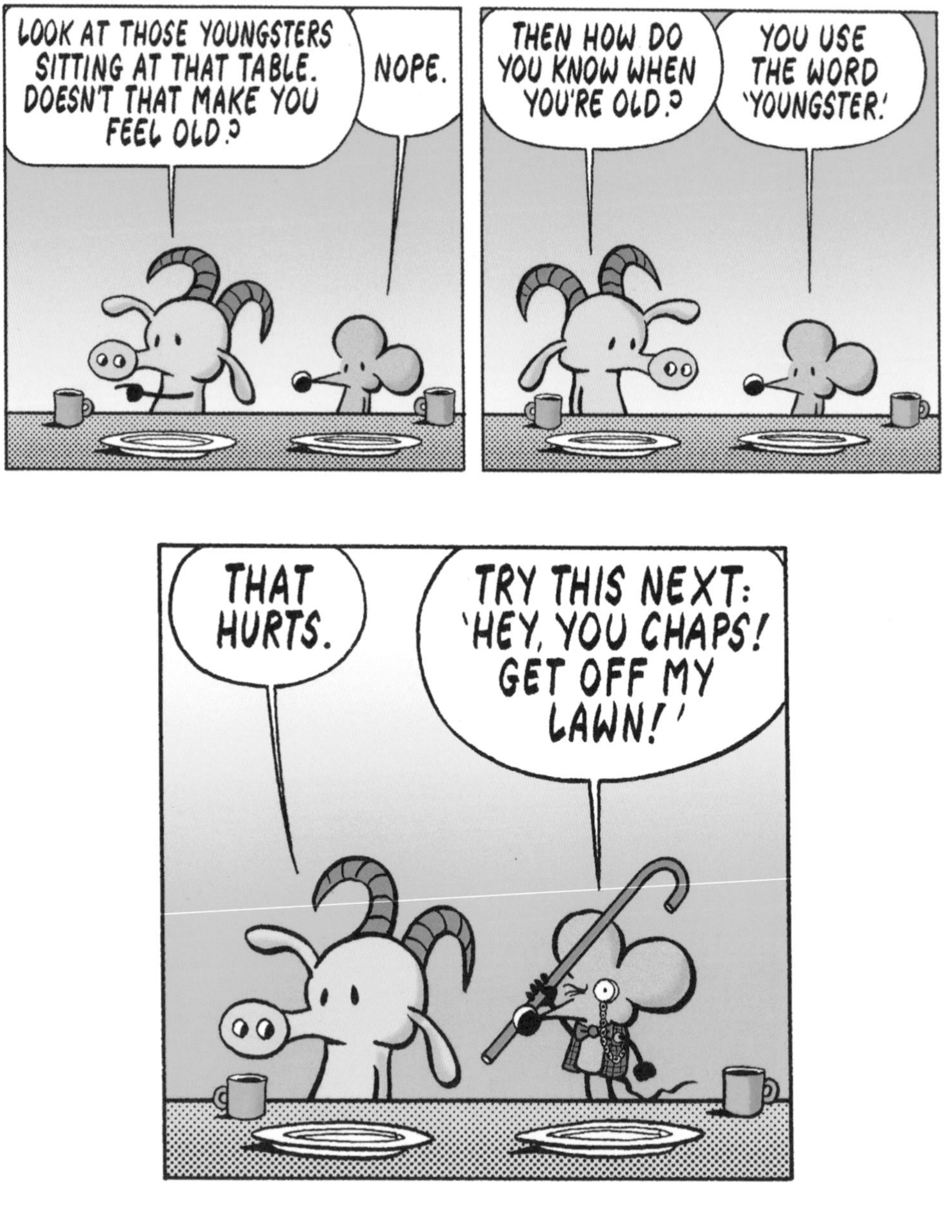
LOOK AT THOSE YOUNGSTERS SITTING AT THAT TABLE. DOESN'T THAT MAKE YOU FEEL OLD?
NOPE.
THEN HOW DO YOU KNOW WHEN YOU'RE OLD?
YOU USE THE WORD 'YOUNGSTER.'
THAT HURTS.
TRY THIS NEXT: 'HEY, YOU CHAPS! GET OFF MY LAWN!'

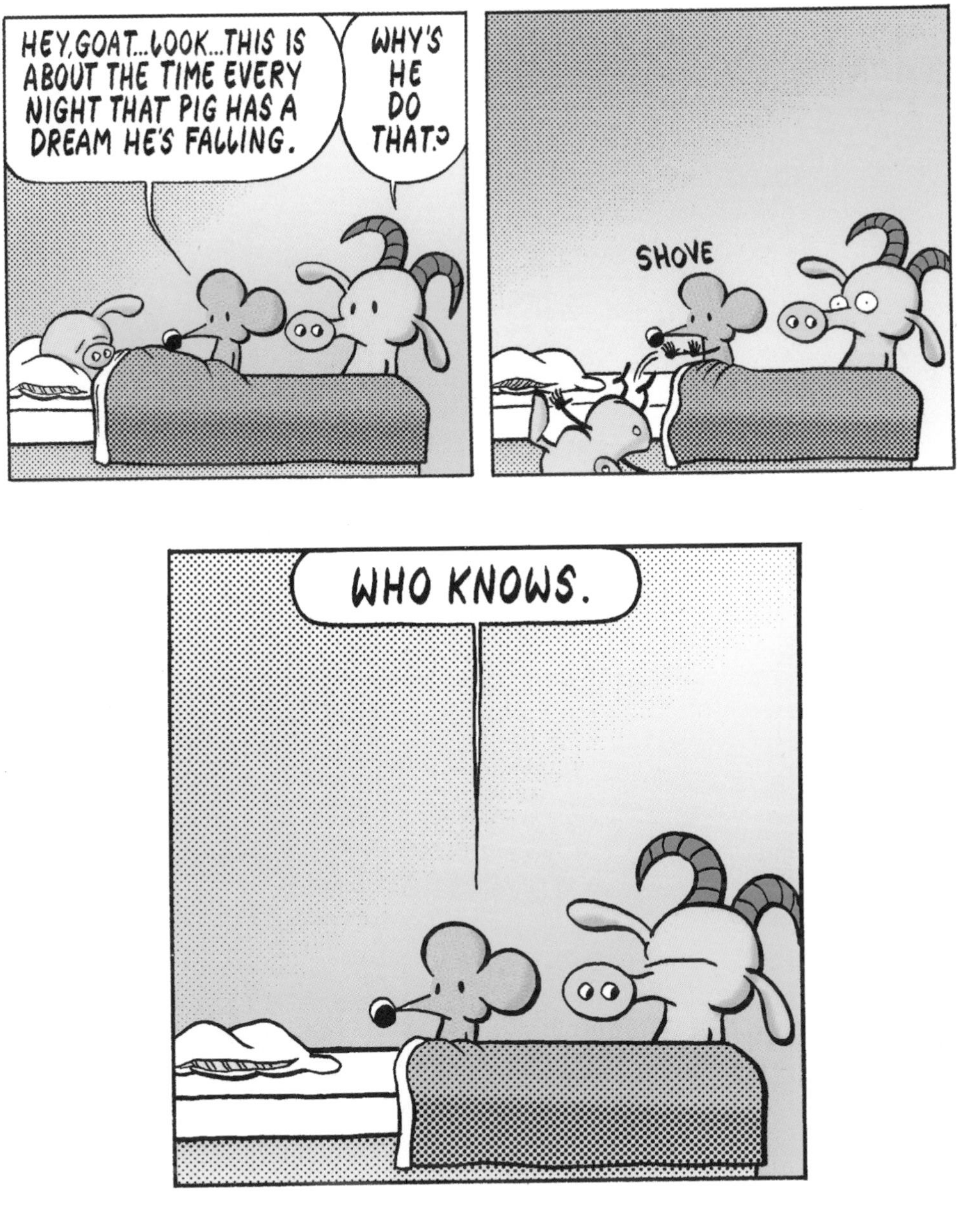
HEY, GOAT...LOOK...THIS IS ABOUT THE TIME EVERY NIGHT THAT PIG HAS A DREAM HE'S FALLING.
WHY'S HE DO THAT?
SHOVE
WHO KNOWS.

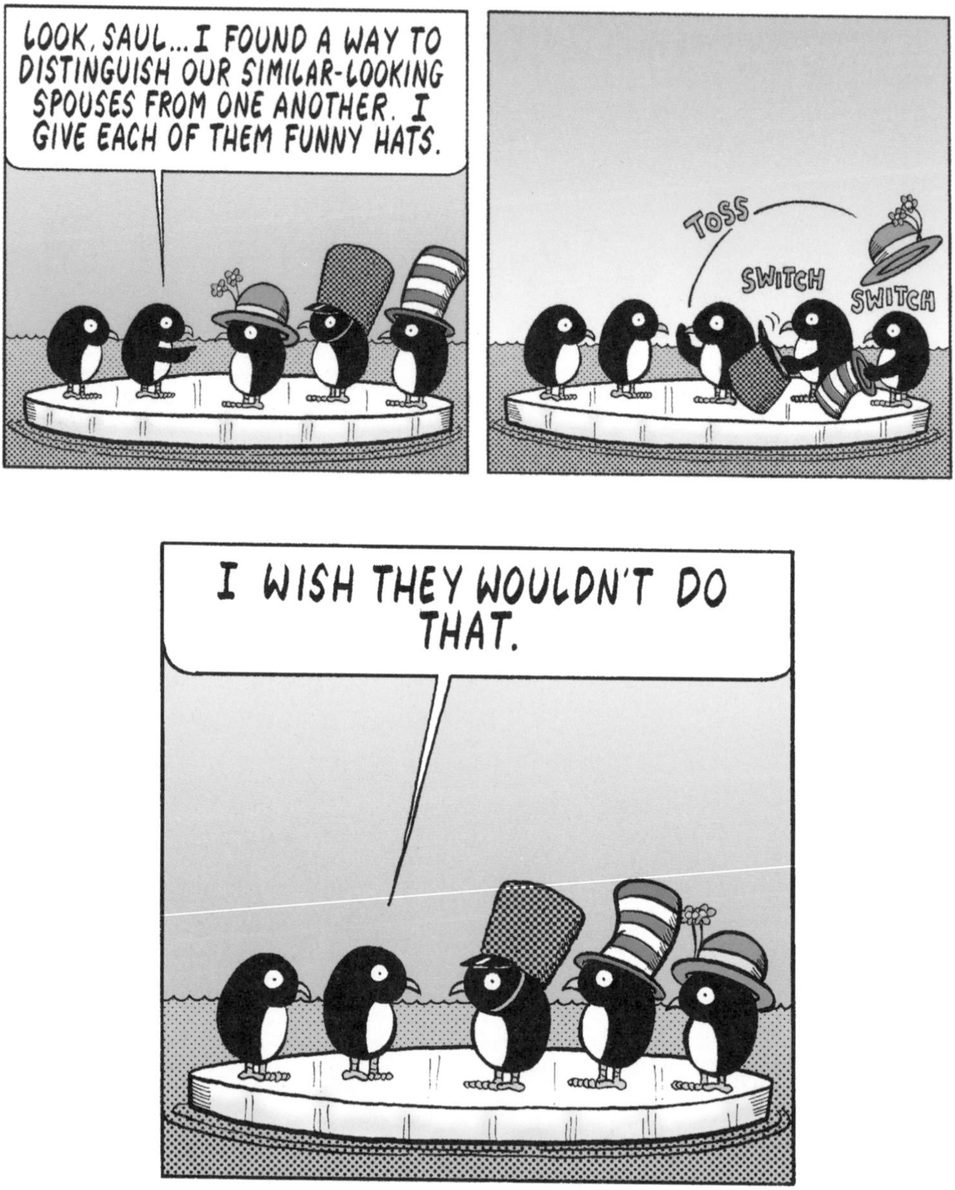
LOOK, SAUL...I FOUND A WAY TO DISTINGUISH OUR SIMILAR-LOOKING SPOUSES FROM ONE ANOTHER. I GIVE EACH OF THEM FUNNY HATS.
TOSS
SWITCH
SWITCH
I WISH THEY WOULDN'T DO THAT.

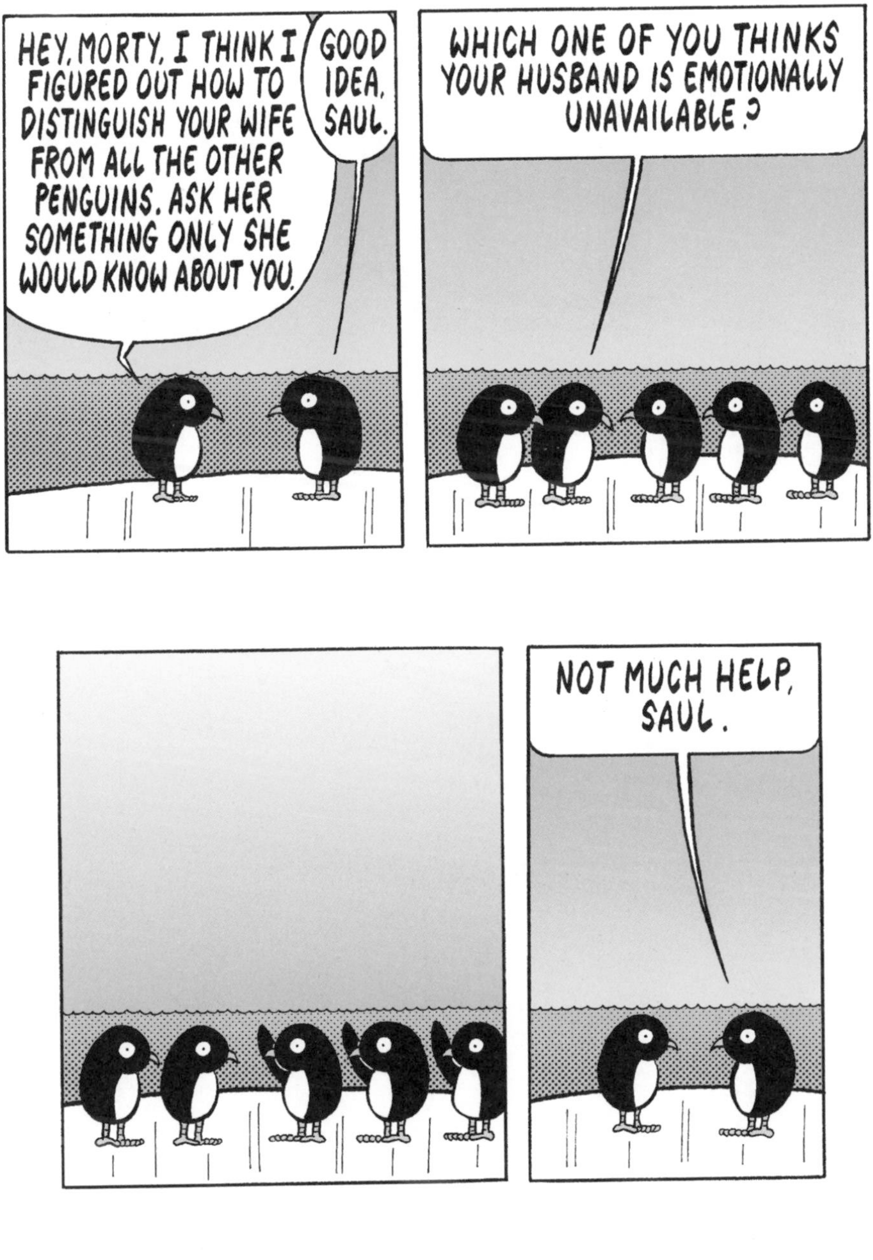
HEY, MORTY, I THINK I FIGURED OUT HOW TO DISTINGUISH YOUR WIFE FROM ALL THE OTHER PENGUINS. ASK HER SOMETHING ONLY SHE WOULD KNOW ABOUT YOU.
GOOD IDEA, SAUL.
WHICH ONE OF YOU THINKS YOUR HUSBAND IS EMOTIONALLY UNAVAILABLE?
NOT MUCH HELP, SAUL.

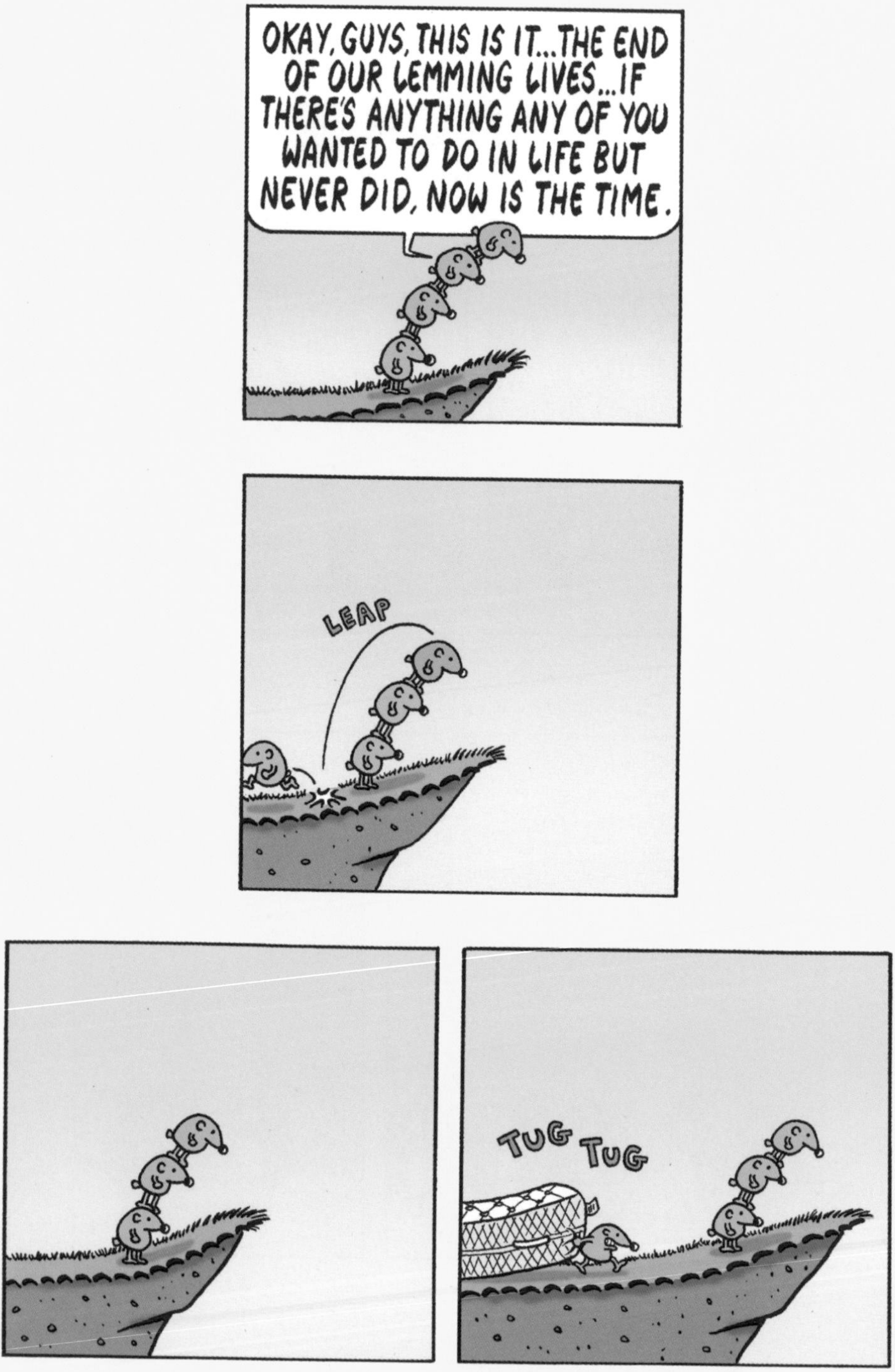
OKAY, GUYS, THIS IS IT...THE END OF OUR LEMMING LIVES...IF THERE'S ANYTHING ANY OF YOU WANTED TO DO IN LIFE BUT NEVER DID, NOW IS THE TIME.
LEAP
TUG TUG

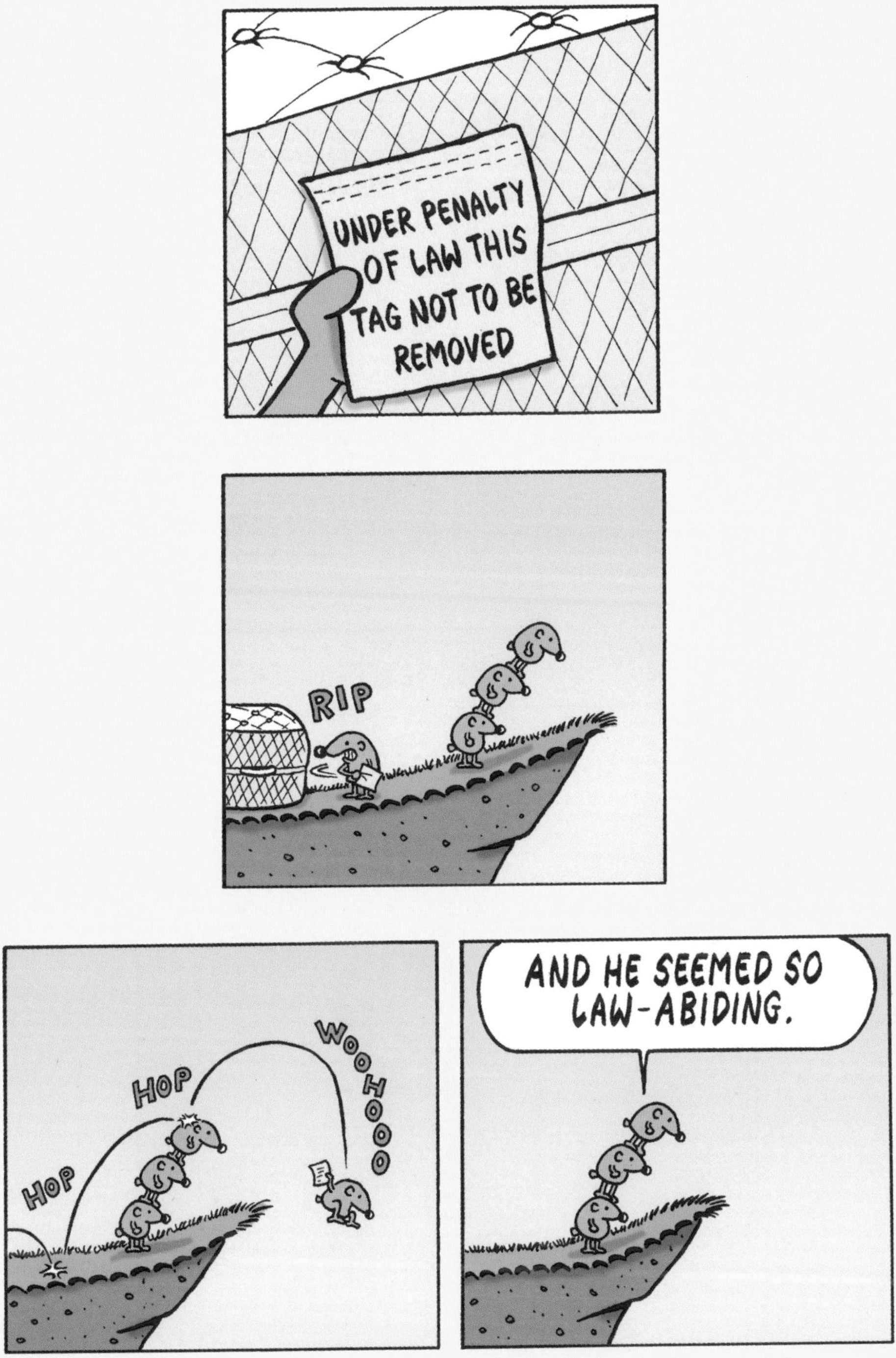
UNDER PENALTY OF LAW THIS TAG NOT TO BE REMOVED
RIP
HOP
HOP
WOOHOOOO
AND HE SEEMED SO LAW-ABIDING.

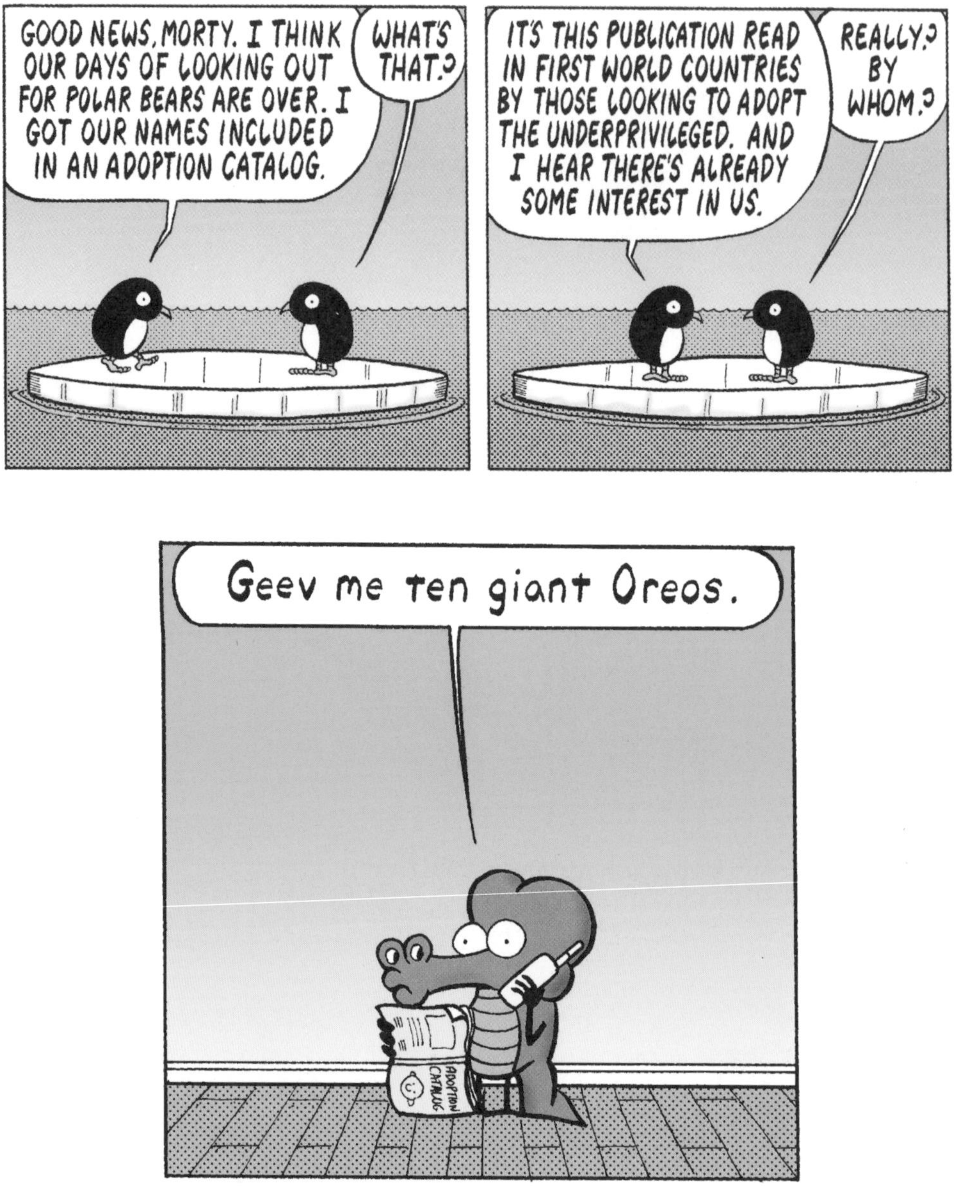
GOOD NEWS, MORTY. I THINK OUR DAYS OF LOOKING OUT FOR POLAR BEARS ARE OVER. I GOT OUR NAMES INCLUDED IN AN ADOPTION CATALOG.
WHAT'S THAT?
IT'S THIS PUBLICATION READ IN FIRST WORLD COUNTRIES BY THOSE LOOKING TO ADOPT THE UNDERPRIVILEGED. AND I HEAR THERE'S ALREADY SOME INTEREST IN US.
REALLY? BY WHOM?
Geev me ten giant Oreos.
ADOPTION CATALOG

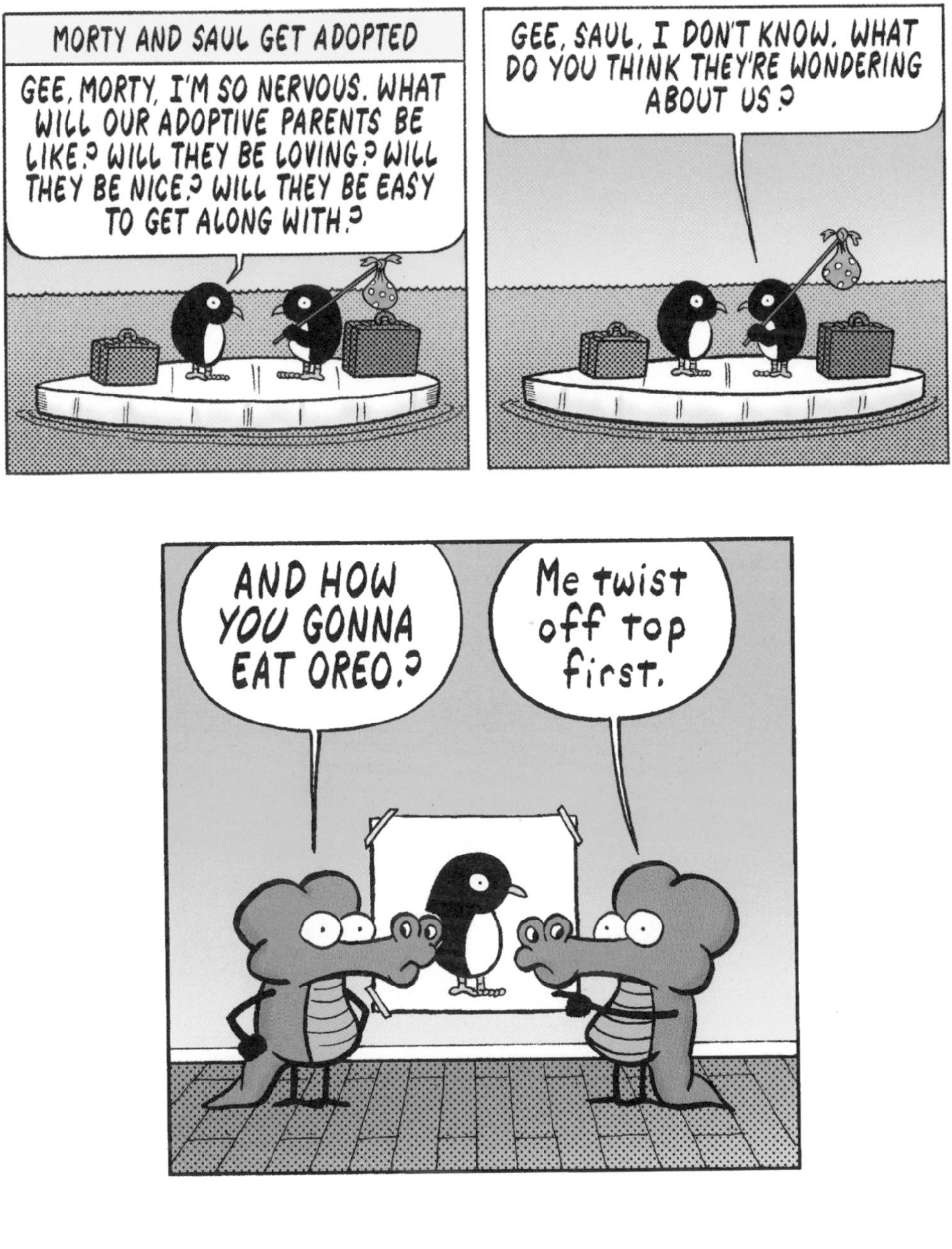
MORTY AND SAUL GET ADOPTED
GEE, MORTY, I'M SO NERVOUS. WHAT WILL OUR ADOPTIVE PARENTS BE LIKE? WILL THEY BE LOVING? WILL THEY BE NICE? WILL THEY BE EASY TO GET ALONG WITH?
GEE, SAUL, I DON'T KNOW. WHAT DO YOU THINK THEY'RE WONDERING ABOUT US?
AND HOW YOU GONNA EAT OREO?
Me twist off top first.

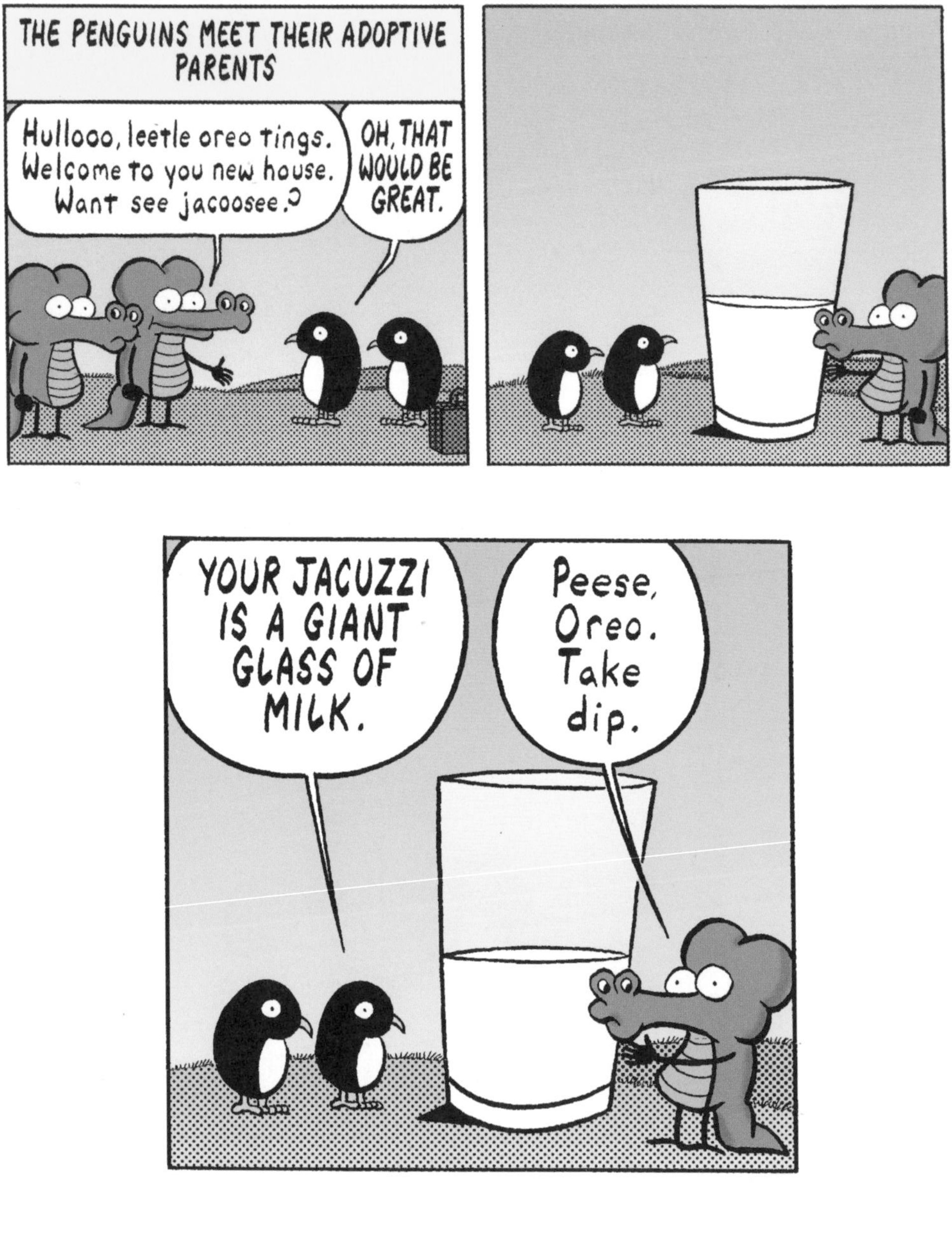
THE PENGUINS MEET THEIR ADOPTIVE PARENTS
Hullooo, leetle oreo tings. Welcome to you new house. Want see jacoosee.?
OH, THAT WOULD BE GREAT.
YOUR JACUZZI IS A GIANT GLASS OF MILK.
Peese, Oreo. Take dip.

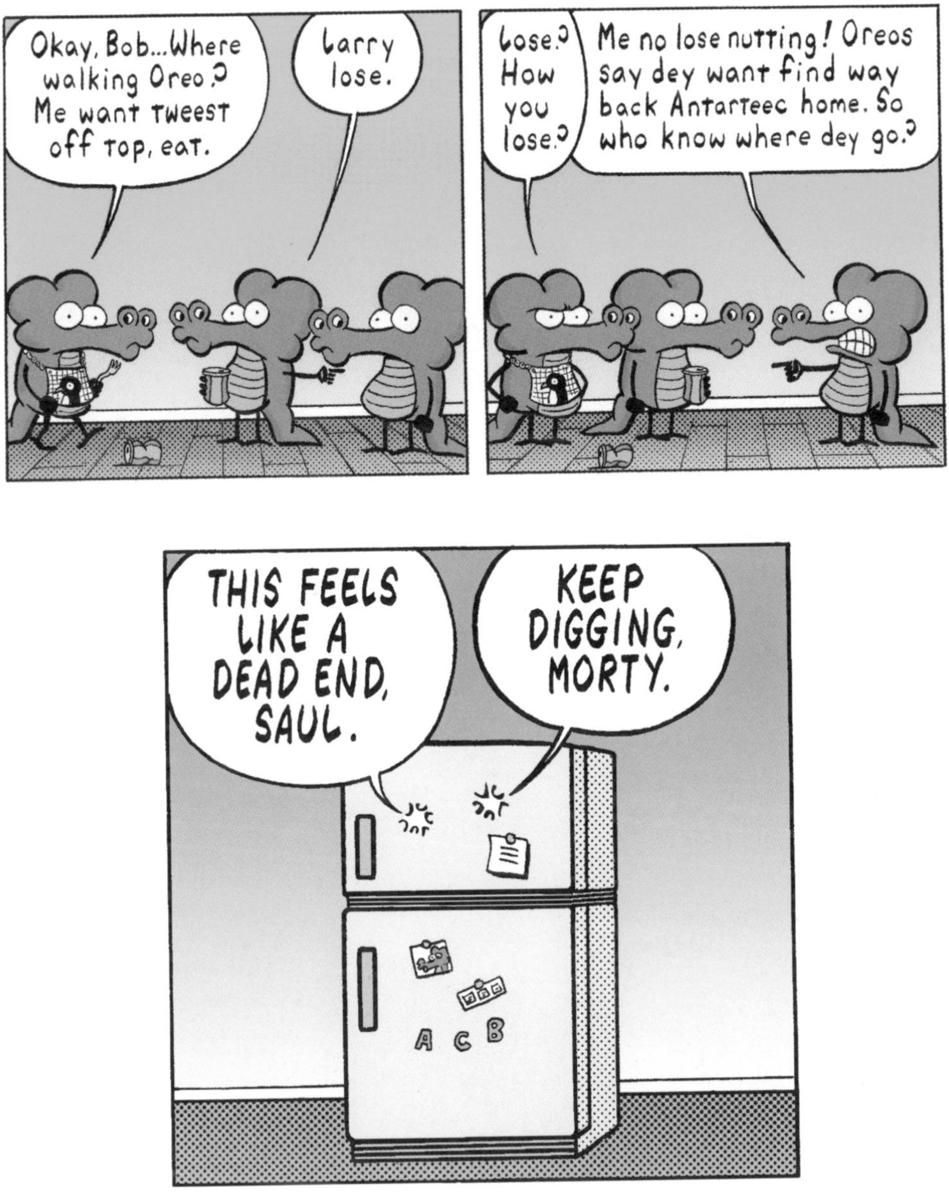
Okay, Bob...Where walking Oreo? Me want tweest off top, eat.
Larry lose.
Lose? How you lose?
Me no lose nutting! Oreos say dey want find way back Antarteec home. So who know where dey go?
THIS FEELS LIKE A DEAD END, SAUL.
KEEP DIGGING, MORTY.
A C B

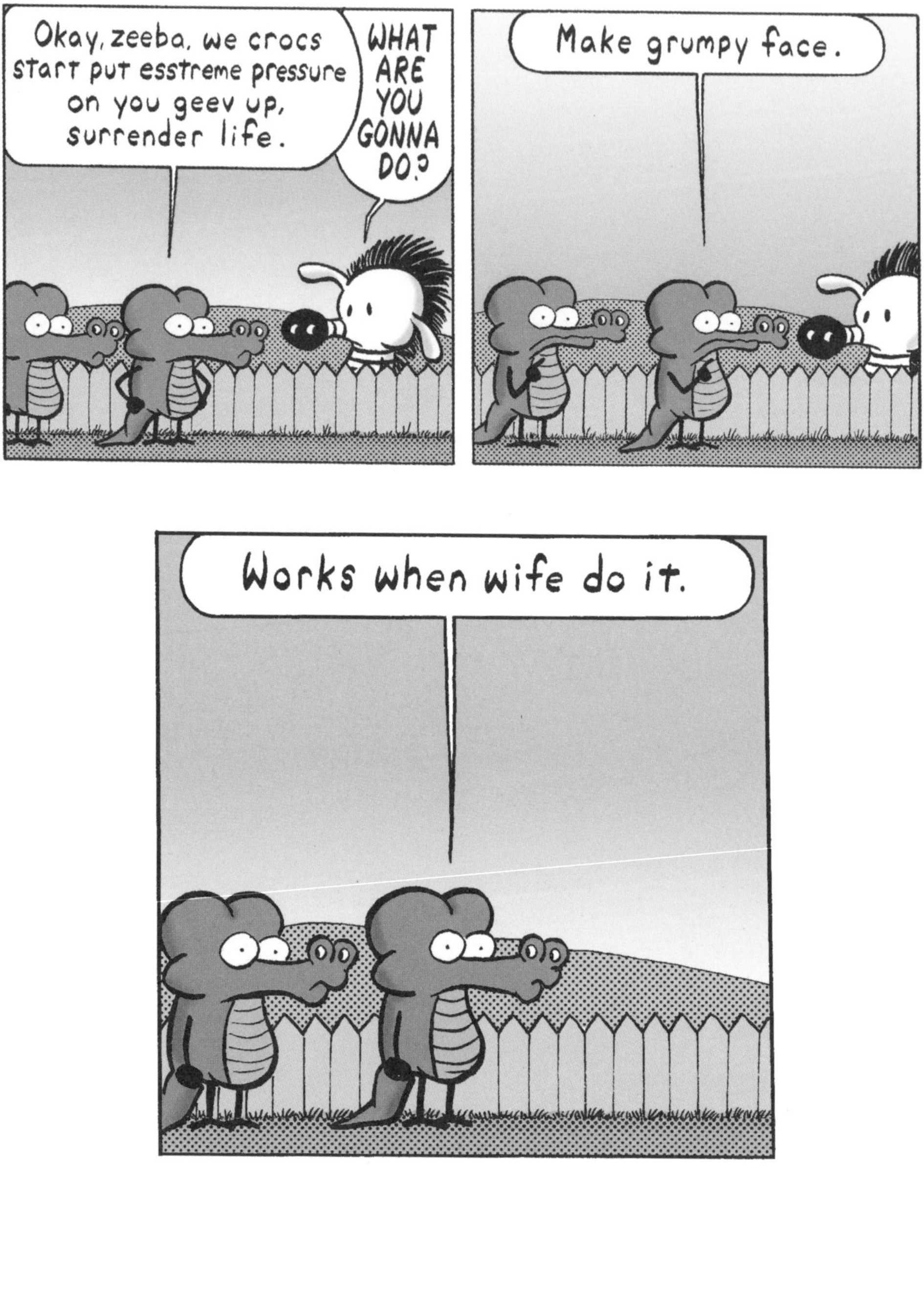
Okay, zeeba, we crocs start put esstreme pressure on you geev up, surrender life.
WHAT ARE YOU GONNA DO?
Make grumpy face.
Works when wife do it.

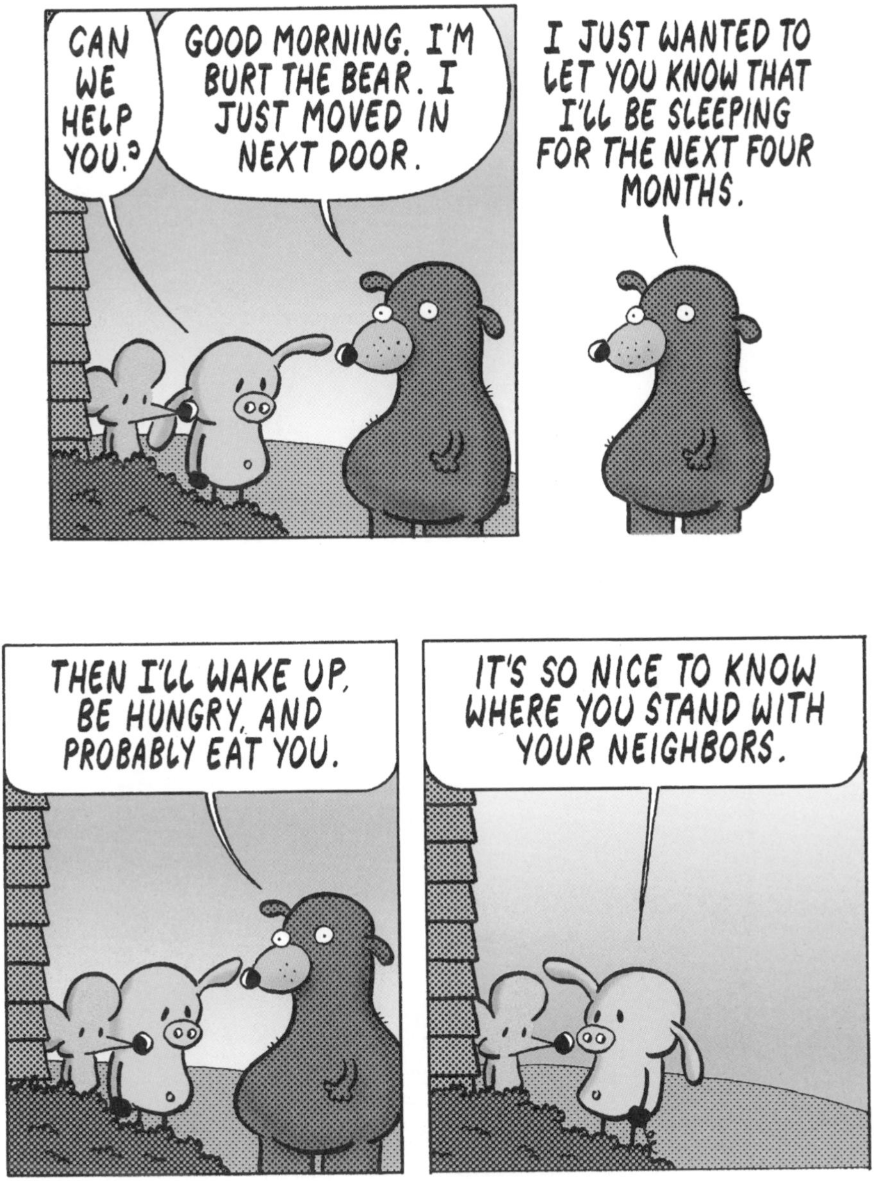
CAN WE HELP YOU?
GOOD MORNING. I'M BURT THE BEAR. I JUST MOVED IN NEXT DOOR.
I JUST WANTED TO LET YOU KNOW THAT I'LL BE SLEEPING FOR THE NEXT FOUR MONTHS.
THEN I'LL WAKE UP, BE HUNGRY, AND PROBABLY EAT YOU.
IT'S SO NICE TO KNOW WHERE YOU STAND WITH YOUR NEIGHBORS.

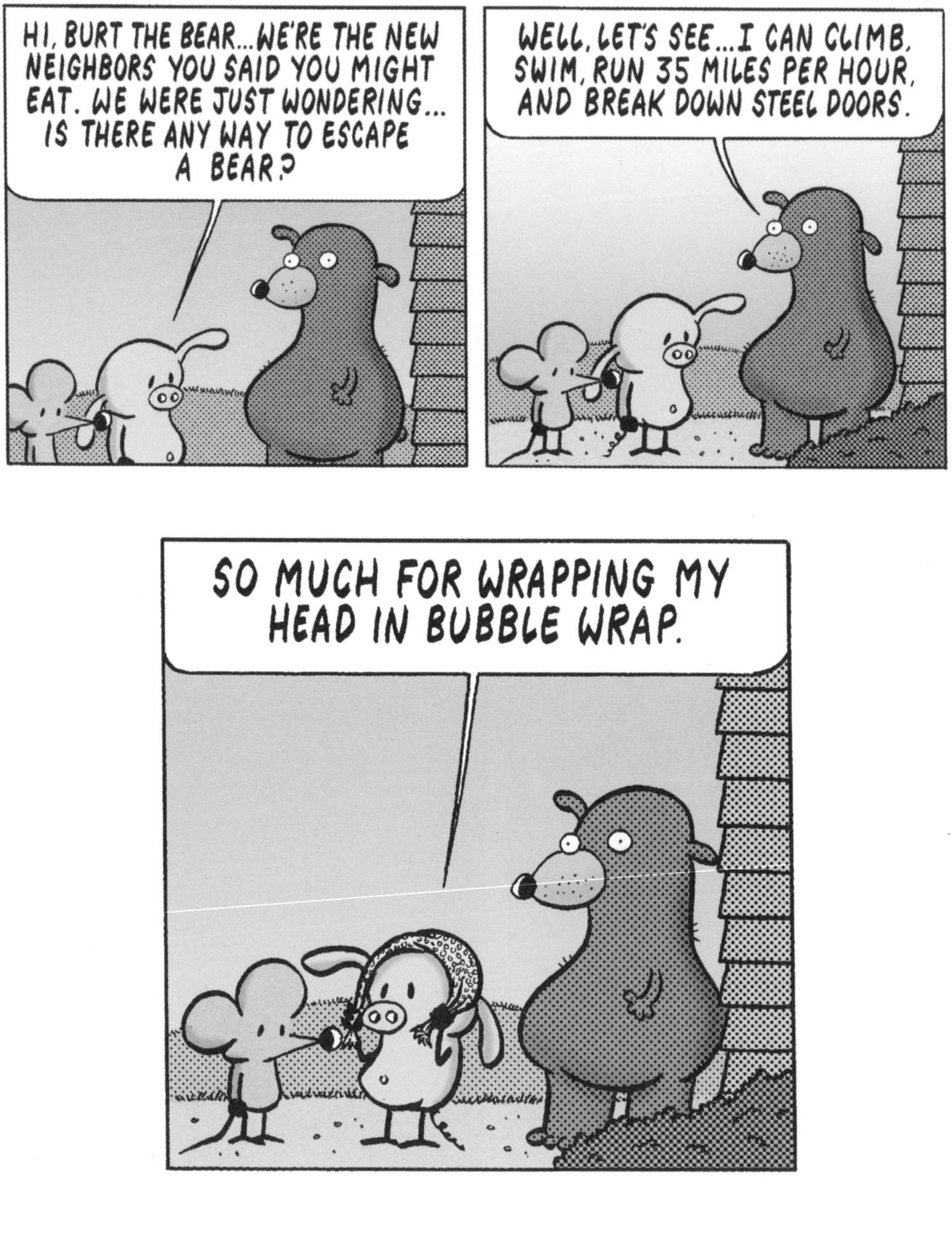
HI, BURT THE BEAR...WE'RE THE NEW NEIGHBORS YOU SAID YOU MIGHT EAT. WE WERE JUST WONDERING... IS THERE ANY WAY TO ESCAPE A BEAR?
WELL, LET'S SEE...I CAN CLIMB, SWIM, RUN 35 MILES PER HOUR, AND BREAK DOWN STEEL DOORS.
SO MUCH FOR WRAPPING MY HEAD IN BUBBLE WRAP.

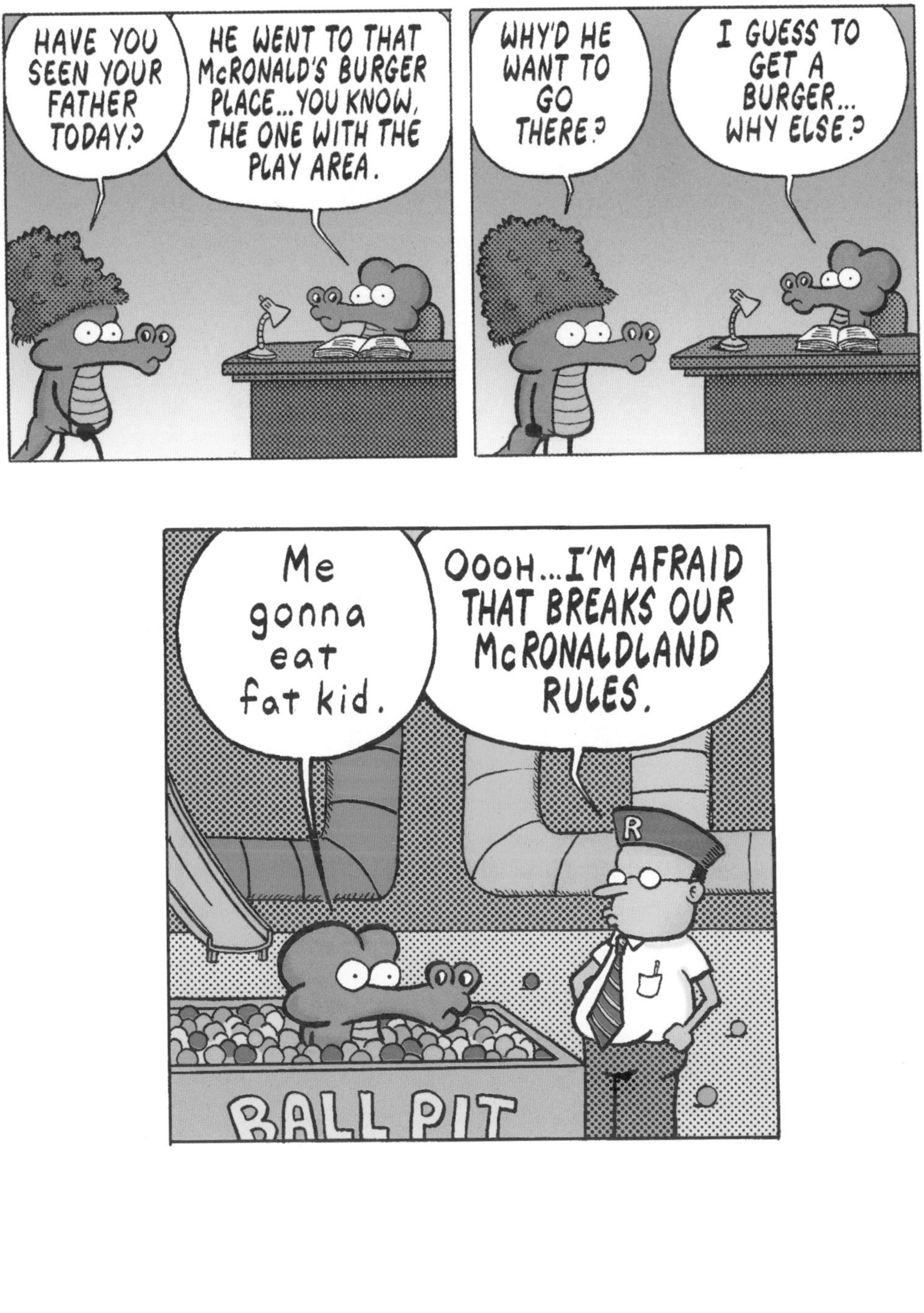
HAVE YOU SEEN YOUR FATHER TODAY?
HE WENT TO THAT McRONALD'S BURGER PLACE...YOU KNOW, THE ONE WITH THE PLAY AREA.
WHY'D HE WANT TO GO THERE?
I GUESS TO GET A BURGER... WHY ELSE?
Me gonna eat fat kid.
OOOH...I'M AFRAID THAT BREAKS OUR McRONALDLAND RULES.
BALL PIT

Bob! Bob! Look whuh me find.
Whuh ees it, Burt?
It say 'defibilator.'
Ooh. Sound like 'alligator.' Must be for reptiles.
Yeah. But how it work? It have instrukshuns, but too hard to read.
Maybe has audio instrukshuns.

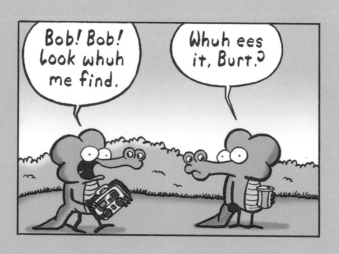

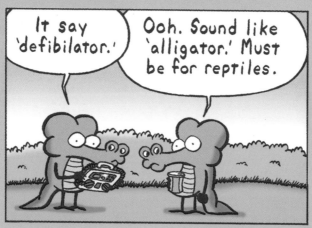

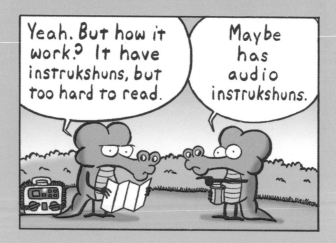

You right. Dis button problee 'PLAY.'... Now where sound come from?
Hedphones.
AREN'T THOSE DEVICES SUPPOSED TO SAVE LIVES?
IN THEORY.
WHUH INSTRUKSHUNS SAY, BOB?

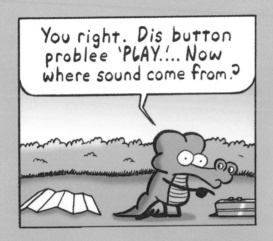

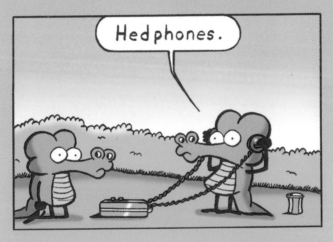

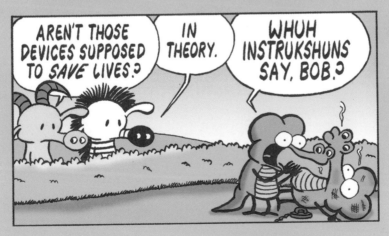

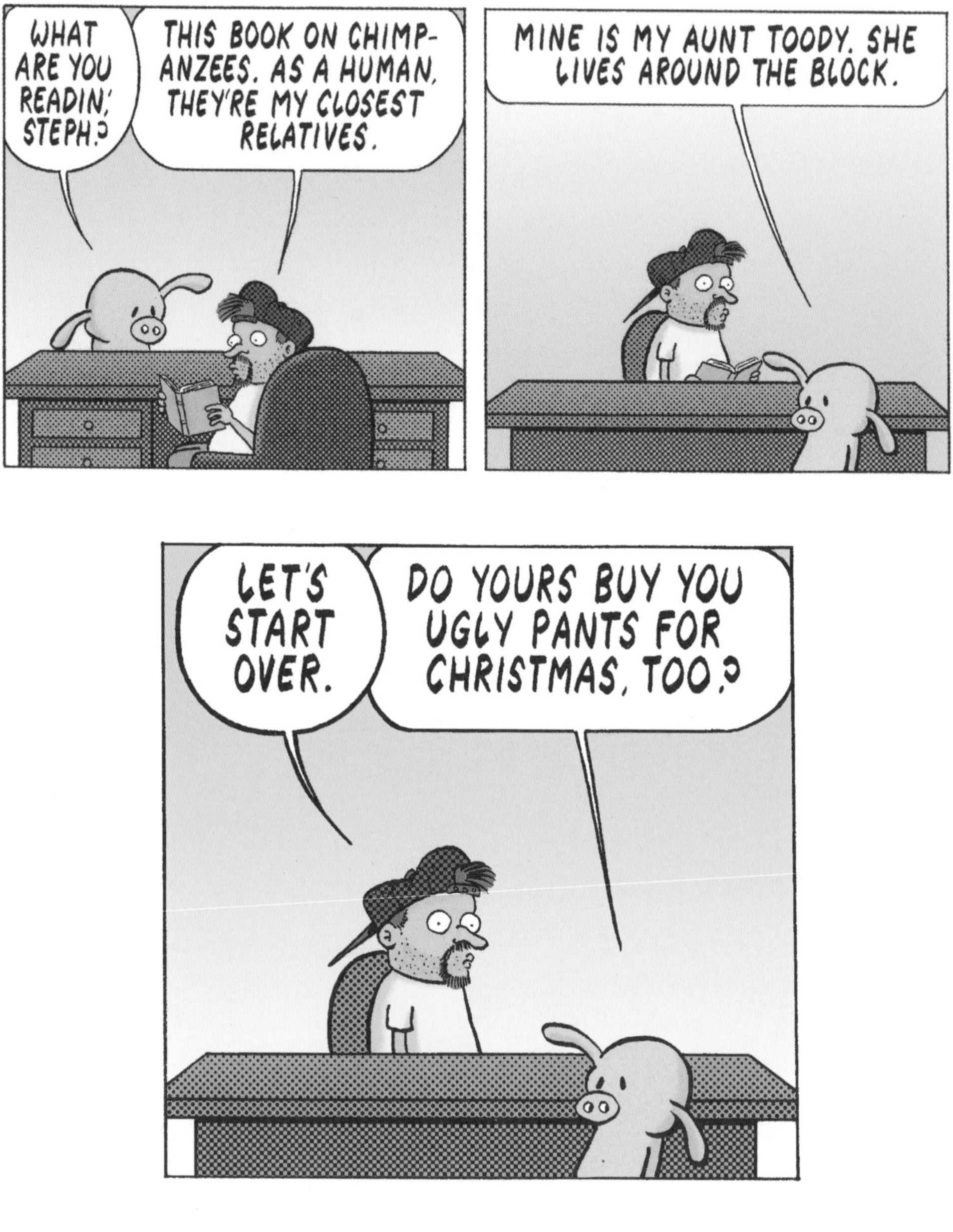
WHAT ARE YOU READIN', STEPH?
THIS BOOK ON CHIMPANZEES. AS A HUMAN, THEY'RE MY CLOSEST RELATIVES.
MINE IS MY AUNT TOODY. SHE LIVES AROUND THE BLOCK.
LET'S START OVER.
DO YOURS BUY YOU UGLY PANTS FOR CHRISTMAS, TOO?

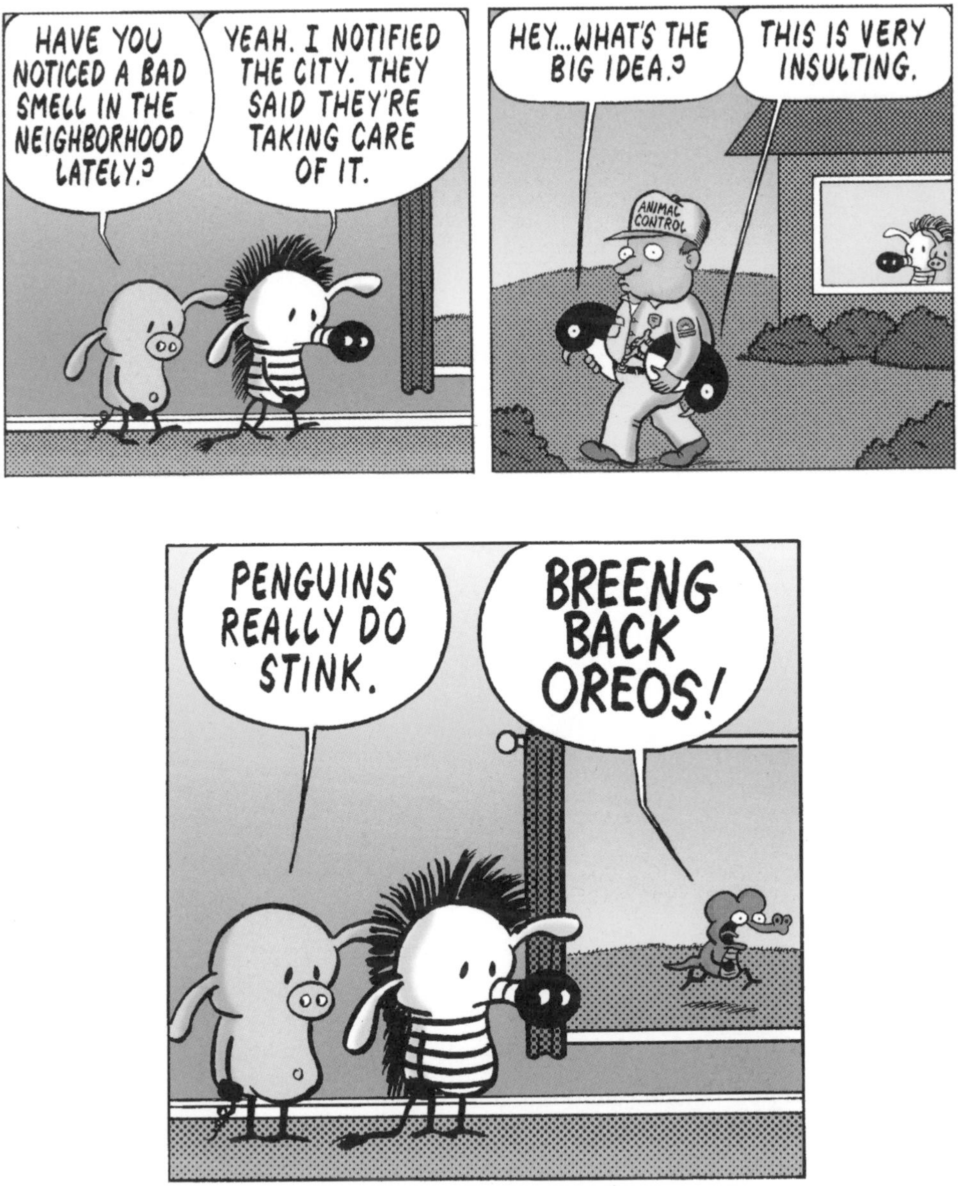
HAVE YOU NOTICED A BAD SMELL IN THE NEIGHBORHOOD LATELY?
YEAH. I NOTIFIED THE CITY. THEY SAID THEY'RE TAKING CARE OF IT.
HEY...WHAT'S THE BIG IDEA?
THIS IS VERY INSULTING.
ANIMAL CONTROL
PENGUINS REALLY DO STINK.
BREENG BACK OREOS!

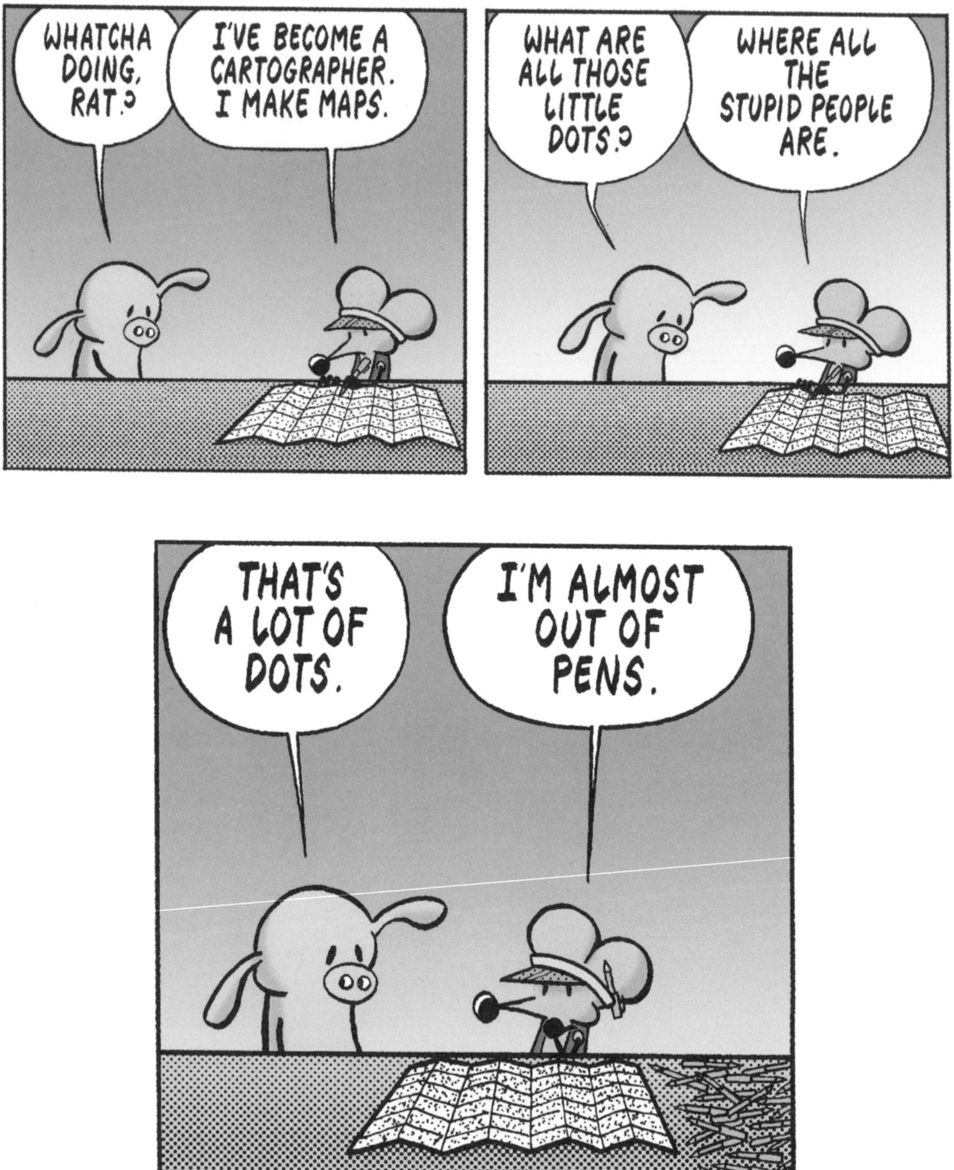
WHATCHA DOING, RAT?
I'VE BECOME A CARTOGRAPHER. I MAKE MAPS.
WHAT ARE ALL THOSE LITTLE DOTS?
WHERE ALL THE STUPID PEOPLE ARE.
THAT'S A LOT OF DOTS.
I'M ALMOST OUT OF PENS.

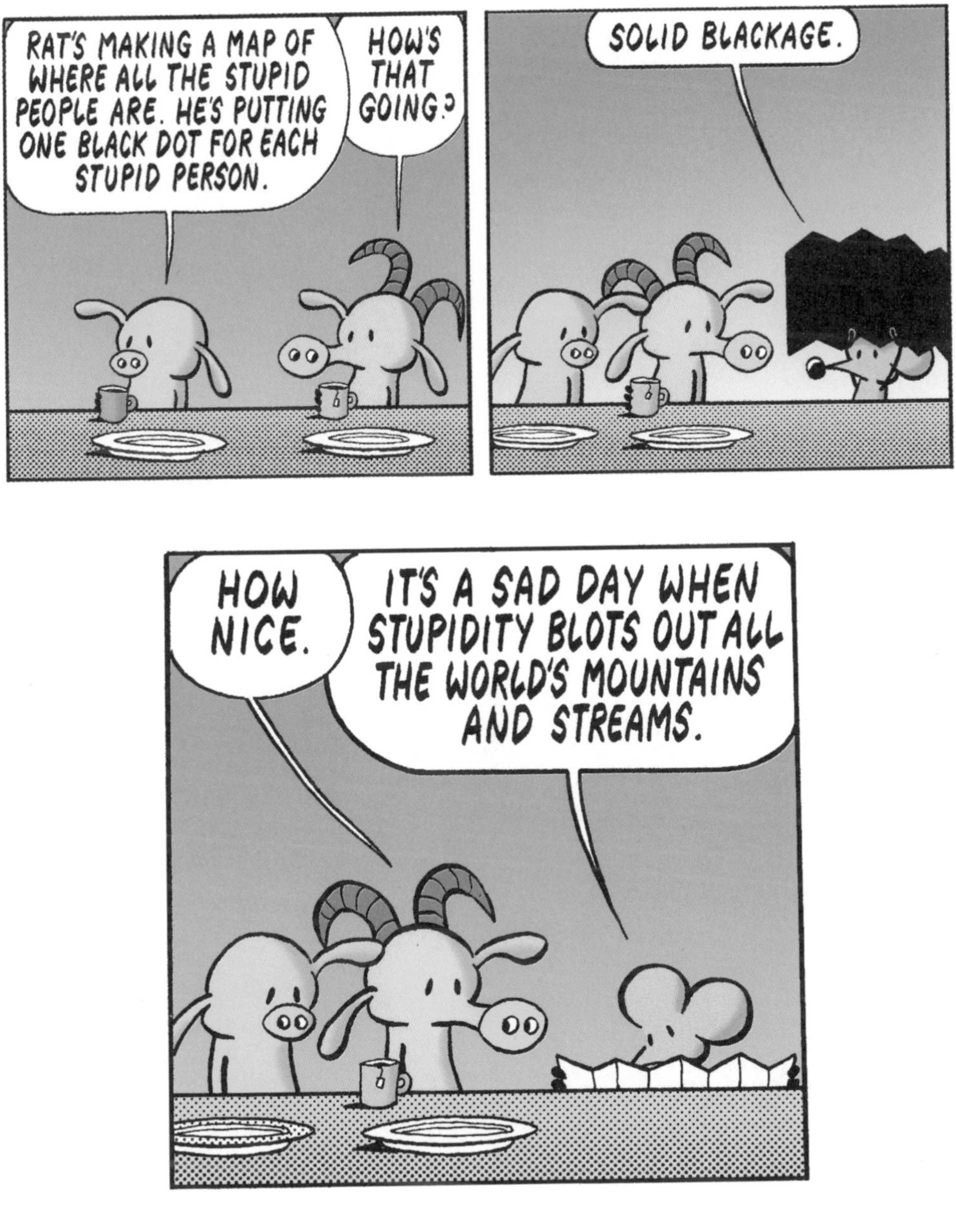
RAT'S MAKING A MAP OF WHERE ALL THE STUPID PEOPLE ARE. HE'S PUTTING ONE BLACK DOT FOR EACH STUPID PERSON.
HOW'S THAT GOING?
SOLID BLACKAGE.
HOW NICE.
IT'S A SAD DAY WHEN STUPIDITY BLOTS OUT ALL THE WORLD'S MOUNTAINS AND STREAMS.

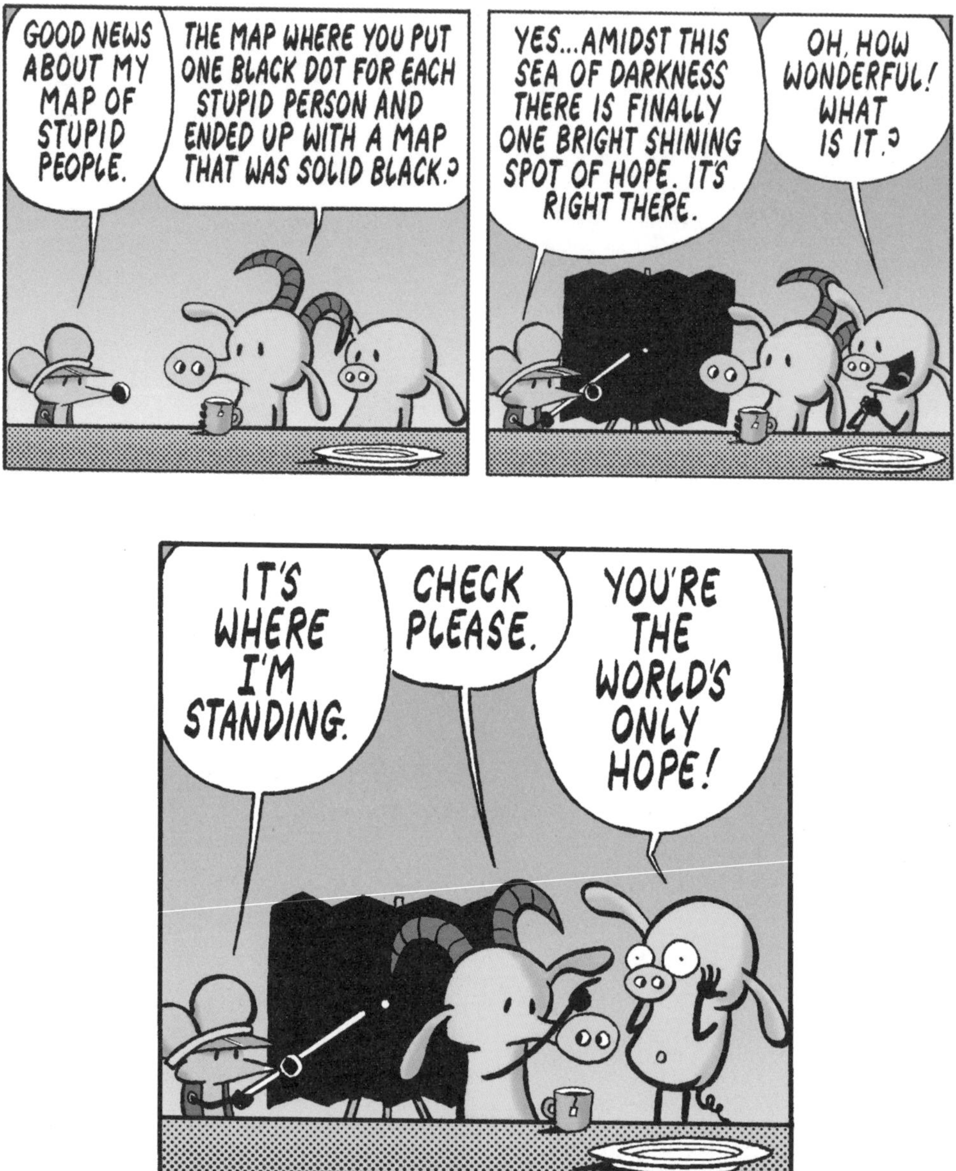
GOOD NEWS ABOUT MY MAP OF STUPID PEOPLE.
THE MAP WHERE YOU PUT ONE BLACK DOT FOR EACH STUPID PERSON AND ENDED UP WITH A MAP THAT WAS SOLID BLACK?
YES...AMIDST THIS SEA OF DARKNESS THERE IS FINALLY ONE BRIGHT SHINING SPOT OF HOPE. IT'S RIGHT THERE.
OH, HOW WONDERFUL! WHAT IS IT?
IT'S WHERE I'M STANDING.
CHECK PLEASE.
YOU'RE THE WORLD'S ONLY HOPE!

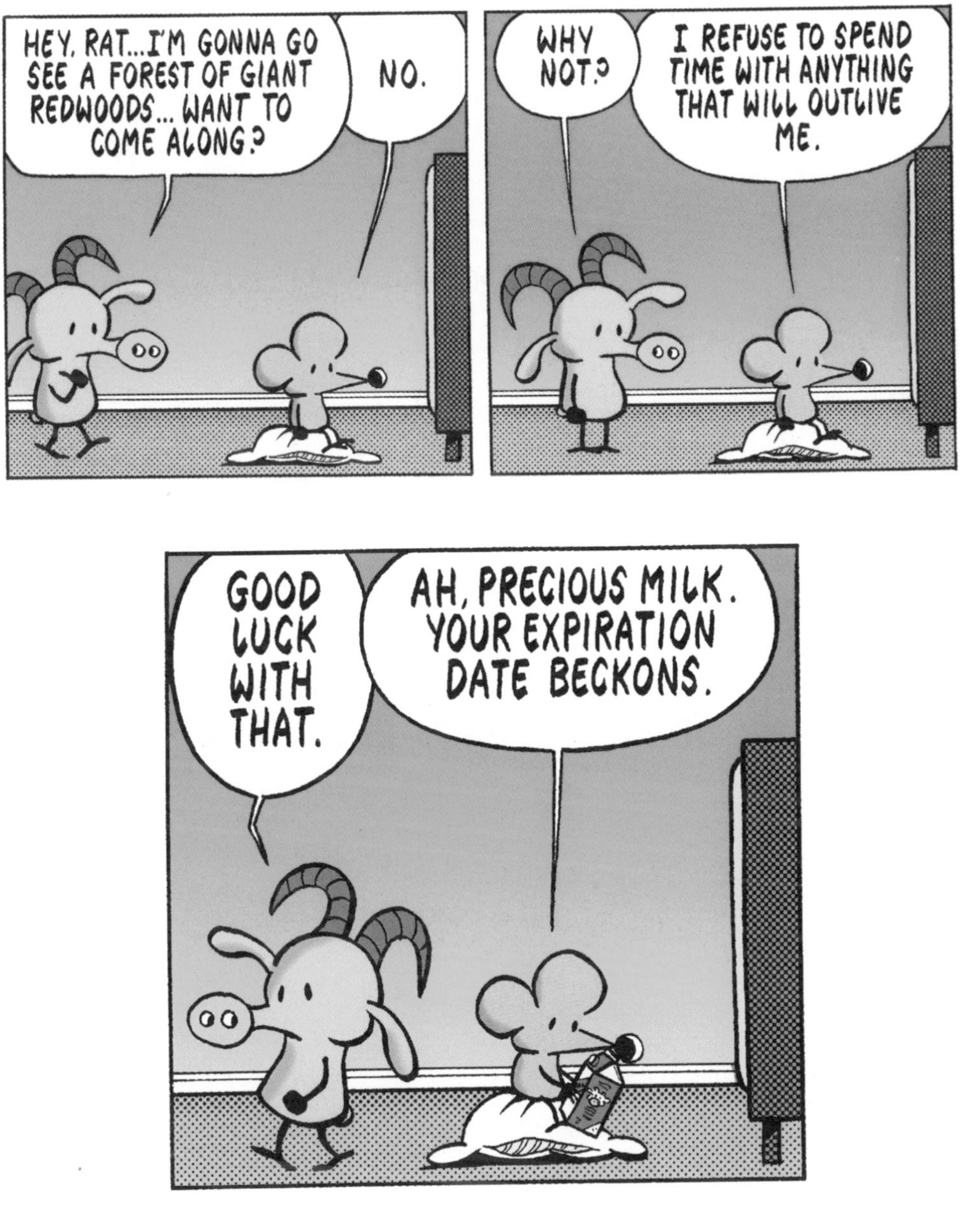
HEY, RAT...I'M GONNA GO SEE A FOREST OF GIANT REDWOODS... WANT TO COME ALONG?
NO.
WHY NOT?
I REFUSE TO SPEND TIME WITH ANYTHING THAT WILL OUTLIVE ME.
GOOD LUCK WITH THAT.
AH, PRECIOUS MILK. YOUR EXPIRATION DATE BECKONS.

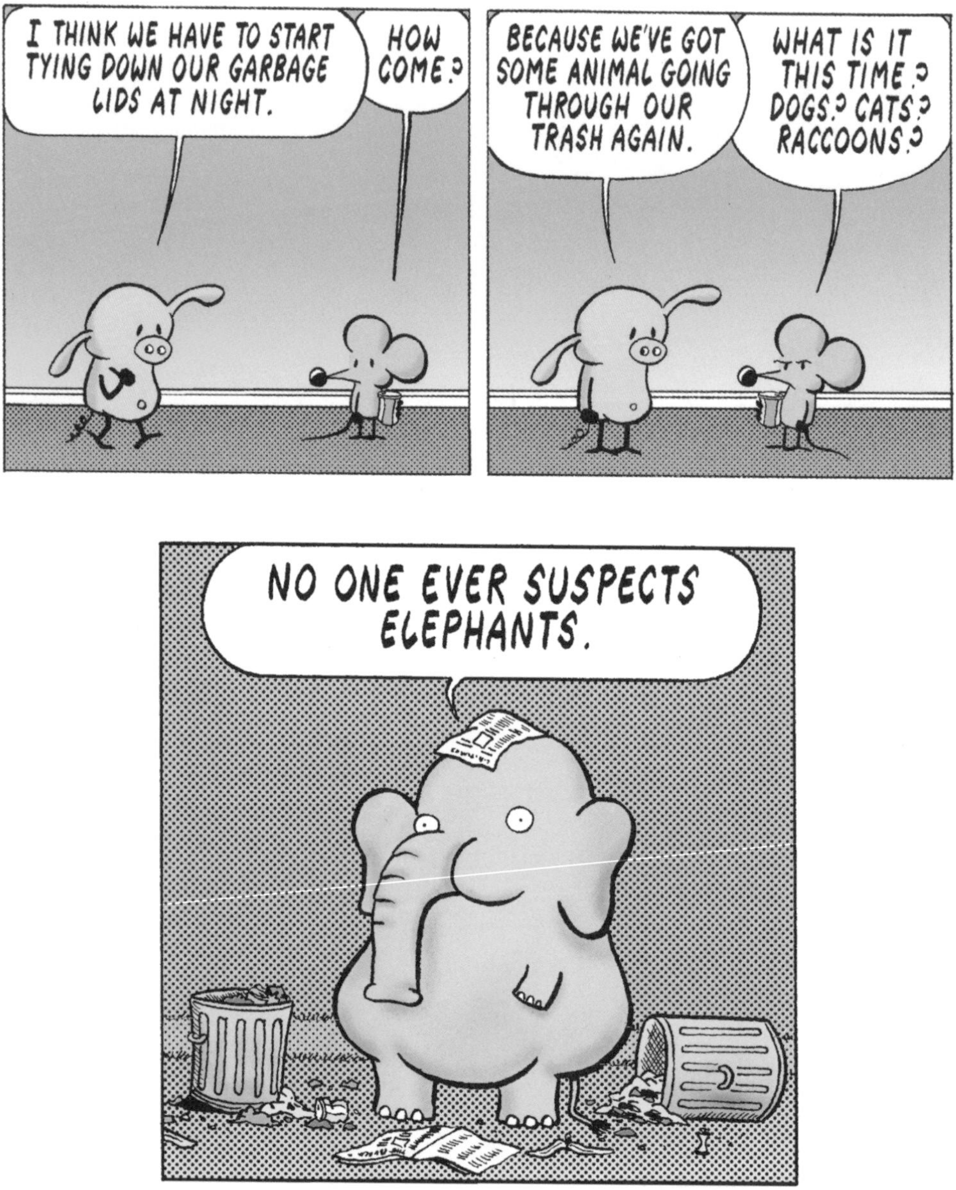
I THINK WE HAVE TO START TYING DOWN OUR GARBAGE LIDS AT NIGHT.
HOW COME?
BECAUSE WE'VE GOT SOME ANIMAL GOING THROUGH OUR TRASH AGAIN.
WHAT IS IT THIS TIME? DOGS? CATS? RACCOONS?
NO ONE EVER SUSPECTS ELEPHANTS.

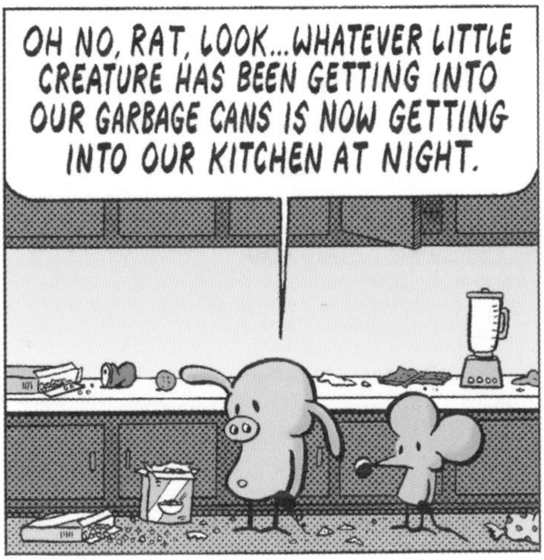
OH NO, RAT, LOOK...WHATEVER LITTLE CREATURE HAS BEEN GETTING INTO OUR GARBAGE CANS IS NOW GETTING INTO OUR KITCHEN AT NIGHT.

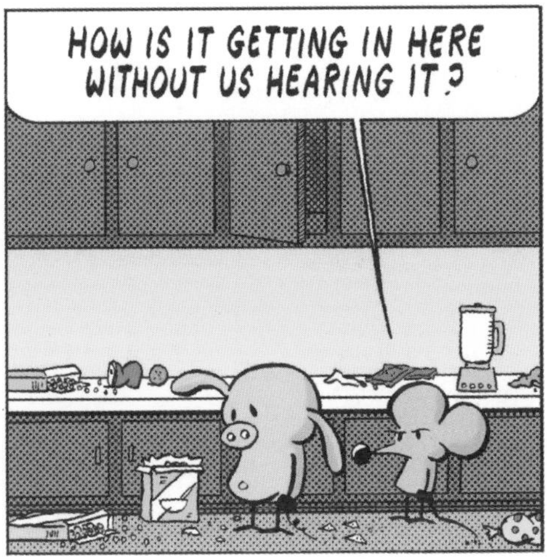
HOW IS IT GETTING IN HERE WITHOUT US HEARING IT?

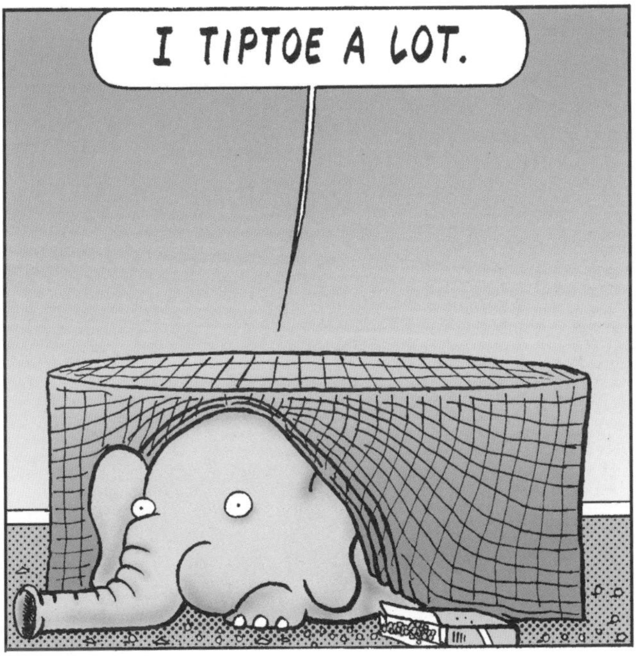
I TIPTOE A LOT.

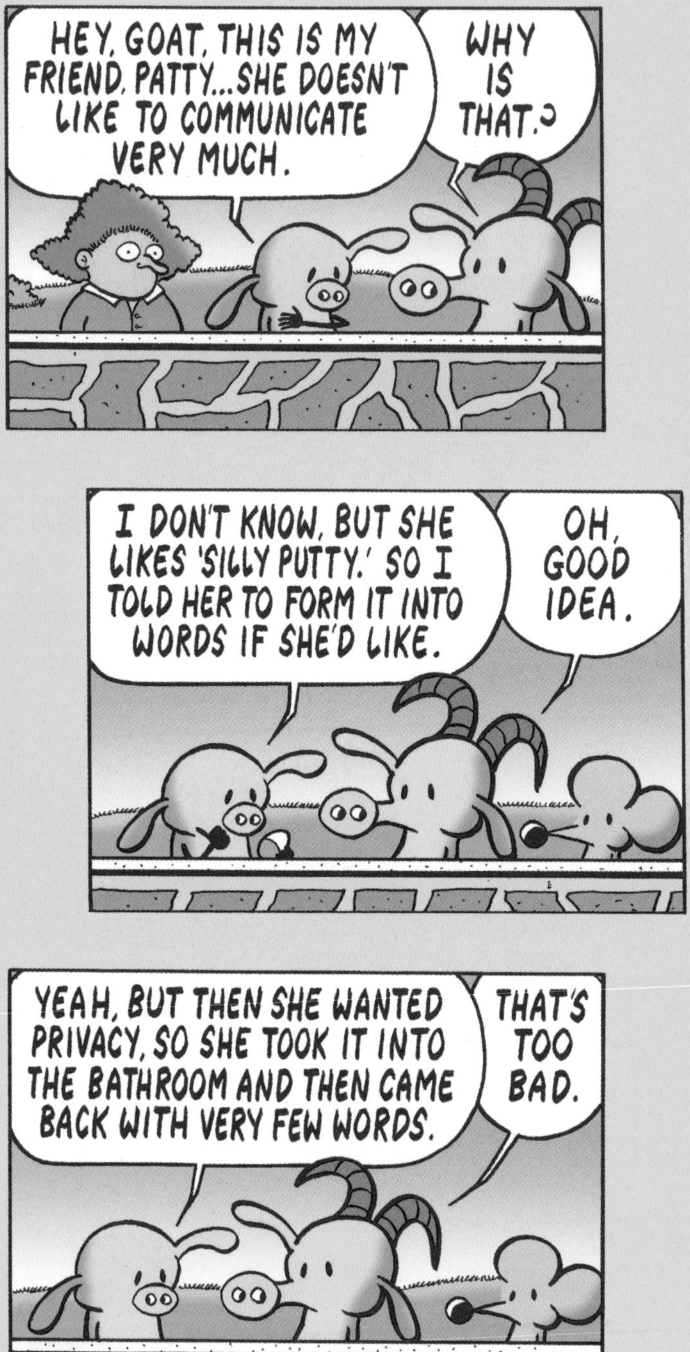
HEY, GOAT, THIS IS MY FRIEND, PATTY...SHE DOESN'T LIKE TO COMMUNICATE VERY MUCH.
WHY IS THAT?
I DON'T KNOW, BUT SHE LIKES 'SILLY PUTTY.' SO I TOLD HER TO FORM IT INTO WORDS IF SHE'D LIKE.
OH, GOOD IDEA.
YEAH, BUT THEN SHE WANTED PRIVACY, SO SHE TOOK IT INTO THE BATHROOM AND THEN CAME BACK WITH VERY FEW WORDS.
THAT'S TOO BAD.

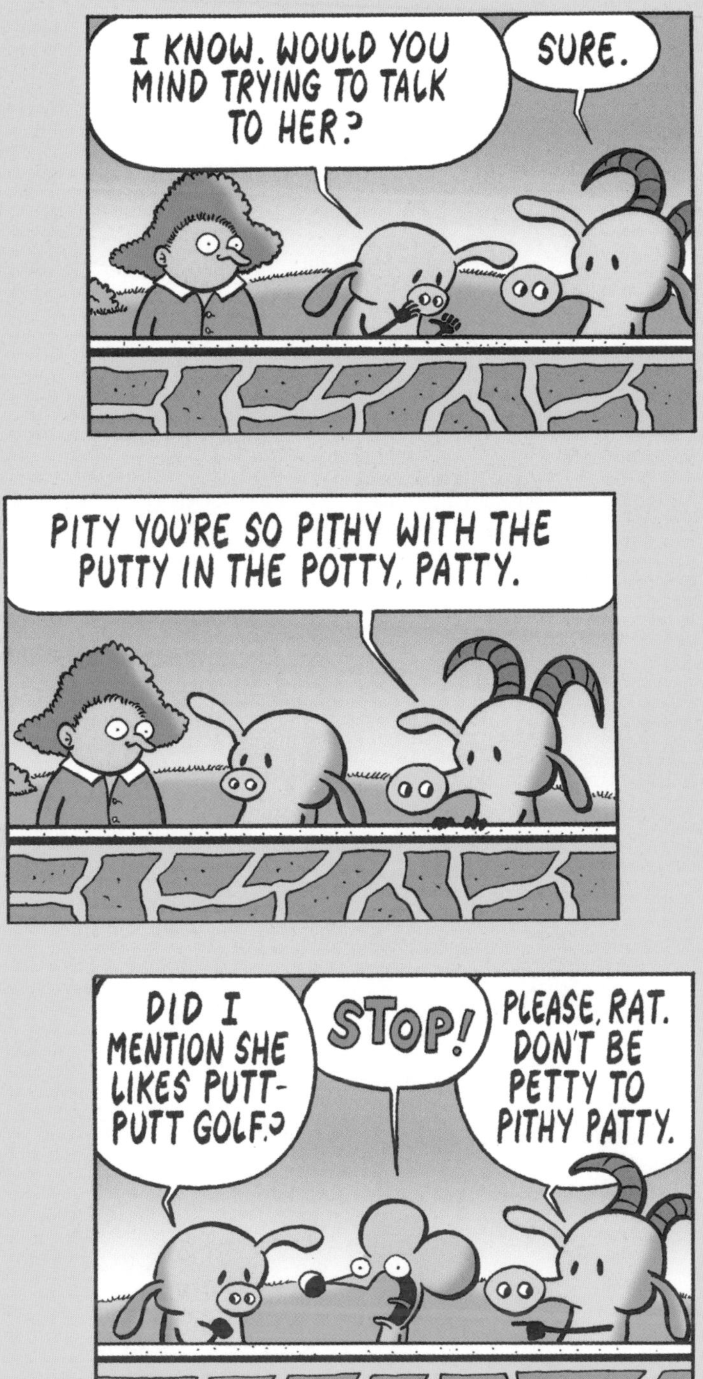
I KNOW. WOULD YOU MIND TRYING TO TALK TO HER?
SURE.
PITY YOU'RE SO PITHY WITH THE PUTTY IN THE POTTY, PATTY.
DID I MENTION SHE LIKES PUTT-PUTT GOLF?
STOP!
PLEASE, RAT. DON'T BE PETTY TO PITHY PATTY.

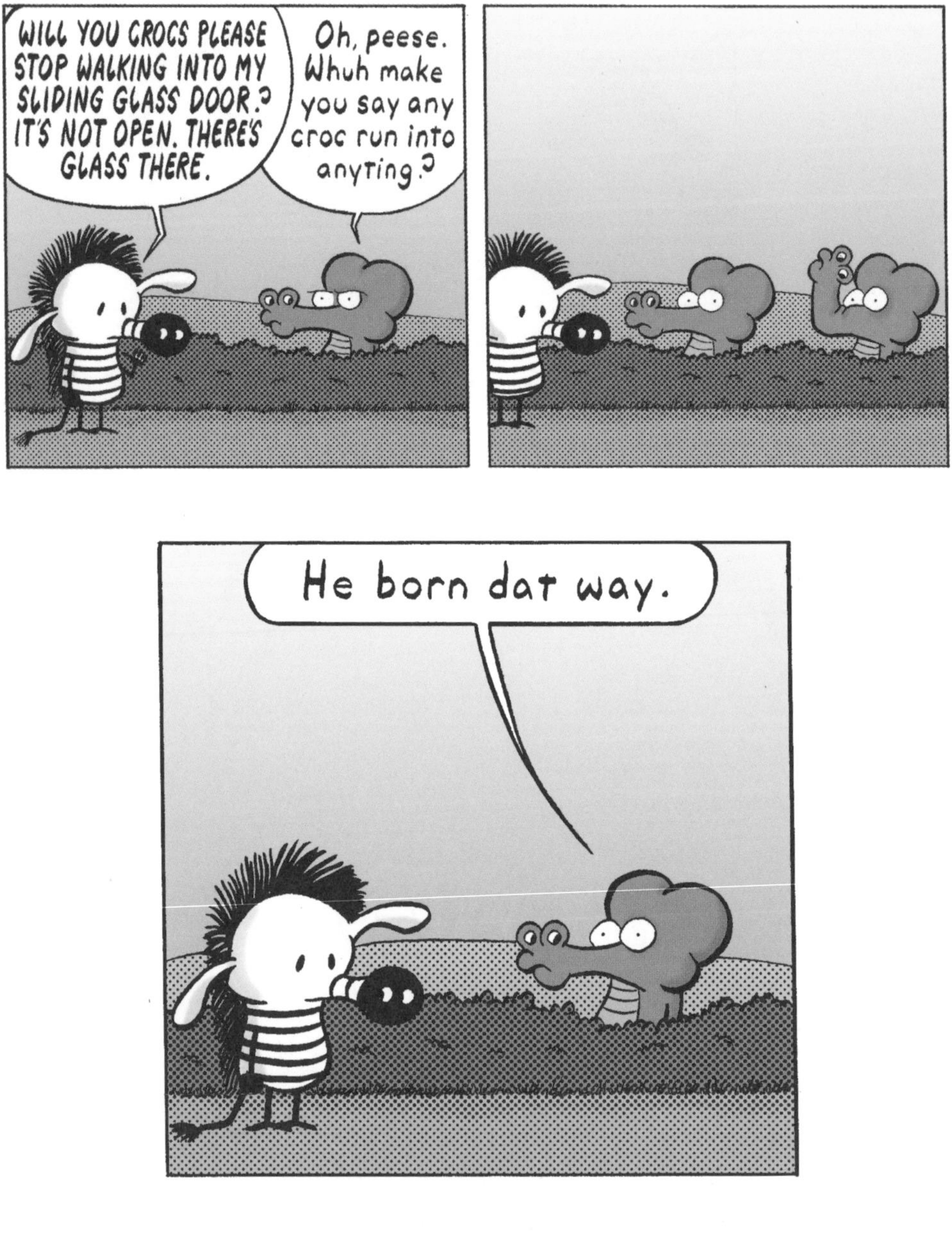
WILL YOU CROCS PLEASE STOP WALKING INTO MY SLIDING GLASS DOOR? IT'S NOT OPEN. THERE'S GLASS THERE.
Oh, peese. Whuh make you say any croc run into anyting?
He born dat way.

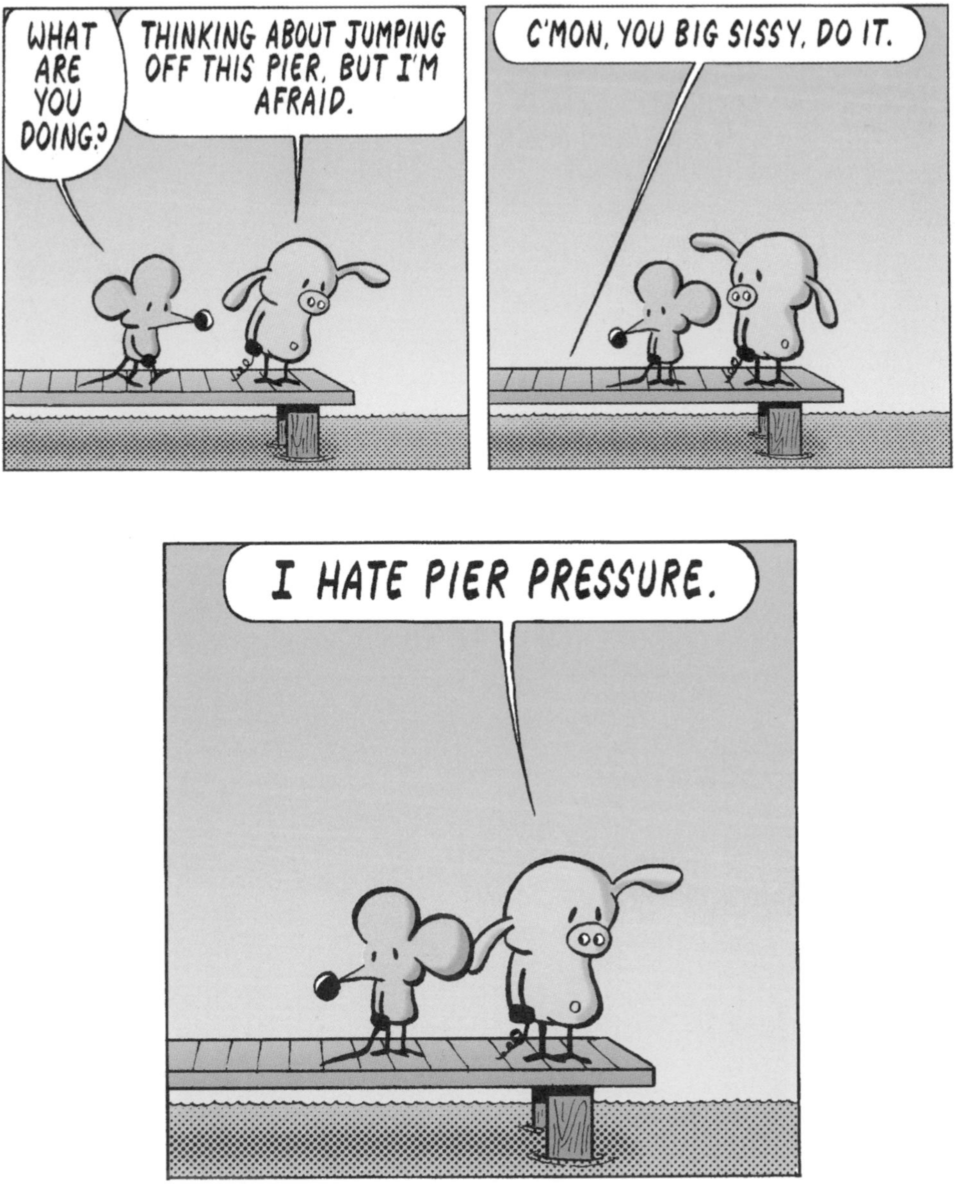
WHAT ARE YOU DOING?
THINKING ABOUT JUMPING OFF THIS PIER, BUT I'M AFRAID.
C'MON, YOU BIG SISSY, DO IT.
I HATE PIER PRESSURE.

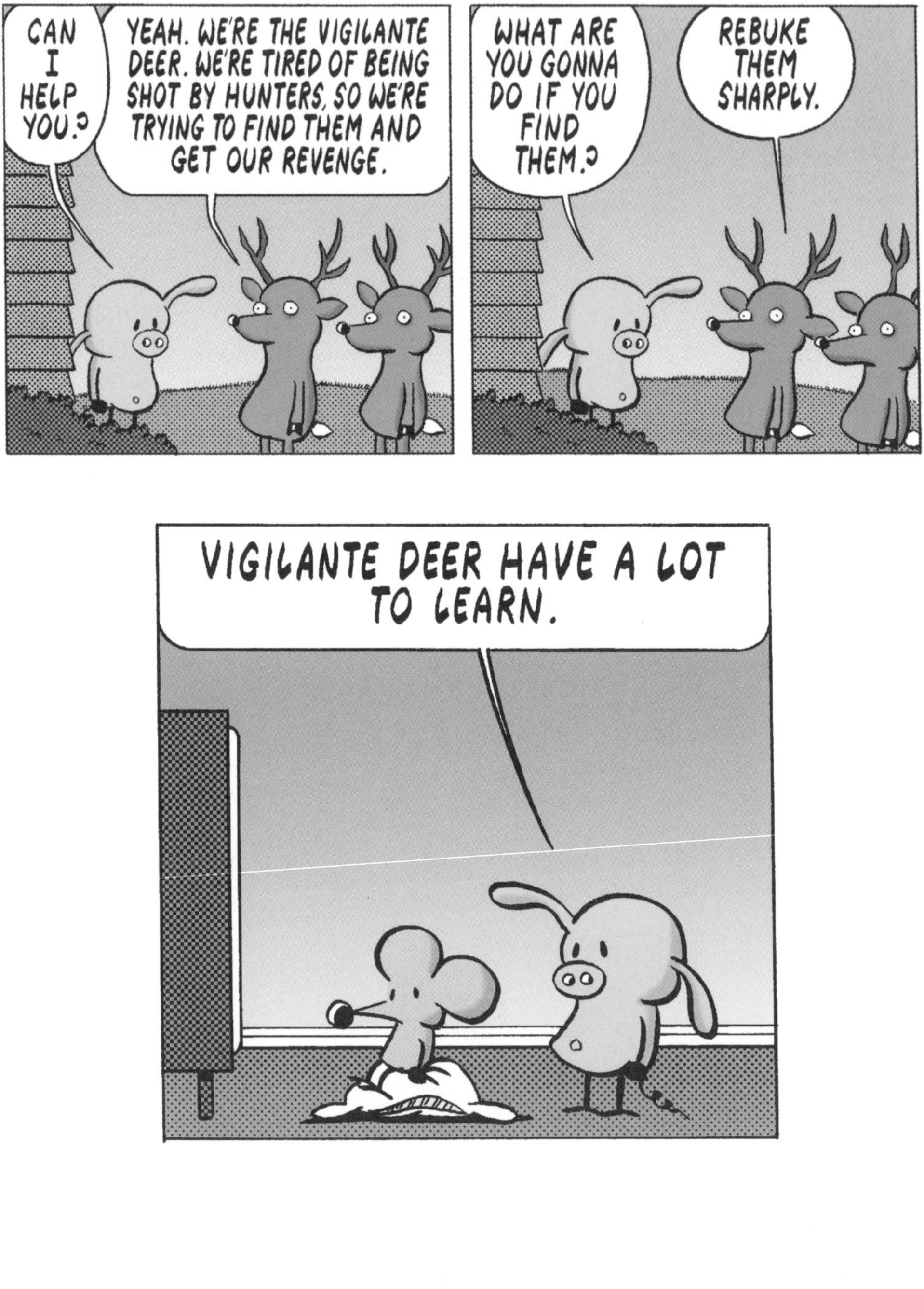
CAN I HELP YOU?
YEAH. WE'RE THE VIGILANTE DEER. WE'RE TIRED OF BEING SHOT BY HUNTERS, SO WE'RE TRYING TO FIND THEM AND GET OUR REVENGE.
WHAT ARE YOU GONNA DO IF YOU FIND THEM?
REBUKE THEM SHARPLY.
VIGILANTE DEER HAVE A LOT TO LEARN.

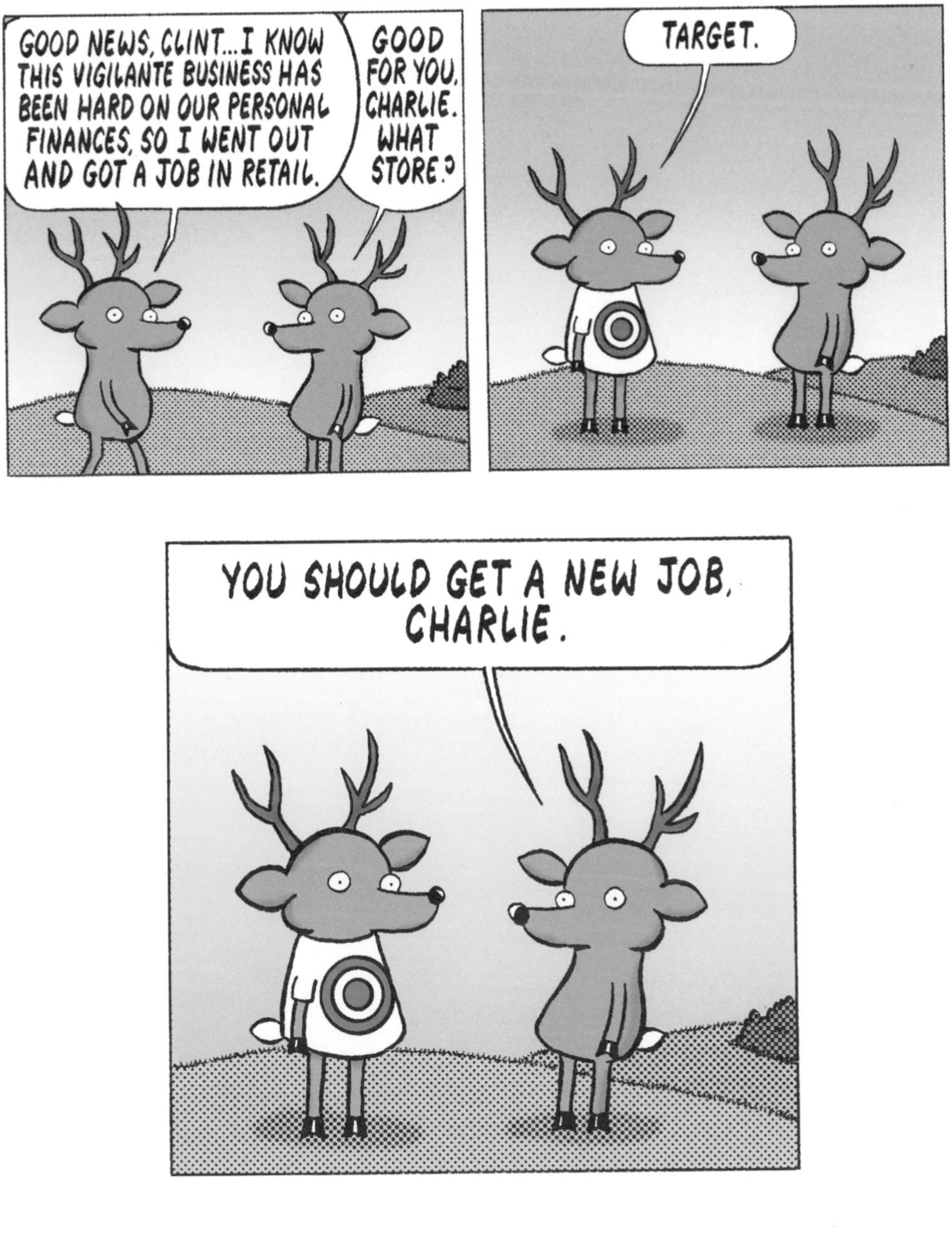
GOOD NEWS, CLINT...I KNOW THIS VIGILANTE BUSINESS HAS BEEN HARD ON OUR PERSONAL FINANCES, SO I WENT OUT AND GOT A JOB IN RETAIL.
GOOD FOR YOU, CHARLIE. WHAT STORE?
TARGET.
YOU SHOULD GET A NEW JOB, CHARLIE.

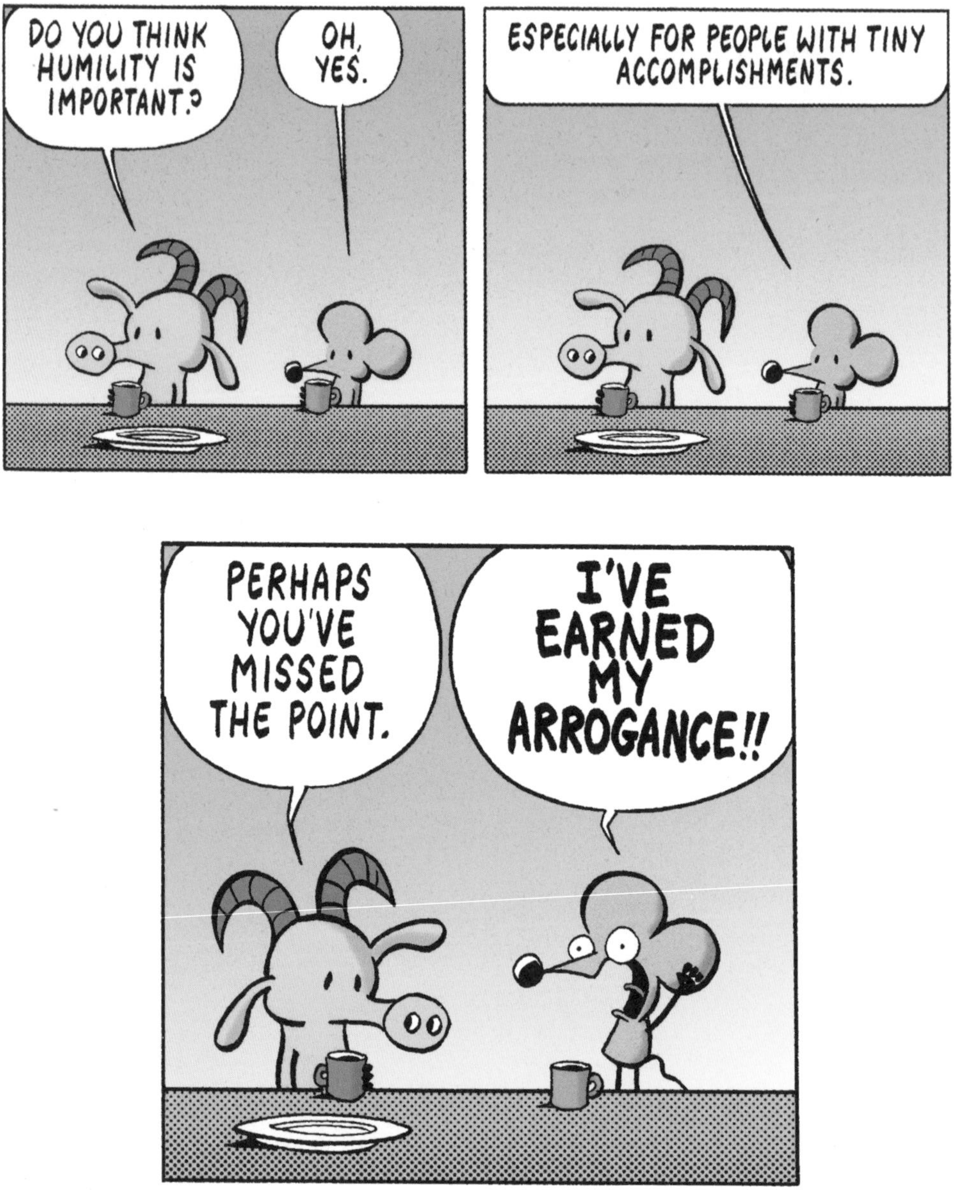
DO YOU THINK HUMILITY IS IMPORTANT?
OH, YES.
ESPECIALLY FOR PEOPLE WITH TINY ACCOMPLISHMENTS.
PERHAPS YOU'VE MISSED THE POINT.
I'VE EARNED MY ARROGANCE!!

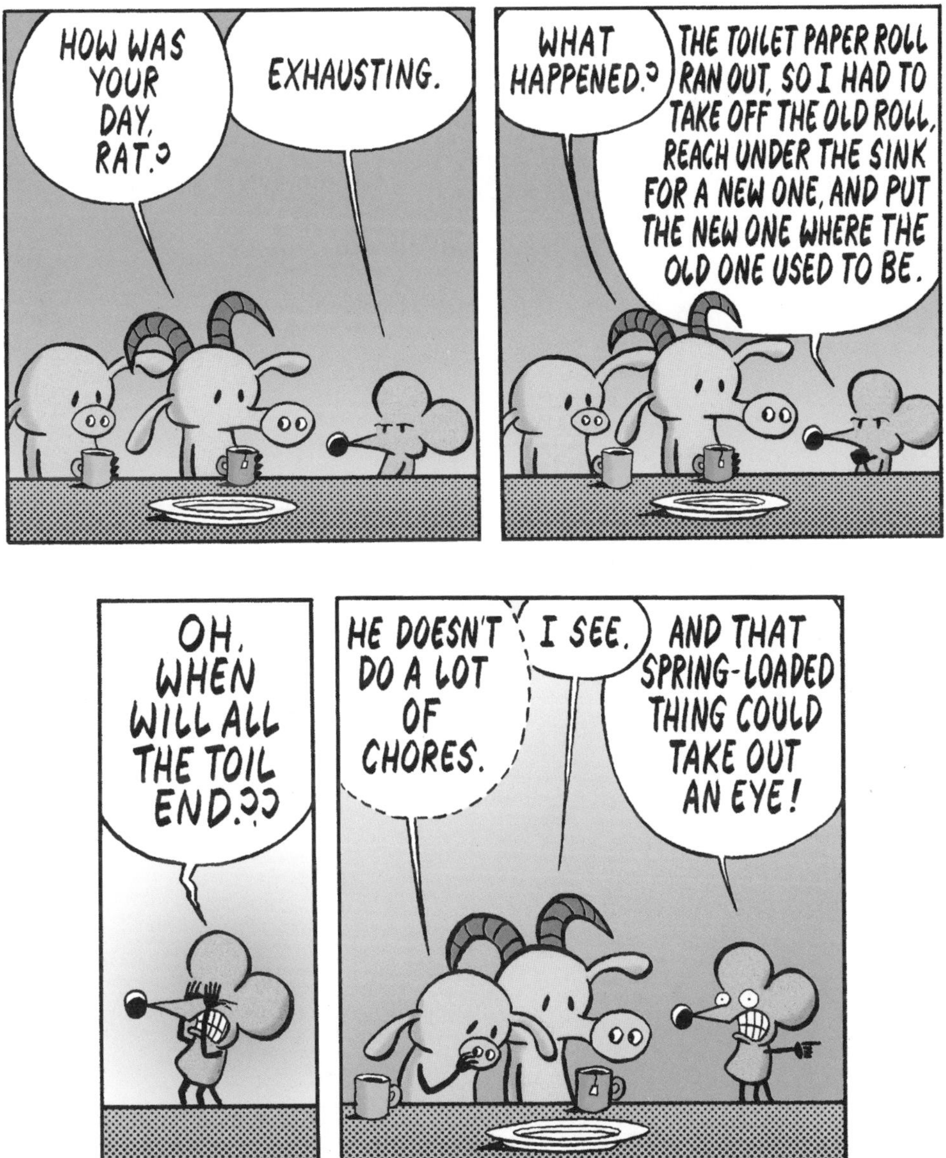
HOW WAS YOUR DAY, RAT?
EXHAUSTING.
WHAT HAPPENED?
THE TOILET PAPER ROLL RAN OUT, SO I HAD TO TAKE OFF THE OLD ROLL, REACH UNDER THE SINK FOR A NEW ONE, AND PUT THE NEW ONE WHERE THE OLD ONE USED TO BE.
OH. WHEN WILL ALL THE TOIL END???
HE DOESN'T DO A LOT OF CHORES.
I SEE.
AND THAT SPRING-LOADED THING COULD TAKE OUT AN EYE!

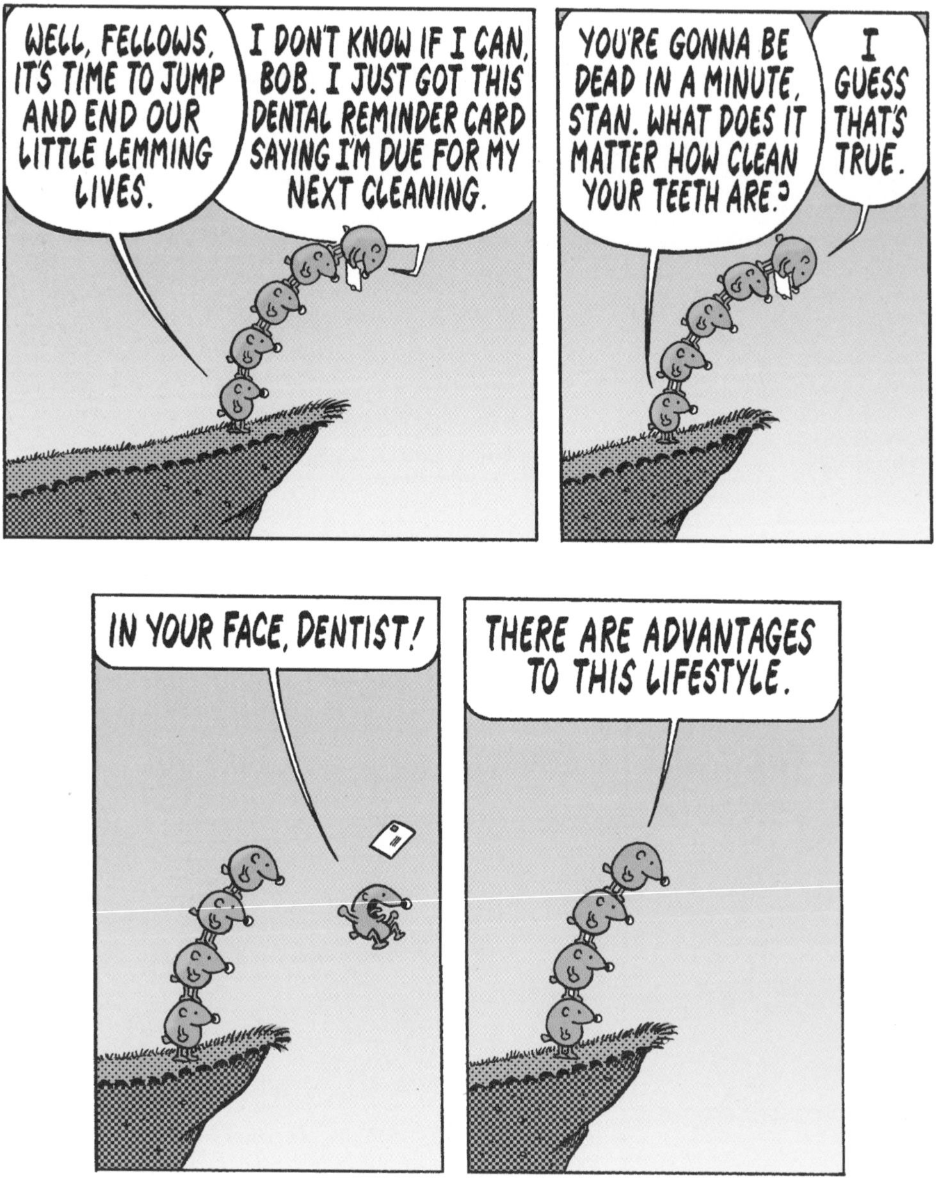
WELL, FELLOWS, IT'S TIME TO JUMP AND END OUR LITTLE LEMMING LIVES.
I DON'T KNOW IF I CAN, BOB. I JUST GOT THIS DENTAL REMINDER CARD SAYING I'M DUE FOR MY NEXT CLEANING.
YOU'RE GONNA BE DEAD IN A MINUTE, STAN. WHAT DOES IT MATTER HOW CLEAN YOUR TEETH ARE?
I GUESS THAT'S TRUE.
IN YOUR FACE, DENTIST!
THERE ARE ADVANTAGES TO THIS LIFESTYLE.

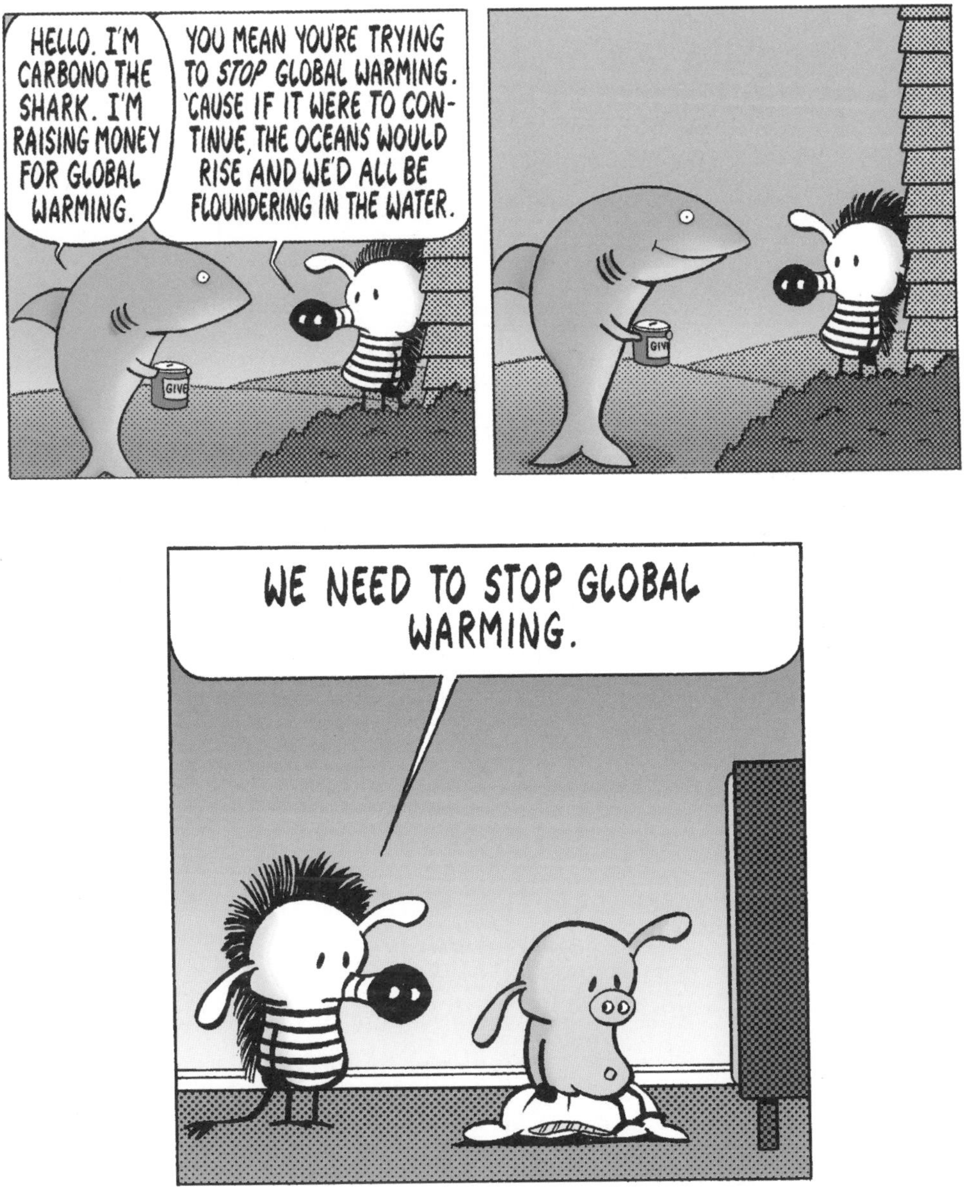
HELLO. I'M CARBONO THE SHARK. I'M RAISING MONEY FOR GLOBAL WARMING.
GIVE
YOU MEAN YOU'RE TRYING TO *STOP* GLOBAL WARMING. 'CAUSE IF IT WERE TO CON-TINUE, THE OCEANS WOULD RISE AND WE'D ALL BE FLOUNDERING IN THE WATER.
WE NEED TO STOP GLOBAL WARMING.

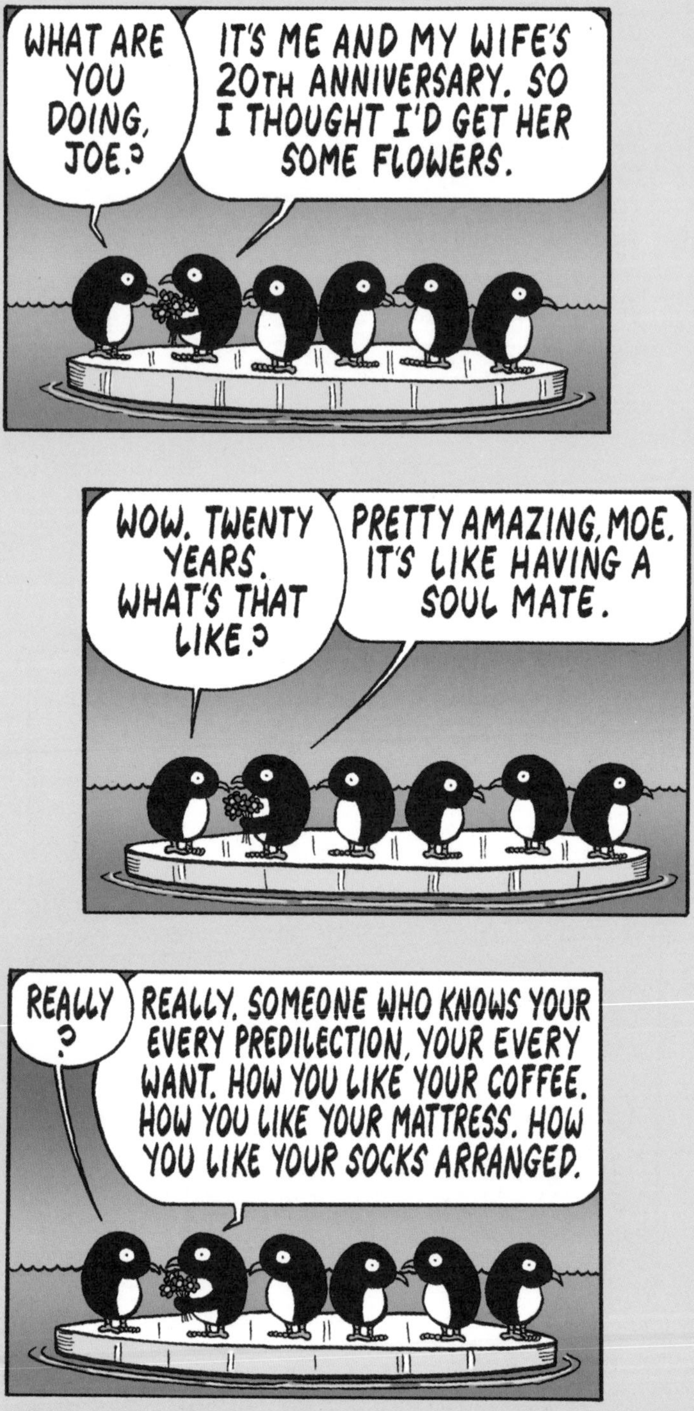
WHAT ARE YOU DOING, JOE?
IT'S ME AND MY WIFE'S 20TH ANNIVERSARY. SO I THOUGHT I'D GET HER SOME FLOWERS.
WOW. TWENTY YEARS. WHAT'S THAT LIKE?
PRETTY AMAZING, MOE. IT'S LIKE HAVING A SOUL MATE.
REALLY?
REALLY. SOMEONE WHO KNOWS YOUR EVERY PREDILECTION, YOUR EVERY WANT. HOW YOU LIKE YOUR COFFEE. HOW YOU LIKE YOUR MATTRESS. HOW YOU LIKE YOUR SOCKS ARRANGED.

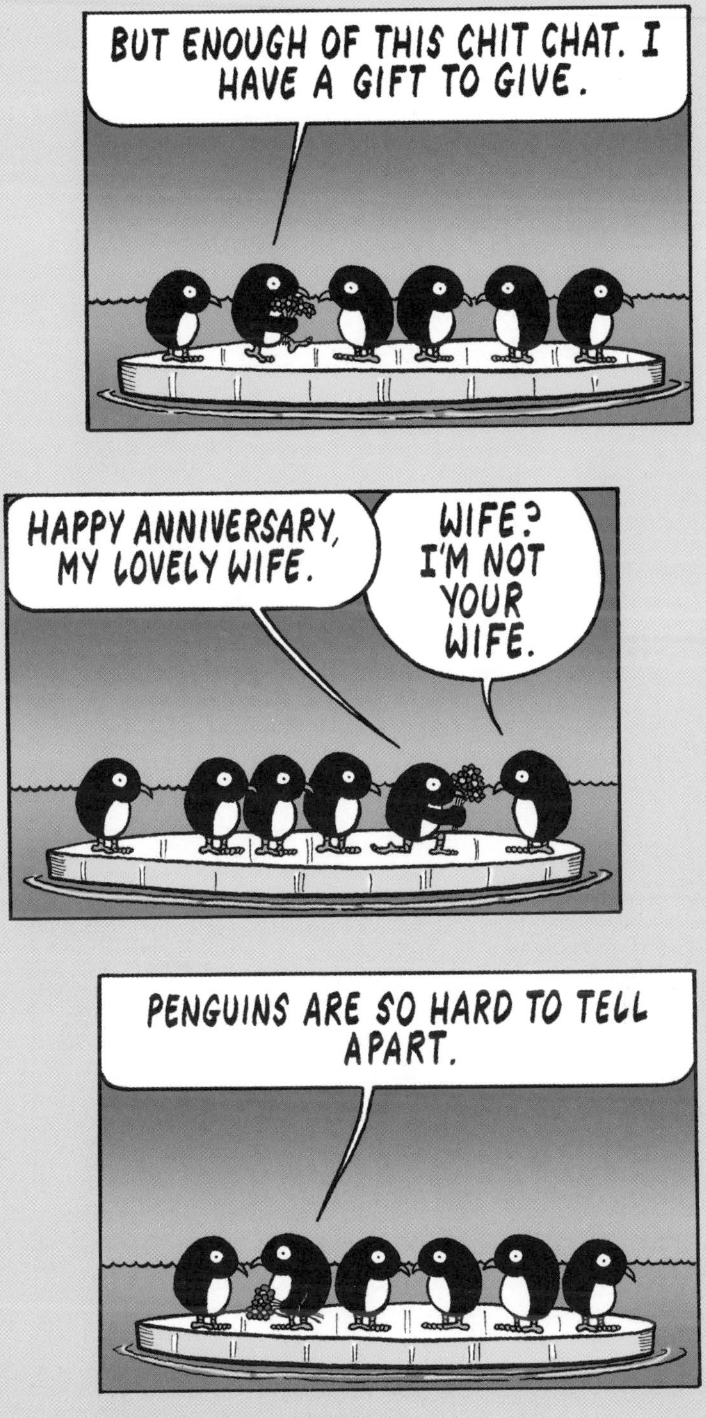
BUT ENOUGH OF THIS CHIT CHAT. I HAVE A GIFT TO GIVE.
HAPPY ANNIVERSARY, MY LOVELY WIFE.
WIFE? I'M NOT YOUR WIFE.
PENGUINS ARE SO HARD TO TELL APART.

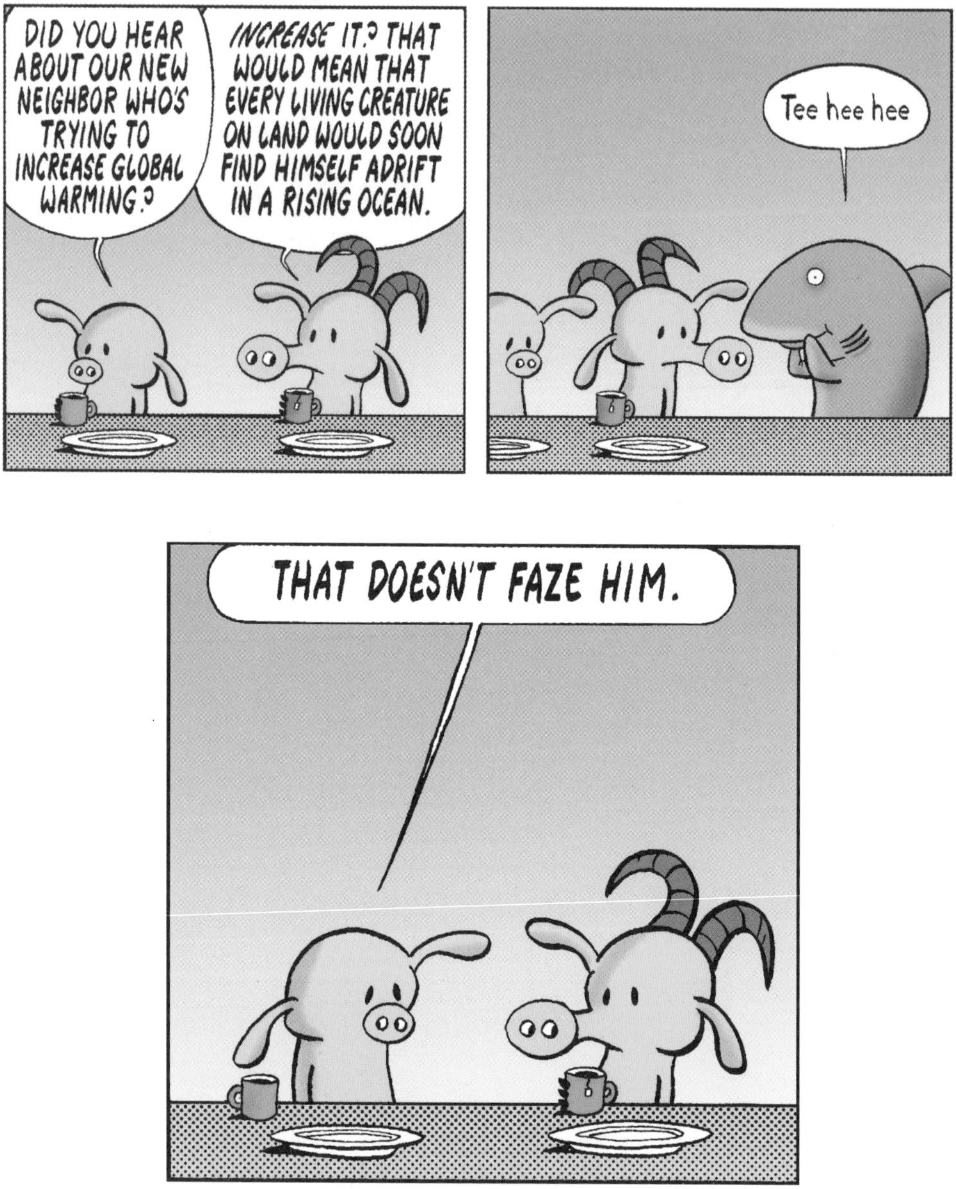
DID YOU HEAR ABOUT OUR NEW NEIGHBOR WHO'S TRYING TO INCREASE GLOBAL WARMING?
INCREASE IT? THAT WOULD MEAN THAT EVERY LIVING CREATURE ON LAND WOULD SOON FIND HIMSELF ADRIFT IN A RISING OCEAN.
Tee hee hee
THAT DOESN'T FAZE HIM.

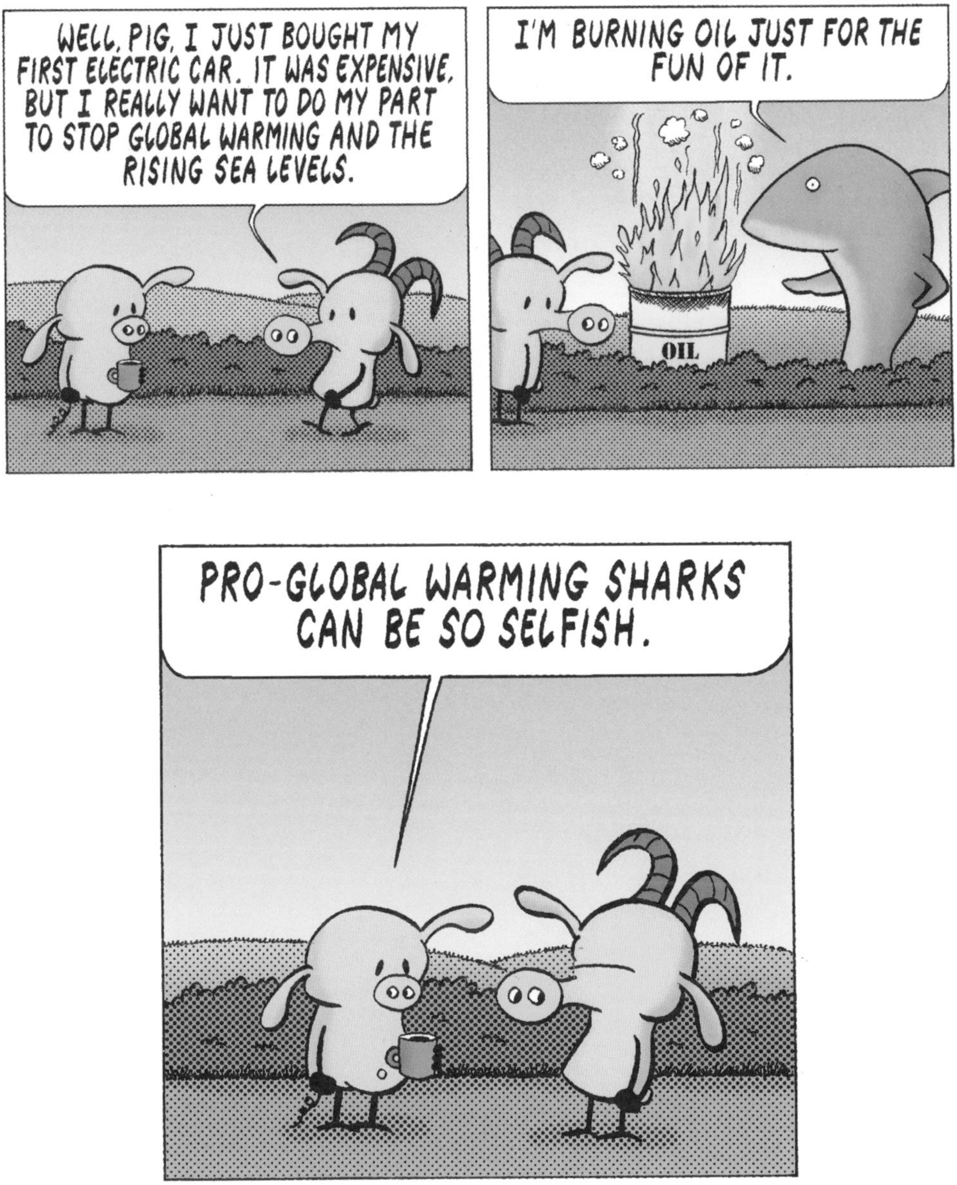
WELL, PIG, I JUST BOUGHT MY FIRST ELECTRIC CAR. IT WAS EXPENSIVE, BUT I REALLY WANT TO DO MY PART TO STOP GLOBAL WARMING AND THE RISING SEA LEVELS.
I'M BURNING OIL JUST FOR THE FUN OF IT.
OIL
PRO-GLOBAL WARMING SHARKS CAN BE SO SELFISH.

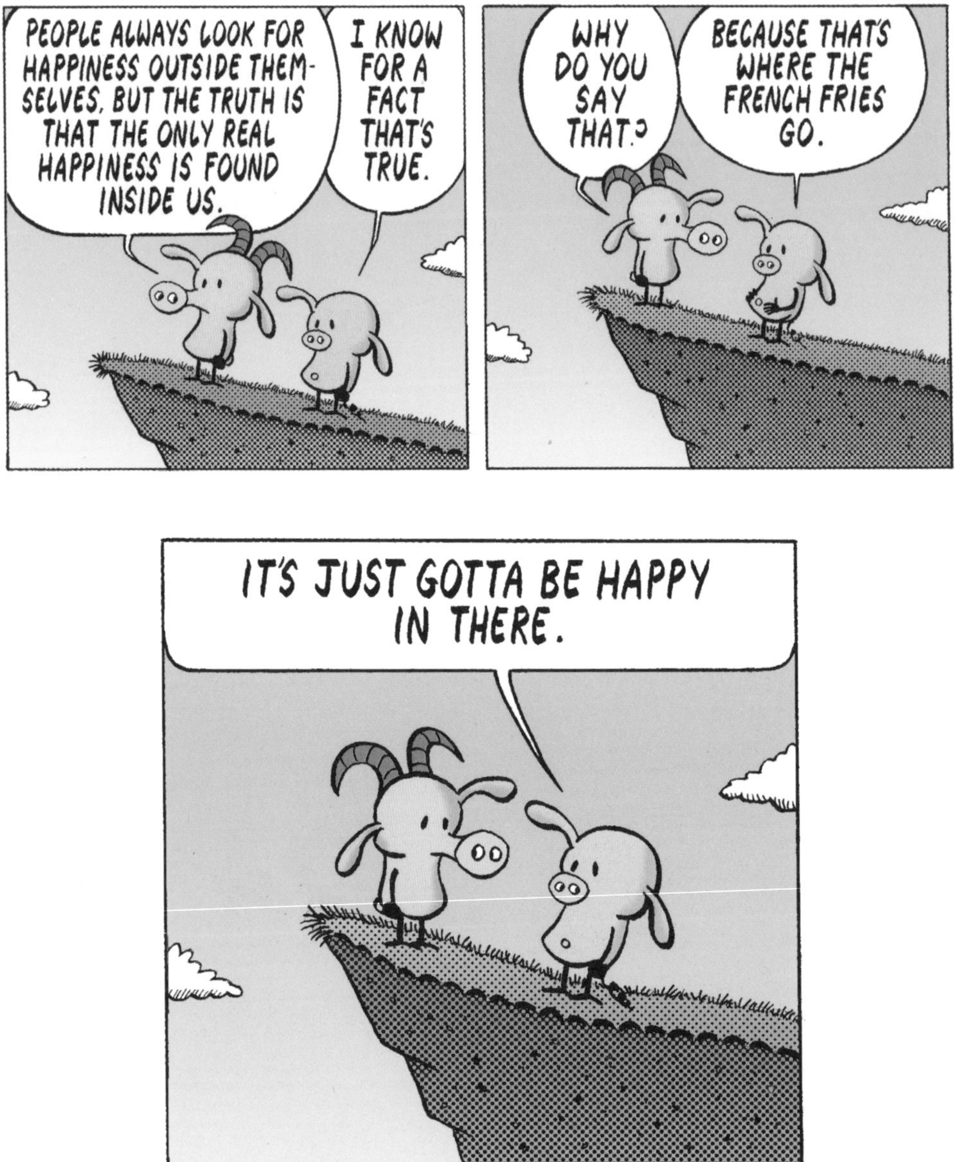
PEOPLE ALWAYS LOOK FOR HAPPINESS OUTSIDE THEM-SELVES, BUT THE TRUTH IS THAT THE ONLY REAL HAPPINESS IS FOUND INSIDE US.
I KNOW FOR A FACT THAT'S TRUE.
WHY DO YOU SAY THAT?
BECAUSE THAT'S WHERE THE FRENCH FRIES GO.
IT'S JUST GOTTA BE HAPPY IN THERE.

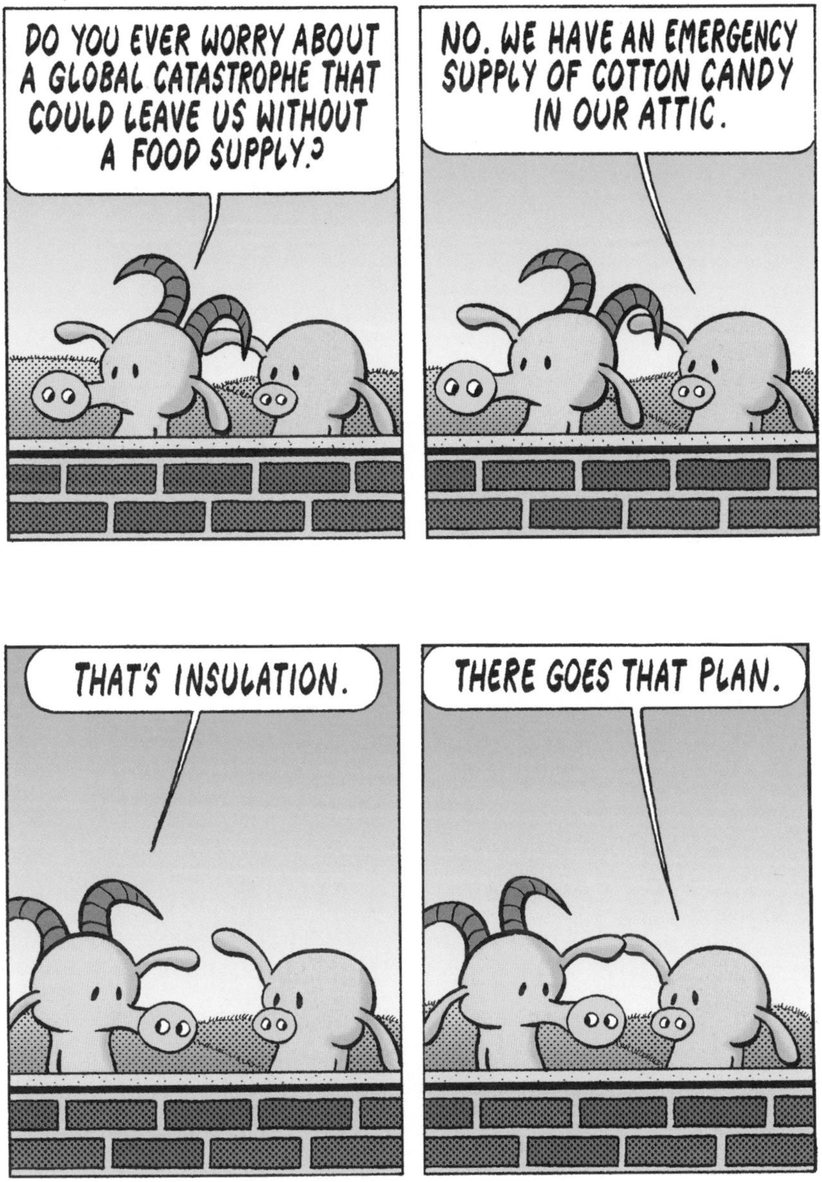
DO YOU EVER WORRY ABOUT A GLOBAL CATASTROPHE THAT COULD LEAVE US WITHOUT A FOOD SUPPLY?
NO. WE HAVE AN EMERGENCY SUPPLY OF COTTON CANDY IN OUR ATTIC.
THAT'S INSULATION.
THERE GOES THAT PLAN.

SO THEN I —
DARN. CALL GOT DROPPED. I BETTER...
...CALL PIG BACK. BUT WHAT IF...
...HE TRIES TO CALL ME? THEN HE'LL JUST GO...
...TO VOICEMAIL. I'LL WAIT FOR HIM TO...
...CALL ME. BUT WHAT IF HE'S WAITING ALSO? THEN I'LL...

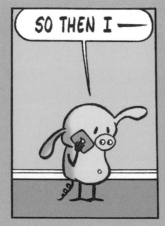

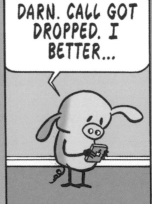

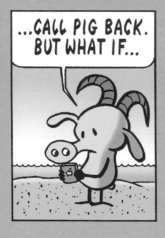

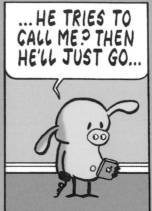

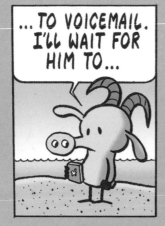

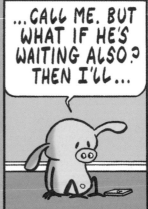

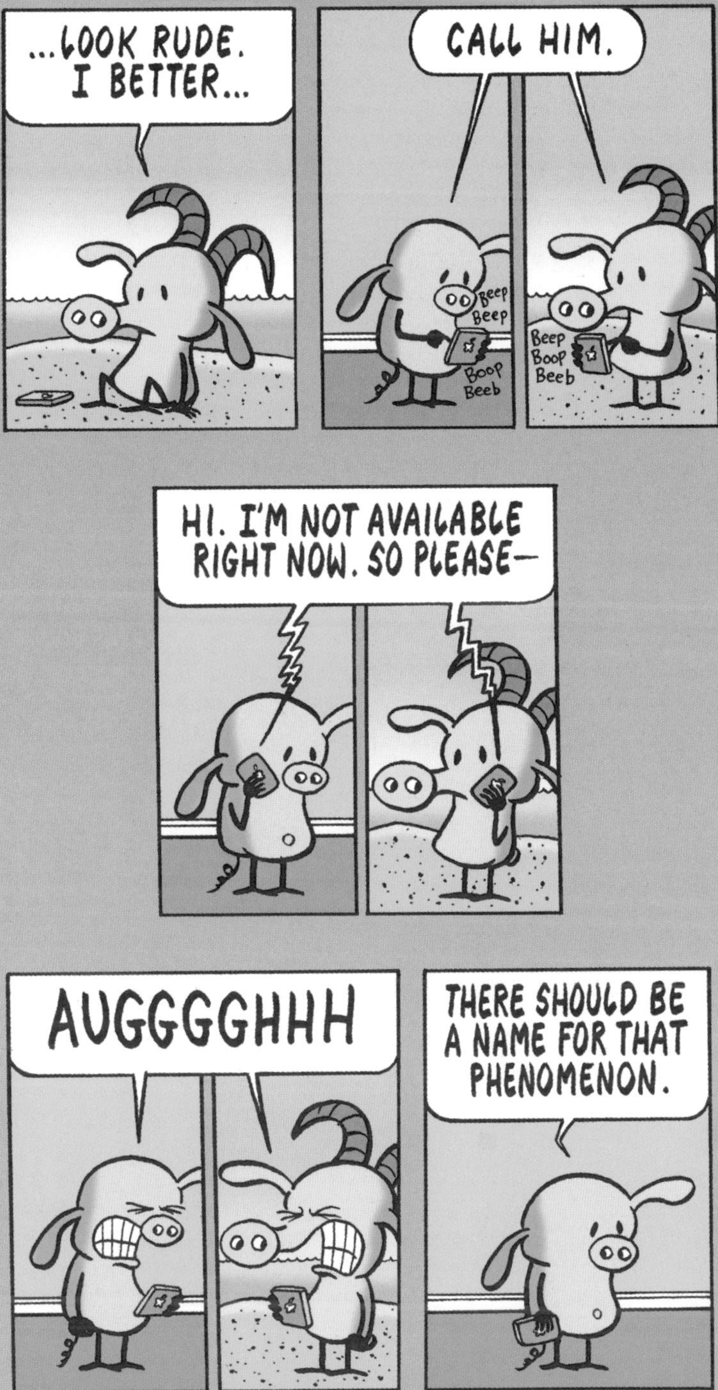
...LOOK RUDE. I BETTER...
CALL HIM.
Beep Beep
Boop Beeb
Beep Boop Beeb
HI. I'M NOT AVAILABLE RIGHT NOW. SO PLEASE—
AUGGGGHHH
THERE SHOULD BE A NAME FOR THAT PHENOMENON.

Pearls Before Swine is distributed internationally by Universal Uclick.

Andrews McMeel Publishing
a division of Andrews McMeel Universal
1130 Walnut Street, Kansas City, Missouri 64106

www.andrewsmcmeel.com

16 17 18 19 20 SDB 10 9 8 7 6 5 4 3 2 1

ISBN: 978-1-4494-7627-4

Library of Congress Control Number: 2015955642

Pearls Before Swine can be viewed on the Internet at www.pearlscomic.com.

Made by:
Shenzen Donnelley Printing Company Ltd.
Address and location of manufacturer:
No. 47, Wuhe Nan Road, Bantian Ind. Zone,
Shenzhen China, 518129
1st Printing – 4/18/16

Be sure to check out other *Pearls Before Swine* AMP! Comics for Kids books and others at ampkids.com.

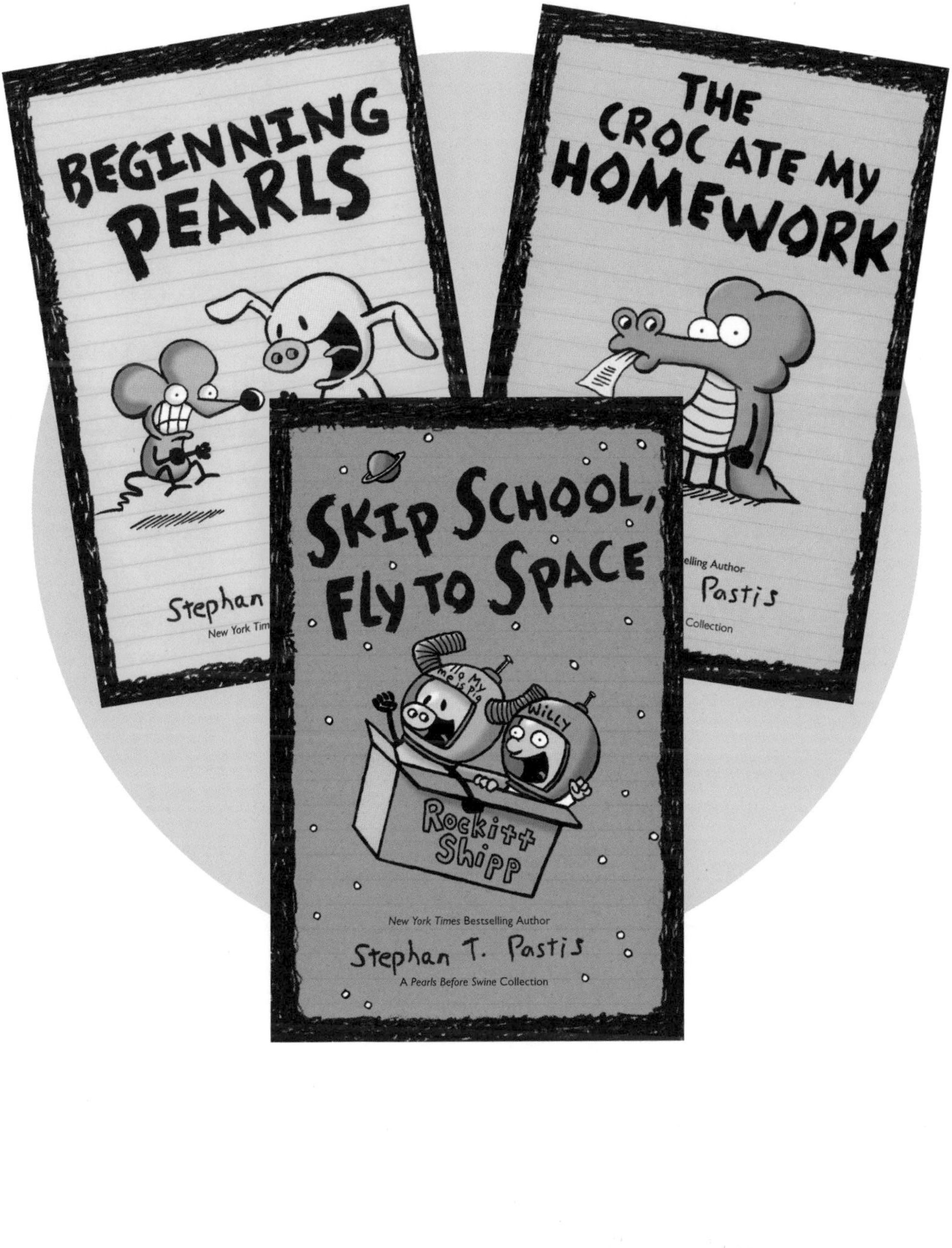
BEGINNING PEARLS
Stephan
THE CROC ATE MY HOMEWORK
Pastis
Collection
SKIP SCHOOL, FLY TO SPACE
WILLY
Rockitt Shipp
New York Times Bestselling Author
Stephan T. Pastis
A Pearls Before Swine Collection

Check out these and other books at ampkids.com

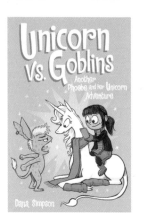

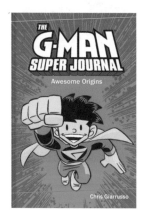